HOLLY FOX lives in Dorset with her daughter. *This Way Up* is her first novel and she is currently working on her next book.

THIS WAY UP

HOLLY FOX

POCKET
BOOKS

LONDON · SYDNEY · NEW YORK · TOKYO · SINGAPORE · TORONTO

First published in Great Britain by Pocket Books, 2001
An imprint of Simon & Schuster UK Ltd
A Viacom Company

1 3 5 7 9 10 8 6 4 2

Simon & Schuster UK Ltd
Africa House
64-78 Kingsway
London WC2B 6AH

Simon & Schuster Australia
Sydney

A CIP catalogue record for this book is available from
the British Library

ISBN 0-671-77379-8

Typeset by SX Composing DTP, Rayleigh, Essex
Printed and bound in Great Britain by Omnia Books Ltd, Glasgow

For Mum, in loving memory of the levitating donkey, a chimney brush in the next street, and the fresh egg wars.

THIS WAY UP

1

While she waited for Virginia Pye, Duck Woman, Chris had read the letter twice over.

Now she leaned on the yellow-and-red rail of the second floor offices, with the neatly typed sheet crumpled in one fist and considered, quite objectively, whether she ought to throw herself over now – or later.

Two floors below her, the Reception of Up-Line Cable TV was full. The noise of the fledgling television station drifted up to her – a noise just like a school playground at dinnertime. In Up-Line Cable, just as in the playground, there would always be a combination of people standing in corners looking shifty, and others running about in aimless circles, usually neighing like horses. And the odd bit of setting fire to someone's plaits was not entirely unknown.

Chris watched a motorcycle courier cross the huge expanse of marble floor below her, passing a gaggle of pensioners who had turned up as a coach-party audience to watch *Cooking Up A Storm*. At the Reception desk, a girl was fanning herself with a photograph of Jude Law. The elderly visitors huddled together, clutching their handbags and each other, obviously fearing that they had been ushered into a high-tech madhouse.

Which, of course, they had.

Chris sighed, and turned her attention to The Wicket.

Dead centre of the shining marble floor beneath her lay Bill Clinton. He was lying on his back saluting the ceiling. Meanwhile, Darcy Bussell was being hoisted into his recently vacated place. She was dressed as Giselle.

'Gorgeous!' shouted a technician. He lifted the ten-foot placard of The Wicket directly behind Darcy's improbably lithe silhouette.

The Wicket was the brainchild of Up-Line Cable's newest boss, Owen Majolica. At twenty-eight, Owen had no time for so-called stars. Instead, he thought it very important that icons should be insulted on a regular basis. As a result, a new cardboard celebrity was lowered into place in Up-Line's foyer every Monday, and a bucket of wet sponges was put by the entrance door. Particularly good shots among Up-Line's staff were rewarded with a bag of sweeties on Friday afternoons.

'Who wants the ducks?' shouted the receptionist.

Chris squinted back at the front desk. There she could see a small, grey-haired woman, who was gripping something so tightly that her knuckles shone white. Chris smoothed and folded the letter, putting it inside the sheaf of notes she was carrying. Business as usual, she reminded herself. The world was not waiting to see if Christine Craven was about to commit suicide over a publisher's rejection letter. There were far more interesting subjects on hand – namely, why any grown person would want to be bound in matrimony to a mallard.

Chris made a steady descent down the stairs.

All this month, she had been trying to follow the advice of *Today!Again!*'s yoga guru. The daily breakfast mantra. Try to relax. Let the diaphragm drop. Embrace the rising sun. Feel the green force. Love everyone. Become one with the world.

Try not to garrotte people who call themselves editors. Particularly the ones who write letters that begin,

Dear Ms Craven, We regret . . .

She gripped the stair railing, trying to concentrate. Which was important on these stairs. Vital, even. The scissor staircase of the building flung itself down the cathedral-like yawning shell of the studios and offices. Chris was convinced that it had been designed by some sort of seven-foot sadist – someone, definitely, with a legspan considerably longer than average. The spaces between the rungs were far too wide, and each step was alternately coloured red and yellow – Up-Line's colours. As a result, most people descended very slowly, usually with one hand over their eyes, negotiating each step with all the grace of a crane-fly stuck in jam.

At the first floor landing, Chris waved at the woman below. 'Here!' she called out. 'Ducks!'

The little lady in the blue hat looked up. Mrs Virginia Pye wore a dazzled, confused smile. Her gaze trailed away from Chris and, for a moment, followed one of the little bleeping trams that were buzzing through Reception. Invariably driven by seventeen-year-old frustrated rally drivers, the trams were another idea of Up-Line's boss, Owen Majolica. He had thought it would be enormous fun to hitch rides on them. In fact, his general business and management policy consisted of one word, and that word was *frolic*.

Frolic! labels were pasted above every door on every floor, and inside every room. Sticky *Frolic!* labels were on the phones, the lavatories and the stationery. *Frolic!* yelled the signs along the stairs. *Frolic, frolic!* boomed the neon lettering by the lifts. *Frolic*, whispered the instruction on the Tampax machines.

Chris came out into the foyer, and Mrs Pye focused on her. The woman was keeping a tight grip around a striped bird, which was stuffed so far under one arm that its body was lost in the folds of an ancient wool coat, and only its beak stuck out. At Mrs Pye's feet was a basket, the kind that took cats to the vet.

As Owen Majolica's personal assistant, Chris had been

detailed to look after Mrs Pye during her appearance on
Up-Line's flagship midday programme, the mercilessly
unfunny *Love At Lunch*. Majolica had pursued this
strange little lady with an almost manic fervour, demanding that she be brought to him. Why, Chris really didn't
understand. And why she should devote herself so avidly
to Mrs Pye – 'Don't let her out of your sight,' had been
Owen's instruction – was another mystery. Shepherding
was usually a researcher's job, and a junior researcher at
that. However, still smiling, Chris strode forward with her
hand extended.

'Mrs Pye? Hello. I'm Christine Craven.'

Mrs Pye lunged at her. 'Oh, it looks so exciting,' she
said. 'I knew it would. I imagined it all the way.'

Smiling, Chris softly dislodged the mittened grip. 'Did
you have a good journey?' she asked.

'Lovely.'

'On the train from . . .'

'West Tolwell.'

'And this must be Archie,' Chris said, nodding at the
bird.

'Oh no,' Mrs Pye replied. She seemed rather stung. 'This
here is Harold. Archie's in the basket.'

'Howzat!' shouted the crew. The Wicket was ham-
mered into place behind Darcy, and the divine diva had
been promptly pelted. Chris and Mrs Pye looked at the
water pooling on the floor.

'What did she do?' Mrs Pye asked, meaning Darcy.
'Why are they throwing things at her?'

Chris shrugged. 'Nothing. It's a new twist,' she said.
'This week they're throwing things at someone who hasn't
done anything wrong at all. Except by being thin.'

They watched for several seconds while the crew lobbed
missiles at Darcy's sublime solar plexus.

'Ha ha,' Mrs Pye said. 'I'm not thin.'

'No,' Chris agreed. 'And neither am I. So we're both safe.'

'Too gorgeous by half!' the team yelled.

Darcy's placard effigy smiled gracefully.

Chris took the frantically quacking Archie – and his wife – over to the lifts.

2

Sally Matthews, journalist, looked at the wall. Then she looked at the floor.

'Rain,' said Eddie Massingham, Editor-in-Chief of *The Corker*, the woman's weekly magazine *extraordinaire*.

Everyone in the editorial meeting looked up – looked right at him, their attention drawn away from the suspended ceiling, the carpet, the double glazing, their paper clip. All around the table, they waited in silence for the Editor to say something else . . . anything else, in fact, as this was the very first word that he had uttered in the last hour.

But Massingham did not oblige.

Sally Matthews considered his profile.

Massie didn't appear to be particularly unhappy. In fact, he had made one or two reflex movements in the last quarter of an hour to show that he was alive. Every now and again, he had leaned forward, opened his mouth, and had taken a loud and deep breath. All heads, as now, had dutifully turned in his direction. Then, he had closed his mouth and turned sideways on to the vast conference table, returning his feet to their position on the next chair, and sticking the cigarette back in his mouth.

'Rain?' Sally asked.

'Hmm.'

She looked at the window, following his gaze. The water rushed down the window in rivulets.

'Well,' she said, eyeing both the rain and Eddie

grimly, 'let's get on.' She glanced round the table. 'Where's Lydia?'

The Business sub-editor flicked a paper pellet at the light. 'She's in Oral,' he said.

'I know,' Sally retorted, 'but where is she?'

'Not *into* Oral. *In* Oral,' he told her. 'Kazakstan.'

'I'd like to live in Kazakstan,' murmured the Fashion Editor.

'She's deeply pissed off,' the sub said. 'She's been sitting in Astrakhan airport since six a.m.'

Sally's assistant, Ellen – a woman of fifty, not known for flights of fancy – leaned forward. 'There's an Ars in Denmark,' she said.

'There is not,' Sally said.

'My aunt lives there,' Ellen replied.

'There's a Poko in Zaire,' the Business sub offered.

'Why Kazakstan, anyway? She's not Russian,' Sally said.

'She went there for the weekend, for a laugh.'

'And a poncho,' the Business sub supplied. 'Someone told her you could buy them off herdsmen for ten pence a time.'

Sally sighed. Unlike Lydia, who had been born with several silver spoons stuffed in her mouth, Sally had fought her way up from darkest Dagenham and now, at thirty, wore her long slog up the journalism ladder well. A petite five foot two in her bare feet, she was, however, not the type to be overlooked. She had a piercing gaze, a size 8 silhouette, acid-white blonde hair, and the electric aura of the A-type achiever. She kept the fact that she also had a soft heart as well hidden as she could.

'Why the hell do we employ her?' she said now. 'Her family haven't got a brain between them.'

'You're not allowed to have a brain *and* a title,' Ellen pointed out. 'It's against the law. And –' she drained the

last of her coffee and plonked the cup down on its saucer
'– we employ her because her father's cousin owns sixty-
two per cent of the shares.'

'We shot some underwear in Big Beaver once,' Fashion
said, from the other planet that he inhabited. When they
stared at him, he spread his hands. 'It's in Canada, cross
my heart.'

Sally glanced at Eddie, but his face was still totally
impassive.

Sally had known him for two years. Eddie Massingham's reputation had preceded him, of course. He had
started out, fifteen years ago, as the nerd-haired, horn-
rimmed-glasses boy who still appeared on the various
photos on his office wall, pictured with his hand on
various office doors where he had once been the youngest
this and the youngest that in living memory. He had been
slim then – not the nineteen-stone monster he now was –
and rather handsome behind his hair and glasses.

Eddie Massingham's star had rocketed quickly. It had
been said that he was the biggest and most self-opinionated
bastard on Fleet Street. Sally had often wondered exactly
what depths he had plumbed to earn himself that accolade.
It was said that he had slept with at least four friends'
wives. He had stolen a story every day as a sort of aperitif
to actually writing anything. And, when he was promoted
to the dizzy heights of Editor on the *Daily Grind*, his
articles had ignited one libel case after another.

He was a different man now, of course. You only had
to look at him to see that. His liver gave him a primrose
pallor. His nails were bitten. His stomach ballooned over
his belt. He had taken to throwing computers out of
windows.

His attempt at the women's market, by setting up and
running *The Corker*, had not been a success. Although it
had started out as the thinking-woman's weekly, the

magazine had recently descended into tat and farce. Every week the staff held on to their jobs with their fingernails, as Sally struggled to halt their lemming-like leap into obscurity. She, it seemed, was in charge these days, whether she wanted to be or not. The Editor, it was rumoured, was suffering a breakdown.

Sally didn't know.

All she knew was that the edge was crumbling from the cliff and that she, along with all the other staff, was dangling above the drop while Massie observed the weather.

She looked away from him, and tried to concentrate on the pictures spread before her. Carl, the Fashion Editor, was just starting his pitch on the beachwear.

'Yeah . . . now this is retro seasonal,' he was saying, spreading his pictures around. 'Post-radical, with a manufacture line . . . kinda high white bluesy, low chic . . .'

As usual, no-one knew what he was talking about. But then, neither did he.

Nor did it matter that it was a desperately cold spring, and that most of the women who read the magazine would never see the sun, let alone a beach, for six months. The magazine was running six pages on Goa, and, adding insult to injury, slapping the readers in the face with skeletons in skins masquerading as models. In the background of the shots were two enormous black guys who appeared to be naked. Sally inspected the black guys with a magnifying glass. She knew how the whole foreign-beach scam worked . . . the readers were supposed to lust after the sun, the thin thighs and the men in the back-ground, and then, sighing, settle for the swimsuit.

Readers did, however, possess a few more brain cells than *The Corker* gave them credit for. Every week the staff received letters demanding to know why the magazine saw fit to spend so much money flying anorexic twelve-year-olds to fantasy locations. *The Corker*'s reply was that they only provided the best for their readers, and that you just couldn't get the right light in the UK. Omitting to mention, of course, that Eddie Massingham liked Goa very much.

'Thanks, Carl,' Sally said.

'Karin Muldano's looking grey,' someone commented.

Carl shrugged. 'At least she was upright.'

'I thought she had a month in the clinic.'

'She did.'

'Couldn't you get anyone else?' Sally asked.

Carl gave her an acid look. 'Have you met her agent?' he asked.

There was a knock at the door. The small, worried face of one of the sub-editors looked in.

'Sally? Celia Hawkins has arrived.'

'OK. I'll be a couple of minutes.'

'She's . . .' A pause.

'She's what?'

'Well, she's crying a bit.'

Sally shrugged. Celia Hawkins was a world-famous academic novelist with a world-famous penchant for picking the wrong man. 'Well, it's her own fault,' she said. 'We had that whole article last time about finding true love, etc. How her heart had taken flight on wings of desire, etc. I mean, anyone could see that a future with a four-foot-six sixteen-stone Chilean mud-wrestler was bound to be limited. Give her a cup of tea.'

'All right,' said the face, and disappeared.

Sally looked around the table. She looked at Eddie, at the wisps of once-nerdish, now very thinning, hair. 'OK. Next,' she said. '"Celebrity Dives".'

The Features Editor, a chinless girl, wriggled in her seat.

'Who is it this week?' Sally asked.

'Harry Venturi,' Chinless replied.

The designer across the room groaned. 'Jesus, I thought

he was embalmed already.'

'What's the house like?' Carl asked.

The Features girl wriggled again. 'Bloody *awful*.'

'How awful?'

'Leopardskin walls. Filthy kitchen. Filipino housemaid who wouldn't stop hoovering. And this huge sticker to one side of the front door. *Jesus Is My Life*.'

'He brought out that song before Christmas,' Carl said.

'"Love Me Again Like Jesus Does",' Sally replied.

'It stank.'

'So does his fridge,' said Features.

'Any revelations?' Sally asked.

'He asked me to measure his testicles.'

There was a prolonged and breathless silence.

'He did what?'

She fidgeted. 'Measure them. Weigh them.'

'*Weigh* his testicles?'

Features shrugged. 'He said that he was very worried about testicular cancer and that he had weighed them last month, and intended weighing them every month, because apparently that's one of the signs, when one starts weighing heavier than it used to, and he said that he couldn't do it properly himself and would like me to . . .' she spread her hands. 'You know – weigh them.'

Sally stared at her. 'How, exactly?'

'On the kitchen scales.'

Someone down the table sniggered.

'He had a brass pair. Of scales. You know, with the little baskets you put things in.'

Sally put her hand briefly over her eyes, then dropped it.

'He was going to stand on a chair and put the scales on the kitchen worktop . . .'

'Oh, spare me,' Sally said. 'No. No. Definitely no.' She was thinking of Harry Venturi, sixty if he was a day, in his

too-tight slick LA suit, with his silk T-shirt straining over
his paunch, and the colour leaking from his hair as he
sweated. 'No more.'

Carl leaned forward. 'Did you?' he asked Features.

'Of course not!'

'Thank God for that,' Sally whispered.

'Not with him standing on a chair,' Features added.

Sally held up her hand to stem the torrent of questions
rushing to everyone's lips. 'I'm finishing this meeting,' she
said. She glanced at her secretary. 'Ellen, please recap.'

Ellen, stony-faced and monotone, ran through the list of
items they had covered that morning.

'"Ten Best, Readers' Husbands, My Dad Wasn't My
Dad, My Dog Is A Drunk, Waterproof Wetlooks, My
Three Thousand Lives, My Wife Wasn't A Woman, Diets
To Die For, My Daughter Wasn't My Daughter" . . .'

'I saw that woman,' Carl said.

'Which one?' Sally asked.

'The "My Dad Wasn't My Dad" woman.'

They all began gathering up their papers, standing up,
eating the last crumbs from the Danish pastry dish.

'Actually,' Sally said, 'she was very nice.'

'She was very *tall*.'

'That too.'

They all looked at Massie.

'Is that all, then?' Sally asked.

The Editor closed his eyes.

'Is that OK, Eddie?' she said.

They watched him in silence. He made no move at all.

'OK,' Sally said. 'Right then.'

And, in a long trailing line, they left.

3

Chris turned the corner of her street.

It was dark by the Tube station, where the streetlight had failed last August and had not yet been repaired. She looked at the distant outline of her own house, the end of a Georgian terrace, a marooned block squeezed in next to a warehouse and facing a row of Victorian cottages.

Reaching the Victorian terrace, Chris stopped at the kerb, waiting for an opportunity to cross. The three-storey Georgian block was in darkness, in contrast to the lit windows on this side of the street. From somewhere behind her, Chris could hear the booming throb of a bass, and the squawk of voices – whether an argument or laughter, she couldn't tell.

Chris harboured a secret desire to live here, on the Victorian side. Life seemed to be more fun in the run-down row whose railings peeled inelegantly into the two-foot concrete squares that used to be gardens. For one thing, the women who lived in these houses seemed to know everyone. In the morning, when they had finished shouting their last instructions to their children, they would stand happily on their steps, leaning on their door frames, while they yelled routinely at neighbours and passing traffic. By some method that Chris had never figured out, they knew the bus drivers and the motorbike couriers and the delivery truck drivers. Even the postman seemed to go to that side of the road first, as if drawn by animal magnetism.

Chris's side of the street, by contrast, was like a ghost

town. No one ever leaned on their door frame here, unless it was to recover for a moment after opening the credit card bill. None of them on the Georgian side knew their neighbours, either. Not in any detail. For instance, all that Chris knew about the couple living next door to her was that the man left his house at about six in the morning, dressed in a suit. And the woman left soon after, dressed in a suit. There were no children. And they ran up and down their stairs squeaking and squealing when they got home, and then made irritating orgasmic noises right next to the party wall.

In fact, it was as if the Georgian side of the street were another country altogether. A No-Kid country. The residents were all just singles with driven expressions and real fireplaces and power showers. Or else business couples with island kitchens and terracotta floors, Ikea catalogues and distressed stairs. But the other side of the street was definitely Kid Country. Kids whose stickers and stuffed toys crowded their window sills, whose bikes were chained to the flimsy porches, whose T-shirts and jeans hung flapping on the lines at the back. Of course, there was never any washing to see on Chris's side. Coming home in the dark, the driven singles and childless couples transferred their clothes from flesh to machine and back again. Nothing Chris wore had ever flapped on a line.

And then there were the bottoms. Bottoms flourished everywhere in Kid Country – in fact, some of the women in Kid Country had positively cornered the flourishing and roaring Bottom market. They owned vast estates of bottoms, enormous sprawling industrial bottoms, rolling landscaped and floral-decked bottoms, conglomerate bums of breathtaking width and influence. They refused to conform to the pedal pushers they were put in. They broke out of jeans and strained the seams of skirts. Some of them were true Gothic arses of staggering breadth and splendour, that waved about grandly under coats, slapping from side to side as their owners walked, the prize-winning result of thousands of white bread sandwiches, fry-ups, bacon butties, pizzas, chips, doughnuts, Jammie Dodgers, finest-quality fried Mars bars, and exceedingly good cakes.

The Georgian side of the street had no bottoms at all.

Here, bums had been scoured from existence, dieted to death. Singles' bottoms were made from vodka and obsession, and No-Kid couples' bottoms were made from pinched frustration. Open any dustbin in No-Kid country and Chris was convinced that you would find several out-of-date bottoms, wrapped up shamefully in black plastic sacks. She often wondered what her life would be like if she woke up with a heritage-style bum one day, a really stunning Caribbean slap-hanging no-nonsense rear end, and hung out of the window with it, calling at gas repair men. Instead of which she crept out of her home soon after Woman In Suit, concealing her barely-upholstered arse as she drifted to the Tube like a shadow.

She waited for a gap in the traffic, glancing at her watch. It was seven o'clock. In Kid Country, cars continually swerved to a halt, disgorged passengers, stood at the kerb letting the engine idle, and then roared off again. It was a cacophony of slamming doors. The No-Kid/No-Bottom side stood mute, with the faint air of someone who has not been invited to a party and, trying to look somewhere else, claims that they don't care.

Chris finally managed to cross over, and put her key in the door. And there in the hallway, as usual, the love of her husband's life was waiting for her.

Electra the cat wore a pained expression. Chris reached down to pick up the enormously fat, yellow-eyed tabby, but it shrank away from her hand. 'I'm not late,' she said.

Looking at Electra eye to eye like this, their mutual

contempt was evident. Chris tried to love Electra –
attempted to display at least a small fraction of her
husband Malcolm's adoration for the cat – but it was
hardly worth it. Electra always stared at her as if Chris
were something dead that even she, a committed
murderess, could not stomach. 'I'm living with *you*?' she
seemed to be saying. 'In this house? How crass.'

Electra stalked back to the door and sat looking at it,
waiting for Malcolm.

Chris put down her bag. She sorted through the mail,
filled the kettle and switched it on. Then she heard the
door crash open next door, and a flurry of conversation,
and rapid steps, and then water running. Then a screech of
laughter, and some relatively half-hearted squealing. The
Suits were home.

Bastards, Chris thought. Sex every night.

It was eight o'clock before Malcolm came in. By that
time, Chris was sitting in front of the fire in the sitting
room on the first floor when she heard his key in the lock.

'Darling,' he said. She could hear him wiping his feet on
the mat in the hallway. 'You lovely girl. What have you
been doing today, eh? Gone for a walk? Had a nice sleep?
Look at you, all lovely. Who's my own best cat . . .'

Chris gritted her teeth.

There was a pause of almost a minute while Malcolm
and Electra admired each other. Then Malcolm called
upstairs. 'Darling? Home?'

'Yes,' she replied.

'Guess what?'

'What?' she responded.

'Thirty-nine pence!'

Chris sighed. She heard him coming up the stairs with
his usual measured steps. He stuck his head in the door.
'OK?'

'Yes.'

'Thirty-nine pence!' he repeated. Malcolm had a thing about finding money in the street.

'Yes, I heard.'

'A twenty-pence piece on the down escalator at Bank.'

'Good,' she said.

'And we had a hatching today.'

'Did you? Great,' she said. Malcolm bred a kind of super-maggot for medical research. She always tried to be enthusiastic.

'I'm just going to take my eyes out.'

He disappeared. She listened to his footsteps going up to the next floor.

Malcolm said the same thing every night. *I'm just going to take my eyes out* – which meant he was going to remove and soak his contact lenses. Long, long ago, several centuries ago, this phrase had been funny. Far back in her memory, Chris dimly recalled laughing at it. Three years ago? Four?

Ever since they had been married, probably, which was six years ago. Six years – how many weeks was that? Three hundred and twelve, Chris rapidly calculated in her head. She had always been good at maths. Three hundred and twelve weeks equalled two thousand, one hundred and eight-four days. And at the end of every day, Malcolm took his eyes out. Two thousand, one hundred and eighty-four times he had uttered that innocuous little joke.

She heard him run water in the bathroom.

He had other phrases, too.

Excuse-em-moir-oh. He never actually ever said, 'Excuse me.'

Dally-baguetty-oh. This meant bread.

Appall-y-ensis. Horrible, disgraceful.

Goggles. Spectacles.

'Oh God, that's *sooooo sweeeeet*!' one of the girls in the office had said when Chris had carelessly confided

Malcolm's private language. 'Oh, I would *love* a man to say things like that!'

It was sweet.

Possibly.

But, repeated by rote daily, it had lost its sweetness somehow. What was that song? 'Does Your Chewing Gum Lose Its Flavour on the Bedpost Overnight?' Like a song out of the dim past, a song from *Family Favourites*, played at Sunday lunch all through her childhood.

Chris sighed. The letter crinkled in the pocket of her skirt.

Malcolm reappeared, dressed in a very old flannel shirt and sad jeans of such antiquity that they had even been ancient when she had met him.

He kissed her on the cheek. 'Good day?'

'Terrible.'

He sat down next to her, tweaked her knee. He was very fond of her, anyone could see that. And he showed it all the time, patting her arm, tickling her chin, and calling her pet names.

'Oh, little poppet,' he said. 'Why?'

'I got a letter.'

'You did?' he said, his eyebrows arched in surprise. 'Not from the publisher?'

'Yes.'

'Not a bad one?'

'Yes.'

'Oh, poppet,' he said. 'They sent it back?'

'Under separate cover.'

'No taste,' he said. He put his arm around her shoulder.

'I don't think they had even read it,' she said.

'It's better than any of the trash on the shelves.'

'I know that,' she told him.

'You're really very, very good,' he said.

'I know that,' she said, 'and you know it, but we are the

only two people on the face of the planet who do.'

'It's better than any of the trash on the shelves,' he repeated.

This was a familiar exchange, one which, by now, was almost achieving the status of *I'm taking my eyes out*.

At first the rejection letters for Chris's novel had really hurt. The few terse sentences. The coffee ring stain that had been on one. The returned manuscript, its pages battered at the edges where it had been used as a doorstop. She remembered the very first time as if it were yesterday.

A couple of years ago, she had sent her novel to a publisher. It wasn't romance. It wasn't slush. It was . . . well, she thought it was compact. Witty. Off-the-wall. Original. A description that now brought a wry, child-just-smacked smile to her face.

She had not known which publisher she ought to submit it to, other than the obvious choice of not handing her baby over to *Roof-Trusses Monthly*. And she would rather have died than confess to anyone at work that she had a book to sell. So, she had sat for a long time in the local library poring over the names of the companies listed in the writers' reference book. The names of the Fiction Directors all sounded fantastically literary, or else very thrusting and businesslike, which was possibly worse. *Camilla Rhineheart . . . James Punch . . . Fabia Gossleigh-Warner*.

Chris had agonised over those names, imagining the people who owned them. Trying to guess their ages. Trying to visualise them at their desks. Eventually, she had decided upon the Fabia, because she had once had a friend at school called Sarah Fabian, who had been very nice because she was enduring an entire school life being bullied over her weight. It gave her a tired, helplessly anxious-to-please look, and Chris imagined Fabia Gossleigh-Warner with the same hesitant expression –

mostly because she was too frightened to imagine Fabia
Gossleigh-Warner as a wraith in Kookaï.

She had taken the book – this precious feat of mental
engineering, this piece of her flesh – to the Post Office, paid
the extortionate postage and given the manuscript a little
pat of encouragement before it was whipped under the
counter partition by the woman in frosted spectacles.
Chris had felt herself flush, as if a child of hers had been
touched by a stranger.

'Has the package any value?' the woman asked.

'It's priceless,' she had responded, laughing self-
consciously, and then immediately feeling stupid. 'No,' she
added hastily, while the woman regarded her with an
expression of extreme boredom. 'No, it's got no value.'

She had waited eleven weeks.

Eleven long weeks.

She had not dared ring up Fabia Gossleigh-Warner and
ask her if she had received the book. She didn't want to
seem desperate. What could be worse than to be a woman
of the advanced age of thirty-eight who has poured all her
hopes into a few hundred pages of A4? How much more
pathetic could one be? In darker moments, she thought of
Fabia Gossleigh-Warner ridiculing her book, pointing at it
on top of a teetering pile. 'Slush!' Fabia jeered in Chris's
dreams. 'Unadulterated slush!'

And yet sometimes Chris allowed herself a small flight
of fantasy.

She would imagine the book – The Book – sitting on a
conference-room table somewhere, while discussion raged
about it and someone in charge of Fabia Gossleigh-Warner
yelled, 'You mean you haven't signed her up yet? Get on
the phone this minute!'

This fantasy sometimes got so out of hand that Chris
would leap every time the phone rang in her office. The
fact that it would be a Neighbour from Hell, or a Police

Sadist, or a Midwife in Leather, or someone from a media complaints authority – which was pretty well daily – would be of less interest to her than the little red light winking at her on the other line. She would be sure that Fabia Gossleigh-Warner was sitting, drumming her fingers on the precious manuscript, waiting to be connected to her new best-selling author.

The manuscript had come back on the Friday of the eleventh week.

The letter said, *Thank you for leting me see your novel. It was interesting but I'm afraid not right for out list.*

Fabia Gossleigh-Warner's name was printed at the bottom, but someone else had signed it – with an unreadable scrawl.

Chris had read that letter – and the signature – twenty times.

Almost as bad as the rejection was the fact that Fabia Gossleigh-Warner had let some illiterate assistant mis-type the reply. And whoever had done it obviously hadn't read her novel and didn't care.

Chris had laid down on the floor that first time and wept.

She wept harder than she had for years, full Technicolor weeping that soaked the carpet on which she lay. It was, sadly and shamefully, as hard as when she had miscarried. Harder than when her first boyfriend had dumped her when she was fourteen. It was true hard-core crying.

Eventually she had got up, cursing herself, her own idiocy, her waiting, and even cursing the manuscript. She had dusted herself down, picking bits of cat litter off herself, cursing Electra for good measure. She had thumped the two nearest doors, so that, even now, the hinges on one pulled away from the wood. Then she had flung the manuscript into a cupboard, slammed the door, and kicked it.

She had turned to find Electra watching her with a knowing smile.

When Malcolm had come home, he had said, 'But it's better than any of the trash on the shelves,' and kissed her.

This very afternoon, after getting Mrs Pye and her quacking husband into make-up, Chris had taken a walk outside, out to the railings by the river. She had looked at the water for ages, while the rain clouds cleared, scudding across the sky.

Eventually she had come to a realisation, one that had been lurking at the back of her mind for some time, but which she hadn't liked to admit until now.

It wasn't the book. *It was her*.

You could always, with luck, fix a book. Edit it, re-write it, throw it up in the air, pick up the scattered pages, and see if it read any better starting at Chapter 17 followed by the Prologue. No probs.

However, she herself was simply not marketable material. Her shelf-life had expired. All her shoes had *Clarks* written inside them, and she knew that, in the world of sexily marketable women writers, that was deeply sad. Whenever she got herself dressed up, she knew that she looked more like a loosely tied bundle of washing than a literary superstar. With her faintly freckled face, brown eyes and reddish hair, she looked more like a spaniel than a femme fatale. And you couldn't put a grinning spaniel on the jacket of a book. You put carelessly barefoot with a cigarette. You put too cool for words on a Paris street. But *not* spaniel.

Plus, she had none of the essential requirements of being famous.

She was not twenty-one and living in a house with three other girls in Chelsea. She was not anyone's mistress. She was not a supermodel, a TV gardener, or a politician. She was not Indian or Mexican or Chinese. She was not a lesbian, a tree campaigner, a defrocked vicar, or a polar explorer. In short, she was of no interest to the publishing world.

And somehow the publishers – all the Fabias of this world – had known this just by looking at her manuscript. They sensed her size 6E shoes, and her chronic spaniel-ness, wafting up from the pages like some weird form of osmosis.

All she could do was write.

And that, she had thought, turning away from the river and kicking the railings for good measure, was no earthly bloody good to a publisher at all.

4

It was six o'clock when Sally saw Massie again.

She was in a hurry, desperate to get home before Dermott. She wanted to be there when her husband got in, because he was so rarely in, and there were things she wanted to talk to him about. There were always things she wanted to talk to him about, but pinning him down was like knitting fog. As she piled papers into her briefcase, she didn't notice Massie coming across the room.

'How are things?' he asked.

She jolted at the sound of his voice. So, she thought wryly, you can speak. 'Fine . . . fine,' she told him.

'Going?'

'Yes, I—'

'Got a minute?'

She hesitated, but Massie had already turned and was walking back in the direction of his office.

'You sod,' she muttered, following him.

As she came in the door, he indicated the two lounge chairs at the far end of the office. Her heart immediately sank. Only the most serious of discussions took place there, and, as she had already been told a month ago that there was no money for pay rises, she doubted that Massie had any good news for her now. The only other reason that she could think of for sitting in the low chairs was to dissect the latest issue, page by page – something that Massie occasionally did when he had no dinner appointment and hated the thought of going home to his empty house.

'Sit down,' he said.

She paused. 'Massie, I'm sorry, but I do have to be home fairly early tonight.'

'Sit down,' he repeated.

She did so. He lit a cigarette, taking an age over it. She realised that she ought not to have said anything; now he would prolong the hour to an hour-and-a-half, for the sheer pleasure of seeing her fret. She tried to compose her face.

'How's everything this week?' he asked.

'Fine,' she said. 'You were at the meeting . . .'

'Yes. Fine, is it? That so? Everything absolutely fine?'

She tried to gauge what he was getting at. Obviously things were not fine. But what exactly had gone wrong, she was at a loss to know. 'Is something bothering you?' she asked.

He said nothing for a moment, then smiled. 'Should it be?'

'I don't know,' she said warily. 'You tell me.'

He took a long drag from his cigarette. 'What is your position on this magazine?'

'Senior Editor,' she said.

'Senior Editor?' he asked innocently. 'And what does that involve?'

What indeed. It had no meaning in itself. Massie had created it, taken her on to do his work.

'Massie . . .' she began.

'Senior Editor.' He considered the tip of the cigarette, then pointed it at her. 'But you aren't, are you?'

'What do you mean?'

'Well,' he said, 'seeing you at the meeting this afternoon, one could be forgiven for thinking that you were several flights above the editors. One could imagine that you were *The* Editor, perhaps. The Managing Director, perhaps. The owner.'

A slow flush crept up Sally's face. She cursed the give-away of her temper. She kept her hands clasped hard in her lap. 'What's the problem?' she asked.

'Problem,' he said. 'Yes, it is a problem.' He sat forward suddenly, thrusting his yellow face towards her pink one. He looked so unwell. 'I hired you as a feature writer, if I recall,' he said. 'And here you are taking over the whole bloody shooting match.'

'That's not fair,' she retorted.

'Oh! Not fair? Dear me, how fucking sad. It's not *fair*, is it – taking the chair of my own meeting?'

'You wouldn't speak!' she accused him. 'Someone had to.'

He snatched a copy of the Christmas issue from the table in front of them. 'And you produce shit like this,' he said, and slammed the copy back down to the table. 'Shit!'

She had seen him work himself into a temper before. It used to happen regularly, until last year when, during a screaming fit, he had suffered what everyone took to be a heart attack and was carted off in an ambulance. High drama – not to mention high hopes – had enlivened the office for an afternoon. But Massie had been right back in work the next morning, telling everyone that he had had an *episode*, and that they were to be bloody kind to him. The experience had sobered him for a fortnight, literally. He had never quite achieved the same level of apoplexy again.

Until now.

Sally had time to wonder, vaguely, what it was that had lit the blue touchpaper, before he started turning the pages of the magazine viciously, ripping a few as he went. 'This – and this – and *this* . . . shit, shit and more shit!'

'You wanted that leader,' Sally objected. 'You told me to find a mismatched couple and I found them. How much more extreme did you want than a seventeen-year-old welder and a W.I. President?'

'Shit!'

'Massie,' she said softly, 'if you say that word just once more, I shall be forced to kill you.'

She had meant it as a joke. Unfortunately, he didn't take it as one. His expression disintegrated into a sneer. 'I took you on as someone with talent,' he said. 'Where did it go? Did you have it removed? Was it sucked off by machine? Abandoned in Left Luggage – what?'

'I have talent,' she said. 'But you never use it.'

He shoved the magazine under her nose. 'Show me your talent,' he said. 'Show me the page.'

She regarded him levelly. 'Massie, I'm going home.' She half-rose to her feet.

'No, you bloody aren't!' he shouted. 'You've engineered this magazine into bankruptcy.'

'Bankruptcy?' she said. 'But it isn't bankrupt, surely?'

'It will be in three months,' he said.

She lowered herself to her seat. There was a long, fraught silence.

She thought of the advertisers he had turned away, of the contacts he had lost. She thought of his scenes at restaurants and theatres. She thought of the rumour that he had slept with the wife of a leading banker, and wondered – not for the first time – if it was the wife of the banker who financed this magazine.

Massie was sitting with his head in his hands. His voice, when it came, was that of a slapped three-year-old. 'You've hurt me,' he said.

'Hurt you?' she echoed, incredulous. 'By doing all your work, by following every instruction?'

'Yes,' he said.

She got up. She really was intending to leave, but had only gone two paces when she turned back to him. 'When you hired me, you lied to me,' she said. 'You told me that

The Corker was going to be an upmarket, satirical, slick weekly. Witty, dangerous, expensive . . .'

'It was,' he said.

'No,' she told him. 'It never was. You lost your nerve.'

'You brought in true life stories,' he muttered.

'Because you told me to!' she said. 'It was only for a couple of weeks, you said. A joke, you said. Now it's every week. Now it's our staple. Except we don't do it as well as the rest, we're a parody, and we don't even do that well. We've got no identity. And that's down to *you*.'

She took a breath, looking at the balding spot in the top of his hair that she hadn't noticed until now.

'I don't want that stuff,' he said.

'But it's what you bloody well demand.'

'I've changed my mind.'

'Well,' she said. 'Fine.'

'I haven't a penny to my name,' he said.

She bit her lip. A cold wave rose in her throat. 'Massie, I don't care,' she said.

'You betrayed me,' he said.

'I was hired as a Political Correspondent,' she said. 'Remember?' This was true. Massie had headhunted her, back in those old glory days a couple of years ago when he was setting up the magazine – with, it was rumoured, a pay-off on a libel case.

For once it was Massie who had been libelled, and not the other way around. He had then pursued Sally Matthews like a fevered suitor – in fact, for one horrible week, she had actually thought that getting her into bed was on his mind, such were the tender little admiring notes with the flowers, the phone calls early in the morning, the little gifts – and then he had persuaded her that he was launching the most outrageous, funny and unusual magazine in the world, and that she would be the best paid, the funniest, the most outrageous name in the media.

Oh God. It sounded so naïve now. Massie had lost one of his backers in the early months. Instead of keeping his nerve, he had argued with another sought-after name, who had had the good sense to leave him to his own devices and bugger off to the *Guardian*. Six weeks later, appalled by low sales, Massie had dropped his price by half. From then on, the writing had been not so much in the magazine as on the wall.

Sally could have had some sympathy with him as his image became ever more ridiculed and tarnished – the speed king farting along on the hard shoulder of the media motorway, his engine coughing, his tyres deflated, while racier models, magazines with titled columnists, award-winning cooks and favoured arts critics thrashed past him in a blur – if only he had shown a fraction of his better nature. But Massie came from the Genghis Khan school of man-management, and staff dropped from him like flies, until Sally was hiring younger and younger starry-eyed trainees. Or, worse still, young hard-faced monosyllabic graduates who hated everything they did and spent most of their time combing the Sits Vac.

She had almost left last year, as a job had been offered to her abroad. Dermott was in one of his particularly absent phases, and she had reasoned that she was as likely to meet him in New York as in Primrose Hill. At that point, before she had time to hand in her notice, Massie had his *episode*.

Feeling that it would be shitty – supremely and Massie-like shitty – to kick him when he was down, she had hesitated, and then Dermott had come home and started fantasising about them having a family.

Without consulting her, he ordered a complete reno-vation of the house and, realising that it would cost a fortune, Sally decided to stay put at *The Corker* until the spring. This spring.

It was nearly here, she reminded herself.

'I'm going to be ruined,' Massie moaned.

She sighed, glancing at her watch. 'It can't be that bad.'

'It is.'

'Well, thank God it isn't your money.'

'It is. I bought in a year ago.'

There was nothing more to say. Bad judgement and a loud mouth had been Massie's downfall all his professional life. She felt sorry for him. That was the trouble. She had always felt sorry for him. And she said so now.

'I'm sorry.'

He made a noise – 'Mmm . . . mmm . . .' like a failing generator. He took out a handkerchief – in a revoltingly filthy state, she noticed – and wiped his nose. She thought he might actually cry.

'When did you hear?' she asked. She thought of the yawning chasm of redundancy facing her. Facing not only the hardened graduates and the innocent has-beens, but nice women like their copy typist Sarah Hardy, who had four children at school.

'I saw the bank today,' Massie said.

'How many weeks have we got?' she said.

'Six. Eight. Sixteen. I don't know.'

'But they must have given you a deadline.'

'They raised their voices,' he said, with a note of contempt.

'How many weeks?' she insisted.

'Nothing I can do,' he murmured.

'How many weeks!'

He looked away from her and pleated the edge of his jacket between thumb and forefinger.

Then, cold realisation hit her. 'You're lying,' she said.

There was no response.

'Are we going under or not?'

'We might well do if you don't pull your fucking finger out,' he said.

She stared at him. He was just unbelievable. Totally unbelievable. 'What has this really been about?' she asked.

'What d'you mean?'

'These last fifteen bloody minutes,' she said. 'What did you really call me in for? You're no more bankrupt than I am.'

'I will be if this rag doesn't shape up,' he said.

She considered him for a long time. One more tantrum. And now Dermott would be home before her, and that would be another tantrum, another sulk. Christ!

'You were bored, weren't you?' she demanded. 'That's what it was. So you decided to while away a few minutes taunting and threatening me and blaming all your faults on me . . .' She felt utterly choked. She picked up her bag and walked to the door.

'Come back,' Massie shouted.

She glanced around at him. 'You self-centred bastard,' she said.

'You're fired,' he told her.

'Good,' she responded. 'I can't stomach you any more.' She put her hand on the door, but couldn't resist the words that came storming into her mouth. 'I'm so sick of your man-of-the-people farce,' she said. 'That's why this magazine is so bad. You think you've got the common touch.'

'I have got the common touch,' he said. 'I know what people want.'

'And how do you make that out?' she challenged him. 'Brought up in your fur-lined carrycot and fed with a bloody silver spade. The last time that a window cleaner came into your office, you practically backed into a corner, you were so afraid of him.'

'I wasn't afraid,' he said.

She gave a short-tempered snort of a laugh. 'You were terrified. He only asked you for a light.'

'Well? I gave him a light.'

'You dropped the matches all over the desk.'

'He looked like a bloody mugger!' Massie objected. 'There I am, working away, head down, concentrating . . .'

'You were asleep,' Sally said.

'I was not asleep. I was thinking.'

'And snoring.'

'I look up, and there's this shaven-headed mugger about to hold a knife to my throat . . .'

'That's your trouble,' Sally said. 'You think that you know the man in the street, and you can't even recognise him when he's right in front of your eyes. As for the woman in the street . . .'

'Look here—'

'What do you know or care about women? You went to an all-boys' prep school and an all-boys' public school and I reckon you somehow paid for a place at Cambridge for three years . . .'

'Where I did bloody well for myself,' he interrupted.

'On the backs of other people,' she retorted. 'You think the world owes you a living. You just have no idea what it's like to have no money to fall back on, to have to live from week to week—'

'Hark at La Misérable,' Massie said. 'Married to Dermott Matthews!'

She fixed him with a look. 'You've got a nerve, the way you lean on Miriam,' she said, her voice dropping dangerously low. 'Getting photographed at Tatler parties next to some grinning fifteen-year-old tart.'

'Watch it,' he said.

'Paying ten thousand quid for a teddy bear at some Tory auction. Turning up at Glyndebourne so smashed that you fall into the flowerbeds.'

'Food-poisoning – the fish was bad!'

'Going on *Start the Weekend* and claiming you're the Voice of Britain, while Miriam picks up your bills, Miriam and her one-brain-celled family. And then you have the gall to call this magazine a failure, when you rarely show your face . . .'

'Take a breath,' he said. 'You're turning blue.'

'And then you fill in a few dead minutes on a Friday night by hauling me in here and ripping me off when you've ruined any career I might have had.'

'Piss off,' he said. 'You never had a career worth mentioning.'

She stared at him for a moment. Then, very slowly, she picked up her briefcase, and opened it. She turned it upside-down and emptied everything out. Papers, files, back copies . . . everything hit the carpet with a thud.

'Goodbye,' she said.

'Don't bother to come back,' he said.

She stopped in the doorway. With her back to him, and still shaking, she considered half-a-dozen different exit lines. In an hour's time, she would actually come up with three devastating throwaway ripostes. But nothing at all came to her right now, except the desire to turn and throw something blunt and heavy at his head.

In the end, she said nothing at all.

As she walked away down the corridor, she heard him shout, 'I mean it!'

Not bothering to wait for the lift, she walked down the 114 stairs to the fresh air.

5

At 1 a.m., the phone rang. Chris was busy at the Whitbread Awards. She was sitting at a table with Tom Hanks, who had just been lowered on a rope through the roof. 'I'm looking for Private Ryan,' he said.

'We're all heroes here,' she told him sweetly.

The cameras were whirring at her back. In the corner, they were nailing crosses to the wall just above the head of a very senior publisher.

'What's your name?' Tom Hanks asked.

She smiled at him coquettishly. He didn't seem to have noticed that she was over twenty-five. Quite a long way over twenty-five, in fact. Over the hill and rolling swiftly down the other side. Instead, he was looking at her with undiluted desire, which was strange, because she still had her slippers on, and they were made out of Shredded Wheat Bitesize boxes. 'I'm Christine Craven,' she said.

He picked an envelope out of his dinner jacket. 'It's you!' he cried. 'Best Screenplay!'

She rose to her feet. The Whitbread Award came flying through the air. She dodged it, knocking it across the room. The Booker judges rushed down the central aisle, dressed as archangels, carrying the Ark of the Covenant between them.

Harrison Ford materialised at her elbow, wearing his hat and carrying his whip. 'Don't look into the light,' he said. 'Close your eyes . . . don't look into the light!'

The angels plucked heavenly music from their mobile phones.

'I must get that call,' she said.

'The light,' he whispered.

'Give me the prize first,' she said.

'The light!'

'The prize!'

A hand grabbed her arm. She flipped over into bed.

'Hello?' said another man.

'I mustn't open my eyes,' she mumbled.

'Wake up,' said the same voice. But this time, it wasn't Tom Hanks, or Harrison Ford.

She opened her eyes. Malcolm was sitting up in bed next to her, the phone pressed to his ear. As she gazed foggily at him, he nodded towards her side of the bed and mouthed, '*The light*'. She rolled over, switched it on, and turned back to him.

He sat a little more upright. 'When?' he asked. There was a silence while he listened to the reply. 'And where is that?'

She watched him. His face was completely expression-less.

'Thank you,' he said. 'Yes.' He put the phone down.

'What is it?' Christine asked. 'Who was that?'

He swung his legs out of bed and paused for a moment, gazing down at the floor. 'It was some hospital in Kent,' he said. He picked up his watch and squinted at it.

'It's five past eleven,' Chris told him. 'What's happened?'

He stood up, and reached for his dressing gown. 'My father's had a stroke,' he said.

As they drove down through London – a sulphur-lit London, one set of traffic-lights after another, no pedestrians, endless yellow-lined roads – and out on to the motorway, Chris thought of when she had first met Malcolm's parents.

She had been thirty-two. Malcolm, only a year older, was still living at home. He was entirely free of any attachments. But Chris came with a full set of emotional baggage.

In fact, when Chris – who had been married before – visualised that emotional baggage, she saw herself staggering out of a door with both arms full, and a harness strapped to her body from which extended a long line attached to a separate overloaded trolley, the kind they dragged with a towtruck to the side of aircraft. Serious, undisputed world-heavyweight baggage.

Her first husband had been called Kevin.

Lives are theatre. As a teenager, Chris had always seen herself modestly centre-stage with, given a fair wind and a bit of luck, some sort of interesting role to play. In this leading role, she would always have a fine line in acid wit, and be married to a man called James. At any moment James would be perfectly capable of throwing off his languid air and, like the Scarlet Pimpernel, become an adventurer. Then he would be called Jack. In teenage fantasies, Chris was always either with James or Jack, floating in and out of literary salons in an expensive dress, or lying on Jack's boat off the Great Barrier Reef while he throttled sharks with his bare hands. Very occasionally, James and Jack would take second place to a Charles or a Rick or a Harry. Never – never, never, *never* – did Chris spend any time at all with a Kevin.

She had often wondered why it was her mission in life to marry the men whose names nobody else wanted. Nobody in their right mind married a Kevin or a Malcolm.

Chris's husband Kevin had been an accountant with a little company in Liverpool occupying a nondescript block near Lime Street, and she, in this past life which she tried very hard not to recall, had been working for the Inland Revenue.

She was twenty-five when they first met. She wore 1980s power suits with ridiculously wide shoulders, so wide that it was a miracle that she didn't, by law, have to have a sign on her back saying *Dangerously Wide Load*. She wore big suits, big heels, and had big, big hair. The hair took hours of dedicated rollering and spraying and welding to achieve its carelessly tousled look, a kind of *When Harry Met Sally* style, but with 50,000 volts run through it. She was positively stunning.

Kevin had big hair, too. He tried desperately hard to look like Bobby in *Dallas*, and spent ages every morning getting his hair to curl under. Unfortunately, it was always a bit too wiry to stay where it was put and ended up resembling three cottage loaves fighting for purchase on a hopelessly narrow shelf. Nevertheless, he was incredibly proud of his crowning glory and, on the first night that Chris had noticed him in a crowded Liverpool pub, Kevin had been in the process of artfully flicking his curls.

The juke box was playing Spandau Ballet.

He came over and said, 'Drinking?'

'Yes,' she said.

'Buy us one,' he told her. And she did.

The next five years were like that.

As the signs for the M3 blared blue through the windscreen, Chris looked over at Malcolm and wondered why she should think of Kevin now.

The answer was probably because he always came into her mind at times of crisis and worry. The themes were inextricably linked, after all. Kevin . . . crisis . . . worry. Worry . . . crisis . . . Kevin. It was Pavlovian. Instead of salivating when a bell was rung, her throat went dry when Kevin arrived in her head. He was accompanied by images of a court bailiff peering into her garage . . . of a woman smirking at her at a party, of a cottage-loaf perm wilting in summer humidity, and a patch of ground by a window where she had buried Kevin's whole Showaddywaddy collection.

She wrenched her attention back to Malcolm, a pale profile in the dark car.

'Who found him?' she asked.

'Mrs Robbins.'

Mrs Robbins was Malcolm's father's home help.

'What time?'

'Half past five.'

Chris considered for a moment. 'And she took all this time to ring you?'

'She didn't ring,' he said, his eyes fixed on the road. 'The Ward Sister in the ICU rang me.'

'But . . .'

'He was on the floor in the kitchen,' Malcolm said. 'She could see him but he had bolted the door. She had to call the police. They broke in.'

Chris said nothing. Mrs Robbins was not very bright. It was amazing that she had managed to call the police, and not very amazing that she had forgotten to call Malcolm. Once Malcolm's father was in the ambulance, she would have gone to bingo.

They reached the hospital at ten minutes to midnight.

The corridors were deserted. Poorly lit, echoing. Smelling of fish and polish. It was a new wing. They hurried to Intensive Care between the worst pictures Chris had ever seen. Someone had been commissioned to draw the hospital's new wing in various stages of construction, and these drawings had now been framed and hung at intervals along the walls to Intensive Care. Passing them was like enduring a slow decline into chaos, as the prints began at completion and worked backwards, so that at the door of Intensive Care you were presented with a painting of scaffolding and several churned-up acres of mud.

'Lovely,' Chris muttered, under her breath.

The Ward Sister came towards them.

'Mr Craven,' Malcolm said. 'How is he?'

'Comfortable,' she said. 'Responsive.'

Well, there's a first, Chris thought. And immediately hated herself for the thought.

Malcolm almost ran to the bedside where Henry Craven, aged seventy-three, was lying, naked to the waist, festooned with wires. His eyes were open.

'Dad,' Malcolm said.

'He's having a problem with speech,' the Sister explained. 'It's his right side.'

Henry flexed his left fist, as if to illustrate.

'Dad, don't worry,' Malcolm said.

Henry looked at his son, and then at Chris.

'Hello, Dad,' Chris murmured.

He stared at her accusingly. It was the same old stare.

'He's all right,' Chris whispered.

'Dad,' Malcolm said, not looking at her.

The Sister touched Chris's arm. 'These are early days,' she said. He is all right, Chris thought. Look at him. 'He has suffered a very serious setback,' the nurse added.

Chris sat down at Malcolm's side and looked into Henry's face. The skin was ochre yellow, a legacy of years of smoking and sitting in the sun. His eyes were pale blue, the whites mottled with yellow. She had read somewhere that that was a sign of cholesterol. Whatever showed up in the eyes was already present in the arteries.

Henry Craven's arteries must have been monuments to the English cooked breakfast. When Malcolm's mother had been alive, he had always insisted upon being served a heart attack on a plate every morning: four rashers of streaky bacon, two fried eggs, fried bread, and one large sausage. On the first weekend that Chris had met him,

Henry had informed her, waving his knife in her direction, that a man needed a lining to his stomach. Over the years, Henry must have perfected a stomach lining of inch-thick fat. She had had to look away that first weekend morning, gripping her cup of coffee tightly and admiring Malcolm's mother's geraniums by way of distraction. Soon after his plate had been delivered to the table, Henry had shocked her by freezing upright in his chair and bellowing like a hippopotamus. 'I've only got one piece of fried bread!' he had cried.

'I'm just coming with the others,' Malcolm's mother had replied, from the kitchen.

Chris had glanced at Malcolm. He had been eating obliviously.

Malcolm's mother had died at sixty-two. As far as Chris knew, no one had ever brought *her* breakfast.

She gazed now into Henry's flecked blue eye. It was very curious to see that the left one seemed entirely as usual, with a perceptive expression. The other had a blankness to it. It was a drawing of an eye, executed in thin pastel. It blinked at a different rate to the other – slowly, as if with effort. She felt a rush of pity for the old man.

It was a rare sensation.

Henry Craven – ex-Army, ex-Civil Service – had always, if not frightened her, then certainly dismayed her. It was as if he had been washed up from some prehistoric storm and left stranded on the shore of modern life. Henry did not simply think that women were inferior, he knew it for a fact. He banged on about brain sizes and body weight and crying and motherhood and mood swings, about hand spans and women not being able to grip a machine gun. About sandstorms and women having no sense of direction. About minefields and women running about in circles. He had opinions so fixed that they were welded to the roof of his mouth, so that they came rolling out every time he spoke. He was rather keen on the idea that menstruating women should not touch fresh meat. He said that women were genetically incapable of driving a vehicle. And, all the time, he was the model of empty gallantry, standing up when a woman came into the room, holding the door open for her, pulling out her chair for her, adjusting the curtain so that the light should not shine too brightly in her eyes, and then, as soon as she was settled into place, charitably insulting her for all he was worth.

Poor Henry.

She couldn't help the thought, much as she hated him.

Poor Henry, struck dumb on a hospital bed. His gaze kept flickering towards her as if he were desperate to tell her that the only decent doctors were men. If he had his voice he would be saying, at this very moment, that women made damned fine nurses, because they were a nurturing and mothering species. But the doctor . . . thank God, the doctor was a man.

As if he were reading her thoughts, Henry's voice rumbled in his throat. No words came out. Everything he wanted to say was churned at the larynx, and sent back into his chest. He gripped his son's hand.

'It's all right, Dad,' Malcolm said.

Deeply embarrassed, Chris looked away.

6

It was Dermott's birthday on Saturday.

That same morning, there was an article in the paper about an elephant with toothache. The cure, according to the vet in attendance, had been to extract the tooth. To do that he would have to use a giant hypodermic needle. There had been a photograph of the vet, the elephant, and the needle.

All through dinner that evening in the restaurant, Sally had looked at Dermott and thought, Elephant, Dermott, needle. For if anyone in the world needed puncturing, it was her husband, the irritatingly famous and charming Dermott Matthews.

His face was puffy in the restaurant's dim lighting, and Sally looked at him, thinking, Elephant, needle, as he roared through another joke. Dermott was the life and soul of any party, even those that had been declared dead. He whipped sick parties until they screamed.

'Why do women have legs?' he shouted.

No one took much notice. Most were so drunk that Dermott's voice was just another resounding drum in their heads, which were already floating several feet in the air, whirling like extras from *The Exorcist*. Sally knew instinctively that Dermott's personal trainer, Mike, felt like this, because he was looking at her with that face of tearful need that he always wore when he was legless.

Why had she ever married an Irishman? she wondered morosely. After all, if she had wanted a load of frantic

Celtic noise, she could have just booked tickets for
Riverdance. She didn't have to go and marry a madman,
even if he had all the usual Irish attributes of being able to
charm birds out of trees, argue black was white, and fight
all comers. She could have had a quiet life. Instead, on a
suicidal impulse last summer, which had a lot to do with
gin and tonics and nothing at all to do with sense, she had
married an Irish actor, whose face was now too famous to
let him out alone on public transport.

Two years ago, Dermott had been the archetypal
struggling thespian, living on baked beans in draughty
bedsits while touring schools with a theatre group called
Mad Bad Socks – until he had been spotted at a parents'
evening by a TV producer. Not any old producer, but the
producer of the national three-times-a-week-with-an-
omnibus-edition-on-Sundays soap, *Beckside Street*.

In no time at all, Dermott had found himself trans-
ported from pretending to be an anarchic carrot frightening six-year-olds, into an anarchic long-lost son of one of
Beckside's main characters. It was just about this time that
Sally had met him, and been bowled over by the breathless,
smiling whirlwind whose very first act on their very first
date had been to walk into traffic on Charing Cross Road
and stand in the centre, cars braking all around him, while
he told the world that Sally was an angel fallen to earth.

He actually had said that. *She is an angel fallen to earth.*

'Get out of the fucking road!' a taxi driver had sworn.

' "For lo, the wished day has come at last",' Dermot had
yelled, his arms outstretched towards her while carbon
dioxide fumes wreathed him like morning mist. ' "Pay to
her usury of long delight . . ." '

Tyres had squealed on the tarmac.

She had stared at him, her mouth open in shock, too
amazed even to be embarrassed.

' "And let them make store of bridal posies . . ." '

At last, he had had to leap out of the way of a Number 29 bus. He came back, laughing, and took her hand in his.

' "Wake now, my love",' he had murmured, pressing his lips to her skin. ' "Awake, for it is time . . ." '

Oh God. Sally Trent, boarding-school pupil since she was four. Head Girl. Hockey captain. Fourteen very lonely years at school, then uni and several more only slightly less lonely years since then, with three or four bland boyfriends notched on her bedpost. As a child, she had long ago learned to suppress feelings and deny she could be hurt. As an adult, she found she coped almost too well. Her life was pristine. No one could touch her heart. She was quite sure that she had the cynical measure of any man. And Sally Trent, whose determination and bright-natured independence was legendary – she had fallen, and been captured, in three minutes flat by an Irish broth of a boy who could quote Edmund Spenser.

It was like plugging into a dangerous drug.

Sensible Sally, sharp and quick-witted Sally, whose brains were turned to rice pudding by a flood of shamrock-stamped tosh.

Dermott's star had risen as fast as her addiction to him. As Lily Blythe's son, he was destined for rapid fame. Lily Blythe was the barmaid at the Beckside Arms, a tarty piece long past her best. The writers of the serial, in a desperate attempt to beef-up the actress's part, had come up with the idea that Lily had had an illegitimate son when she was a wee poor colleen in Ireland. Cue Dermott as Feargal Blythe, the rascally twenty-four-year-old son with a song in his heart and nothing in his pockets. Cue Feargal, with a line to charm the ladies and break their hearts. Cue Feargal, lately, with a secret heart condition of his own that had launched several tense scenes in the *Beckside* hospital, while young nubile nurses wept for him behind hastily-pulled curtains, and the consultant doubted that he was long for this world.

Dermott hadn't liked that storyline much. It had been started early this year, after Dermott had had an argument with the producer about his pay. The producer – the universally feared Audrey Barnett, whom Sally had never met – had told him that eighty thousand pounds a year was seventy-five thousand pounds a year more than Audrey herself had got when she had first started with Middle England TV, and that no actor, even one as popular as Dermott, was bigger than *Beckside Street* itself.

And so Feargal Blythe languished on various hospital trolleys and under various pieces of giant hospital machinery, trying to get back into favour.

Dermott – this short, bouncing Irish boy – had become Sally's husband three weeks after meeting her last year. Sally was his very first wife. As he kept on telling everyone.

It was now ten minutes past midnight. The waiters in the restaurant were lined up like a desolate firing squad behind the bar, waiting for Dermott to grow tired, or preferably fall unconscious.

'Geoff,' Dermott called across the room to his manager, while slinging his arm around Sally's shoulders and kissing her enthusiastically on the cheek. 'Geoff, why do women have legs?'

Geoff Elgin was laboriously counting change out into a saucer for a tip. His glasses were perched on top of his head.

'Come on! Come on!' Dermott said.

'I don't know, Mott.' Geoff dropped a two-pence piece, and felt around the floor for it. 'You tell us.'

Dermott rolled his eyes.

Sally thought, Elephant, needle. She could do with a large elephant needle right now – one that could put Dermott to sleep.

'No, no,' he yelled. 'You've got to guess. No friggin' fun

if you don't guess.' He stared around at the disintegrating crowd of friends and hangers-on.

Jo-Anne Williams and her husband were putting on their coats, talking to another couple at a nearby table. Jo-Anne and her husband looked relatively sober – but then, Frank Williams was Dermott's psychotherapist and she had never seen him lose control. As Sally watched them, she realised that Jo-Anne and Frank were apologising for Dermott, whose voice could probably be heard on the other side of the city. The city being Aberdeen.

And she noticed something else. She noticed Frank give Dermott a slow, appraising stare, and then flash her a look of pity.

'Why . . . do . . . women . . .'

Sally got to her feet. 'Pack it in, Dermott,' she said. 'It's time to go.'

He stuck out his bottom lip.

'Dermott.'

'No bugger's giving me the punchline,' he said.

'Nobody cares,' she replied. 'Get up.'

'You owe me eighty quid,' Geoff said, edging alongside them.

'What for?' Dermott demanded.

'Dinner. I paid your bill.'

Sally reached for her purse. 'I'll pay you, Geoff,' she said. 'Here.'

'Don't give him money!' Dermott yelled, swaying from side to side. 'He'll only buy Premium Bonds with it.' He turned around and shouted at the waiters. 'This is the only man in Britain who buys Premium Bonds! He never wins! He still buys the Bonds! He still buys them!'

'Dermott, shut up,' Sally said.

Geoff gave Sally a sympathetic grin. 'I'll call you a taxi,' he said.

'That's all right,' Sally said. 'I've got the car.'

'You haven't had too much to drink?'

'I haven't had anything to drink,' she told him.

'That's why you're so bloody miserable,' Dermott said.

All around them, the party dissolved. The last four couples pushed back their chairs; the phalanx of waiters moved in, sweeping up crumpled napkins, empty party poppers from the floor, paper hats from the chairs.

'WHY DO BLOODY WOMEN HAVE LEGS!' Dermott cried wildly.

Sally opened the door to the street, and the blissfully frosty air blew in.

'Happy birthday, Mott,' Geoff said, as he passed.

'You miserable bastard!' Dermott yelled.

Nobody took a blind bit of notice.

They were home within half an hour.

As she pulled into the drive, the car's headlights picked out piles of builder's sand, another pile of horrendously expensive reclaimed bricks, and a tangle of cast-iron pipes. Sally stared at it all for a moment, then turned off the engine.

Two months ago, one night when she had come home from work, Dermott had informed her that every man needed a son.

'A son?' she had echoed, peeling off her coat in the hallway.

'A man needs a son. A son binds people together.'

Sally had frowned at him. 'That was in last week's episode,' she said.

'It was not,' he objected.

'It was, Dermott,' she replied resignedly. 'It was where Tony was leaning on the pub counter and Lily was crying. Tony said . . .'

'Well, what if it was?' Dermott replied airily. He stepped forward and hugged her – his great, bearlike, unbreakable hug. She had smiled at him. Dermott really had the most amazing eyes – full of light, full of humour. When the publicity machine had called him (rather sickeningly, she had thought), 'the man with the dancing eyes', she had, however reluctantly, had to agree with them. Dermott's eyes were almost all his allure: big, greenish-blue eyes, the eyes of a small child, filled with apparently innocent delight. Looking into them, Sally continually forgave him his excesses. Of which, she was slowly discovering, there were many.

'I want us to start a family,' he had said.

'Now?'

'Forget your blueprint,' he said, which had been a private joke since their first few days of married life.

'Can we have dinner first?' she'd said.

The next week, when she had come home wearily on Friday, Dermott had told her that the builders were starting on Monday morning.

'Starting what?'

'Renovations.'

Sally had stopped dead. 'Not here?'

'Of course here.'

Of course. Here. The big Victorian house they had bought on impulse and almost immediately regretted. Clanking plumbing. Rising damp. Leaking roof.

'I'm going to have it all put right for the children,' Dermott had said, edging her up against the wall.

'Stop that,' she told him. 'What children are these?'

He gave her an aghast expression. 'You mean you aren't pregnant yet?' he demanded. 'We'll have to see about that.'

Sally looked across at the great man now as she took the keys out of the ignition. The birthday boy was sound asleep, head on chest. When he woke up, he would have excruciating neckache. That gave her the energy to smile.

She got out, swinging the keys between thumb and

forefinger. The security light blasted with a spot worthy of a West End début. Another of Dermott's brainwaves – he was worried because Lily Blythe had been burgled by a masked man intent on stealing the pub's entire supply of dry roasted peanuts – the light came blinding on whenever a cat peed in the hedge. Sally stood on the dramatically-lit threshold, and looked back at the car. Then she opened the house door, stepped inside, and locked it.

She bolted it top and bottom. Then she ran up the hall, and into the kitchen. The room was merely a cavern now, filled with cement, and the skeletons of unfitted cupboards, and loose wiring hanging from the ceiling. She deadbolted the back door. Darting next into the sitting room, she double-bolted the French windows.

Then she stood back and waited.

It must have been a good ten minutes before Dermott woke up. She had turned off the lights. She heard the car door bump open, then his muttered curses, followed by the sound of him falling over.

She crept to the window and saw her husband slumped over the bonnet of the car. Almost immediately, he straightened himself and stared down at the car accusingly, as if it had no right at all to have suddenly glued a bonnet to its front half. She watched him feel his way round it. Then he looked up at the dark house.

'Sally!' he shouted. 'Help me!'

She winced. They lived in a quiet street, a family street, where a lot of babies and small children would no doubt be snugly asleep in their infant beds. The last thing anyone needed was for Dermott to wake them all up. But her heart hardened. She was damned if she was cleaning up after his drinking any more.

She hadn't forgotten the last time yet, when Dermott had single-handedly pebbledashed the downstairs loo – the only room in the house that had, so far, been untouched by the builders. He had thrown himself heart, soul and stomach into redecorating it in curried carrot. After that, he had lurched upstairs and redecorated the bedside rug. Half way through the night, he had woken her in tears, claiming that he had something stuck in his throat.

Try as she might to ignore him, at about four o'clock in the morning, after he had told her that he couldn't breathe, and was going to die, she had driven him – sobbing in the passenger seat and clutching at his windpipe and telling her that he would certainly lose his voice and never work again – to the local Casualty Department. There, among drug addicts and other less comfortably-heeled drunks, they had waited for an hour. An hour during which Dermott cursed the entire nursing profession and warned them that if the delay resulted in his being struck dumb for life, he would sue the Health Authority for millions.

At five-thirty in the morning, they were finally seen by a weary Asian registrar. He examined Dermott, and then told him that he had a swollen epiglottis, caused by Dermott attempting to pull it out.

All the way home, Sally was silent.

'But I thought it was something stuck in my throat!' Dermott had whispered. 'I was only trying to pull it out to see what it was.'

That was a month ago.

The next day, Dermott had promised her faithfully that he would not drink heavily again.

'Sally!' Dermott screamed now, from the garden. 'Oh Sally . . . Sally, please.'

She looked out again at him. She saw him try to see the face of his watch. He leaned forward, to get the light to reflect from it, and promptly fell head first into a pile of sand. He stayed there, inert, for a moment or two, then prised himself up, stared outraged at the sand, and wheeled towards the house with purpose. She stepped back, behind the curtains.

When the doorbell stopped, the silence in the house was almost as shattering. Dermott began rattling the letterbox.

'Sally, I bloody love you!' he yelled.

She did nothing.

'Right,' she heard him mutter.

He passed the door, and went around to the back of the house. She waited for the sound of him tripping over the concrete mixer, and the '*Ooomph!*' as the breath was knocked out of him. Then he got up, tottered to the patio, and fell over some pipework. She steeled herself for his screams and curses, but none came. After a couple of minutes, she could stand the suspense no longer, and crept downstairs again to the kitchen window.

Dermott was lying in the hydrangeas, crying.

She opened the window. 'You can lie there all night,' she told him sternly.

'Sally, please help me,' he sobbed.

'You're not coming in.'

'But I think I've broken my leg.'

'Good.' She went upstairs, threw off her clothes and took a shower. When she had finished, she looked out into the garden. Dermott was standing underneath their bedroom window.

As she watched him, the phone rang. She glanced at the clock. It was almost one o'clock in the morning. She lifted the receiver. 'Hello?'

For a moment, she thought she heard an intake of breath. Then the receiver was gently replaced.

Sally gave the phone a querying look, and put it down. She opened the bedroom window; beneath her, Dermott was standing in exactly the same place, looking up at her, his hands clutched to his chest. He was mumbling something. 'Shut up,' she hissed.

He held his arms out to her. ' "My delight and thy

delight, Walking, like two angels white, in the gardens of the night",' he said.

She looked at him hard for some time. 'Oh shit,' she muttered.

Half an hour later, in the darkness of their bed, she ran a hand over his chest, feeling the thumping of his heart, tracing the rise and fall of his breathing.

'Dermott,' she whispered.

He roused himself for a second. 'What?'

'Why *do* women have legs?'

His laugh spluttered into a cough. At last, he managed to get out his reply, between gasps of rasping air.

'So that, my darling, they don't leave a trail like a snail.'

She listened to him fall asleep.

Then she sat up, got out of bed, and went to the spare room.

7

Chris climbed the stairs of Henry Craven's house. It was Sunday, and Malcolm was visiting his father at the hospital. By now, Henry had shown some improvement, and had been moved from Intensive Care into a general ward.

She and Malcolm had been here all weekend, invaders in Henry's private territory. Henry Craven owned a period house opposite Prystock Cathedral. It was a truly lovely place. With its sloping roof and warm-stoned face, it looked like the last refuge of a retiring spinster. The heavily flowered curtains at the windows had been made by Malcolm's mother twenty years ago; the heavy oak door opened on to a flagstone hall hung with two self-effacing, faded paintings of English landscapes. There was a neat shelf of china dogs, and of enamelled flowers in porcelain wheelbarrows.

Malcolm's mother haunted the hallway still, with her quiet, apologetic face. Chris could feel her hovering somewhere just out of her line of vision, shifting hesitantly from one foot to the other. If she listened hard, Chris could still hear her footsteps pattering along the landing upstairs. Blue court shoes with a blue fabric bow. Running to get her gloves for church. Opening the windows for air. Closing them all again on Henry's instructions.

Chris paused on the landing now.

As you went upstairs, Malcolm's mother did fade. Henry had taken away the frothy nets from these windows, and they were bare. He had also taken down the picture of Inverness – Malcolm's mother's home town – and replaced it with a group picture of his Regiment.

Chris passed along the upstairs landing. She paused only for a moment at the door at the end, before taking the key from her pocket and opening it.

The room was always cold.

'You don't want heat anywhere near these artefacts,' Henry used to say. 'Artefacts like these . . .' A dreamy look – the closest to delight that Chris ever saw on Henry's face – would transform his deepset frown lines into a smile. 'Yes, artefacts like these . . .'

He would never finish the sentence. It was as if Henry's artefacts were simply too sumptuous, too sublime, for words.

Although Chris could easily have found words for them.

She looked at the face of Thomas Fowler now. Thomas Fowler stood in his World War One uniform at one end of the room. He was desperately creepy – a full-size shop mannequin, the very old-fashioned kind, with a smooth shiny face and arched brown eyebrows. He stood permanently gazing into Henry's private war, his private trench, his private Western Front. Thomas Fowler's arm was extended; in his hand was a rifle with the bayonet fixed. Thomas Fowler's uniform gave off a violent stench of mothballs, and bore a brown stain on one shoulder.

'Blood,' Henry had told her.

'My God, how awful,' she said, horrified.

'Awful?' he repeated. 'That is *war*, Christine.'

'Yes,' she replied weakly.

'Noble,' Henry said. 'A time of tremendous sacrifice. And that is the real Thomas Fowler's uniform.'

'How sad,' she had tried.

'You know,' Henry had said to her last year, turning to

her as he had dusted Thomas Fowler's ears, 'you ought to devote your talents to something like this.'

'I'm sorry?' What on earth did he mean?

He had bunched the duster into a yellow fist. 'History,' he said succinctly. 'You've got a degree, haven't you? What's it in?'

'Economics.'

He nodded sagely. 'You're wasting your time in that television place.'

'Am I?'

'Yes, when you could be devoting yourself to something worthwhile.'

'It's a long time since I took my degree,' she had said quietly.

'You should have used it.'

'I did use it, Henry,' she reminded him. 'I was a Tax Inspector for eight years.'

'Hmmph,' was all he said in reply. This – Chris's past – was a dangerous area, possibly every bit as dangerous as parts of Thomas Fowler's original Front Line. In Chris's past, lives had been dismembered, blows struck, careers ruined. Hers, mainly.

Henry had fiddled with Thomas's shoes. 'Got to get over these things. Life. Crises.'

Chris regarded him impotently. 'I did get over it,' she told him. 'I moved down to London to get over it, and I met Malcolm. And I really can't see myself doing that now.'

'Book-keeping,' Henry said.

'Not that, either.'

'Insurance, then. Or a solicitor's clerk. A bank. Steady. Worthwhile.'

'Well,' she had said, slowly. 'I believe entertaining people is worthwhile.'

'Entertainment?' Henry said disbelievingly. 'Dish television?'

'It's called cable.'

'Nonsense.'

'Yes, sometimes.'

'All the time,' he insisted.

'It's great fun,' she said. 'I wanted a bit of fun. Tax was so dry. I enjoy what I do now.'

'Fun?' Henry echoed, horrified. 'A woman of your age? You ought to have got over fun.'

Centuries had ticked past while she looked at Thomas Fowler's shiny face and listened to the blood circulating in her ears.

'All that nonsense, on Up-Line TV,' Henry grumbled. 'Trash and nonsense. Quizzes. Confessions.'

'Yes,' she conceded.

'*Call My Bluff*. Now that's a proper programme. Radio Four.'

'Yes, but—'

'*Sharpe*. There's another proper programme. Or *Question Time*. I enjoy that. BBC, of course.'

'Yes, current affairs.'

'And what's on *your* station?' he demanded. '*Hotel Fires*. Is that properly informative?'

'Well . . .'

'*Paint My House Pink*.' He snorted.

'That's been shelved, actually.'

'I should hope so. It's rubbish.'

'Yes, that was rubbish,' she agreed. 'But you know, it's very lively, every day is different . . .'

'Every day is the same,' he snapped. 'Complete obscene rubbish.'

Henry did have a point. A great deal of Up-Line's output was close to obscene. And quite a large proportion of it was rubbish.

For a start, they had weathered a storm at the end of last year after having been accused of fabricating whole confessions programmes, buying actors and actresses to pretend that they were ordinary people. The case had been made, the point accepted, with a lot of breast-beating in public by Owen Majolica.

Although Owen couldn't keep his face quite straight. At first, he had dutifully done whatever his father had told him in running the station, but over the last year or so Chris had noticed that his heart wasn't in it. She suspected that, far from being a witless foil for Jefferson Bluehorn Majolica Senior, Owen did, in fact, have both a head and a heart. Often, lately, she had caught him staring out of the window with a faraway look on his face. And he just couldn't seem to take the industry seriously.

Which was probably deeply in his favour.

On *Newsnight*, he had almost wept for five minutes, declaiming that he had never known that his researchers could sink so low as to hire actors, and that he had indeed fired every one of them the moment that he had been informed. Jeremy Paxman had almost cracked and believed him. Unfortunately the camera had caught Owen, while someone else was speaking, sniggering into his handkerchief.

Chris had been summoned to Owen after that. She thought that he might have had a severe ticking-off from the Great Bluehorn. Owen had told her that he trusted her above his other personal assistants. He had said that he wanted to reinforce her position, her authority. She had blushed – sad, but true – with pleasure at the compliments, and imagined a huge pay rise, and a blue glass office like the one Fabia Gossleigh-Warner must surely possess. She had imagined – just for a flashing fraction of a second – that Owen had genuinely recognised her talent, her flair with words, her calm and, naturally, her rather under-stated sexual allure.

Then, Owen – who was not yet thirty – had hugged her,

and said she reminded him of his mother.

'And that's what I want you to be,' he had said.

She was gripped in his embrace in the centre of the floor, while her dreams of empire ran out of her body through her shoes. Well, at least he hadn't said that she reminded him of his dog.

'You want me to be your mother?' she asked puzzled.

He laughed. 'I want you to mother this lot,' he told her. 'You know, headmistress them. Kind but fearsome.'

'Like Pauline on *The League of Gentlemen*?' she had offered, joking, watching in horror as he appeared to take her seriously for a while.

'No,' he mused finally. 'More cuddly.'

'Cuddly?' No, surely not. No, not that. Rounded, squeezable – yes, she was certainly that. But *cuddly*. Dear Lord God in heaven. She was only a size fourteen! And that was only on the hips! In fact, that was only on *one* hip. She was only ten stone – only *just*. She did dance aerobics. Sometimes. When she remembered. She was hardly juggernaut material, was she? Hardly headmistress, surely?

Of course, there was the size 6 shoe that looked like a shoe, and not a piece of board with straps on. There was the extreme age. And there was the spaniel face . . . She had looked deep into Owen Majolica's eyes. The pity of it was – and this was so shameful that she hardly dared admit it even to herself – that she liked Owen. No, that was not right. That was not truthful. In the dark wasteland reaches of the night, under the duvet, she was sometimes able to admit to herself that she fancied Owen Majolica. Fancied his neat, trim body, his closely-cropped dark hair, his wide-open and rather wild expression. She also fancied his wealth.

Up-Line Cable was a toy that Majolica Senior had bestowed upon his eldest son, a kind of test to see if Owen deserved to inherit his newspaper empire in the States.

Owen was doing quite well when he concentrated, bouncing his little cable TV network in the faces of more prestigious organisations. Of course, Up-Line was brash and tasteless. Of course, it was hideous. But it was a game. A big, brightly-coloured game complete with boxes that beeped and lights that flashed and little men and women models crying and laughing and showing their operation scars on demand.

She had had to look away from Owen's face. She was sure that he would be able to read her matronly, motherly desire in her face.

Owen, in fact, would have been very surprised to hear some of the thoughts that ran through Chris's head. Not so much perhaps at the idea that she liked him – most women did, awkwardly for him – but that she saw herself as so ancient. The mothering idea was a sort of joke to him, because Chris did not look like anyone's mother at all. She had, he considered, a very nice mouth for a start. Full and kissable. Nice skin that was always slightly flushed. Nice eyes, with hidden depths that amused him. Nice brain to go with the all-woman body that was curvy enough to make a man want to put his arm round it.

Chris, of course, to whom mental self-flagellation had always come just a tad too easily, would have been staggered to hear his version of her. Her gaze at the moment had landed on the giant oar that was suspended on the far wall, and the collection of prints of sailing ships. In an office filled with executive toys, the oar and pictures struck an incongruous note. Someone had once told her that Owen had been an Oxford Blue, the Stroke in an Isis crew; but he never referred to it, even if his own eyes often strayed to the same wall.

'I'll give you a title,' he said.

'Queen Mother?' she asked.

He had laughed. 'Chief Whip,' he said. 'Chief Whip Queen Mother.'

'Thank you, Owen,' she murmured.

'I want you to make sure we don't have more than thirty per cent actors, all right, Madeleine?'

'We don't need actors at all,' she had said. 'And my name's *Chris*.'

He actually blushed. 'Chris. Sorry,' he said hurriedly. 'Well, right . . . that's the spirit. And hey, you can have an office, yeah? Right up here with me.'

'With furniture?' she had asked. 'Or just the iron cup chained to the wall?'

He had roared with laughter. 'Ah, you kidder, you!'

She stood in Henry's mausoleum now, staring at Thomas Fowler's bayonet and the brown bloodstain.

'The world is dumb enough,' she murmured to herself.

When she had got home that night from work, she had told Malcolm what Owen had said, turning it into a joke. Well, it was a joke. God save her from taking herself too seriously. If she took herself seriously she would have to lock herself in the attic for her art until someone from a major publishers talked her down with a large megaphone.

'My father is right,' Malcolm had said.

She had stopped stirring the pasta sauce, and stared at him. 'He's *right*?'

Malcolm fiddled with a fork on the table. 'You could come and work for me,' he said. 'That TV station is beneath you.'

This had been a complete revelation.

'With you?' she had asked. 'You told me there was no money.'

'We've been given a grant.'

This was news. 'Who from?'

More fiddling of the fork. 'Trepantex Industries.'

She had paused, then turned the gas off under the sauce.

Slowly, she had drawn out a chair and sat down opposite him. 'Malcolm,' she said. 'Genetically modified foods.'

'It isn't the genetic division.'

'But Trepantex!'

'They are a world leader in research,' he mumbled. He still hadn't met her gaze. 'They're very go-ahead. Fired-up.'

'But Trepantex!'

'Look, stop saying that,' he said, finally raising his eyes to her. 'All they want is my maggots.'

She considered him. 'Since when did Trepantex have anything at all to do with medical research?' she asked.

'They have a medical division.'

'But they're soya farmers, aren't they?'

'They recently bought up Fromish Laboratories.'

Her mouth dropped open. This was like being told that Mad Games Inc. had taken over Boots. 'You're joking.'

'It's not a joke,' he said obstinately. 'They're pouring money into us.'

'But why?'

'I've told you – to aid research.'

'Into wound sterilisation?'

'Yes.'

She shook her head in disbelief. 'Malcolm, they're lying.'

He started to look offended. 'They are not lying. We've had a presentation.'

'At work?' she asked.

'They were there all day. They brought in caterers.'

'Oh,' she said. 'Oh, I see. They brought in caterers, so that makes it OK. They've suddenly become the saviours of the world.'

'You're very cynical,' he said.

'I'm realistic,' she countered. 'Surely you can't believe them.'

'Why shouldn't I?'

'Because they're into world rape.'

He laughed indulgently. 'Oh, come on. Really.'

'Yes, really. Look . . . what did they say to you?'

He sat back in his chair, confident. 'They said they were fantastically excited.'

'By the sterile maggots?'

'Yes.'

'And what else?' she asked.

'They came around the laboratories. They were very impressed. In fact, they've promoted me,' he announced triumphantly.

'To what?' she asked. 'You're already Head of Division.'

'To Research Fellow.'

'But what does that mean? Are they giving you an academic scholarship somewhere?'

'No.'

'Membership of something?'

'No.'

'What, then?'

'We get to go to America three times a year,' he said. 'To Florida.'

She remained staring at him. Staring at her husband, involved in a strange brand of medical engineering – so strange that she dared not tell anyone at Up-Line Cable because they would surely bring him in for a programme and call it *The Man Who Puts Maggots In Your Body* – a husband whose life was very quiet and calm and straight, and whose idea of a holiday was a week on the Pennine Way, here he was, talking about going to Disneyworld and selling his soul to the devil.

Malcolm Craven had worked for eight years on refining his maggot programme. Although, at work, they never called them maggots. They were known as larval therapy. Or, as Chris called it, *The Old Ways Are The Best*.

Sterile maggots – very, very sterile maggots, bred with supreme care and delicacy, the aristocrats of the maggot world, never touching anything but a sterile surface, never breathing ordinary air, never running in the long grass, growing body hair, having girlfriends, drinking Pils or going clubbing – such were the maggots of Malcolm's world.

When they were grown-up, their job was to eat away rotten bits of flesh in human bodies. Which they did with clean success. Not pretty, but effective. Very New Age.

Chris had remained staring at Malcolm's profile. Trepantex was a giant in the food world. A monstrous, gobbling giant. Trepantex would undoubtedly crush Malcolm's maggots, and they would never see the light of a test tube again. In fact, Trepantex would probably crush them so successfully that they would flavour them, sesame seed them, and turn them out as Protein Fancies.

'Malcolm,' she began.

'It's all above board,' he told her. 'Why can't you just be happy for me?'

'I am,' she said.

'You're not,' he said.

'I'm worried,' she admitted. 'Worried that they're selling you a line of some kind.'

'Why can't you believe the best about people?'

'Because . . .' She hesitated. 'It's not their style, is it?' she asked. 'Not this very prolonged, careful stuff.' She paused again, trying to find the right approach. 'I mean, look how long it was before you refined the strain, before you could get hospitals even to consider them on trial . . .'

Malcolm fiddled some more with the placemats, the forks, the knives, the salt and pepper. Then he got up and said, 'I'm going to take my eyes out.'

She watched him walk, like a little boy disappointed by his football suddenly deflating, to the door of the room.

'Malcolm,' she said. 'I know that you *do* see the best in people. But it's all you see. You don't pick up signals. You don't read between the lines.'

He had said nothing in reply.

She had stared for some time at the opposite wall, knowing that he was the same with her. Always taking her at face value, never picking up subtle hints, always disappointed if she was upset or depressed or tired, as if by being so she had somehow let the side down.

Malcolm lived in a Stepford world, where everyone smiled and said what they meant, and no one meant anything very much.

She put her head in her hands, annoyed at her condemnation of him, annoyed with him and his stock phrases and responses, annoyed at bloody avaricious rapacious Trepantex, preparing to swallow Malcolm's decent little unfashionable research project whole, leaving no trace of it at all except a nasty aftertaste, just like one of their chicken curries.

She sighed deeply now at the memory, and started to dust Thomas Fowler's face.

That had been six months ago. Sure enough, Trepantex were bearing down hard on Malcolm's maggots, just as she had predicted.

And Henry lay in hospital, a desperate problem in waiting.

8

In the little village of Deadham Markham, all was quiet. In London, fifty miles away, Chris was beating off an old bat with a stick and, further across town, Sally was enduring another old bat called Trixy.

Chris's bat was a real one, the common vampire *Desmodus rotundus*. It had got loose in a morning chat-show about phobias, and its owner was at this very moment trying to dissuade it from mistaking Chris for a belfry, while certain phobic members of the audience were stretchered away in a state of shock.

Sally, on the other hand, had Trixy Bushell – once a 1960s model, now the possessor of a positively pintucked face – on the phone. Trixy was trying to sell her story of alcohol abuse to the highest bidder. The more that Sally insisted that she no longer worked for *The Corker*, the more Trixy laughed like a drain and talked over her. Sally had taken to staring out of the window, too fed up even to put down the phone.

Strangely enough, Deadham Markham also had a problem with bats.

The Reverend Michael Blood stood in the parish church of St Benedict's and gazed up into the cavernous roof. It was a beautiful roof – listed, sixteenth-century, vaulted. Especially beautiful this morning, with the dusty sunlight streaming in across the aisle through the stained glass and spreading the colours over the ancient stone.

Listed, vaulted, beautiful . . . and infested.

During services, when a faint breath of heat finally
filtered through the congregation and floated heaven-
wards, the bats would stir. You could hear them as the
evening progressed, twittering contentedly to themselves
as they dropped dung on the faithful below.

It had caused an unpleasant scene in last week's PCC
meeting.

'You must do something about the bloody fucking
bats,' Mrs Wright had said. She was not a woman to mince
words. Not anywhere. Especially not in church gatherings.
When tackled about it, she would proudly declare that she
called a spade a spade and there was too much farting and
arsing about in this country.

Michael had gazed at her bucolic face.

It was rarely that one saw such a face on a woman,
although he had seen plenty of them on men – ex-India
men, red of face and purple of nose, with broken-veined
cheeks and fleshy mouths – in short, the prime of English
bloodstock. Mrs Wright was such a species, hewn from the
same granite, smelling of sherry and dry rot, living in a
thatched house dating back to the Restoration, which had
never and would never be restored if she had anything to
do with it. She was barely five foot four, but she must have
been a full metre across the shoulders.

'Built like a brick privy,' Philippa, Michael's wife, was
fond of observing.

'Don't say that,' he would reply. 'Vicars' wives aren't
supposed to say that.'

'Built like a brick shithouse, then,' she would retort,
barely lifting her head from the *Financial Times*.

The rest of the PCC always fell silent when Mrs Wright
spoke.

The Reverend Blood's voice fell like the proverbial seed
among thorns. 'There simply isn't any money,' he'd replied.

Mrs Wright turned a deeper shade of puce. 'There's

money enough for this arsing ridiculous scheme of yours,' she said.

'A project for the community,' he countered, as calmly as he could. 'And it's funded by local government in conjunction with the Church, not by this parish.'

Mrs Wright glared at him. 'Why here?' she said. 'That's what I want to know. Why can't St Bede's have them, in town? Hanging around sodding street corners and chain smoking. Prison – that's where they belong! Or the bottom of the river with a millstone round their necks. *After* they've had a few licks of the cat.' She had stared at the rest of the meeting to canvass support. 'I don't want to look out of my window and see some arsing oik leaning on my hedge.'

'They won't be leaning,' Reverend Blood had replied. 'They'll be working.'

'I should like to see it. Troublemakers,' she added, for good measure. 'Shooting – that's what they want. That'd sharpen them up.'

'The scheme is not only to benefit the young unemployed, but the elderly, too,' Michael had said. 'We shall send the first team to you, Mrs Wright, to help with your hedge and not lean on it.'

It was a mistake.

It was a mistake on two counts. First, by suggesting that Mrs Wright was anything other than a mere slip of an innocent child and, secondly, by implying that her hedge was in need of repair.

The hedge had been a bone of contention in the village for over ten years, ever since Colonel Wright had died and Mrs Wright had been left in solitary splendour in Manor Lodge. The hedge had grown colossal, leaning right out into the road, obscuring traffic, landing on unsuspecting passers-by, and having to be regularly propped up with a selection of poles and sticks. To suggest now, in open court, that Mrs Wright was in any way to blame for the mighty development of the Manor Lodge hedge was akin to Mel Gibson flashing his bare buttocks at the English army in *Braveheart*. The Colonel's widow rose in her chair, all her fury rushing in a red tide to her neck and ears.

Dear God, Michael Blood had thought, she's going to have a seizure.

'They will cross my threshold over my dead body,' she thundered.

'They are just boys,' he pleaded.

'They are beasts!' she'd cried.

'No, no,' he said soothingly. 'Philippa and I will make sure they're no trouble to anyone. The opposite, in fact. We'll make sure that they're a *benefit* to everyone.'

'Is Philippa organising it?' another member asked.

'Not organising exactly.'

'She's giving up her job?'

'Just my point,' Mrs Wright said, with some triumph. 'A woman can't run a bank *and* a half-arsed plot like this.'

'She's given me a lot of helpful advice already,' Michael said.

'You need more than advice,' a local farmer, Tim Marchant, replied. 'You need the Parachute Regiment to keep little buggers like that in line.'

Michael had fisted his hands so tightly in his lap that, for several days afterwards, the marks of his fingernails had showed in his palms. 'They are not criminals,' he'd said.

'You are utterly bastard mistaken, as usual,' Mrs Wright sniffed.

Tim Marchant had leaned forward at this point and placed his immense arms on the table before him. 'Why don't you drum up some cash from these people buying homes in the village – these newcomers?' he asked.

'Which newcomers?'

'Nova Scotia's for sale. And Lindley House is sold. And the old Tangent Farm. All bought by Londoners.'

'Oh?'

'Money pouring in, you mark my words,' Marchant said. 'Frank Bellingham's already been asked for quotes for Lindley and Tangent. Ripping out perfectly good gas fires in nice little tiled fireplaces, and putting in wood burners. Chipping out inglenooks. And he's been told for Lindley, that if he don't find an inglenook and a bread oven, he's to bloody well build them.'

The meeting shook its collective heads.

Marchant pressed his index finger to the table. 'The way I see it is this,' he said. 'If they got so much money, let them give some of it to these boys in Wetterton, give them a youth club or something, and stop them coming round here.'

All eyes turned to Michael.

'It isn't to keep them occupied,' Michael replied, speaking as slowly as he could. 'It's to give them work. Real work. Some self-esteem, you see? Then find them real jobs.'

They all stared at him as if this confirmed what they had always suspected, that he, like his predecessor before him, was weak in the head.

The Reverend Mount – from whom Michael had taken over – had started lashing himself to trees and prophesying the end of the world in April 1995, before the psychiatric hospital had taken him away and released him into another, more distant, community.

Now, the PCC's expressions said, their next vicar was going the same way. The way of sandals and guitars. The way of brown rice and tolerance. The way of doom.

When they had all left, Michael Blood looked down at his dog, Angus. Angus looked back at him with plaintive eyes full of wisdom.

'I wonder who the new people are?' Michael asked him.

9

Sally and Dermott had almost spent their honeymoon in France. They were going to Paris, the city of lovers. All they had to do was to get on the Eurostar at Ashford.

That was how they found themselves in Deadham Markham.

Dermott had a theory, Sally discovered that first married morning. Dermott had many theories, all of them deeply cherished. This particular one was that men could both drive and navigate far better than women. He was devastatingly charming about it, of course.

'I don't want you worried about driving,' he'd said, kissing the inside of her wrist lingeringly before placing her hand gently on the steering wheel. 'But someone has to navigate.'

'Dermott,' she said, 'I drive through the Hanger Lane gyratory system every morning.'

'My darling little love,' he said, settling into the passenger seat.

Sally had been faintly amused at his outrageousness. She thought that his chauvinism was probably a joke, and that if she had appeared offended, she would lose points. So she took it in good heart as she drove from the hotel, and he told her in great detail – as they passed under the leafy summer shade of the lanes of Kent – how Prehistoric Man, scouring the great plains for food, had needed no compass. Apparently, there was an in-built, pre-programmed ability in all males to go by the landscape, picking up subtle geographical clues; women, their coarser sensibilities undoubtedly fixated on such frivolous details as keeping the children away from flash floods and wild beasts, had never had this slotted into their female hard disk. Using this ancient ability, men would arrive at their chosen destination as if by magic, and with the minimum of fuss.

That morning, Dermott pointed them west.

After an hour, Sally slewed the car to a halt in a secluded lay-by.

'Ach, that was a little hard on the brakes,' Dermott chided, smiling.

'Dermott,' Sally said, 'we just passed a sign that said *Welcome To Wiltshire.*'

'No, we didn't,' he told her.

'We did! It's just back there . . .'

'No, no,' Dermott murmured, laughing.

'Yes – look. That sign there.'

'There's no sign.'

She gaped at him. 'Dermott, turn around and look. There is a sign back there in that hedge.'

He finally glanced back.

'Wiltshire isn't anywhere near Ashford. Ashford is in Kent,' Sally continued. She was furious at herself, for not noticing their fundamental error before now. Where the hell was her brain, for God's sake? *Back in bed*, came the whispered thought.

'Now it'll be quite close,' Dermott said. 'Not to get yourself worried.' He was casually leafing through the road atlas.

'Please can I have the map?' she asked.

'This road will bring us to the M4.'

'The M4?' she'd echoed. 'But the M4 is miles out of our way!'

'No, no . . . it isn't.'

'We don't want to *be* on the M4, Dermott.'

'Yes, we do.'

It was one of her husband's tricks, she learned, to simply contradict you until you gave up. Or shot him.

'Dermott, please give me the map.'

He did so with a cavalier resignation. She flicked to the index.

She turned the car around, and they drove in silence for another hour. Dermott sulked, refusing to look at the map again, while Sally became ever more panicked.

At last, stopping the car again, she turned to him. 'We're going to miss the train,' she said.

'There'll be another one along,' he said.

'To Paris?'

'It's only across the water.'

Some distance ahead, she could see a tiny black-and-white road sign saying *Deadham Markham*. 'Dermott,' she said, in desperation, 'let me navigate. You drive.'

'I can navigate perfectly well if only you had faith in me,' he told her.

'Yes,' she said. 'Please drive.'

He started to frown. 'So you don't trust me?'

'Maybe you're tired,' she said.

'I am *not* tired,' he'd said.

'Please swop seats, Dermott. I want to go to Paris. *Please*.'

He had got out of the car. But instead of walking around to the other side, he had leaned on the gate of a field. Sally went to the passenger door.

'Dermott,' she said.

He opened the gate, and started walking.

'Dermott!' she cried, astonished.

She ought to have got back in the car, and run him down there and then. No one would have known. She could have stuffed his body into a hedge. Generations of women would have thanked her. Instead, she had watched him in amazement. Hands in pockets, he was strolling down the grass of a paddock. It was a slope. Soon she had lost sight of his feet. She quickly realised that, in another few moments, she would lose sight of him altogether as he wandered off into the middle distance.

'Dermott!' she called.

He didn't look back.

'Jesus *God*,' she muttered, and stood fuming, thinking of the Eurostar easing smoothly out of England.

She went to the gate. Dermott had reached a stile down the hill about a hundred yards away. He climbed it. When he had climbed it, he picked a piece of grass and stuck the end of the stalk in his mouth.

'Dermott!' she yelled.

Ignoring her, he walked on.

Seething, she locked the car and jogged after him down the slope, climbing the stile in her turn. By this time, Dermott was already halfway across the next field, a little green patchwork with a stream running through it. On the other side of the stream was a small row of houses, sheltered by a row of chestnut trees.

The breath caught in Sally's throat. It was the scene from *Tess of the D'Urbervilles*, where Angel Clare crosses a midday field, the farm buildings before him, the heat rising from the summer grass. As she watched, Dermott lifted his battered Panama to his head, and crushed it on, swinging his free arm.

She fell in love with the picture. She carried it forever afterwards, wholesale: Dermott, the village, summer.

But he had never looked back for her.

The field path emerged into another lane; this one had larger houses. Various small children were cycling up and down. She walked towards the church, hobbling slightly in her sandals, past the last shielding tree, and was instantly rewarded with an archetypal village green, complete with pond and geese and a thatched pub with its doors obligingly open. Dermott was standing at the pond, looking at a house that faced them.

It was a little house, with a low tiled roof. It had a porch, and squat windows like curious white eyes in its sandstone face. There was a beech hedge around it, and a paddock to one side. As Sally reached Dermott, he was still staring at it. He glanced at her and smiled, as if there had never been any disagreement, as if his manhood had never been called into question by her reading the road map. As if he had never stalked off and left her.

'Isn't that perfect,' he said.

She looked again at the house. It was. And it was also, apparently, empty.

'I should like to live there,' he said, putting his arm around her shoulder. 'I should like to live there with you and have six children. Six little children all like you, all little tiny ones and all blonde.'

'Children are all tiny until they grow up,' she pointed out.

'That's right,' he agreed. 'All tiny like you.'

She bit her lip on her response. It wasn't her fault that she was only five foot two and seven stone. She ate like a horse. 'Only six?' she said.

They went into the pub and had lunch.

'What is the house called across the way?' Dermott had asked.

'Nova Scotia,' the landlord told them.

'Really? Why?' Sally asked.

'Mrs Wick owned it. Her husband came from Canada. Canadian airman. Last war.'

'Does she still live there?' Dermott asked.

'No,' said the landlord. 'Kidneys finished her off three weeks ago.'

'Oh,' Sally said. 'Renal failure?'

'No,' he said, wiping glasses. 'Bates's pies.'

'Is it for sale?' Dermott asked.

The remark was treated with derision. 'Sell it?' the landlord said. 'She's got three children, and they all want it. Can't agree who's having it.'

Dermott had looked sadly at Sally as they sat at one of the tables. 'And they were going to be such a nice lot of children,' he said.

'Whose?' Sally asked. 'Mrs Wick's?'

'No,' he said. 'Ours.'

'But we can raise children anywhere,' she said.

'Not in London.'

'Well, not in your flat or mine,' Sally said. 'Maybe we should buy a house.'

'A house to have children in? In London?'

She had smiled. 'First things first,' she said. 'House in London, few years' savings behind us, children.'

He had regarded her for some time. 'The best laid plans.'

She shook her head. 'You won't deflect me from my blueprint,' she said.

'Ah, a blueprint,' he murmured. 'So you've got me married, and now I hear there's a blueprint. And I thought I'd swept you off your feet.'

'You did,' she said.

'But there's a blueprint.' He shook his head. 'And how long have you had this blueprint?'

'Always,' she told him. 'Job, husband, house, savings, children, schools, pension, second house . . .'

'Stop, stop,' he said.

'You have to think ahead,' she said.

'No, no, no . . .'

'No thinking ahead?'

He smiled. 'You're a little iron hand in a little velvet glove, aren't you?'

She smiled back. 'What little velvet glove?'

He lifted her hand and pressed it between both his own.
' "In frolic dispose your pounds, shillings and pence",' he
said.

'Sorry?'

' "In frolic dispose your pounds, shillings and pence,
For we shall be nothing a hundred years hence".'

'Ah,' she said. 'Gordon Brown?'

'Thomas Jordan,' he told her. 'Born 1612.'

Sally looked at Dermott now, recalling that day six months
ago when she was newly married and oh, so naive and
trusting.

It was evening. They were at *Strange Eclipses*, a new
avant-garde art exhibition.

The Corker had received an invitation to the gallery,
and Dermott had shown an unnatural enthusiasm for
attending the opening. Normally, he hated modern art. He
had once asked Sally to promise to help him burn down
Bankside on the day it opened. And yet he was here, somewhere – she hadn't seen him for the past half an hour –
immersed in a heaving mass of Stella McCartney and
Versace.

Sally leaned against a wall, ostensibly studying the
display of a hedgehog that had been sawn in two, had its
back feet replaced with casters, and then been arranged in
a Chivers marmalade jar full of formaldehyde.

'Sensitive,' said a man at her side.

'Mmm,' she said, turning away. But she was not thinking
of the poor benighted beast. She was thinking of the house
repairs. Of the cans of Farrow & Ball paint in the hallway,
of the book of Colefax & Fowler textiles on the stairs. Of
the bill from the reclamation yard for sixteen Art Deco
fingerplates. And, every time she thought of the house, she
would immediately think of Eddie Massingham's voice

booming along the corridor as she had left the building.

'Oh God,' she murmured, for the fiftieth time that day. How the hell were they going to pay for it all now? Dermott had been on a reduced salary since his character had developed the heart condition, but that hadn't stopped him from spending £80 last week on flowers for the assistant producer on her birthday, and another £90 on a prolonged consultation with his therapist to reduce his anxiety levels.

Sally wondered what was going to reduce *her* anxiety levels. She hadn't told him yet that she had lost her job – that they couldn't afford a single yard of Colefax & Fowler, let alone an entire household.

As she walked around a set of dentures on a plinth covered with frogspawn, quite suddenly, she could smell food. For some reason, ever since she had walked out on the magazine, she had been permanently hungry. She had taken to grazing as a serious business, stuffing whole Twix bars into her mouth while standing at what used to be the kitchen sink. She could smell bacon now, and she hoped very much that some enlightened person was making bacon sandwiches, and that she would not follow her nose to the buffet only to find a warm chicken and bacon salad in a frangipani dressing.

'I can't,' said a female voice, from behind a ten foot empty canvas.

'Ach,' said a male.

Sally stopped dead.

'I'm in Berlin then,' the female continued. There was a rustle of paper. 'Look,' she said. 'You see? It's true. Berlin, then Perth, then Flushing. There is nothing but tournament everywhere I go.'

Sally knew that voice. She had heard it somewhere. Not at the magazine.

In her bones, she knew it was a voice whose whole aura

she disliked. It immediately brought to mind roaring associations with tortured green turf, cat gut, and Miss Weston from Sally's school, games teacher and tyrant.

'I see,' said the man.

'But you do, really . . . look . . .'

Tennis.

Sally paused. There was small riffle of laughter from behind the canvas. That voice was famous. Very famous indeed.

'No, you must look . . .'

'I am looking.'

She could be wrong. How many words had she heard? Five, and an *ach*.

'You must not do that,' the woman purred.

More laughter.

'No,' she said naughtily. 'That is my strained tendon.'

Sally put her head around the canvas.

Dermott looked up. In his hand he was holding the extended leg of Maria von Elbock, tennis player and all-round desirable object. Six foot one inches tall in her heavily-advertised tennis shoes – although she was wearing little black stilettos tonight, Sally noticed.

'Darling!' Dermott said. He held out his free hand to his wife, while still balancing Maria von Elbock's thigh on his hip. 'Darling, there you are! Come and look at poor Maria's poor little tendon.'

She walked towards them, smiling. She held out her hand to Maria. 'How do you do,' she said.

Dermott grinned. 'She does tennis,' he said.

'And husbands?'

Maria disentangled her leg. 'I am pulling a tendon in my thighs,' she said grumpily.

'How awful,' Sally replied sweetly. 'Perhaps you should try not wrapping them around strangers.'

Maria did blush, Sally would give her that. She blushed

and tried to hide her appointments diary in her inch-square handbag.

'Did I hear you say you were going to Berlin?' Sally asked Dermott.

'Me?' he said.

'I am going to Berlin on Friday,' Maria said.

Sally regarded her levelly for some seconds. 'You have got enormous shoulders, haven't you?' she said.

Dermott grabbed her arm. 'Come on now,' he whispered.

She shrugged him off. 'No, I want to look at Maria's shoulders,' she said. 'Have you at any time worked on a building site?'

'Sally,' Dermott said.

'A sight?' Maria said.

'And the nose.'

'I am sorry?'

'N-o-s-e,' Sally spelled out. 'I hear it's been done. Couldn't they take any more off? Didn't they have a big enough skip?'

'Sally,' hissed Dermott.

'What is skip?' Maria said.

'Lovely to have met you,' Dermott said.

'Are we going?' Sally asked.

Dermott dragged her out through the crowd, past the hedgehog on castors, the teeth, the bricks and balloons, the flashing neon knickers, the plastic penguin, the ship's boiler, and the singing cod, wrenching open the doors to the street, and practically throwing her out on to the pavement.

'How could you do that!' he shouted.

'Do what?' Sally asked.

'Disgrace me like that!'

'*Disgrace* you?' Sally echoed.

'One of the world's leading tennis players,' Dermott ranted. Passing pedestrians glanced at them.

'And noses,' Sally said.

'With *one of the world's leading managers*,' Dermott gritted out.

'Manager? Who?'

'McClintock Brady MacKenzie.'

'Aah.'

'Aaah – yes, quite.'

Sally stood with her hands on her hips. 'Nothing to do with thighs, then?' she asked.

Dermott raised his hands to heaven. He wheeled around with them extended, as if begging understanding from the entire population of London. The mobile rang in his jacket pocket, trilling innocently as a bird. He reached inside and turned it off. A passing taxi driver rolled down his window and yelled, 'Awright, Furrgull?'

'No!' Dermott yelled back. 'I am married. *Married*!'

'Shut up,' Sally said.

Dermott dropped his arms and stared at her. 'McClintock Brady MacKenzie, who can swing deals with a dozen noughts in them,' he said.

'You're under contract,' Sally reminded him.

'Do you think that means anything to MacKenzie?' her husband retorted. 'He can get me out of *Beckside Street* without breaking stride.'

'But why do you want to be out of *Beckside*?' Sally asked.

Dermott made a show of tearing his trademark hair out. 'To get into *Limey Batman*, you stupid bint!'

'*Limey* . . .' Sally's voice tailed away temporarily. 'But that's just a rumour.'

'They're over here casting!'

'You never told me,' she said.

'I wanted to surprise you.' Dermott shrugged. 'Ach, what the hell. I wanted to give you everything. Go on – ruin it for me. That's all right.'

Sally stared at him. An apology was on her lips when the light dawned.

'You bloody liar,' she said.

'What?'

'You lying bloody lying . . .'

'Ouch!' She had caught him with the flat of her hand right on the mouth.

'MacKenzie doesn't manage Maria von Elbock,' she said. 'It was in *The Corker* last month. He manages Sabina Gulstadt. Maria von Elbock is managed by her brother. And they're not casting *Limey Batman*, either.'

'They bloody are!'

'Oh no they're not,' she said. 'The director changed his mind at the last minute. He's filming *Shakespeare in New York* with Bruce Willis.'

She could see the various alternatives, the desperate contradictions, chasing over Dermott's face. He just wasn't quick enough to catch any of them up. *Liars.* She was stuck with a whole cast of liars in her life.

'She had her leg around your waist,' she said.

'She was feeling unsteady.'

'She was talking about meeting you.'

'She wasn't.'

'She was.'

'She wasn't,' he said. He gazed at her with that pleading puppy look. 'But forgive me anyway.'

She couldn't say anything. Two bloody liars in one week, she was thinking.

'I bought you a present,' he said.

She closed her eyes.

'I bought you a dream,' he said.

'Oh Dermott, cut it,' she said.

'A little dream, just for me and you.'

Sally turned away. She started to walk. Slowly at first. Then faster.

Dermott ran after her. 'She does not mean a thing,' he cried. 'Here – here!' He was holding something out on the flat of his hand.

They were at a road junction.

Dermott put up his arm, hailed another taxi. It slewed to a stop. 'Awwright, Furrgull!'

He opened the door. 'I bought you Nova Scotia,' he said.

She frowned at him. 'What?'

'Half a day in a dank bloody pub standing next to people with balaclavas sewn to their heads,' he said. 'Stench of fucking cow muck, everybody staring at me, auctioneer drunk, three sets of warring families egging me on, clutching for money, had to take the three lots out the back, strike a deal, pay the whole bloody lot off, stump up a fortune for the place, just to buy you a dream.'

She stared at him. 'Dermott,' she said. 'I don't know what you're talking about.'

He threw a set of door keys at her. 'I shall never forget how you have shamed me tonight,' he said haughtily. Then he got in the taxi, and was driven away.

She picked the keys up from the street. *Nova Scotia*, said the fob. *Deadham Markham*.

10

Chris was called into Owen Majolica's office at 8.30 a.m. on Monday morning.

At first, he didn't seem to see her; he was sitting on the window sill looking down at the Thames ten floors below, a phone jammed to his ear.

'Yes, Dad,' he was murmuring.

Chris looked round at the room.

There was a life-size poster of Belinda Bass, the Up-Line Cable weather girl, right by the door. It had made Chris jump the first time she had seen it, thinking for a moment that the seriously pneumatic Belinda had been wafted into Owen's presence and made to pose by the door to demoralise other women, a cunning woman-management ploy.

After all, it was hard to distinguish a life-size placard from Belinda herself, for neither spoke, both grinned, and both could only move if helped, such were the weight of Belinda's charms.

Until last year, Belinda had been a civil servant in the local Ministry of Agriculture, Fisheries and Food office, processing whelk stocks. Then she had made a serious career move. She had decided to inflate her breasts. This simple procedure had catapulted her straight into the media spotlight, as the size she chose to inflate to was 40DD.

Soon, the whelk stocksperson was on every tabloid cover. Somewhere along the line she added the letters 'b' and 'e' to the front of her name. Then she had appeared on a confessions show. Owen had seen the confessions show – it was his own, after all, at 9 a.m. and this episode had been called *I Love My Look* – and he had immediately booked her. There was a great deal of comment on weather fronts and Belinda's front. She knew nothing about weather, of course, and, as it transpired, she knew nothing about the country she lived in, regularly pointing to Scotland and referring to it as the south-east, and leaning forward over Wales and calling it The Channel Islands. Belinda was terminally dim, but that didn't matter. Televisions all over the land were switched on every morning so that pre-pubescent boys – some of them in their eighties – could salivate over Belinda, and so that Outrageds all over the country could write reams of hate-mail to the programme controllers.

It was marvellous, Owen said.

Marvellous.

These days, rumour had it that Belinda was now the mistress of a Cabinet Minister whose one delight was to have her throw buckets of seafood over him.

Chris stood by the door and gazed at Belinda's image.

'Yes, Dad,' Owen repeated.

He saw Chris, smiled and waved her in, indicating a chair in front of his desk. As she did so, he mimed at the phone and made a despairing face. She smiled back at him, sitting down hurriedly, hiding her elderly and crinkled and crumpled legs as far under the desk over-hang as she could.

Owen finally put the phone down.

'Dad,' he said.

'Oh yes?'

'I don't know, I don't know,' he muttered, as if to him-self. Then he looked around, as if searching for a neutral subject. 'Seen my sick dog?' he asked.

Chris looked into the small conference area, where he was pointing. On the expensive yew table sat a mechanical black-and-white terrier with a plate in its mouth. It must have been three foot tall. Owen picked up a remote. 'Look at this,' he said. He pressed a button, and the dog's ears sprang outwards.

'Aah,' Chris said.

'No, no – it gets better. Look.' He pressed another button, and the dog put the plate on the table. Owen chuckled. 'Brilliant, isn't it?'

'Brilliant,' she agreed.

'Ah, but look – just look – watch.' He pressed another button. The dog was sick on to the plate.

'Ha ha,' Chris said.

Owen laughed. 'Brilliant!' he repeated.

'But what is it?'

'Oh, just food colouring and gloop,' he said, 'in a compartment inside.' He flung the remote on his desk.

'Frolic.' Chris said faintly.

'Yeah,' he agreed.

She could see he was bored now. He fiddled with the case of the mobile.

'How is your father?' she asked.

'Usual,' Owen said. 'World domination, that kind of thing.'

'Is he going up in his balloon again?' Majolica Senior was a bit of an adventurer.

'Next month,' Owen said.

'I hope he doesn't get brought down over Iraq this time,' Chris murmured.

'I hope he does,' Owen muttered.

They regarded each other solemnly for a moment.

'Chris,' said Owen.

'Owen,' said Chris.

He seemed curiously deflated. A bit like his father's

round-the-world balloon hopes. Then he suddenly looked
up. 'How is *your* Dad?' he enquired.

'Dead,' Chris told him.

'Is he?' Owen remarked. 'Why did I think he was alive,
then?'

'I don't know, Owen,' Chris said.

'Hang on – it isn't your father, it's your father-in-law,'
he remembered. 'How's your father-in-law?'

'Not too bad.'

'Out of hospital?'

'No . . .'

Of all the subjects Owen could have chosen, this was
the one that Chris least wanted to think about. Every time
she did so, she pictured Henry not being able to negotiate
his way through cutlery and cups of tea without help. And
then she would think of the house in Prystock, with its
narrow stairs, and the only bathroom up those stairs. At
the moment, Henry could sit up, but walking was out of
the question. Talking was a jumble of blurred consonants
and vowels. And there was something else, far worse than
that, a change in Henry that was more unnerving than all
the other things put together.

'Chris?'

She looked up at Owen's face. 'Yes?'

'Are you OK?'

'Yes . . . yes, fine,' she lied.

Her boss walked round to the other side of the desk and
pressed the intercom. 'Sophie, could you bring us some
coffee,' he said.

Chris slipped down into her seat. That's it, she thought.
He's going to fire me. He's going to soften me up with
coffee and then fire me for being thirty-eight and not
possessing a single lilac twinset.

She thought morosely of the days when owning a
twinset had been the height of Tory middle-aged frigidity

and pathos. She still couldn't get her mind round the fact that it was now exactly the opposite, so much so that her fingers twitched and clamped around her credit card when she had at last decided to buy one. She just hadn't been able to do it, to buy the thing that her auntie used to wear under a gabardine mac and a headscarf decorated with horseshoes. Even when Meg Ryan had looked stunning in one in *You've Got Mail*, she couldn't do it. And now she was going to pay for not being able to wear one.

Fired for not wearing fashionable knitted garments. She could see it on her P45 now.

'Chris,' Owen said. 'This is a bit delicate.'

Here it comes, she thought.

Owen strolled to the window and stood for a moment with his back to her. Then, turning, he walked over to the sailing prints and the Oxford oar. His fingers touched the oar once, very briefly, almost surreptitiously, as if it held some kind of secret allure.

Chris, meanwhile, was trying very hard not to look at Owen's bottom. It still looked tight even in a pair of baggy chinos. Instead, she looked at the back of his neck, and suddenly found that that was worse, because he had a rim of shell-pink skin just above his collar and before his understated sandy-coloured tan. To her horror, she had a desperate urge to put her arms around him from behind, rest her lips gently on that inch of skin, and then lay her head on his shoulder.

He turned around.

She looked away, rigid with embarrassment – stared at the arrangement of toys on Owen's desk – his axe-murderer pencil sharpener, his rotating head, his Play-station, his Mont Blanc pen with the pink furry snake jammed on the top.

Please God, don't ever let us invent videos for thoughts.

'Chris,' he blurted out. 'I need you.'

The world lurched abruptly to a halt.

'I'm sorry?' she said.

'You're the only one,' he said.

Sophie came in with the coffee.

Sophie was wearing a twinset. She looked fantastic.

'Thanks,' Owen said, without even glancing at his secretary.

Warmth rushed to regions in Chris's body that had been buried in permafrost for some time. And yet it wasn't physical, it was emotional. No complaints had actually ever formed and taken substance in Chris's mind over Malcolm's performances in bed, or hers, for that matter. Their sexual relationship was a bit like a traffic queue on the Embankment: you always knew it was going to be there, and sometimes it bounced along, and sometimes it came to a dead stop, and sometimes you thought of your shopping list while you waited for the green light, and sometimes you thought of your shopping list while you had your foot on the accelerator, and mostly the other motorists, even those alongside you, took very little notice of you as long as you kept pace. And it got you where you wanted to go, and you didn't have to stand out in the rain or get splashed by other cars because you were safe inside your own little car stop-starting routinely along in a vaguely forward motion.

Chris had never really wanted to be in another car.

Not really.

But she did want to talk to the driver.

And, as Owen leaned over her while he passed her the cup of coffee, he looked into Chris's eyes, and there was a connection. She rarely, if ever, looked into Malcolm's eyes, and he had certainly never looked into hers with rapt attention, or intrigue, or amazement. They had existed for years on their shorthand, glancing at each other for odd moments.

Malcolm was not one for expressing his feelings. In fact, Chris often wondered if he had any. Outrageous, blinding, heart-stopping feelings. Wild schemes and ambitions. Impossible dreams. Desperate fears.

She had never seen an emotion like that ever cross Malcolm's face. He had everything taped. Boxed. Labelled. His life was an organised pattern – a very comfortable place to be. Chris had never been threatened or worried by Malcolm, a fact for which she was eternally grateful after Kevin.

And yet . . . and *yet* . . .

Dreams, improbable dreams, lived in Owen's face. And now, as Chris looked at him, she saw the dreams racing through him, and it opened a very small and utterly forgotten door deep in her battered and disbelieving heart.

'Are you sure you're OK?' he repeated.

She took a sip of coffee. 'Yes,' she said. 'I am fine.'

He brought a chair up close to her, and sat down on it. 'Look,' he said, 'I want to ask you something. A favour.'

She smiled at him. 'Ask away.' *Dinner? The weekend?*

He fiddled with the trim on the edge of the chair. 'It's a bit of a cheek really,' he murmured, 'taking you away from your husband at a time like this.'

She put down her cup. 'My husband . . .'

'Now, I mean. With a crisis on. With your father-in-law.'

'Well . . .'

'But I need someone I can trust. Someone to act for us.'

'To act for you?' she said.

He nodded. 'There's someone I'm supposed to see, but I can't see them today, and I need to see them today. But I've got a meeting in Canary Wharf I can't get out of. And I'm meant to be speaking at the Young Entrepreneur Lunch.'

She continued to stare at him, not understanding.

'Dad wants me to get someone,' he explained.

'Get someone?' What was he talking about?

'Mrs Pye.'

Fantasies – whole worlds of fantasies, whole solar systems of fantasies, spinning universes, parallel dimensions, infinite aeons of fantasy – screeched to a stop in Chris's head. The car that she was, in her imagination, already travelling in with Owen Majolica – a sex-red Ferrari, speeding away from the Embankment and out into never-never land – did an emergency stop, catapulted her out of the passenger seat, out through the windscreen and into the road.

'Mrs Pye?' she said faintly.

'Yes.'

'You don't mean Mrs Duck Pye?'

'Yes, the woman from West Tolwell. She was here last week.'

'That Mrs Duck Pye,' Chris confirmed. 'She's married to a mallard.'

'That's the one.'

Chris took a deep, calming breath. 'Just a minute,' she said. 'You want to have some sort of relationship with Mrs Pye – and you want me to set it up for you?'

Owen laughed. 'Well, you could say that,' he said. 'Dad wants to sign her up.'

'What for?'

'To write a book.'

If he had said, 'Dad wants to sign her up to sit naked on the Albert Memorial', she would have been less shocked.

'What kind of book?' she asked.

Owen shrugged. 'Doesn't matter. Life-story, novel . . . whatever she wants.'

'A novel?' she said, outrage in her voice, which rose several pitches.

'Well, you never know, do you?' Owen said. 'She might have a novel tucked away. Some people do.'

'Yes,' Chris said. She started to hyperventilate. 'Some people do.'

She bit the inside of her cheek to get a grip. 'Since when did your father buy books?' she said. 'I thought he was an engineer.'

'He is,' Owen agreed, 'but he recently acquired a car company in the USA, which has a printing company attached to it – publishes a whole range of classic car books, he says. Dad liked it, so he bought it along with the parent company'.

'He did?' Chris asked. 'What's it called?'

'Pueblo Country.'

'I've never heard of it.'

'It's a kind of holding thing, a tax thing,' Owen observed off-handedly. 'Owns a couple of publishing houses over here.'

'Good heavens! Which ones?'

'Dunno,' Owen replied. 'Big enough to get him interested in publishing things.'

'Novels?'

'Yeah.'

'And Mrs Pye . . . you want her to write a book.'

Owen got up, and began pacing up and down. 'There may be a TV series for her, and Dad says he'll sign her up for a tie-in book deal.'

Chris clenched her hands tightly. Her mouth had gone totally dry.

'One of the researchers took her back to West Tolwell the other day,' Owen said.

Chris wrenched herself away from the mental picture of Owen Senior throwing her own manuscript off the top of the Majolica Industries building in Cheapside, yelling, 'I don't want no one who ain't married to a duck!'

'Yes,' she replied slowly. 'I know. It was Mike. He had a dentist's appointment. It was on his way.'

'Did he tell you?' Owen said.

'Tell me what?'

'What it's like, Mrs Pye's place?'

'No,' Chris said. 'What is it like?'

Owen grinned. 'She lives in a couple of converted railway carriages, and runs a sort of bird rescue centre from it.'

'Yes, I do know that,' Chris said. 'That's how we found her. We were doing a programme on I Love My Pet and someone phoned us and said Mrs Pye had been in the paper because she needed funds, and that, for a stunt, she'd married one of her ducks.'

Owen nodded. 'That's it, that's it,' he agreed. 'But when Mike got there – didn't he tell you? These birds came from everywhere. It was like Hitchcock or something. They flew all round her. She told him that she can talk to them.'

'Did she?' Chris asked woodenly. 'Lovely.'

'But don't you see?' Owen said. 'Virginia Pye – living in the middle of nowhere with no money, devoted to her animals, innocent abroad, lovely old-fashioned lady. Who does it remind you of?'

'Doctor Doolittle?' Chris offered.

'Hannah Hauxwell,' Owen told her.

Chris suddenly saw where Majolicas Senior and Junior were coming from. Hannah Hauxwell, a wonderful old lady from an isolated farm high up in the Pennines, had been the media scoop of the 1980s. Her sweet face had reminded a tired population of a simpler, more caring time. Her observations on modern life had been salutary and touching. The nation had taken her to their hearts.

And here, in the shape of Virginia Pye, was another Hannah Hauxwell.

'I get it,' Chris said.

Owen smiled. 'I knew you would.'

'And you want me to go there today?'

'There's a car waiting.'

She nodded, then sighed. 'OK.'

'Great,' he said. 'Great. Just charm her . . . you know. Be nice, and wave lots of money at her.'

'How much?' Chris said.

Owen shrugged. 'Hundred thousand?'

Chris was in the process of standing up; she took hold of the back of the chair for support. 'A hundred-thousand-pound advance,' she said. 'From Majolica Industries?'

'Mmm.' Owen was already sorting through some other papers on his desk. He waved a hand vaguely in the air. 'Just get her on our side, OK?'

'Will you just tell me one thing,' Chris said.

'Yes? What is it?'

'Why me?'

Owen dropped the piece of paper he was holding and ignored the phone as it began to ring again. He came around the side of the desk and took her hand in his.

'Because I trust you,' he said simply.

She laughed briefly. 'You have a building full of people here,' she told him.

'You've got a degree in economics,' he said.

She raised her eyebrows. 'How do you know that?'

'I looked in your records.'

'That still doesn't answer the question,' she said. 'You've got people with PhDs in Advanced Networking, Lying and Delusion working for you. Marketing men. PR girls . . .'

'Mrs Pye liked you,' Owen said. 'She told Mike.'

'Oh . . . right. OK.'

'And I like you,' he said.

'OK.'

'No . . . really, I do. You're not like the others.'

She savoured a faint image of the sex-red Ferrari for a second, then let it go. 'Thank you, Owen,' she said.

He opened the door for her. 'You're so mature,' he said.

Chris walked out, smiled at Sophie, went through the wide glass doors, and started down the stairs.

On the way out of the building, she slapped Darcy Bussell.

Hard.

11

Malcolm was not comfortable with tears. He hadn't cried in thirty-five years, ever since he was five.

He sat at the side of his father's bed now, in the overheated afternoon silence of the hospital ward, and thought back to those school gates at Capperstone Road, and his mother standing at them, waiting for him, searching the lines of children as they left in the hometime swarm.

On that particular day, all those years ago, he had been last out. His calm had been perfectly controlled until he had seen his mother, her hands clasped anxiously in front of her. Something in his five-year-old mind had snapped as he had crossed the playground, clutching his satchel and screwed-up plastic bag that still contained his lunch.

'Malcolm,' his mother had said, and clasped him to her. He could still, if he tried, recall the scratchy material of her coat, the curiously fishy smell of her support stockings, and the cream that she used to rub into her rheumatic knee. Even now, just to pass the Scholl counter in the chemist's brought a strange sensation of relief and comfort to him, the relief of his mother's arms, the comfort of her all-enveloping unseasonal coat, worn even in summer. The slight shame of needing her at all.

She had taken the plastic bag from his hands. 'You haven't eaten your sandwiches,' she said, surprised.

All the sorrow in his five-year-old heart had welled up, and he started to sob. Sobs that wrenched his stomach and brought a long tight band of pain to his chest, the pain of utter injustice.

'He wouldn't let me,' he gulped out.

'Wouldn't let you? Who wouldn't?'

'Mark Bowman,' he snivelled.

Mark Bowman. The name still had a faint tang of scorching even now. Mark Bowman, who had matches in his pocket, and threatened to set fire to you. Mark Bowman, who always stood on the top of the wooden fire engine and wouldn't let anyone else climb up. Mark Bowman, who wound the swing chains around your wrist.

'Bowman?' his mother queried. She knelt at his side and wiped his eyes. 'What did he do?' she asked him.

'Peed on my lunch,' he blubbed.

His mother's fury had been interesting to see. It was short-lived but violent, like a summer storm. She had marched him straight to the empty classroom, where the form teacher had been wearily clearing up. Incandescence flickered about her like ball lightning. He recalled only a torrent of words, the hitched gulps on his mother's breathing, the high pitch of her voice. And then he remembered her sitting down with the teacher, collapsing like a punctured balloon, and crying herself in a patter of sighs and gasps.

When his father came home, the story had been re-told.

Henry Craven had listened, frowning, then a deep, disapproving sound had escaped him – somewhere between a moan and a cough. He had taken hold of Malcolm's shoulder.

'This will never happen again,' he said.

Over his father's shoulder, Malcolm had seen his mother's face lit with relief. His father, Henry Sanderson Craven, ex-Quartermaster Royal Marines, was going to do something. Malcolm's five-year-old brain thought of Mark Bowman being tossed bodily off the fire engine. He thought, very briefly, of pissing on Mark Bowman's own sandwiches. Better still, his crisps.

His father's hand had tightened on his flesh until he felt his bones bend.

'Never again,' Henry Craven had said, towering above his son like Colossus, 'will you cry in a public place. *Never again!*'

And he had not.

It was not that he thought his father was right any more about crying – after all, he was as new a man as anyone else, and accepted that crying was possibly mandatory for the truly successful young male, especially for getting women into bed. He knew, intellectually, at the front of his brain, that crying was a natural release, and that women were psychologically healthier for it, and that men snapped like twigs under emotional pressure, because they could not weep.

But the back of his brain was a slightly different matter.

There, at the back, Henry lurked, a shadowy monster several feet taller than himself, his hand on Malcolm's metaphorical shoulder. And so, even at times when he felt like crying – even, more importantly, when he *should* have cried, even when Chris had been in hospital, pale-faced in a raised bed, her arms crossed over her stomach, her mouth turned down in grief – even then he had not cried. He had felt Henry's fingernails digging into his neck, and stopped dead, the tears halfway.

He had said something awful to Chris that night three years ago. Something that she had not remarked on at the time, and had never mentioned since. But, nevertheless, he had said it. As he stood next to her, and held her hand, and wondered what they were going to talk about for the next seven months if they were not going to talk about babies, he had heard himself say, *Well, we must always look on the bright side.*

'The bright side?' Chris had echoed, with desperate pathos.

'You're fit and well,' he had said.

She had said nothing at all.

Leaving that night, seeing himself reflected for a second in the plate-glass doors of the hospital foyer, he had wondered who the man was in the silhouetted image. A fool blundering along looking on the bright side, swallowing his grief.

And the next day, they had not referred to it. He didn't know how to raise the subject. He didn't know if he should. And, whenever he looked at Chris, she would smile quickly, as if to prove that she was being optimistic.

He knew that things had never quite been the same since; there was not the same solidity, the same unerring trust. He was not the hero any more, the man who had saved Christine from the horrible memory of Kevin the Creep – a man who hoovered up money and slept with other women in Chris's bed. Malcolm had once saved her from that – or, perhaps more accurately, he had picked up the scattered pieces afterwards, carefully repairing Chris's shattered finances and putting her quietly back together, so that she no longer flinched at the sight of bank statements and gas bills.

No, he was not the hero any more. He was the man who looked on the bright side. Which was why the last two or three days had been so hard to deal with.

His father had been moved into a ward and now occupied the middle bed in a line of ten. It was a ward that seemed to be devoted to circulatory diseases, and Henry's fellow patients were in the various early stages of recovery from heart attacks and strokes. It was a dismal, god-awful bloody place, the walls decorated in acres of magnolia, the bed curtains and blankets a particularly sick-making pastel blue. All around Henry were similarly elderly faces, and it had struck Malcolm hard the first morning that he had walked in here, that his father was just that – an elderly man. Such a thing had never really occurred to him before.

Henry's life up till now had been written in capital letters, in headline tones of black and white; what Henry said was right, and what Henry said was important. The rest of the world was at best misguided and at worst criminally wrong.

Of course, Henry was a racist and bigot. Even Malcolm knew it, and he would have known it even if Chris didn't always tell him so. But even being a racist was somehow right in Henry's eyes.

When South Africa had still been in the grip of apartheid, Henry had said that the reason why black people couldn't get a vote was that they were far too excitable.

'Excitable?' Malcolm remembered Chris saying. They had been watching the TV news at the time.

'That's right,' Henry had confirmed. He waved his hand at the TV set. 'Look at that.'

A news item was being broadcast from a football stadium where ten thousand ANC supporters had gathered. The whole crowd was moving as one, arms extended, voices raised in a flood of feeling.

'You see that?' Henry had said. 'Jumping up and down like a load of bloody monkeys. Would you give a vote to that?'

It drove Chris mad. Being with his father brought her close to chewing the carpet. 'Get him out of my sight,' she would tell him, if Henry came to visit. After only two or three hours, Chris would go out into another room, where Malcolm would invariably find her mercilessly tidying things that didn't need tidying. 'For God's sake, Malcolm,' she'd whisper, 'take him out! Take him for a walk. Take him to the zoo and let him meet his other relations.'

But something had happened to Henry in the past few days. The headlines and capitals were no more. He had been re-written in lower case, in the kind of text you find in footnotes at the bottom of insurance forms.

Henry Sanderson Craven had shrunk.

Malcolm went into the ward on Monday morning, and saw his father propped up on pillows in his bed. On the other side, a very old man of ninety-two was sitting in a chair alongside his bed wearing an air of total bewilderment. The other neighbour was asleep and snoring loudly.

'Hello, Dad,' Malcolm had said.

Henry had looked at him.

'How are you?' Malcolm asked.

Henry's face had dropped on the left side, as if his skin were made of wax that had melted a little. His eyelid was almost shut. His mouth drooped. The plug had been pulled from the left side, leaving a ghost in its place, a shadow.

'Treating you all right?' Malcolm had said.

And then, Henry had started to cry.

Malcolm had looked away, pleating the bedspread between thumb and forefinger, while Henry made little guttural noises of distress. He had never before touched his father, never kissed him, never hugged him. And he couldn't do it now.

It had never been what his father wanted.

He had wanted a silent upstanding boy, a boy who said things like, *Look on the bright side*. And that was exactly what he had got, a son who hated any kind of confrontation, any kind of scene.

And so it was impossible now – *impossible* – to find a way to stop Henry crying. Malcolm couldn't raise his own eyes to the shameful sight, let alone hold his father's hand. If Henry were ill, he would never forgive Malcolm for taking pity on him, or even noticing that he was distressed. When Henry got better, Malcolm thought, he would despise him if he remembered that Malcolm had weakened. It was just not done. Not their language.

And so Malcolm had sat in agony, looking away.

After a minute or two, a nurse came to the bedside. 'What's the matter?' she asked.

Malcolm had looked up. She was no more than eighteen, very pretty.

The nurse moved round the side of the bed. 'Oh, Mr Craven,' she said, taking Henry's immobile hand and squeezing it hard. 'There's nothing to cry about, is there?' Then she wiped Henry's eyes, and had turned back to Malcolm with a smile. 'It's frustration,' she explained. 'It's very common.'

As she'd smoothed Henry's pillow, Malcolm watched as Henry looked up at the girl with the devoted expression of a beaten dog.

'You'll be all right, won't you, Mr Craven?' she said kindly. 'You'll see.'

Then she'd walked away, heels clicking on the suicidally-polished floor.

Malcolm had looked back at Henry. 'You'll be all right, Dad,' he'd echoed weakly.

But he had known in his heart it wouldn't be all right at all.

12

It was midday on Monday before Sally found her way to Pinbarrow Studios. She hadn't seen Dermott since Saturday night at the gallery.

She had expected Pinbarrow to look like the entrance to the lot in *Sunset Boulevard*, with an arch over the top saying something like *Pinbarrow – We Dream the Universe – The Home of Beckside Street*. But instead, the studio was hidden away behind a seemingly endless series of warehouses, next to a railway line on the outskirts of St Albans, and the only sign over the gate was one which said *Headroom Six Feet, Deliveries At Rear*.

It was painted grey, with a security fence around it, and a grey security box manned by a grey man who didn't care.

'*Beckside Street*?' Sally had asked, winding her car window down.

'Fourth on the left,' he said, with a mouth full of Peppermint Aero.

'Do I need a pass or anything?'

'Are you dangerous?'

'No,' she said.

'Fourth on the left,' he told her.

There was no office, no Reception. A fine drizzle floated over open hangar doors, inside which Sally glimpsed stacks of brown cartons. She pulled the car over, and got out, hugging her coat around her to keep out the cold.

'*Beckside Street*?' she asked a man who walked out of the hangar with an electric cable.

'Go through.'

'Just anywhere?'

'Follow the screams.'

She gazed at his retreating back.

The hangar was cavernous inside, a mass of apparently discarded equipment, boxes, pallets. At the far end, metal doors were slightly open. Behind them, she could see a sliver of light.

As she opened the door, she saw a girl sitting on a plastic chair, dressed in an overall and in full stage make-up.

'*Beckside Street*?' Sally asked.

'The hell with them,' the girl said.

Sally eyed her warily. 'Is Dermott Matthews about?' she enquired.

'That shit,' the girl snorted.

Sally walked on, unshocked. The girl obviously knew Dermott well. There were two trailers parked in the gaping black hole of the sets, but she didn't know whether either belonged to the cast. As she emerged from behind them, she saw a row of doors, all open. In the first, a fight of astonishing proportions was taking place.

A chair came flying out of the door.

'And don't mention hotpot!' yelled a voice. 'Don't you ever mention bloody hotpot again, you bastard, you bloody bastard!'

A woman in her fifties came storming out of the door, wig askew, glasses on a gilt chain bouncing around on her huge bosom. A few steps out of the room, she tore off her blonde wig, and stamped on it. In the shadows, a crew stood silent and watched her dance on the wig.

Sally crept towards the door. She could hear another two voices now, one of which was Dermott's. He was singing.

She got to the door and peered around the frame. Dermott was standing in the centre of the small rehearsal

room, his head tipped back, and his hands over his ears.
He was just starting the chorus of 'My Way'. On
the other side of the room was a woman Sally didn't
know – short, fat and dark-haired. She had her hands on
her hips.

'It won't work,' the woman shouted.

' "When there was doubt . . ." ' Dermott sang.

'Not a single second, not a minute of airtime, not an
inch of film, not ever, so you can stuff it,' she continued.

' "I ate it up . . ." '

'Right up!'

' "And spat it out . . ." '

Sally withdrew her head. So he's the same here, she
thought. She looked back at the crew. They looked like a
group of mourners at a funeral. As she walked over they
regarded her with sympathetic calm.

'It's a bad time,' Sally said, to the nearest man.

'Yeah,' he replied.

'Are they filming today?'

'Yeah. Film every day.'

She glanced down at his T-shirt, which said, in bold
jazzy capitals, *Evita*.

'You've come down in the world,' she commented.

'Yeah,' he said.

'Is it always like this?'

'Lately.'

'What're they arguing about?'

'Dying.'

Sally raised her eyebrows. 'Someone's dying?'

'Dermott Matthews.'

She nodded slowly. 'I see. How long has he got?'

'Forty seconds of script.'

'To die in?'

'Long enough.'

'Is it?' she asked.

'Yeah,' he told her. 'Betty Brindley had fourteen seconds in *Snow's Drift* last week. See that?'

'No,' Sally said.

'Major character, that. Fourteen seconds to fall in the canal.'

'And . . .' Sally glanced around. She could hear Dermott yelling. It wasn't 'My Way' any longer. It was a stream of dancing Gaelic curses that a six-year-old in a school in Glasgow had taught him while Dermott was being a banana with the *Mad Bad Socks*.

'He's taking it awfully well, isn't he?' she said.

All at once, the door was slammed. Then it was opened, then it was slammed. Finally, the woman came out. She made a beeline for one of the trailers.

'Who *is* that?' Sally asked.

'Audrey Barnett, the producer. Who are you, any road?' the crewman enquired. 'A reporter?'

'No,' Sally said. 'Just an innocent bystander.'

A continuity girl broke off from the crew and trotted after Audrey.

The producer turned on the trailer steps. 'Get me Alex here!' she shouted.

Sally looked at the man alongside her. 'Who is Alex?' she whispered.

'Script,' he told her.

'Take lunch!' Audrey yelled. 'Forty minutes!' She disappeared into the trailer, the continuity girl closing the door after them both.

The crew drifted away.

Sally stood hesitantly in the shadows, waiting for Dermott to make an appearance. When he did not, she walked back to the door of the rehearsal room. Dermott, she saw at once, was sitting in a chair, dialling a number on his mobile. As she came in the door, he glanced up, did a double-take, and switched it off.

'So it's you,' he said. He made no move to get up.

She sat down slowly opposite him. 'I hear you're fired,' she said.

'Yes, I'm fired.'

'Dermott, I'm sorry.'

He shrugged. 'Plenty more parts where that came from.'

She frowned, surprised. 'Are there?'

He looked down at the phone in his lap.

'Are you coming home?' she asked.

He said nothing.

'Where have you been for the last two nights?'

'Here,' he said.

'A hotel here?'

He nodded.

'Well, aren't you coming home?' she persisted.

He picked up the phone and weighed it from palm to palm.

'Am I stopping you making a call?' she asked.

'No, no.'

She looked down at the floor. There was a long silence.

'I lost my job, too,' she said.

He glanced at her.

'We must sell the house,' she said.

He shrugged again.

'Dermott? I lost my job,' she repeated.

He started to hum.

'Dermott, don't do that.'

He stood up. 'Ach, I'm getting awful tired of being told what to do,' he said.

She gazed at him. 'We've got no money,' she said slowly. 'There is nothing coming in at all, if you're out of *Beckside Street*.'

'Don't worry about that.'

'But I *am* worried!' she said. 'And now there's Nova

Scotia. What on earth possessed you? Is there a mortgage, or what? Will there be more bills coming in?'

'There'll be no bills.'

She frowned, puzzled. 'You paid cash for it?'

He started to pace the room. 'It's a present.'

'But . . .'

He turned to her. 'Look, live there,' he said. 'Sell the London house. Do what you want.'

'Live there? Both of us, you mean?'

'No,' he said, not meeting her eye. 'I'm going to America.'

She thought she had misheard him. Perhaps he had said, *I'm going to lunch*, or *I'm going to Erica*. Perhaps Erica was someone on the crew.

'Erica?' she said.

He laughed, and ran a hand through his hair. 'Jesus, Sally.'

'I didn't hear what you said . . .'

'I'm going to America.'

She clasped her hands. They were suddenly shaking. 'For an audition?'

He looked at her for some seconds, then sighed, and walked over to her. He squatted down next to her, taking her hands in his. 'It's my fault,' he said. 'I'm awful sorry. Truly I am. Awful, awful sorry.'

'What's your fault?'

'Look . . .' He paused.

'It isn't your fault you lost your job,' she said hurriedly. 'I lost mine, and it wasn't my fault. Sometimes people are hard to work with.'

'Sally . . .'

'Go and apologise,' she continued. 'You can apologise.'

'Sally, for Christ's sake,' he said. 'Don't be so bloody dense.' He dropped her hands and stood up. 'I'm going to America because I've been asked.'

Her stomach lazily flipped over, the first true premonition of his deceit.

'Don't look at me like that,' he said.

'I'm sorry,' she told him. 'I can't alter my face for you.'
She stood up beside him. 'Why don't you just spit it out,'
she said. 'Like the song says.'

He smiled, a smile full of embarrassment. 'I've been
seeing someone,' he said.

Her stomach gave up the battle to remain on an even
keel, and dropped out of sight, somewhere below the floor.
Somewhere through the core of the earth, and out the
other side, and flung itself into deep space.

'Someone,' she repeated. 'Who?'

'Divina Delaney.'

She looked away. She looked at the far wall, where
there was a *No Smoking* notice decorated with cigarette
burns. Divina Delaney, oh God. Very Hollywood. Very
big.

'You don't know her,' she said. She turned back to look
at him. 'Or do you?'

'I went to see her in *Rabbit* at the Royal Ionian.'

'When?'

'Last month.'

'You didn't say.'

'No.'

She rubbed her hand over her forehead. Divina Delaney
had been playing a twelve-week season at one of London's
largest theatres, to popular acclaim. Mostly because she
took her clothes off in it and revealed her cosmetic
surgeon's expertise.

'You had it all planned,' Sally said.

'Yes.'

'You went to the Ionian and planned to see her.'

'Yes.'

'You told her who you were, and saw her . . .'

'Yes.'

'And she . . .'

'We went out for dinner.'

Sally nodded. 'I see.'

'No, you don't see at all,' he said.

She smiled. 'Oh yes I do,' she said. 'But I wonder if she does.'

'Now, Sally . . .'

He had put his hand on her arm. She pulled away. 'Don't touch me,' she said. 'I told you her marriage was over. I told you the rumour. *I* told you!'

'Yes.'

'Two months ago. We ran a piece on her.'

She recalled it now. Divina looking thoughtful on the terrace of her Los Angeles home. Divina considering two new film contracts. Divina holding the script to the London play and looking wistful and saying that she hoped so much that she was good enough to play on the London stage.

And then there had been a few more shots of Divina looking very lonely, Divina looking very hurt.

Divina had dumped her older boyfriend now that he had got her where she wanted to go. Poor wizened old guy with a rubber goods inheritance, who had helped launch her into her acting career and, it was rumoured, a hundred beds on the way to the top. Now she commanded five-million-dollar parts, and the seventy-year-old rubber goods baron had been pensioned off, thrown aside. Five million dollars a film was still just chickenfeed for Hollywood, of course. But she was getting there.

'What the hell use are you to her?' Sally demanded.

Dermott looked wounded, but only for a moment.

'You're the same, the pair of you, aren't you?' she said. 'Well-matched.'

'Yes,' he admitted.

'Good in bed, is she?'

'Yes,' he said.

It hurt. It hurt so much that she took a step backwards, as if he had physically hit her. 'Oh God,' she whispered. 'You cruel bastard.'

'I'm sorry,' he said. 'It was a whirlwind thing, I—'

'Like us?'

He gave a twisted little grimace.

'What can you give her?' she said. 'She'll drop you in two months.'

'She's going to introduce me to people,' he said. 'She already has.'

'Then she'll drop you,' she said.

'No.'

'Oh, you bloody fool,' she muttered. Then, another sickening betrayal occurred to her. 'How'd you get her number?'

'I rang Michael at the magazine,' he said.

'You . . .' Words temporarily failed her. Dermott had rung the Entertainment Editor and, bloody man that he was, Michael had given her husband Divina Delaney's hotel number. The shit. The *shit*.

She sat down again, as if winded.

'Sally, I'm sorry,' he said.

She stared at the floor. 'Only last week you were talking about a family.'

'I know.'

'Talking about a family when you were already seeing her.'

'Yes, I know.'

'Getting builders in to renovate the house, Dermott . . .'

He shrugged, guilty. 'Well, yes . . . there is that.'

'Did you tell her?'

'What?'

'That you were married?'

'Yes,' he said.

She shook her head. 'It wouldn't mean anything to her, of course,' she murmured.

'I am sorry, Sal,' he repeated.

She frowned as she gazed at her feet. 'Only the other night you were messing about with that bloody tennis player,' she said.

'That was nothing,' he muttered.

'Nothing,' she said. 'Yes, right. Nothing.' She stood up, still not looking at him. 'Lying to me about *Limey Batman*.'

'It's not a lie,' he said. 'Well, *Limey Batman* is a lie, but Divina's got me the next Bond. It's a formality, Sally – the director told me so. They start filming in Canada soon. Then Arizona.'

'English villain?'

'Irish villain.'

'How very appropriate,' she murmured.

'Sally, look . . .'

'Don't come anywhere near me,' she warned.

'Sally . . .'

'I suppose Divina Delaney gave you the money for Nova Scotia,' she said. 'To pay me off.'

'She did not,' he told her. 'I paid for it with my handshake from here. From *Beckside Street*.'

Sally walked to the door. He came after her, trying to turn her round so that he could look into her face.

'Leave me alone,' she said.

'Sally . . .'

'Leave me alone!'

'Sal . . .'

She wheeled round and looked at him. 'If you don't leave me alone, good and alone,' she said softly, 'I shall fucking well kill you.'

She left.

The second long exit, in a very long week.

Out through the shadows of the studio, and into the rain.

13

Chris was not having much better luck at West Tolwell. It was on her road atlas – marked in the centre of a green patch labelled *Crackle Down* – but when she actually got to the area, she found herself in a maze of nameless lanes without signposts.

She was parked in a field gate when a tractor came past. She wound down her window and waved.

'West Tolwell?' she shouted.

The driver opened his cab window. A blast of *Sweet's Greatest Hits* wafted out. 'Where?'

'Tolwell. West Tolwell?'

'Five miles the other way up,' he said, closing the cab window and churning past in a spray of mud.

'Thanks,' Chris muttered. She looked at herself in the driving mirror. 'Up,' she said. 'Super.'

Ten minutes later, travelling obediently up a narrow hill, she met a right-angled bend. She was thinking of Henry at the time, and of Malcolm, and so didn't appreciate the sharpness of the turning until it was too late. She crammed on the brakes, and the car slewed gracefully sideways into a hedge, then abruptly dropped with a thump.

'Oh, shit,' she muttered.

She took her foot off the brake and gently put the car into first. She hit the accelerator. The engine whinnied like a horse. She opened the driver's door and saw that the car was quite spectacularly wedged between hedge and verge, with a small stream running underneath. It was resting on its body, with the wheels spinning uselessly. She closed the door.

'That was really a very difficult thing to do,' she told herself. 'Take note now, because in all your years of driving, you will never see that happen again. Congratulations.'

She pulled on her raincoat while still sitting in the driver's seat. Glancing at the lane, she saw that it was running with water, a fact that had not really registered as she was comfortably swishing along in warm comfort. She grimaced. Heels and water. Heels and grit and a slippery hill. Wonderful.

She got out, leaving the hazard lights flashing. The car rocked a little as she stretched her legs for the road, and then wriggled her body out. She slammed the door and looked at it, perched like a giant green slug in the bushes. 'Owen will be pleased,' she whispered to herself.

She set off up the hill.

There were no houses to be seen. In fact, there was no countryside to be seen either because the rain was folding a grey blanket over Kent, and tucking it in at the edges like a devoted mother putting her child to bed. Chris soon had the sensation that there was actually no way out of Kent at all, particularly this piece of Kent, and that she would be wandering forever in a damp little pocket of the world, like a ghost.

Fifteen minutes later, she reached a crossroads.

There was a signpost.

In one direction, it said *Blagd* and in another it said *Pul*, because some rural joker had thought it fantastically witty to pull the names off. She turned left, for no reason other than *Blagd* sounded more like an obscenity than *Pul*, and she had taken to swearing routinely as she walked along.

She thought of Kevin, just as she always thought of Kevin when she was pissed off.

The first car that she and Kevin had owned was a red Reliant Robin. Kevin bought it because he didn't have a full driving licence, but he did have a motorcycle licence, and that was all you needed to drive a three-wheel Reliant. Most of the time it was easy to forget that it had three wheels, because it was built of fibre-glass and hurtled along roads like a bat out of hell. Especially with Kevin driving.

Kevin was a determined driver with a kind of superiority complex that Chris had never seen equalled. You would have thought that he was piloting a Lotus. If he ever approached some sort of obstruction in the road where other normal, cautious drivers would stop, or at least brake and change down, Kevin would simply put his hand over the horn, ready to blow it should he encounter opposition. His favourite saying was, 'You could get a bus through there.' The number of times that Chris had seen fear frozen on other drivers' faces, rapidly followed by disbelief, was far too many to count. Once they had recovered from their brush with near death, you could see the next momentary thought cross their faces: *God Almighty! I've just been cut up by a Reliant Robin.*

Chris didn't give a damn what kind of car they drove. Which, on reflection, was probably just as well. She did notice, however, that the other drivers who gave them a friendly wave – other Reliant drivers – were all over sixty. They were all a particular brand of person, too. Not proud people. After all, you couldn't be proud behind a Reliant wheel. You could be quirky, you could possibly be eccentric, even fun, but no way could you be arrogant.

And the other Reliant drivers who waved at them were always men, with a snug-looking woman in the passenger seat – the kind of woman in her middle sixties who always looked pleased to be out, cuddling a basket on her lap with a Thermos sticking out of the top. There would be little signs in the rear window saying things like *A Dog Is Not Just For Christmas* and *Pulboro Steam Fair 1978*. What the hell these people made of Chris and Kevin – Kevin dressed in his business suit and Chris in her Civil Service two-piece, God only knew.

And there would be another difference, too. The cuddly Reliant drivers would always be progressing at a civilised potter of 30 mph along the road, whereas Kevin and Chris would be careering around corners on two out of their three wheels because they were always late.

Once, they had been pulled over in Kirkby. The policeman had a terrible job keeping a straight face.

'Do you know that you were driving at fifty-nine miles an hour in a built-up zone?' he had asked Kevin.

Kevin had assumed the choirboy expression. 'I can't believe it,' he said.

The policeman had grinned. 'Neither can I.'

Kevin never did pass his driving test.

He took it twice, and failed, and decided the whole thing was a waste of money. You didn't want, after all, to be spending hard cash on lessons when you could more enjoyably be pissing it up a wall after ten pints of John Smiths. Kevin couldn't pass either his driving test or a pub. They always called in on their way home from work. Kevin believed that he drove perfectly after four pints. He had never had an accident, he told her.

'Never had one, but witnessed thousands,' she would say.

It was her fear of his driving while drunk that had forced her into taking lessons herself. She had passed first time. But by then she and Kevin had split up, and when she came out of the Test Centre, so excited, so relieved, she had rushed to a phone box to share the good news. And it was only when her hand was on the receiver that she realised she couldn't phone Kevin any more – and yet he was the only one she really wanted to tell.

She had stood in the Liverpool street with tears coursing down her face, feeling for the hundredth time how much she missed him. How much she missed him and how glad she was to be rid of him, all rolled into one.

She had bought herself a Volkswagen Beetle. It was yellow. The people in her office called it the Musical Custard, because she always had a tape going full blast. She purposely turned herself into the kind of woman she had always disapproved of before – someone who smoked, had one-night stands, debts. It was a time of revolt. Revolt against the five years she had spent propping up Kevin and *his* debts. Five years standing by while Kevin had *his* one-night stands. Five years watching Kevin light up one cigarette after another. She actually became Kevin for a while, staying out at clubs until they closed, taking home lovers whose names she never knew, having very little fun out of it and a lot of humiliation, until one day she woke up and wanted out of Kevin's life for real. She applied for a job in London, a copy typist on a newspaper.

And then she met Malcolm.

She had trouble explaining to Malcolm what life with Kevin had been like. It was light years away from Malcolm's responsible existence, and she didn't know if he really believed her. Sometimes she didn't believe it herself. She had met Kevin when she was a shy girl grateful for attention.

Shy was a dreadful death sentence. It meant that you were too insecure to question bad behaviour, especially when – and this was the card trick – he said that he loved you, and swore eternal loyalty, while treating you like something dredged from the bottom of a slurry pit. She had wrestled for five years with Kevin and this problem, the problem of being a nice girl with a shit for a husband, a nice girl who wanted to believe the best, while feeling her faith in the human race draining away slowly every day, until the face in the mirror was no longer a shy, insecure girl but a sardonic, weary, insecure girl who hated herself for being so stupid, so gullible.

And the end came all wrong. To be properly satisfying, Chris's conversion to the-buck-stops-here-woman should have been to cut up all Kevin's suits and burn his floppy discs, then strut off down the street – preferably into a sunset – with a bag packed and her head held high. Instead of which, she had been lying on the couch nursing flu when Kevin had come back after being out all night at a stag party. Or so he said.

She hadn't even asked where he had been. She was too tired, too ill.

'I'm off out in a minute,' he had told her.

She struggled to a sitting position. 'Do you love me?' she croaked.

'For God's sake,' he muttered.

Ice had closed over Chris's heart. No rush of blood to the head. No flare of temper. No big scene. Just ice.

'Don't come back,' she told him.

'All right,' he shrugged.

He had gone upstairs and showered and changed his clothes. When he came back down, he stood for another moment in the doorway, looking at her. 'Is this what you want?' he asked.

'Yes,' she'd said.

And, as she had watched him walk away up the road, she had still wanted him. That was the crazy thing. Still wanted to touch him. It was as if she had purposely taken a part of herself – some vital, living part – surgically removed it from her body and thrown it in the fire. A needful incision. Heart surgery. A re-routing of blood. A necessary by-pass. Her throat ached as if already anticipating the scar, and she knew she would never be quite the same again, not quite so whole. She would go on all her life – comfortable, effective, outgoing, loving – but she would never be entirely the same again. Because she had had the heart by-pass, the essential operation to remove the obstruction. The full monty, without anaesthesia.

She had watched him go, turn the corner of the street, the same corner she had watched so often, waiting for him to come home, waiting for him to come around that bend on his way from the station.

He never did come home again.

She never knew who the woman was. She supposed there was a woman.

And to meet Malcolm – Malcolm, who had never knowingly done a wrong thing in his life, never even had a parking ticket, or a library fine – well, that was like stepping into a pool of fresh water. From the moment she met him, she trusted him, and was grateful. She was so grateful to him for rescuing her from the residue of the Kevin debts, for treating her like a human being, and for being the exact opposite of Kevin in every way.

Grateful.

She paused now on the featureless road, the rain sloshing into her shoes and running down her neck under her coat collar. Funny thing, gratitude. The other person didn't have to be particularly clever or gifted or attractive. They just had to be there at the right time. They just had to be different, a negative image of the positive one. Or, conversely, a positive image of the negative one. Which one was Malcolm? she wondered. Was he positive, because he didn't drink, have other women, or stay out all night? Was he positive because of the list of things he didn't do?

The funny thing was, the Reliant came back to haunt them both.

She and Malcolm came home from work one day –
three years later – to find a man standing at the front door
of the house. He had held out his hand and called her by
her first married name.

'I'm Christine Craven now,' she told him.

'I've come to repossess the car,' he said cheerfully.

'What car?' Malcolm asked.

'A Reliant Robin.'

Christine had caught her breath. 'I don't have a Reliant
Robin,' she said. 'I've never owned one.'

'But your first husband owned one.'

'Yes,' she agreed.

'And on the divorce, you took the car,' the man said.

Christine and Malcolm had looked at each other. 'No,'
she said slowly. 'My husband kept the car. We got a
divorce, and he kept the car.'

'That's not what I've been told,' the man said.

'I suppose he owes money on it?' Malcolm said.

'Yes. I have to repossess it,' the man answered.

'And he told you that I had it?' Christine said.

'He said that he doesn't see any reason to continue
paying for the car when you have it,' the man told her.

'I haven't got it,' Christine replied, angry now.

'Can I look in your garage?' the man asked.

They showed him their own small Renault parked in
their own small garage at the back of the house.

'Did you sell the Reliant and buy this?' the man asked.

'How dare you,' Christine had retorted. 'I actually sold
a nice little yellow Beetle to buy this, and I have never had
the fucking Reliant.'

'Now, Chris,' Malcolm said.

It was Malcolm, of course, who sorted it out. Malcolm
who suggested that they sit down with a cup of tea. Over
the teapot and the biscuits, Chris had given the man a
quick resumé of The Life of Kevin.

'You know what's happened?' Malcolm said. 'He's sold it, but not for enough to pay you off.'

'He's not allowed to sell it while a hire-purchase agreement is running,' the investigator stated firmly.

'That won't make any difference to him,' Chris had replied.

And that was the last they saw of the investigator. It was also the last that Chris ever heard of Kevin, and the last time that the Reliant was ever mentioned. Sometimes, if she saw one trundling along in the street, she would still prickle with resentment and a feeling of injustice and sadness – the curious, never-healing irritation and attachment. The internal adhesions from the operation.

The surgery scar.

'Can I help you?' said a voice.

Jolted from her memories, Chris turned towards the speaker. A woman was standing at the side of the road. If she hadn't spoken, Chris might well have passed her by, because she looked far more like a hedge than a human being. In fact, even now, Chris was only assuming it was a woman because the voice was female. She peered through the curtain of rain at a large square heap of greenish brown material, suddenly distinguishing an ancient camouflage jacket, a pair of slime-green cord trousers, green wellies caked with mud, and a large hat of the kind favoured by round-the-world yachtswomen while negotiating Cape Horn. Except there was nothing jaunty about this hat. It fell to the wearer's shoulders, drawstrings dangling, brim almost covering the face, and was, to complete the whole ensemble, the same fetching shade of sludge.

'I'm looking for West Tolwell,' Chris said.

'You're in it.'

Chris looked up and down the empty lane. 'Am I?'

'Its Christine, isn't it?' said the hat.

Chris peered even closer. 'Mrs Pye?'

A right hand emerged from the slime-coloured sleeve
and gripped hers like a vice. The left pushed back the brim
of the hat and revealed Virginia Pye's red face and broad
grin. 'Lovely weather for the family!' she cried.

Chris smiled back. 'Ducks?'

'Aha!' Mrs Pye said triumphantly. 'The very same. And
did you come on the bus?'

'No,' Chris said. 'My car's sitting in a stream down the
hill.'

'Cobble Hill Corner,' Mrs Pye said knowingly. 'You're
soaked through.'

'Yes,' Chris admitted.

'Follow me!' Mrs Pye said.

She had the voice of a Girl Guide leader. Opening the
gate behind her, she ushered Chris into a field. It was one
long tussocky swathe of rain-soaked grass, with two large
boxes in the corner. As they got closer, Chris could see that
the boxes were abandoned railway carriages, once maroon
and now faded to pink, with a roof of green mould. At one
end was a makeshift chimney, out of which dribbled a little
plume of smoke. The windows were steamed up.

By the time that Chris had struggled to the door, Mrs
Pye was standing looking up into the trees.

'Oh, they're such bastards to each other,' she said.

'Who are?' Chris asked.

'Robins,' Mrs Pye said.

She opened the door. Warmth rushed out. Chris smelled
coffee and – it was not possible – bread. And something
marvellous, a smell like a French restaurant. Garlic,
vegetables, pepper.

Mrs Pye went first, pulling off her jacket and kicking off
her boots. She hung the jacket on a hook, and took Chris's
coat from her.

'Is it ready?' Mrs Pye asked.

'Yeah,' said a voice.

Chris looked down the carriage. A man was standing naked at the stove.

'This is Steve,' Mrs Pye said. 'Steve, this is Christine from the television.'

He walked towards her. Taking a deep breath, Chris realised that he was not naked, but only almost naked. He wore a towel round his waist. A tiny, weeny towel.

The thought that immediately ran through her head was that the soft drinks people really ought to meet Steve. Because when they next did an advert for an eleven-o'clock appointment, and showed a window cleaner or a builder halfway up his ladder and an entire female office population lusting after his body, they really ought to have Steve on the ladder. For, even though Christine had actually met the impossibly handsome man who currently starred in the ads, and even though he was twice as handsome in the flesh as he was on the screen, he would have looked like Quasimodo next to Steve.

'The Vicar sent me a man,' Mrs Pye said, looking into the coffee-pot on the stove. 'Isn't it marvellous? You can get anything in this village. Though it isn't this village, its the next village, Deadham Markham, but its the same parish. And they sent me Steve. Lovely, isn't he?'

Chris swallowed hard. 'Yeth,' she said.

Yeth?

'Yes,' she added swiftly. 'How do you do, Steve.'

'All right,' he told her.

'Good, good,' she said.

'He's smashing, isn't he?' Mrs Pye said. She was pouring out three mugs of coffee. 'He's been here since eight this morning, and got soaked and now I'm giving him his lunch.'

'Oh,' Chris said. She took the mug of coffee.

Steve sat down next to Chris.

It was very hot in the room. Or perhaps that was just Chris. She tried not to look at the towel. Steve was no more

than twenty. Six foot three or four. Dark. Very dark.
Smooth-skinned. Big hands. Big, sexy hands . . .

'Steve's just got out of prison,' Mrs Pye said. She was
now stirring the pot of stew on the stove.

'Oh?' Chris said.

'Two months,' Steve said.

'Oh yes?'

'Bodily harm,' he told her.

'Right,' Chris replied.

'Bit of trouble,' he explained.

'Yes, of course.'

'Bit of a mistake,' Steve continued. 'He tripped when I
picked up the hammer.'

'Ah.'

'Wasn't going to hit him,' Steve told her calmly. 'Fixing
a fence, like. He hit his face on it.'

'The fence?'

'The hammer.'

Mrs Pye turned around, smiling broadly. She came to sit
beside them on the narrow wooden bench. 'Well,' she said,
nodding around herself at the railway carriage. 'What do
you think of it?'

Chris, remembering Owen's instruction to keep Mrs
Pye sweet at all costs, started to say that it was really very,
very nice. And then, looking about herself for the first time
in any detail, she stopped mid-sentence.

For Mrs Pye's house was not nice at all. It was anything
but nice.

It was quite possible that Mrs Pye had been living here
for a couple of hundred years, and in all that time had
never cleaned the place. It was Quentin Crispian in its
layers of dust. It was a symphony to muck, muck in its
highest incarnation – a full-throated, cannons-and-all,
Tchaikovsky symphony in filth. The floor was brown.
Possibly lino, possibly cow dung. The walls were dark

mushroom. Not just the colour, but actually dark mushroom in several places, blooming, no doubt, on a river of damp. The sink was a large Belfast stone one, balanced on a pile of bricks, with two ancient taps appearing out of the wall above it. Chris put down her coffee cup, thinking suddenly that the coffee had been made from water that had come out of those taps. The furniture was a mass of recycled bins and boxes, except for the table at which they sat, which had once been a very nice table indeed, possibly Georgian, the kind of table that Chris couldn't afford for her real Georgian dining room. Pans and crockery littered every available surface. In one corner stood a large open hutch, in which three white ducks, looking very smug, were sitting on a mound of straw.

Then she saw the painting.

It was propped against the wall in a large gilt frame, so huge that Chris's eye had skated over it at first, obscured as it was by the shadows of the far reaches of the railway carriage, the cloud of steam from the stove, and the general cloud of decay. She stood up and walked over to it.

It was a portrait of a face so familiar that Chris felt an immediate pang of recognition. A famous face in an unknown pose. A man with a large red satin sheet draped over him.

'Who is this?' she asked.

Mrs Pye was busy extracting three plates from the pile on one of the boxes. 'Him?' she said, over her shoulder. 'That's George.'

Chris peered closer. 'It looks like George Bernard Ransome,' she said.

'It is,' Mrs Pye said.

Chris turned to look at her. 'It *is*?' she repeated.

'My father,' Mrs Pye said.

Chris stared at her. 'George Bernard Ransome was your father?' she echoed.

'Oh yes,' Mrs Pye said.

'But I . . . I didn't know he lived here,' Chris said. 'He lived in Los Angeles, didn't he?'

'He was born here,' Mrs Pye said.

'In West Tolwell?'

'Yes,' Mrs Pye said. 'My mother worked at his mother's house. Got pregnant by him at sixteen. Before he went to London.'

'But he married Ava Morini.'

'Yes.'

'And Bette Morris.'

'Yes.'

'And he directed *Gone with the Day*.'

'Yes, dear.' Mrs Pye was spooning stew on to the plates.

'And he was murdered by the Mob.'

Mrs Pye shook her head. 'He drowned in a swimming pool when he was eighty-five,' she tutted. 'Drunk.'

'One of the greatest directors in Hollywood.'

'Yes, I expect so.'

'Born *here*?'

'He went out to America in 1930,' Mrs Pye said. 'His mother gave him £50 and told him never to come home again.'

'But I thought he was American.'

'Oh no,' Mrs Pye said. 'He just liked people to think that. Think he was rags-to-riches.' She wiped her nose while holding the stew spoon. 'Spoil his image, you know, coming from gentry.'

'You're titled?' Chris asked.

'Not me.' Mrs Pye laughed shortly at the very idea. 'Wrong side of the blanket.'

Chris stared again at the picture. 'And this . . . this is surely by . . .'

'Salvador Dali,' Mrs Pye nodded. 'Got it in my father's will. Came here in a courier van.' She laughed throatily.

'Should have seen the palaver. Sign this and that. Am I insured and all that.'

'And are you?' Chris asked.

'Don't be daft,' Mrs Pye said and plonked the stew down on the table.

Chris looked at Mrs Pye and then she looked at Steve. The blood thumped dully in her head while the room revolved a little. 'This is an original Salvador Dali and you are George Bernard Ransome's daughter,' she recapped.

'Sit down and have your stew,' Virginia Pye told her.

14

The Reverend Michael Blood and his wife Philippa were in bed when the doorbell rang. It was half past six in the evening.

'Don't answer it,' said Philippa.

The echo of the bell drifted away in the Rectory. All that could be heard outside was the swish of the trees along the lane, heaving in the wind like great ships at sea. Michael tried to concentrate but his nerve failed. 'It might be a death,' he said.

'There might be a death in here if you try and go downstairs,' Philippa warned him.

They lay and listened. There was silence in the house.

'You see?' she told him. 'If it was anything urgent, they'd ring more than once.'

The doorbell rang again.

'I'll have to go,' Michael said.

'Mike . . .'

'It could be an emergency.' He got up.

'Yes, it could be an emergency,' Philippa sighed. 'The stapler could have failed while they were making up the Parish Magazine.' She watched him pull on his trousers. 'You are a martyr to this village.'

'Only if they burn me at the stake over this employment scheme,' he said, smiling.

She swung her legs out of bed. 'Did you send Stephen Harris to Virginia Pye?' she asked.

'I did.'

'To do what?'

'Clean out the duckpond and dig another latrine.'

She considered. 'He'll like that.'

Michael kissed her briefly as he opened the bedroom door. 'I love you,' he said.

'Get out of my sight,' she told him.

As Michael went down the stairs, he noticed that it was raining again, the drops beating against the window. He glanced at his watch.

He opened the door to a stranger's face, a small blonde woman of about thirty, looking deeply defeated, despite her very expensive suit and very expensive calfskin portfolio case. He couldn't remember the last time he had seen anyone looking so sophisticated in Deadham Markham, and wondered if she was someone from the County Court, someone who knew that he had not paid a parking fine in Ludlow in 1978 and had been sent to finally catch him.

'Hello,' he said. 'Can I help you?'

'Is this the Vicarage?' she asked.

'Yes.'

'Are you the Reverend Blood?'

'Yes, I am.'

The woman's gaze flickered to his crotch, and rapidly shot away again. He did up his flies. 'Why don't you come in?' he said. She paused. 'I really don't own a dirty raincoat,' he reassured her.

She smiled. It was a tenuous, trembling expression. She stepped over the threshold and he closed the door.

'Now then,' he said.

'I can't get in my house,' she murmured.

'Ah . . .'

'It's Nova Scotia.'

'Right. You must be . . .'

She held out her hand. 'Sally Matthews.'

He shook it. She felt as fragile as a bird.

'The key fits in the lock, but I can't get either door open,' she said. 'I realise you aren't a locksmith, of course, but I thought you might know of one.' She gazed away from him, at the floor. 'There wasn't anyone about, I didn't want to go in the pub, my mobile isn't working, I don't have a *Yellow Pages* . . .' She looked back up at him. 'I'm terribly sorry,' she said.

And started to cry.

It was very handy to have a wife at a time like this.

Philippa was just coming down the stairs as Sally dissolved into tears, and at once bundled their guest into the warmth of the study. By the time Michael Blood came back in with a tray of tea, both women were comfortably curled on the small sofa.

'And then they said that they would set fire to the house,' Philippa was saying.

'Who's this?' Michael asked, setting down the tray.

'The villagers,' she said. 'Over this employment scheme.'

'They did not.'

'As good as,' Philippa told him. 'They were predicting death and dishonour and the end of civilisation as we know it.'

'They'll come round,' he said. He handed Sally a cup of tea.

'It sounds a good idea,' Sally murmured.

'Oh, it is,' Philippa said. 'There are lads in this village who have never worked at all, and they need occupying. The church is acting as sponsor, setting them tasks and so on, and they'll be paid by the Manpower Action Department.'

Sally nodded.

'We've got some strapping great lads on it,' Philippa said. 'You should see one, he's built like a sh—'

Michael coughed. 'They would come and help you with

Nova Scotia, I'm sure,' he said. 'The garden is a bit of a jungle.'

Sally gave him a watery smile. 'I've turned into a good cause,' she said.

'No, no.'

'It's OK,' she said. 'Believe me, I need help.'

Philippa glanced at Michael as she stirred her tea. 'Have you bought Nova Scotia as a weekend cottage?' she asked.

'Is that what people do?'

'Yes. One or two around here. There's a merchant banker down the road.'

'I'm sure there is,' Sally said. 'I'm married to one.'

'Oh?'

'No,' she said. 'Joke. Forget it.'

'So . . . you're here for good?' Michael asked.

'Yes.'

'With your husband?'

'No,' Sally said.

They all drank their tea.

'I think I know how to get into the house,' Michael remarked, after a few moments. 'There's a pantry window behind the trellis at the side. I helped Mrs Wick through it once.'

'That's right,' Philippa said. She smiled at Sally. 'Her children used to lock her out of the place. Actually changed the locks once while she was at bingo.'

'But why?' Sally was bemused.

'She had three grown-up children living there at one time, and no one got on with anyone else.'

'And they locked her out?

'Yes, because she threatened to sell the house and cut them off without a penny. She was always doing that – threatening to give it to a cats' charity.'

'Oh.' Sally put down her cup. 'And you think that one of the children's done the same thing now?'

'Probably.'

'But my husband said that they put the house up for auction, and they got a very good price.'

'They did eventually,' Philippa agreed, 'but that won't stop them being awkward. It's probably the eldest. He always wanted to live there, and he got voted down. House sold, proceeds divided equally.'

'And he thought he should have it all?'

'I think so.'

'Great,' Sally muttered. 'So I've got a man with a grudge hanging round the place.'

'No, no,' Michael reassured her. 'This is probably a parting shot.'

Philippa poured Sally another cup. 'So . . . you're divorced?' she asked.

'I will be soon.'

'Oh. Recent split?'

'This morning.'

'Good God,' Philippa said. 'Only a tiff, surely.'

'He's gone off with another woman.'

'This morning?'

'Yes. Literally.'

'Christ!' Philippa exclaimed. 'How long have you been married?'

'Six months.'

'The bastard!'

'Philippa,' Michael warned.

'It's OK,' Sally responded. 'She's right. I had to get out of London.' Her gaze flickered away again. 'This was going to be our little piece of paradise,' she said. 'We saw the house on the first day we were married.'

'The utter shit,' Philippa said.

'He was only talking about babies last week,' Sally told her.

'No!'

'And quoting poetry to me,' Sally continued.

'Deviant.'

'And all the time he was with her.'

'May he burn in hell,' Philippa said. 'They're just bloody useless, men, aren't they?'

Michael got up. 'I'll fetch my coat,' he said. 'You're small enough to get through that pantry window with no problem at all.'

Sally and Philippa embraced.

'I'll come round tomorrow,' Philippa promised.

'You've been such a comfort,' Sally told her.

Michael went out into the hall, where Angus was lying like a draught excluder across the kitchen door.

'Don't look at me,' he told the dog. 'I know nothing. I'm just a useless, clapped-out, feckless bloody male.'

15

It was almost ten o'clock before Chris got home.

The only light shining in the house was in her and Malcolm's bedroom, and she went upstairs with her head still buzzing from her encounter with Virginia Pye.

'Malcolm,' she called. 'Where are you?'

He was sitting on the edge of the bed. She kissed his cheek.

'You won't believe the day I've had,' she said. 'Did you get the message?'

'Yes,' he said.

'I had a devil of a job finding West Tolwell,' she told him, dumping her bag on the floor and running her hands through her hair. 'It turns out that Virginia Pye lives in this sort of railway shed. She had a naked man in there and – wait for this – she's got an original Salvador Dali painting *hanging on the wall*. When the director from Up-Line came, she wouldn't let him in because he had a beard.'

All the time she was talking, she was stripping off her clothes. 'Do I smell of anything?' she enquired.

He hesitated. 'Silage.'

'Do I? Jesus.' She started stuffing her clothes into the laundry basket.

'A man was here,' Malcolm said.

'She doesn't mind the TV series, but she won't deal with a bloke over thirty,' Chris carried on. 'Did Owen ring?'

'No,' Malcolm said. 'A man was here.'

'You can't have a crew under thirty.' Chris went into the shower room, and pulled a towel from the cupboard. She started laughing. 'She's got this thing with birds . . . they come running, they sit on her shoulder, you should see it . . .' She paused, then came back out into the bedroom. 'What man?'

'From Social Services,' Malcolm said unhappily.

She stopped in the doorway. 'Social Services?'

'About Father.'

She walked back into the bedroom and sat on the chair opposite him. He looked away from her, at the hands hanging over his knees.

'They're going to move him,' he said.

'From hospital? Why?'

'He's getting better.'

Chris looked hard at his down-turned head. 'But where will they move him to?' she asked.

'Home.'

She frowned. 'He can't manage at home, Malcolm.'

'No,' he said.

'Well, then . . .'

'Not without help.'

She opened her mouth to say that there was no one to help her father-in-law because his wife, Malcolm's mother, was dead. Then she had a sudden premonition of where Malcolm's conversation with the Social Services had led. 'Who is going to help him?' she asked.

At last, Malcolm looked up.

'Not you,' she said.

'How can I help him?' Malcolm said. 'I've got my job. Trepantex won't hear of any time off.'

'But they must,' she said. 'Just a few days.'

'No days at all,' he said.

She narrowed her eyes. 'The caring sharing company with caterers,' she said.

He sighed, and took to examining the thread of the pattern in the duvet. 'They fired Helen,' he said.

Chris stared at him. Helen was Malcolm's assistant. She was fifty-nine, with an invalid husband. She had never, and would never, set the world on fire, as she had a great deal of time off to cope with her husband, but when she did come in she worked with a vengeance. Moreover, she was a very sweet person.

'For what?' Chris asked.

'Absences.'

'My God,' Chris breathed.

Malcolm looked up again. 'So I can't take time off,' he said. 'Not yet.'

She gazed into his eyes and read the answer in them. 'Malcolm,' she said. 'I can't look after your father.'

'He would get better with the right help,' he said. 'The doctor told me about it.'

'Malcolm,' Chris repeated slowly. 'I can't do it.'

'I don't see why not.'

She gaped at him, and then laughed. But not for long. 'Because I'd kill him within twenty-four hours,' she said. 'Malcolm, when have we ever got on?'

'He's not the same man,' he said.

'Yes . . . I know.'

'He needs help.'

'I know that too.'

'He wants to be at home.'

She glanced at him. 'Has he said so?'

'No,' Malcolm said. 'But he would want to be, I know.'

'Then we'll have to get a nurse.'

'We can't afford it.'

'No, but Henry can, surely?'

'No,' Malcolm said. 'He can't. He's got no health insurance at all.'

Chris sat back in the chair. 'Malcolm,' she said, 'it's not

just that I wouldn't have the patience or the ability. It's not just that Henry and I hate each other—'

'He doesn't hate you.'

'OK, he doesn't hate me. But he dislikes me, Malcolm. And I can't honestly put my hand on my heart and say that I love him. He isn't lovable. He's never made any attempt to be lovable. Even to be necessarily friendly.'

'He's different.'

'Yes,' she said. 'He's ill. And I'm very sorry that he's ill. He needs care, but I couldn't give him care. I'd give him impatience and frustration, and he'd be frustrated too.'

'He . . .'

'I haven't finished,' Chris said. 'There's my job.'

Malcolm shrugged. 'Well, you would have to give that up,' he said.

A silence settled. During it, Chris looked very hard at the man she had married.

'And you feel that would be right?' she said.

'It's a solution.'

'That's not what I asked,' she told him. 'I asked what you felt about it.'

He looked puzzled. 'I'm just trying to find an answer.'

'And the answer is that I give up my job and nurse your father.'

'It might not be for long.'

'And do you care what *I* feel about it?' she asked.

'Well,' he said, 'obviously I need to hear your thoughts.'

She shook her head. 'We're not talking the same language,' she said. 'I ask what *you* feel, I ask if you want to know *my* feelings, and you talk about solutions and opinions.'

'I don't understand you,' he said.

'No,' she replied. 'You don't.' She got up and paced the room for a few seconds. 'Do you know,' she said, 'in all the time we've been married, you've never told me what you really *feel* about anything?'

'Oh, come on.'

'No, honestly,' she said. 'Not really *feel*. You're full of facts, and you're brilliant at all the household things – the Council Tax, the Income Tax, the bills, the insurances – and you can hold forth at length about the fuel capacity of the car, or the cost per unit of electricity, or the effectiveness of the double glazing, or the exact bloody distance between Arbroath and Coventry, but you never *tell me what you feel*.' She paused. 'And you never ask me what I feel about anything.'

'I do.'

'You don't!' she retorted.

'I asked you about the wallpaper downstairs.'

'I'm not talking about the fucking wallpaper!' she cried.

'Now, Chris.'

'And don't *now Chris* me either,' she said. 'I'll tell you what you want. You want a sort of plastic doll, don't you? You can't bear it if I get angry or frightened or unhappy . . .'

'Naturally I don't want you to be unhappy,' he said.

'But you back off, you just back off from me if I am.'

'I do not.'

'You *do*,' she said. 'You don't get involved. Nothing touches you. Everything's at arm's length, where it's safe. It's as if I'm not allowed to have weaknesses. You don't show anger yourself, or fear, or impatience.'

'I would have thought that was a good thing,' he said.

'What?'

'A lot of women would be very grateful to be with a man like me,' he said.

'What!'

'I've never kept anything from you. Not a penny. I don't go out drinking . . .'

'I'm not talking about money or drinking.'

'You can spend what you like,' he said.

'Oh, Christ.'

'Well, can't you? I never spend a penny on myself. Do I ever object?'

'Why should you bloody object?' she shouted. 'I'm not careless with money! Who are you, anyway – The Lord High Giver of Bounty or something? Like you deign to give me some of your money and you're a really good person to let me rush out like a crazed person flinging cash around?'

'You know that's not what I meant,' he said.

'And I wish you bloody well *would* spend something on yourself,' she said.

'I don't want to,' he told her.

'Just some clothes or something.'

'There's nothing wrong with my clothes.'

'Or a haircut.'

'But *you* cut my hair.'

'Oh Jesus Christ,' she snapped. 'You don't spend anything, and you don't begrudge me spending, it's like a really big magnanimous thing you're doing, depriving yourself, watching me run up debts . . .'

'I didn't say that.'

'Sitting on the sidelines watching life played out in front of you, never taking a chance, never making a mistake, being very very careful.'

'And that's a fault?' he said. 'I can't believe I'm wrong about being careful. Carefulness is a virtue, not a crime.'

'Listen to you,' she said.

'This is ridiculous,' he murmured.

She stared at him. 'Even now, you're not angry,' she said.

'I don't see how screaming and shouting is going to solve anything,' he said.

She stood still, trembling.

'Sit down,' he told her.

She did.

'Now, let's talk calmly.'

She stared at him. 'Does it hurt?' she asked.

'Does what hurt?'

'To see your father so ill?'

He frowned, thinking. 'Its very worrying, yes.'

'Hurt?'

'Sorry?'

She placed her hand on her chest, over her heart. 'Do you hurt in here?' she said.

He got up. 'I shall make a cup of tea,' he said. 'I expect you'd like one.'

She lay back on the bed and looked at the ceiling while he went downstairs. When he came back, she was in the same position.

He put the tray on the bedside cabinet.

'Chris,' he said, 'I realise that you like your job very much, and how much of a sacrifice this would be, but Henry does need our help and its the only way out.' He poured the tea.

'He could go into a nursing home,' Chris said.

'I don't want him in one of those places,' he said.

'We could find a nice one.'

'They would need to be paid,' Malcolm said, 'because father has a large house worth quite a bit of money, and he's also got savings.'

She sat up, slowly. 'Then we would have to use his savings,' she said.

'I'm not going to do that.'

'But why not?'

'Because he's not in a position to think carefully about how his money is used, and I have no power of attorney, and I wouldn't dream of getting one. Its not as if he's mentally ill.'

She looked at the tea tray, her eyes tracing the pattern on it over and over again. 'Let's just get this straight,' she said. 'Henry is coming out of hospital, and needs nursing care. He has a house worth two hundred thousand and savings. We both work. There is no one else in the family. But you won't consider a nursing home, even temporarily, or a nurse to be with him at home, or you yourself staying with him at night.'

Malcolm considered for a moment. 'No,' he said. 'None of those are reasonable alternatives.'

'But you want me to look after him, and that *is* reasonable?'

'I know it's not ideal.'

'And give up my job.'

'Yes.'

'For how long?'

Malcolm shrugged. 'Its hard to say.'

'Will there be a permanent disability?'

'How long is a piece of string?' Malcolm said. 'He might get better very quickly, or remain disabled. Apparently it's impossible to predict.'

'So you want me to nurse him perhaps indefinitely?'

'Well . . .'

'Even though we don't like each other?'

'We could perhaps see how it goes for three months,' Malcolm said. 'Then review it.'

She clenched her hands tightly together. 'But if I stay down there, won't you miss me?' she asked.

'Of course I will.'

'There isn't any of course about it,' Chris said. 'Will you miss me? Is Henry's situation reason enough to part us?'

He smiled. 'That's a bit melodramatic,' he said. 'We're not parted. I'll come down on Fridays.'

She looked, briefly, at her feet, unable to bear his bland, reasonable, tolerant, sensible expression any longer.

'But I must give up my job,' she said.

Malcolm did not reply.

Chris went into the shower. She spent some considerable time soaping away the day, closing her eyes against the stream of water and, finally, weeping. Then she got out and towelled herself slowly, and put on her dressing gown.

When she came back out into the bedroom, Malcolm was reading a book. She sat on the edge of the bed next to him.

'Malcolm,' she said. 'Hold me.'

He put down the book, marking the page carefully with an advert for Scottish Widows Pension Fund.

As he hugged her, he said, 'Poor little poppet.'

She stiffened, and drew back from him. She took a deep breath.

'Malcolm,' she said, 'I'll compromise with you. I'll go down to Prystock and stay with Henry overnight. But you will have to get a nurse in during the day.'

'No, no . . .' he began. 'Because, you see . . .'

'Get Henry to release some of his money.'

'But . . .'

She stood up. 'I am not giving up my job,' she said.

'Now, Chris . . .'

Her face fell. She walked to the door.

'Where are you going?' he asked.

'The sofa, poppet,' she said.

She opened the door, and saw Electra sitting on the landing, looking superior.

She picked the cat up, shoved it into the bedroom, and went downstairs.

16

Sally woke up at an unearthly hour.

She felt around her on the floor for her pocket alarm, and then realised that it hadn't sounded. She pushed her head over the edge of the sleeping bag and peered at a supernatural grey oblong that had appeared in the room, thinking, God! Arthur C. Clarke! for a few dazed seconds, until it struck her that, far from being a pulsating monolith from another planet, it was only the window. A window without curtains. And it was getting light.

Sally hadn't seen the dawn lately.

When she had, it was with Dermott at the Casualty Unit, and she had driven home through a seeping ochre shadow, the best that London could do at daybreak.

She forced herself on to one elbow and stared at the sky. It was pearlescent pinkish blue, the kind of colour that she had always assumed only happened over the Greek Islands in August.

'God,' she muttered. 'Please don't let it be beautiful. Let it be bloody miserable, so I'll feel at home.'

She wriggled her way out of the sleeping bag. When they had finally broken in last night, she and Philippa and Michael Blood had found a house entirely stripped of any sign of human habitation. The Wick children had taken everything: every carpet, every light bulb, every stick of furniture. They had even prised tiles off the wall in the kitchen, taken the sink plugs, dug up what Michael Blood said had been several beautiful shrubs in the garden, and hacked the units off the wall in the kitchen. There wasn't even a sink. There was a light patch on the wall, and a tap emerging from the plaster.

'Oh good,' Sally had said, when they had finally stood in the empty shell of the kitchen. 'They've left some wallpaper! Fantastic.'

Philippa had run upstairs to see if the loo was still there. Meanwhile, Michael had given Sally a deeply apologetic smile. 'We're not all like this,' he said.

Sally had tried to smile back.

Leaning over the banister, Philippa had called, 'It's OK. You can pee in comfort.'

Relative comfort, anyway. When Michael and Philippa had gone, Sally had found the bathroom by torchlight. And she had also found a whole population of woodlice and spiders, sitting in the bath, glaring at her.

She'd been too tired to scream. Much as she loathed spiders and expected them to launch themselves out of the bath and sink their fangs into her bare arse, she had used the loo. Downstairs, she shook out the sleeping bag on the exercise mat she had brought with her and had lain for a while gazing into the blackness, ready and able to cry, ready to feel her soul constrict with longing for Dermott. Nothing came though. Pity. She could have done with a good tearing of hair, scouring of spirit, ashes on forehead, clothes-rending seizure.

Eventually she had turned over, and fallen asleep through sheer exhaustion.

She pulled on a sweater now. Then, after standing for a few moments, feeling the cold seep swiftly into her bones, she rummaged in her bag, took off her jeans, put on a pair of thick tights, put the jeans back on, and dragged on another sweater. She went out into the kitchen and looked at the tap on the wall. Then she opened the Thermos that Philippa had given her, and drank some of the lukewarm tea.

She opened the back door, and walked out into the garden. A blackbird flew up in her face, twittering hysterically.

'Piss off,' she told it. It flew up into the lilac, where it continued complaining to itself.

'I know where you live, so shut up,' Sally said.

She walked up the path, pulling aside overhanging branches, showered with moisture from the trees. There was, she saw, a little bench behind the trees. It was in front of what might once have been a pond and was now a tight mass of rampant water lilies. She went further, down a grassy slope that looked out over a field. Here, leaning on the fence, she watched a mist drain off the pasture. She could hear the stream, probably the same stream that Dermott had crossed six months ago just before he found the house. She wondered where he was now.

She hadn't planned to leave London, exactly. She had decided to come down here and see what sort of a state Nova Scotia was in, but she hadn't planned to move out. Not until Dermott's call last night.

'You mean you'll be in and out of this house?' she had asked.

'Now and then,' he said.

'Until when?'

'Ach, I don't know that, do I?'

'But I thought you said you were going to Canada to film. Or to America to see *her*. Or what-bloody-ever.'

She could hear him smile. 'So I might, I might.'

'And you might also be coming here from time to time?' she had asked. 'What – to get clothes, or something?'

'I can't just pick up my bed and walk,' he said.

'You already have,' she told him. 'Where exactly are you now?'

He didn't answer her directly. 'Now I don't want you to be bitter,' he said. 'I'm not throwing you out, am I? You can potter about and get yourself sorted, and I'll see you before you go . . .'

'See me,' she had repeated.

'For a few little chats and the like.'

'Chats,' she whispered, permafrost fastening around her heart. 'About what, Dermott?'

'Ah now, Sally, are you over me just like that?' he'd said.

At that point she had pulled the phone cord out of the wall. 'You bastard!' she yelled at the dead receiver. 'Go to her, and don't you – ever – set – foot –'

She'd abruptly stopped kicking the kitchen door. Of course Dermott would come back. He might, for all she knew, be standing at the end of the street right now. Perhaps he'd had an argument with Miss Delaney.

And he'd turn up at odd hours and expect tea and sympathy in his troubles. Sally could see herself sitting in the London house waiting for his knock on the door and his arms around her waist.

'Oh no,' she muttered. She experienced a sudden desperate horror of hearing Dermott's key in the door, and an even more desperate fear that she could not stand up to him, and was a sucker – had *always* been a sucker – for those merry green-blue eyes.

She'd packed a bag, driven to a local estate agents, instructed them to sell and given them a key and her email address. Then she'd driven off. Driven all the way down here, knowing that Dermott wouldn't bother to follow. She would be out of the M25 zone, and he couldn't navigate himself beyond the M25 even if he had a car. *Especially* if he had a car. And she was damned sure he wouldn't know the phone number of Nova Scotia. Not that it would still be connected anyway.

She glanced at her watch. Half past seven. In the morning.

'God,' she muttered. She went back in the house, and pulled a pad of paper from her bag. On it, she wrote:

> *electricity, phone, locksmith*
> *bed*
> *have I got any money?*
> *see bank*
> *no money*
> *or job*
> *husband*
> *kill somebody*
> *Dermott*
> *myself*

She stared at the list for a moment, then scribbled out *myself*. Then she wrote:

> *electric fire in bath*
> *poisoned condom*
> *drug to bring on complete alopecia*
> *write to Divina and tell her I've got herpes*
> *gonorrhoea*
> *infectious hepatitis*
> *photographs*

She paused, then scribbled out everything after *alopecia*. She would never write to Divina. She might send the poisoned condoms, though.

At eight o'clock, now so cold she was shivering uncontrollably, she walked over to the Vicarage. Philippa came to the door.

'Come in,' she said. 'Christ, you look frozen.'

Sally stepped inside. 'Are you allowed to say Christ in here?' she asked.

'No,' Philippa said. 'The last thing any vicar dare mention to anyone is Christ.'

They went into the kitchen. Michael was sitting in an armchair and Angus was sitting on Michael. Both appeared to be reading the *Independent*.

'Sally is hungry,' Philippa said.

'Oh no,' Sally interrupted. 'I didn't come for breakfast.'

'Why not?'

Sally held up her laptop. 'I came to borrow a cup of electricity.'

'And you're not hungry?'

'I . . .'

'Sit down,' Philippa said. She brought a pile of toast to the table and a jug of coffee. 'The boys will be here soon,' she said. 'I've taken to toasting several loaves every morning.'

'You mean I have,' Michael said.

'All right,' Philippa conceded. 'You have. I was just trying to impress Sally with my non-existent domesticity.'

'They come here every morning?' Sally asked.

'And we dole out the jobs,' Michael said. 'Shall we send someone round to the garden?'

'I can't pay you,' Sally said. 'I don't think I've got any money.'

'You don't have to pay them,' Michael said. 'They get paid by the Government.'

Philippa poured the coffee. 'Are you unemployed?' she asked.

'Tactful,' Michael said.

'It's OK,' Sally replied. 'Yes. I resigned last Friday.'

'From what?'

'*The Corker* magazine.'

'*The Corker*?' Philippa repeated.

'Yes, I know.'

'I wouldn't have associated you with stuff like that,' Philippa said. 'You mean you're a writer, a journalist?'

'I was once a political columnist,' Sally said. 'I lost my way.'

Philippa considered her. 'You've had quite a week,' she said.

'You do look weary,' Michael commented.

Sally looked hard at him. 'I don't feel weary,' she told him. 'I feel bloody murderous, if you must know.'

'Of course you do,' Philippa said.

Sally put down her cup. 'I mean it,' she said. 'I thought I'd kill Dermott, but now I'm just going to kill Divina Delaney instead.'

Philippa glanced back at Michael. 'Whoa,' she said. Then she smiled at Sally. 'Michael's quite keen on Divina,' she remarked. 'He's seen *Looking for Linda* three times.'

'She's a bitch,' Sally said.

Michael leaned forward in the chair, much to the dog's disgust. 'Are you saying your husband has left you for Divina Delaney?' he asked.

'Yes.'

'The real Divina Delaney?'

'She isn't real,' Sally said. 'She hasn't been real since the last operation.' She pushed her plate away from her.

'Is he an actor?' Michael asked.

'Yes,' she said. 'Look, do you mind if I plug this laptop in for a minute?'

'Go ahead,' Philippa said. 'I must get off to work.'

Sally went out to the hallway for privacy's sake. She squatted down on the floor and watched the screen load up its programme. Then she logged on to her email.

The first message waiting for her was from Eddie Massingham. It was nothing if not succinct.

Sally, where are you, you silly bitch? She erased it.

The second was from the estate agents confirming a viewing of the London house that afternoon and asking for a phone number and address where she could be contacted.

The third was from Sally's assistant, the redoubtable

Ellen. *Sally, we miss you*, it read. *We heard about Dermott. Don't come back. Be happy. Happy, near Amarillo, New Mexico. And Hope is in Arkansas.*

Sally smiled. 'Bless you, Ellen,' she whispered.

The fourth was from Eddie Massingham. *Sally, I've got some bloody cosmetics account in here. Who are they?* She erased it.

The fifth was a mailshot.

The sixth was Eddie. *Is your period finished yet?* She erased it.

She thought for a moment, then typed, *Gone far away into the silent land*, and sent it.

She sat back on her heels and thought of Dermott quoting poetry to her. Now she was doing the same thing. She had brought a little bit of Dermott with her, inadvertently smuggled out of the war zone. She wondered which poems he serenaded Divina with, which songs he sang in the shower in her hotel room. She wondered if he were going to honour his contract with *Beckside Street*, or whether he had already left them high and dry, and was in all kinds of legal trouble. She wondered if he ever thought of such things, if he would ever be more than five years old, and then she thought of bitter young-boy-genius-grown-bad Eddie.

She must be a mother figure, she realised. She must give out vibrations, messages of some kind. They thought they could behave badly and that she would still be there to tolerate them and pick up the pieces.

She thought of her own parents, who were currently in Hong Kong; her father, Company Man, and her mother, Company Woman. They were archetypal, thriving ex-pats who worked for a cigarette company and were presently involved with hooking the Third World on to tobacco. They were lovely people who saw nothing at all wrong in their job, and who breezed through life.

Somewhere along the road, Sally had become the picker-upper. In all her closest relationships, she had been the apologist, the mender, the support.

She shut off the laptop, and pulled the plug from the wall. 'What the bloody hell am I doing here?' she whispered.

As she sat there, she could hear a rising crescendo of voices in the kitchen. All male. All young. Every now and then, the back door of the house opened and closed. Not wanting to face a crowd of boisterous seventeen-year-olds – not outside her favourite fantasy, at least – she went to the front door, and opened it.

A man stood on the doorstep, his hand poised over the doorbell. 'Ah!' he said. 'You must be psychic.'

'No,' she said. 'I'm leaving.'

'Mrs Blood?'

'No,' Sally said. She looked back to the stairs. 'Philippa!' she called. 'Someone to see you.'

The man hesitated on the doorstep, then held out his hand. 'John Donoghue.'

'Are you Irish?' Sally asked.

'My grandfather.'

'Excuse me?' Sally said.

'I come from Islington,' he said. 'I wouldn't know one end of a shillelagh from another.'

'Even so,' Sally said, half out of the door past him.

Philippa came down the stairs.

'This is an Irish person,' Sally said.

She was a little way down the path when she heard him say, 'John Donoghue. Up-Line Cable TV.'

'Oh God,' she murmured to herself as she emerged into the lane. 'I can't get away from them.'

17

It was half past five in the morning when Chris left London.

She had slept for precisely two hours – two hours of luridly disturbed sleep, of unpleasant dreams in which Malcolm climbed into Reliant Robins, or Kevin sat in their kitchen, reading her novel, smoking one cigarette after another. She woke at four to find Electra on her chest. The cat was flexing her claws, pummelling her softly as if to determine the depth of her flesh.

Chris had got up, and gone back into the double bedroom.

Malcolm had been fast asleep, snoring gently. He sounded like a distant small aircraft. She looked hard at his face, revealed by the streetlight shining through a crack in the curtains. She looked at the bedside table. At the pile of small change he had taken from his pockets, at the photograph of his mother in its small black frame, at the car keys with the key ring she had given him which said *If You Don't Like The Way I Drive, Stay Off The Pavement.*

It had been a joke, of course. Malcolm was a very careful driver. He had frowned, and said thank you, and then methodically, politely, threaded it on to his keys.

He never laughed at her jokes. Just smiled, puzzled. He didn't find her funny. He found her curious, she thought. Interesting and curious.

She sat down on the chair at the side of the bed and stared at him, realising that, actually, she didn't know what Malcolm thought of her at all. He said that he loved her, but she didn't feel that love radiating from him. She felt his own need for security. And hers. Sitting by his side, she sensed deeply the unspoken contract between them that somehow she was a very wayward person whom he had saved from a fate worse than death, and that he was a very selfless person who ably fitted the role of saviour.

She had got up, gritting her teeth, hating herself for her own thoughts, knowing, with desperation – a quiet, still desperation, the worst kind – that the contract was broken, and she was not grateful any more.

Had not been grateful for some time.

She had packed a case, not trying especially to be quiet, hoping even then that Malcolm would wake. But he didn't. Gathering her things, she had gone downstairs and written him a note, saying that she was going to Prystock.

By four that afternoon, she was sitting with Virginia Pye and John Donoghue in the Black Dog in Deadham Markham.

'You see,' Virginia was saying, 'why I never got married.'

It was nothing to do with Malcolm. Chris had not breathed a word about her own situation, and was trying hard to forget the visit to the hospital that she had sandwiched between leaving London and sitting here. She wrenched herself away from her thoughts and tried to concentrate on what Virginia was saying.

'It isn't that I don't like men,' Virginia continued.

'But you're a Mrs,' John Donoghue said.

Virginia held up a nicotine-stained forefinger. 'Aah,' she said. 'Camouflage.'

'To stop unwanted admirers?' Chris asked.

'Exactly,' Virginia replied. 'Classic diversion, is that. Like the Polynesian Flycatcher pretending to be a tree.'

John Donoghue leaned forward. 'To pretend to be married to put men off?'

'Just some men.'

'What kind?' Chris asked.

'Old ones,' Virginia said.

They watched her weave through the pub on her erratic way to the toilet.

John Donoghue looked at Chris, his eyebrows raised. 'Is she sane at all?' he asked.

'More than I am.'

'That's not saying much,' Donoghue told her. 'You work for Up-Line.'

'So do you,' she retorted.

'Freelance,' he said.

Chris leaned back in her seat and regarded him levelly. The first that she had known of his existence was a phone call from Owen, received while she had sat in the Ward Sister's office at the hospital. Owen had told her that he had hired a writer, John Donoghue, and that he was already in Deadham Markham to recce and to meet Virginia.

'He's brilliant,' Owen assured her over the phone. 'He's done eight *Hired To Kill* and three *Blunderers*.'

So she had been prepared to hate him, this successful writer. This prized hired gun. This very laid-back-looking man in his comfortably worn leather jacket and comfortably frayed blue jeans.

'How did you manage it?' she asked.

Donoghue drained his glass. 'Manage what?'

'To start writing professionally.'

He smiled. 'By accident. I started as a picker-upper on a film unit.'

'And?'

'And what?'

'And how did you start writing?'

He shrugged. 'I had this girlfriend . . .'

Chris laughed. 'Oh, right. That certainly figures.'

'What do you mean,' he said, 'it figures?'

Chris sighed. 'People who make money from writing. It's not what you know, it's *who* you know.'

He eyed her steadily. 'And I'm one of these people?' he asked.

'You're one of these people.'

'And who did I know?' he said.

'Your girlfriend. I expect she was someone's daughter.'

His mouth tightened into a line. 'Yes, she was someone's daughter,' he said. 'Mr and Mrs Watling of Cardiff. I was going to say that my girlfriend got ill, we shared a flat, she couldn't work, my job didn't pay enough, so I started moonlighting on another film production company.'

'And someone snapped you up,' Chris said.

'And I wrote fourteen scripts before anyone showed any interest,' he told her.

'And hired you to write a series.'

'And hired me to re-write someone else's stuff, and I needed the money,' he said.

Chris heard herself make a sour little noise, a petty little dismissive noise, in her throat.

'And,' Donoghue added, 'it took me four years to get anything accepted and another five years before I could give up the other jobs.'

They regarded each other in silence for some moments.

'You seem very bitter about something,' he observed.

'Me?' she said. 'No, no.'

'Do you write?' he asked.

'No,' she said.

'You do,' he told her.

'Look,' she said. 'Well done on your success.'

'You write,' he said.

She felt herself redden. 'I do not write scripts.'

'Novels,' he said. Then slapped his hand on the table. 'No, no . . . let's see. Not novels. *A* novel. One single novel. Much rejected.'

She bit her lip.

'And that's all you've ever done, and of course it's brilliant,' he said.

To her horror, she felt her face turn magenta.

'Ah, that's no good,' he said. 'You've got to have a lot on the boil, and don't get fixated on one.'

'I have not got a novel,' she said.

'Write another one,' he told her.

'Look . . .'

'Write four. Write ten. Write articles. Write scripts. Write gags.'

'I can't write gags,' she said.

'Short stories.'

'I want to write a novel,' she objected. 'I've *written* a bloody novel.' At once, she realised what she had said. He started to smile, and she leaned forward. 'And I'm never writing another one as long as I bloody well live,' she told him.

There was no time for him to reply. Virginia was back. She sat down opposite John.

'How old are you?' Virginia asked him.

John hesitated. Chris could see him weighing the worth of this job against his dislike of the two women in front of him. 'I'm thirty-six,' he said eventually.

Virginia shook her head. 'I don't like them over thirty,' she remarked.

John's foot began to tap against the floor.

'Tell John about your father,' Chris prompted.

'I'm getting a bit bored,' Virginia told her.

'And the painting,' Chris went on. 'Tell him about that.'

'You see,' Virginia said, 'my step-father was eighty . . .'

John Donoghue stood up. He looked at Virginia

steadfastly, then turned on his heel and walked out.

Leaving Virginia, Chris ran after him, and found him in the car park, unearthing his car keys from his pocket.

'Where are you going?' she asked.

He gave her a crooked grin. 'Home,' he said.

'But – why?'

He gestured in the vague direction of Virginia. 'I'll never get on with her,' he said. 'In fact, there's no one in this village I can get on with.'

'That's a sweeping generalisation, isn't it?' Chris said. 'You've only been here eight hours.'

He took a deep breath. 'Look,' he said, 'the first person I met here this morning didn't like Irish accents, Virginia Pye doesn't like men over thirty, and you hate writers. The vicar appears to be running some sort of male brothel, and a madwoman caught me by the coat this morning and told me not to touch her hedge.'

Chris began to smile. 'Sounds like a brilliant story to me,' she said.

'I notice you don't deny any of it,' Donoghue commented.

'No,' Chris said. 'Especially the bit about writers.'

Donoghue paused, looking down at the car keys in his hand.

'I'm sorry,' Chris said. 'It's been a long day. Things not going well, etc.'

He glanced up at her, still hesitating.

'How is your girlfriend now?' she asked.

He said nothing.

'How much is Owen paying you for this?' she said.

A sly grin worked its way over John Donoghue's face. For a moment, they exchanged the unspoken conspiracy of any two writers put together in any of the world's car parks.

Money.

He took her arm and turned them back towards the pub.

'You're right,' he said. 'It's worth another eight hours.'

18

Sally had spent a half-profitable day.

Profitable in that she had managed to buy a bed. Profitable in that, by pretending to weep in the electricity showrooms, she had also managed to get the electricity turned back on in Nova Scotia. Unprofitable in that, even by pretending to weep to BT, the phone giant was implacable in the face of hysteria, and could not connect her until a week on Thursday. It was also unprofitable in that, when she finally found a bucket and turned the water on by way of experiment in the kitchen, a deep brown muck glugged out of the pipes.

At midday, in despair, she had gone into Canterbury, had a very expensive lunch with a high calorie starter, main course and dessert, and bought an electric fan heater and ten five-litre containers of water, and – for some reason she didn't quite understand – a sweater with a laughing sheep on it. She then drove back to Deadham Markham feeling comforted, at least, by chocolate eclairs.

An interesting sight greeted her as she pulled up at the house. Or as near Nova Scotia as she could get.

A furniture van was parked by the gate, its back down to reveal the solitary splendour of Sally's new bed. A water company van was parked next to it, its doors open to reveal at least a mile of blue plastic piping. And a very dirty green van was parked next to *that*, open doors revealing four faces, four pairs of torn jeans, and four pairs of hands gripping four mugs of tea.

'Hello,' Sally said to the furniture men. 'That was quick.'

'Slumberlux Intersprung Drawer Divan double?'

'The very one,' Sally replied, fetching her keys from her handbag. She opened the gate to the garden, saw a deep trench snaking around the side of the house. Down the trench was a very small gnome.

'All right?' he said.

'Who are you?'

'Water.' He held up a piece of blue piping.

'But I didn't call you.'

'Mrs Blood called us. Check water,' he said. 'Problem.'

'Problem?'

'Leak.'

'Where?' Sally asked.

The gnome shrugged. Obviously, if he couldn't answer in one word he wasn't going to bother.

'The house?' Sally persevered. Any minute now, she'd have to jettison words entirely, and do mime instead.

'Outside,' he grunted.

'A leak in the old pipes?'

'Fit new,' he said.

Sally felt a squawk rising to her throat. 'Cost?' she whispered.

'Some.'

'Mine, or the water company's?'

'Yours. Your land.'

'Much?'

'Three, four hundred.'

'On bill?' Sally said. 'Instalments?'

'Lump.'

'Oh God,' Sally breathed. 'Bloody great.' She got to the door, key in hand, before turning back to him. 'When will you switch it on?' she asked.

'Tonight.'

She opened the door. 'Thank heavens for small mercies,' she muttered, and stepped back to let the Slumberlux Intersprung squeeze past her, a man attached to each end. As she did so, she noticed the four heads peering round the side of the green van. Carefully avoiding the gnome in the trench, she walked over to them.

'Can I help?' she asked.

The nearest head, very round and shaved and belonging, it seemed, to an even rounder boy, grinned. He was obviously deep in conversation with his neighbour, and barely broke pace in a breathless explanation, while eyeing her from head to foot.

'And they go in,' he said, 'and it goes *weeeee*, and they shut the door, and they go upstairs, and they're terrified like, and they're sweating like, and the thing, it's sitting in the airing cupboard, got a dead dog, got no teeth, got no face on it and no nose, it goes, *weeee, weeee* . . .'

'I'm Sally Matthews,' Sally said. 'Did you want something?'

The last head rose. Unfolding a body from the back of the van, it sailed six foot four into the air, and moved towards her, towing a pleasant face, a large chest in a white T-shirt, and low-slung jeans. The head nodded. Sally registered blue eyes, black hair.

'Hello, Mrs Matthews,' he said. 'I'm Steve. Mrs Blood sent us.'

Sally pursed her lips. 'She has been busy,' she remarked.

'We've done the back garden for you,' Steve said. 'Or made a start, any road.'

She glanced over her shoulder, then back at him. 'Have you? Oh well . . . thanks.'

Steve smiled. She willed herself to look away, look at the hedge, look at the gate. Anything but look into the eyes. She had a thing about eyes and had learned her lesson with Dermott. If she looked deep into eyes, she was liable

to crack and become a heap of dust, like a cartoon
character struck by lightning. Big city girl. Strong female.
Political columnist. Tough and streetwise. Hardened by
life. But eyes . . .

Not twice.

Got that white T-shirt already.

Not twice.

Steve leaned forward. 'There's just a bit of a problem
with your sewage,' he said.

She stared intently at his kneecaps. 'Pardon?'

'You've got a cesspit,' he said. 'Out the back.'

'A *what*?'

'Sorry, but it's overflowing.'

Sally clapped her hand to her forehead. Inside the
house, she could hear her Slumberlux bouncing off stair
treads to the accompaniment of curses. 'No,' she said. 'No,
dear God. No.'

Steve gently took her hand. She allowed herself to be led
around the back of the house.

'They go *aaaaargh*,' said the head in the van. 'There's a
knife. See the knife slash, like. Tons of blood. Splatter all
over. It goes *wooo* . . .'

'It's at the bottom,' Steve said to her.

'How appropriate,' Sally murmured.

He walked ahead of her down the narrow path. The
grass had been cut with a scythe, and looked yellow and
tufted, like a very bad haircut in Walsall, or perhaps a very
expensive haircut on a Milan catwalk. Bushes had been
hacked and thinned. When they emerged by the pond,
Sally saw a fringe of stones, a little waterfall, an arc of
gravel that had all been obscured before.

'You've got loads of frogs,' Steve said. 'And tadpoles.
And lilies.'

'Oh,' Sally said, unsure. 'Good.'

What had evidently once been a vegetable patch had

been dug over. Weeds and roots stuck out at odd angles from the roughly-turned soil. The nettles had been cut, but not taken away. Now that they were nearing the field, Sally could see a huge lilac that she hadn't noticed before, and a lump came to her throat, a rapid association from the past, from the days when her parents had a house in Cheshire. She had been five or six, and it had been a treasured two weeks, a rare two weeks when they were all actually in the same country together, and it was Easter, and white lilac had hung down over their path and spread its wedding confetti petals on another lawn. She remembered sitting under that lilac and gazing through it at a blue sky, feeling secure, feeling princess-like, being showered with white blossom.

'Lilac,' she murmured.

Steve turned to look at her. 'Sorry?'

'Nothing,' she said. She swallowed hard on the tears, then abruptly stopped. She put her hand to her nose. 'What's that?' she demanded.

'That's it,' he said. 'That's your trouble.' He pointed at the cleared ground. It looked very boggy.

'That's a cesspit?' she said.

'Yes,' he told her. 'We found it when we were digging.'

'God, how bloody horrible for you,' she said.

'It was a laugh,' Steve said. 'Mark fell in.'

She gave him a weighted look. 'And what am I supposed to do with it?' she asked.

'You'll have to ring somebody. "Suck Waste." Somebody like that.'

'And what will they do?'

'They'll park out front, pull a pipe down the garden, stick it in the tank. Suck it out.'

'Suck . . .' Sally paused. 'How delightful,' she shuddered.

'It'll be all right when it's done.'

'And you mean, every time I flush a toilet . . .'

'Be all right,' Steve repeated. 'It eats all the muck. You might need a new pump, though.'

Sally looked at him. 'You mean someone's job is to go in there and fix a pump, inside?'

'Yes.'

'How deep is it?'

'Eight or nine feet.'

'And . . . and people do that *for a living*?' Sally said.

Steve gave her a lazy, appraising smile. 'Ever lived in the country before?' he asked.

19

Chris was terminally tired by the time that she got back to Prystock. She let herself in and stood for a moment on the doorstep, absorbing Henry's atmosphere, listening to the silence. Then she picked up the letters from the mat and walked to the kitchen. Waiting for the kettle to boil, she sorted through the mail.

There was a circular telling Henry that he had probably already won £150,000; all he had to do was to sign up for ten years' subscription to *Lovely Monthly* to have his name put in the draw.

A leaflet from the local church reminded him that God loved him.

There was another circular, addressed to Malcolm's late mother, informing her that she could lose her surplus fat for ever.

And a telephone bill.

Chris made herself coffee, and sat down at the kitchen table.

The long day replayed itself in her head. The solitary drive down to Kent, punctuated by a stop at the services, where she had sat in the car and cried doggedly for a quarter of an hour, then, for good measure, and as a kind of punishment for being ineffectual, she had banged her head a couple of times on the steering wheel. After that she made a call to Virginia Pye, who was too busy re-netting one of the makeshift aviaries to talk to anyone and told her so. Then she went to visit her father-in-law in the hospital.

Henry was sitting in a chair in the television room, watching Richard and Judy on *Good Morning*, and was apparently enthralled by a talk on wedding dresses. Chris sat down beside him.

'Hello, Henry.'

He glanced at her. One side of his mouth twitched in what might have been a smile.

'I hear you're feeling much better.'

He looked back at the television.

'That you're ready to go home.'

On the TV set, Richard said that no one ever saw wedding shoes, and that the camera was now going to pan down to the shoes, which cost £120. 'Wonderful shoes,' Judy said.

'Shoes,' Henry echoed.

Chris stared at him. It was the first word she had heard her father-in-law utter since the stroke. She pulled her chair around so that she was almost facing him. 'Henry . . .' she said.

She hesitated a moment, and then held his left hand. It was desperately cold. A reflex reaction passed over his face. It was hard to tell what it meant, though it bore a close resemblance to disgust. She got up, and went to see the Ward Sister.

'Is it usual,' she asked, 'to send people home so early?'

The woman looked at her with a kind of tired resignation.

'There's such competition for beds,' she said.

'Is that a reason to send him home?'

'Stroke patients recover very much better at home.'

'Do they?' Chris said. 'I thought they recovered very much better in a Stroke Unit.'

The Sister smiled faintly. 'We don't have a Stroke Unit here.'

Chris returned the grim smile. 'Not the right post code?' she enquired.

'Mr Craven will get physiotherapy here,' she said.

'You mean he'll have to come back?'

'By ambulance, once a week. And the district nurse will call.'

Chris tried to keep her temper. 'But doesn't he need something every day, some sort of remedial care, some sort of exercise?'

'Well,' said the Sister, 'I understand you're employing a nurse.'

Chris had taken a long walk through the hospital corridors. Finally, coming to a landing that overlooked the car park, she had balled her fists, rested them on the window, and leaned her head on her fists. 'Fuck the National Health Service,' she had muttered.

Going back to Henry, she had watched him from the doorway. Richard and Judy were now doing an item on phobias. A woman was demonstrating how she had overcome her arachnophobia by balancing a tarantula on the palm of her hand. Just then, the spider moved. The woman dropped it with a squeal; there was a momentary flurry while the handler retrieved his spider, and Judy claimed solidarity with the guest, who was now standing on the *Good Morning* sofa.

Henry began to laugh. It was a rumble in the chest and throat. His head knocked briefly on his right shoulder and he stared down at his left leg. The limb twitched and stilled.

Chris walked over to him, and kneeled down at his side.

'Henry,' she said, 'you're going home tomorrow. I'll be there to look after you at night, and a nurse will look after you during the day.'

He rotated his head laboriously towards her.

'All right?' she said.

'Sod leg,' he said. 'Sod sodding bloody leg.'

'Yes,' she agreed wholeheartedly. 'Sod the bloody sodding leg.'

Absent-mindedly now in Henry's kitchen, Chris opened the telephone bill. She ran her eye briefly down the pages, the itemised calls. There were very few, in comparison to her own bill. Most were local. There were no calls to mobiles, or premium lines, or freephones. Henry was not the kind of man to enter competitions, ring sex lines, or ask for any kind of advice. He didn't mix with anyone who was coarse enough to own a mobile – yet another perversion of modern life which he hated. He had once said that, one day, he would personally go out and rip down the transmitters that were beginning to litter every hillside. She had some sympathy with that, though. She had even offered to come with him in the dead of night and wage war against Orange and Vodaphone. He hadn't taken her up on her offer, however. Instead, he had looked at her as if she might be taking the piss out of him.

Her eye rested on a long number on the page in front of her. It was an overseas call. She peered at it. 006635, followed by other digits. Suphan Buri.

Where was Suphan Buri? she wondered. It sounded like something you would order in an Indian restaurant as a starter. Perhaps it *was* in India. Had Henry ever been to India, served over there? She knew that he had been posted to what had then been called Burma. Was Suphan Buri there?

Another number caught her attention, directly under the first. It was 00638822. Cagayan De Oro.

That didn't sound Indian. If Suphan Buri was an Indian starter, then Cagayan De Oro was a Mexican main course. Tortillas stuffed with green chillis. Or deep fried cockroach.

She frowned. Just the two numbers, but four calls to the

first and two to the second, each one about a week apart. The calls began about two months ago. She considered, for a moment, ringing them, her curiosity getting the better of her. Then, instead, she got up and went to the telephone directory and turned to the international dialling codes. With her coffee rapidly getting cold, she ran her finger down the countries.

Almost straight away, she found 0061. Australia.

She looked back at the bill. Not Australia.

00679 . . . Fiji. No. Malaysia. The Marshall Islands. Montserrat. Nauru. She didn't know where half these places were. New Caledonia began with 006, and New Zealand. Norfolk Island. Philippines.

She stopped. *Philippines*. 00638822, Cagayan De Oro.

She gazed at the far wall for a while, then continued down the pages. She eventually found Suphan Buri, which was not in India, but in Thailand. She looked away from the bill, and her gaze lingered on the phone. The plain black phone, just another relic from the past, the kind of phone that used to grace Government offices forty years before, and were now collectors' items at antiques fairs. The dial disc was yellow with age, the once-shiny Bakelite finish dulled with prolonged use. She rested her hand on it.

Who had Henry been talking to?

As if to answer her, the phone rang.

She nearly jumped out of her skin, then shook her head at herself. She picked it up. 'Prystock 7784.'

'It's me,' Malcolm said.

'Oh . . . hi.'

'Just got there?'

'Yes,' she said. 'Just got here.'

'Roads all right?'

She paused. 'Yes. The roads were all right.'

There was a rustle of paper on the other end of the line.

'I've got the nurse's number here,' he said. 'She's called Mrs Villiers. She'll be there at eight a.m.'

'OK,' Chris said. 'What's she like?'

'She's got thirty years' nursing experience.'

'What's she like, though?'

'She'll be carrying identification.'

'I mean . . .' Chris paused. 'Never mind,' she said.

'Heating on there?'

'Yes,' she said.

'Don't forget to double lock the back door.'

Chris's fingers strayed to the telephone bill. She opened her mouth to ask about Thailand and the Philippines, then suddenly realised that opening the bill had been an intrusion. An infringement of Henry's privacy. She had been so preoccupied that the thought had never occurred to her until now, and she blushed, and actually put her hand over the torn envelope, as if Malcolm were capable of seeing it down fifty miles of phone line.

'OK,' she said softly. 'I'll lock the back door, Malcolm.'

20

Hunscrete House stood about eight miles from Deadham Markham, on the top of a low hill. It had been built for a King's mistress several centuries ago, and was a very feminine-looking building even now. A discreet swathe of parkland surrounded it like a skirt, undulating appropriately in all the right places. Close to, it revealed itself as a demure square with an inner courtyard of herb gardens. It was breathtakingly pretty, with its arches and arbours and pale stone. Every inch of it had once been laid out for delight.

Pity, Sally thought, as she drove up the mile-long drive, because there was very little delight to be had at Hunscrete now.

She hadn't even known that the estate was anywhere near here until last night. Of course, like everyone else in the country, she had seen its delicate tracery windows in a hundred tabloid shots last year, and she had known that it was fairly close to London. But she had had no idea that the most photographed house in England was barely five miles away from Nova Scotia.

She might not have known now if it hadn't been for Steve lying on the floor in her bedroom. Of all the things that might be interesting to do in a bedroom, putting paper over the floorboards to keep out the draughts was possibly one of the least interesting, *definitely* the least interesting with a man who looked like Steve – but then, Sally reflected morosely, beggars couldn't be choosers.

Philippa Blood, in another flash of efficiency, had sent Michael round with a pile of newspapers. He had grinned at her as she opened the door.

'It looks like the Somme out here,' he said. 'Is your water back on yet?'

'It is,' Sally said. 'Thanks very much. Though, apparently, I have to fill the trench in myself.'

Michael handed her the stack of newspapers. 'The lads will do that tomorrow,' he said. 'Philippa sent these.'

She looked down at the assorted *Telegraphs*, *Guardians* and *Independents*. 'A little bedtime reading?' she asked.

'No,' Michael said. 'Philippa says if you lay newspaper over the floorboards you'll keep more heat in.'

Sally had smiled. 'She's right, of course,' she said.

'She always is,' Michael told her.

Steve had offered to help her put the paper down, obligingly holding the bed ends up while she stuffed paper underneath.

It was while laying out the last few sheets that she had spotted the article about Alicia Hunscrete. She had sat back momentarily on her heels and gazed for a while at the photograph of Alicia's face. The woman had been pictured standing outside Hunscrete House, alone. The word *disgraced* hissed in the caption beneath.

'Look,' Sally said, showing the page to Steve. 'Doesn't she look different? Who would have thought she'd ever look like that?'

'Like what?' Steve asked. He sat down beside her on the floor.

'Defeated,' Sally said. Blood suddenly coursed through her veins and she had a mental flash of Celia Hawkins, her arms wrapped round her Chilean mud wrestler, dwarfing him. Only this time, it was Sally in the picture, being dwarfed in the arms of Steve. For God's sake, she told herself, don't get any hormonal rushes. He's a man, right?

Remember what men are like, for Christ's sake.

And she forced herself to recall being let down and walked over by the last man she loved. Nevertheless, some other and more primitive part of her brain gratefully stored the extraordinarily seductive scent of Steve's toil-stained T-shirt.

'Who is it, anyway?' he asked, leaning towards her.

Sally stood up abruptly, page in hand. 'It's your local Conservative MP,' she said. 'Or was.'

'Why's that, then?' he asked. He was sitting on the floor at her feet, looking up at her with a lazy grin.

'Why's what?' she said.

'Why *was*?'

Sally started to laugh. 'Don't tell me you don't know.'

'I don't know,' he said. He leaned back on one elbow, and she tore her eyes from his crotch, outlined rather fetchingly as it strained the seams of the well-worn jeans.

'But the place must have been crawling with press a few months ago,' she muttered, smoothing the page of the paper in an effort to distract herself.

'Wouldn't know,' Steve said.

'Aren't you interested?'

'In a bloody MP?' he retorted, laughing. 'Not much.'

Sally raised an eyebrow. 'I suppose politics just passes you by, does it?'

To her surprise, his face darkened. He got up, brushing himself down. 'Everything passes us by down here,' he said. 'Probably because we're all thick and marry our sisters.'

Sally blushed. 'I didn't mean that,' she said.

'Forget it.'

'No, I . . .' she hesitated. 'I'm sorry.'

His expression softened slightly. 'I can see past the pub and the skittles team,' he told her. 'I just can't stick politicians.'

Sally smiled. 'Well, nobody can stand this woman,

either,' she said, glancing back at the paper. 'She got six months for fraud.'

'Yeah?' Steve said. 'What did she do?'

'Embezzled some Party funds. Drove a car at her husband and broke both his legs.' She gazed for a moment out of the window, thinking aloud. 'She never really explained it,' she murmured. 'Her husband told the press she'd gone mad.'

Steve had merely shrugged.

When he had gone, Sally sat for some time in the newly stark brightness of her bedroom, under the shadeless light bulb, thinking about Alicia Hunscrete, who would surely, by now, be released from prison and, if so, would be living alone five miles up the road.

After a single cup of tea and slice of bread the next morning, she had set out for Hunscrete.

She looked now at the lovely landscape unrolling before her. Twenty years ago, Alicia Wentworth had married into the many-titled, many-housed, many-landed gentry that was the Hunscrete dynasty. Hunscrete House was just a little pied-à-terre to them – a whimsy, useful for huntin and shootin and fishin.

The estate was stuffed with all sorts of living targets to keep the male Hunscretes occupied. Rabbits roamed within blast of their guns; foxes obligingly populated the woods; the rusty-gate call of pheasants announced that there were plenty of feathered victims on call. All over the Hunscrete countryside, wildlife trembled at the regular rumble of four-wheel drives tearing up the scenery and full of humans who would blast away at anything that moved.

As if to demonstrate his willingness to be murdered, a hare crossed the drive a hundred yards in front of Sally's car. She kept glancing back at him as she drove on, eventually pulling into the gravelled circle in front of the house.

She got out, and waited.

She fully expected someone to emerge and tell her that she was trespassing on private property. If not Alicia Hunscrete herself, then some whiskered buffoon in a Barbour jacket, accompanied by a couple of hysterical Jack Russells.

But there wasn't a sound.

Hunscrete lay modestly in the morning sun, wearing its years with ineffable calm. Sally walked to the front door. She rang the bell and waited, and heard nothing at all. She tried the door handle and found it locked.

Undeterred, she walked around the side of the house, noticing that the gardens, once the subject of various magazine layouts, looked neglected and grey. There was no spring bedding. Nothing had been pruned, no grass cut, no soil turned. Ghosts of old roses hung on their spindly stems, blackened by frost.

When she reached the kitchens, she knocked on the back door. There was no reply, but this time the door was ajar. Sally poked her head into a kind of wasteland, a sorry attempt at a kitchen, housing one small table and a pockmarked farmhouse chair, and a dresser completely devoid of any crockery. A plate lay on the table, next to an open packet of digestive biscuits; a half-drunk cup of tea stood next to the plate. Someone, Sally thought, had had less breakfast than her.

'Who the hell are you?' asked a voice.

Sally turned round. Alicia Hunscrete stood a couple of yards away.

'Sally Matthews,' Sally said, holding out her hand.

Alicia ignored it. 'What do you want?'

'I'm a journalist,' Sally said. It was like confessing that she was the carrier of some deadly disease; Alicia stiffened and lost what little colour her face had possessed.

'I'm not here to do any hatchet job,' Sally said quickly.

'I wondered if you could tell me your side of the story.'

Alicia looked at her sourly. 'I've told my side already,' she said. 'So if you wouldn't mind, kindly piss off.'

She tried to get past Sally, who stood her ground. 'You might have told it, but no one reported it,' Sally said.

Alicia laughed shortly. 'Oh, and you would, I suppose?' she said sarcastically. 'You're so different from all the rest.'

'Yes,' Sally said.

Alicia shook her head. 'Get off my land.'

'Is it your land?' Sally asked.

Alicia stopped dead, and her eyes narrowed. There was a heavy silence. 'No, it isn't,' she said finally. 'As you obviously know.'

'It ought to be,' Sally persisted. 'He ought to have left you something.'

'Well he hasn't,' Alicia said evenly. 'He's fucked off with his secretary and his lawyers are taking me to pieces, all of which the great British public seems to find extraordinarily amusing.'

'Where will you live, when they turn you out of here?' Sally asked.

'I expect I shall be given a two-up and two-down some-where,' the other woman told her.

Sally nodded slowly. 'I've been given that already,' she remarked. 'And my husband's mistress is younger and thinner and more famous than your husband's mistress, so there.'

Alicia stared at her without speaking.

'Look, I *don't* want to do an article for the chattering classes to read over Sunday breakfast,' Sally continued. 'I want to write a book about you, and I want to make a great deal of money for us both.'

For some seconds, Alicia Hunscrete looked at the ground. Then she pushed the door wide open.

'You'd better come in,' she said.

21

Chris had only surfaced at eight o'clock that morning.

The noise that woke her was like a dentist's drill, the kind that sounds as if it's tunnelling through the skull while it grinds out the cavity. Chris rolled over in bed and stared at the ceiling, at the unfamiliar bowed plaster of Henry's guest room, at the beam that ran the length of the wall, at the leaded lights of the window. The grinding drill repeated its sound, and she sat upright. It was the doorbell.

She grabbed the alarm clock. 'Oh, shit,' she muttered. Dragging on a dressing gown, she staggered downstairs and opened the front door.

Mrs Villiers stood on the step. She wore a green uniform and a green hat, and a green cape. She looked for all the world like a fifty-year-old Norlands Nanny.

The vision extended its hand. 'Emily Villiers.'

Chris smiled. 'Chris Craven,' she said. 'Sorry. I've overslept. Come in.'

Emily Villiers stepped over the threshold. For an instant, she looked at Chris, then seemed to dismiss her. Chris had the feeling that, in those two seconds, she had been assessed, and immediately rejected as a waste of the earth's natural resources. The gaze had now snapped upwards to the ceiling. 'Is there a light?' Emily asked.

Chris fumbled around the wall. 'Yes . . . here, somewhere.'

'Might we switch it on?'

Chris did so.

Emily frowned. 'You will need a good hundred-watt bulb in there,' she said. 'Low light can be very disorientating.'

'Oh . . . right,' Chris said. She watched Emily Villiers put down her bag and remove her cape.

'I haven't seen a cape like that since *Emergency Ward 10*,' Chris said.

'Emergency what?'

'*Ward 10*. It used to be on the telly . . .'

'I don't watch the television,' Emily said.

'No, of course not.'

'Is there a downstairs toilet?'

'No.'

'Oh dear,' Emily said. She opened her bag, and took out a notebook and pencil. 'A commode?'

'No, I—'

'We do need a commode.'

'Of course we do,' Chris said. 'Yes.'

'A bed?'

'I was going to bring the bed down this morning.'

For the first time, Emily Villiers gave the merest ghost of a smile. 'Well,' she said. 'Shall we do that now, Mrs Craven?'

It was midday before Chris could get to Deadham Markham.

She arrived at Virginia Pye's to find the field in the grip of an invasion. The two railway carriages stood in one corner, with their doors firmly closed, while the grass slope was full of people. A large trailer had been towed into the field and stood by the gate, looking glaringly out of place, all aluminium and glass and far too clean; a huge four-wheel drive with the Up-Line logo – a mouth with ten tongues waving out of it – was parked next to the trailer; a green van with no one in it was stuck by the fence, and John Donoghue's sports car was on the verge.

Chris eyed him warily as he came towards her, all smiles.

'How're y'doing?' he asked.

'Filthy,' she said. 'I'm doing filthy.'

He grinned. 'Oh? And why's that?'

'I've been invaded by Mary Poppins. I expect Dick Van Dyke will be there by the time I get back.' She winced. 'Believe it or not, I've been commode shopping this morning. My father-in-law's leaving hospital today.'

'What's he been in hospital for?'

'Stroke.'

'Sweet Jesus.'

She grimaced. 'Quite.' She looked round. 'What's happening?'

John stuck his hands in his pockets and dug a line in the turf with the toe of his shoe. 'Well, we've got a slight problem,' he said.

'Let me guess,' she said. 'Virginia.'

'Yes and no,' John said. 'Virginia's fine when Owen isn't here.'

'Ah,' said Chris. She glanced again at the four-wheel drive. 'When did he arrive?'

'First thing. Along with the trailer.'

'Which is whose?'

'First of many, apparently. Make-up, lighting . . . that's who all this lot are.' He gestured past the trailer where, Chris could now see, several other cars were parked, with their occupants sitting around on various bonnets, looking philosophically pissed off.

Chris sighed. 'Money to burn. He's going to film straight away.'

John spread his hands. 'How can I write a script when I can't get near the main character?' he said. 'I can't even rough anything out. I got in there at eight o'clock, she made me breakfast . . .'

'She likes to cook,' Chris said.

'Then we're just getting round to how she first arrived here, and Owen's trailer turns up.'

Chris shook her head. 'And where is he now?'

'God knows. Gone walkabout with the location director.'

'And Virginia?'

'Locked herself in and won't come out. Says she won't come out until the trailers go.'

'Oh great,' Chris murmured. 'Just great.'

They looked down the hill at the railway carriages. The plume of smoke trailed away at right angles, drifting only slowly without a breeze.

'How's the book?' John asked.

Chris looked at him sourly.

'I can take a look at it if you like,' John said.

'And why would you want to do that?'

He shrugged. 'To help?'

'And how many novels have you had published?' Chris asked.

'None.'

'Or written?'

'None, but—'

She picked up her portfolio. 'Blind leading the blind, wouldn't you say?' she told him, and set off down the hill.

'Please your sweet self,' he muttered.

Chris knocked on Virginia's door.

'Go away,' said a voice.

'Virginia, it's Chris Craven.'

'Fuck off.'

Chris stepped back in surprise, staring at the peeling paint of the door as if it could shed clues on the owner. She leaned forward, and put her ear to the wood. From somewhere deep inside the antediluvian silt of Virginia's house, she was sure she could hear crying.

'Virginia,' she said. 'Are you all right?'

There was a long pause. Then, 'No.'

'Why? What's the matter?'

Nothing. Except a choked snuffling sound.

'Please let me in,' Chris said.

'I will not.'

'Please let me in,' Chris repeated. 'My whole life has gone completely arse-shaped, and if you're going to cry, I want to cry with you.'

Long, long silence.

Then, at last, Virginia opened the door a crack. Rather than looking upset, she looked belligerent, like a bull terrier spoiling for a fight. The redness of her eyes was the only clue to her distress. She looked Chris up and down. 'Men?' she asked.

'Men,' Chris confirmed.

Virginia flung open the door. 'Come in,' she told her.

22

Sally had never really liked claret, but now that she and Alicia Hunscrete were halfway down their second bottle, she was changing her mind. It seemed to have an astonishing ability to blank Dermott from the face of the earth.

She couldn't quite remember what he looked like now. She couldn't even remember his middle name. For a moment, she looked hard at the bottle and tried to remember *her* middle name, and then realised that she didn't have one.

She looked up at Alicia. Between them on the table were the family albums. Alicia pointed to the largest, which was open at a society wedding in 1923. 'And that's my uncle,' she was saying. 'Algernon Pettigrew-Mumber, the iron man.'

Sally peered at the very short person holding the arm of the bride. 'He looks more lard than iron,' she said.

'He *made* iron,' Alicia said, snorting at the absurdity. 'Bridges, ships. Heads for the Royal Family. Statues and heads and horses, civic busts, polo trophies.' She got up. Despite the wine, she was very steady on her feet, Sally noticed. Perhaps you couldn't be upper class unless you could drink the middle classes under the table. Perhaps if you drank regularly like this – at midday, before lunch – and could still tread a straight line, you were allowed to marry a country estate.

'Come with me,' Alicia said.

Sally followed her into the deep recesses of Hunscrete

House. It was as pretty inside as it was out – or, rather, it had once been. Like the garden, the house now drooped with a low-grade despair. Dust lay on the satinwood Pembroke table in the hall, and on the huge vase of dead flowers that sat on top of it. Dead poinsettias flanked the display.

'He had a house party here at Christmas,' Alicia said.

'Before you . . .'

'Before I was let out.' Alicia's eyes ranged over the furniture with contempt. 'See that over there?' she said. 'It dates from 1860. Worth five thousand. This Pembroke . . . maybe forty thousand. That credenza . . . eight thousand. Staffordshire creamware in the cabinet . . . twelve thousand.' She turned and looked at Sally. 'When we first got married, he gave me a job,' she said. 'I had to catalogue the whole bloody house. Took me three years, working eight hours a day. I found things in cupboards that would buy an entire house in their own right. Whole collection of sporting guns in one of the outbuildings, campaign swords, musketry. Shelves of Sitzendorf figures locked away in the dining hall, too fussy for his mother's taste, thirty-two of them, cheapest worth a hundred and fifty.'

'Good God,' Sally said.

Alicia ran her finger through the dust on the Pembroke. 'So, you're a writer?' she asked.

'I used to freelance,' Sally said. 'Then I worked for a magazine. Then I walked out.'

'I knew a writer,' Alicia said. 'An MP.'

'Oh yes?' Sally said politely. 'One or two of them are novelists, aren't they?'

'They need to be,' Alicia commented. 'Politicians are all storytellers. You might as well make some money on the side. You don't need talent.'

'So I hear,' Sally said.

'Thrillers,' Alicia said, as if musing to herself. 'Bonking

in the Commons, spies in the Lords. White knuckles in Whitehall.'

'Very readable,' Sally said.

Alicia raised an eyebrow. 'You think so?' she said. 'If only representing one's constituents were really like that.'

'And it isn't?'

'Cold tea in Committee rooms,' Alicia said. 'Last train out of Waterloo.'

Sally pinched back a smile. 'But you weren't an MP when you were first married,' she said.

'No,' Alicia agreed. 'I did the estate accounts.'

'That must have been a full-time job, too.'

Alicia seemed suddenly lost in thought. 'Three years,' she murmured. 'Saved him thousands, reorganised the staff, sold off the tied cottages he hadn't bothered to re-occupy with tenants . . .' She gave a great sigh. 'He was worth about fifty per cent more than he realised.'

'*You* were worth fifty per cent more,' Sally said. 'As a couple.'

Alicia gave a cold smile. 'In theory,' she said, 'although the Hunscretes don't see it like that. Wives are belongings, you know. Like dogs.'

Sally leaned on the table. 'So you did these accounts,' she said, 'but you didn't have a right to the money?'

'I had an allowance,' Alicia said.

'And your salary as an MP.'

Alicia looked away. 'We were in debt long before that.'

Sally started to laugh, then stopped abruptly. 'In *debt*?' she queried. 'Sitting on this lot?'

'You don't understand,' Alicia said. 'This is all in trust. You can't touch it. You can't sell it. You can't live off it.'

'But surely . . .'

'Not a penny.'

'But the income from the estate . . .'

'Oh yes,' Alicia said. 'There's the income from the

estate, which goes into the estate accounts.'

'What about a private income? Stocks and bonds or savings – something like that.'

'We are Lloyds Names.'

'Oh.' Sally knew how many had been ruined in that particular débâcle.

'No ready cash,' Alicia said, 'is what it boils down to.'

Sally considered her. 'So you stole some.'

'Yes.'

'And that's it?'

Alicia crossed her arms. 'You've read the newspapers.'

Sally frowned. 'What – you couldn't pay the game-keeper, or something? You couldn't keep the yacht in Cannes?'

'I couldn't pay Charles's gambling debts,' Alicia said.

She turned on her heel, with Sally trotting after her. They walked into an enormous dining hall, with a long Jacobean table in the centre, and portraits of Hunscretes on the walls.

Alicia pointed to the first. 'Bartholomew Hunscrete, 1542,' she said.

Bartholomew wore a supercilious expression and had his foot on a dead Catholic.

'Wilfred, 1588, his son,' Alicia said, moving on to the next.

Wilfred had a sword in his hand and his foot on a dead Spaniard.

'Robert Hunscrete, 1714,' Alicia continued. Robert had an axe on his shoulder and his foot on a dead Scot.

'Thomas Hunscrete, 1796, slayer of the revolutionary French,' Alicia chanted. 'Charles Hunscrete in his Irish estates in 1845 . . . William Hunscrete, district officer in Malaya, 1886 . . .'

Sally stopped at the last picture. 'And where are *your* ancestors?' she asked.

Alicia laughed. 'My family was in trade,' she said. 'We don't have portraits. We have family snaps.' She sat down heavily on the couch at the end of the room. Sally sat alongside her.

'He let me stay here for three months,' Alicia said. 'Very generous, you know. To show there were no hard feelings. He let me stay here while he went to the Caribbean with the next Lady Hunscrete.' She smoothed the pleat in her tweed skirt. 'He'll be back in less than a week.'

'And then you're homeless.'

Alicia shrugged.

'And penniless.'

There was no response.

'Why did you never tell anyone about the gambling,' Sally asked, 'even when you were investigated last summer by the Party?'

'One has one's loyalties.'

'To your husband.'

'Quite.'

'But you lost your seat in Parliament.'

'Charles never wanted me to run for office.'

'Oh,' Sally said. 'So that was very convenient for him, wasn't it?'

Alicia looked away from her, out of the window. 'He was really awfully nice at the time,' she murmured. 'Promised it would never happen again, that sort of thing. Told me how much he appreciated what I'd done for him.'

'Big of him,' Sally said.

Alicia smoothed the hair back from her forehead. 'I was protecting my own name, too,' she said. 'What good would it have been to disgrace the Hunscretes?'

'So you stole for him,' Sally said.

'He swore it was only temporary,' Alicia told her. 'That it would be back before anyone noticed. He was desperate. He had borrowed from some rather unsavoury characters.'

'You stole for him, ' Sally repeated. 'At the cost of your own job. At the cost of your own reputation. When you could have just walked out of this house with a sideboard and made fifty thousand in an afternoon.'

At last, Alicia looked directly at her. 'Well,' she said, 'I'm sure we all do stupid things for love.'

There was a silence.

In the enormous echoing space of the hall, the male Hunscretes looked down their noses and centuries at another ruined and suppressed wife.

'What happened in the autumn?' Sally asked.

'Nothing of note.'

Good God, Sally thought. Nothing of note.

'But you tried to kill him.'

'Not really.'

'You drove your car straight at him.'

'No,' Alicia said. 'I drove my car at the call girl. It was her I was trying to kill.'

Sally paused a double beat. 'What call girl?'

'The one who ran away. He stepped in front of the car to protect her.'

'But I never saw a call girl mentioned.'

'No, you wouldn't. He has his friends. Friends with influence.'

'But he said you had gone mad and it was an unpro-voked attack. He said the disgrace of the embezzlement had unhinged you.'

'Perhaps it had.' Alicia sighed deeply, and got to her feet. 'Too many people in his pocket. So you see, Sally, even if you write the story, no one will want to publish it.'

'Are you joking?' Sally said. 'Your husband, Sir Charles Hunscrete, is a Cabinet Minister.'

'You will never get anyone interested,' Alicia repeated. 'He is fireproof.'

'They'll snap you up,' Sally retorted. 'You sacrificed

your whole life for him, and now he's turning you out.'

'I'm rather sick of the whole subject.'

'You'll be even sicker when you're living in a council flat and can't pay the gas bill.'

'People are tired of scandal,' Alicia said.

Sally smiled slowly. 'Oh, I don't think so,' she disagreed. 'I think you'll find that isn't so.'

23

Malcolm sat in the laboratory at lunchtime and watched the sterile tank in front of him. Everyone else had gone out; the staff were glad, these days, to leave the offices. Since they had taken down the rusty pewter sign on the front of the building, and put the Trepantex logo in its place, it was as if the whole building had changed its nature.

There were fewer staff, and those who remained were too busy to stand about in corridors chatting. Where there had only been vague targets for tests, there were now deadlines set in place. A new Administration Wing had been set up, and every communication was copied through it, so that Malcolm couldn't chew the fat with his academic colleagues any more in the old way.

He had to go to meetings now and explain himself. Explain why he had needed to make certain phone calls, and what relevance they had to his experiments. What doctors were charged which fees, and why. What clinics. What hospitals. What departments. Next month, he had been told, all conversations with academic institutions would carry a fee. He would be loathed, stamped through and through with the Trepantex stamp like a piece of seaside rock.

Worse still, there were a lot of women in the building.

Not the kind of women he was used to, who were glad to get their hands dirty and set up experiments and whose talk was usually about their children's football matches, and tonight's tea. These women were some other breed,

some other race. It wasn't as if they even wore suits. They
wore what he only knew were strangely cut things. Skirts
with odd hems, and bag-like sacking jackets and
fascinatingly horrible underwear showing through their
clothes. One woman who seemed to have been assigned to
his section, and whom he avoided like the plague, often
came into work in a leather shirt that someone said came
from Hermès, whatever the hell *that* was.

They all carried laptops and mobile phones, and had
mysterious titles and an air of importance. They were, it
was rumoured by the baffled staff, the *creatives*. 'Like
think tanks,' someone had said darkly, one afternoon in
the canteen.

He didn't understand women, and he couldn't explain
himself.

It was the same with Chris. Sometimes he simply didn't
know why he had done something, only that he had
thought it needed to be done. He couldn't explain to
Trepantex why he had spoken to Alex in Edinburgh about
hormonal synapses any more than he could explain to
Christine why he had all the household bills in little paper
folders with different coloured tabs on them, with a five-
year projection attached to each. He just had to, that was
all. It was like touching base. Keeping in touch. Keeping
the world straight.

The music tape came to a halt.

He reached over to switch it, glancing at the cover to
make sure it was the right kind of sound. He had once
made the fatal mistake of playing Mantovani to hatch-
lings, thinking it was soothing. It had been months before
he had found out that they preferred Chumbawamba.

It was so important to get these details right. And he
liked details. Most of the scientists he knew liked details.
His father liked details. Even Trepantex liked details. It
was only Chris who hated details, who writhed in

frustration at the sight of a timetable or a flow chart. If anything could move Chris to fury, it was the sight of him doing the accounts, with his handwritten list of cheque stubs, and his aligned row of black and red pens.

He sat back and stared at the wall.

He just couldn't understand it at all. But he had been trying very hard, lately, to do just that. In a fit of unaccustomed extravagance, he had actually bought an audio tape of a best-selling book and, all this week, he had been playing it to himself in the car.

It was called, *Why Women Are Rainbows and Men Are Not*. The elderly Chinese author was wildly successful. There was already a sequel out, called *Women Are Daffodils and Men Are Trees*.

He also had the sequel. Sometimes he would stop his car and run a piece of the tape back, and then make a note in a little spiral-bound book. Last night, he had written down: *Women have specialness and danciness, and men have trunkiness and rootiness*. It looked daft when it was written down in black and white like that, but it was, word for word, what the best-selling Chinese woman had said. *Women have danciness and men have rootiness*.

Apparently it was fatal to try and change this order of behaviour, which had been ordained by logic since the world began. The author was very keen to get this message across, so keen that she kept repeating it every few pages in a weird, sing-song voice. Women couldn't change, and men shouldn't change. Women would always be lovely and dancy and men would always be solid and trunky. Nothing, it transpired, would be worse for the history of mankind than to have men and women trying to change roles.

Civilisation would grind to a halt, for instance, if a man tried to be a bit dancy, or a woman tried to be a bit trunky. Women just did not possess trunks at all. In their special dancy existence, they liked only to talk and laugh and feel. Being feely was an integral part of being dancy, and if you took feely-ness away from women, they got very unhappy. In fact, they got *windlike*.

Malcolm had had to check that twice to make sure he had heard right.

The worst thing you could do to a woman, apparently was to force her into *windiness*, a horrible state where all her danciness disappeared and she got very fraught and threw things and called your mother a bitch.

It wasn't wrong at all for women to do this. What was wrong was if the man, forgetting that he had to be rooty and trunky, forgot to give lots of hugs.

Everything was all right if you hugged someone. A windy woman could be cured in an instant if you hugged her and said that she was a beautiful person. Of course, you mustn't say anything else. Malcolm had underlined that sentence in his notebook. *You must not say anything else.* All that was necessary was to show you knew what a hug was and that the word 'beautiful' was in the English language. If you carried on in this vein, however, you ran the risk of ditching every manly rooty quality and becoming dangerously close to dancy.

Imagine, said the author, how awful it would be to have a world full of feely men. Men were built to think, to be trunky, to be dependable and responsible. Men had ideas. Women had urges. Urges were a primeval thing, in tune with the earth mother's winds and waves and tides. Women were spiritually aligned to growth and the seasons, and bimbled along in a state of waviness and feeliness and motherliness, grabbing handfuls of soil and bunches of flowers and bagfuls of food to nurture all those around them.

Men, on the other hand, were never happier than when closeted, alone, in the dark forest. Trees were deep and steady beings. With their feet deep in the ground, they were able to take a long view of life. To make important decisions. Decisions and thinking were the life blood of men, and they had to be left alone to be thinky and trunky on their own.

Last night, Malcolm had had to stop the car in a bus lay-by. His head had been reeling with *nesses*. He had felt rather sick, as if he had eaten a couple of pounds of Belgian chocolates, or been force-fed cake. And it was, unfortunately, with a distinct sensation of *cakiness* and *sickiness* that he had finally found his way home.

Still. It was not so bad today.

The spiral-bound notebook was at his side, and Malcolm found that he could look at it quite normally. More than that, he thought it all made a lot of sense.

Without Chris around to snort derision in his ear, he read all his notes from the tape, and had come to the conclusion that the author was, indeed, a genius. An absolute genius. Because her books described exactly what was wrong with himself and Chris.

He *did* feel very uncomfortable with tears, with feelings. He never knew what to say and, when he did say something, it always sounded inept. Chris was an intelligent person, but for all her intelligence, she was keen on feelings. The mistake they had made was in trying to talk the same language when they were fluent in their own languages, and should be left to speak them. He felt very strongly now that he ought to sit back and just listen kindly when Chris wanted to talk, and that she, in turn, ought just to sit back and give him space when he wanted to do his graphs and accounts.

Neither of them properly appreciated the other. Chris was forever trying to drag him out of his forest into the light, and he had made the disastrous error of beginning to

think that he really ought to be hanging about outside
trying to talk like Chris, when all he wanted was to be left
alone.

And the gap that remained could be easily bridged. Not
by trying to be like each other, but by hugging, and telling
each other that they were great people.

He paused for a moment now, looking down at his
maggots. He wondered what Chris would say if, when she
went on about her book, he hugged her and told her she
was a beautiful person. Didn't he do that already? Didn't
he reassure her that she was marvellous? Didn't he give her
little cuddles?

Perhaps he just didn't come across as confident enough.

From today, he would just hug her regularly and be
brisk about it. He wouldn't try to talk about feelings,
because that was not his job. And he would try to get Chris
to see that being feely was *her* job, and he was very proud
of her doing that job. And that he didn't want her to be a
tree at all.

As he sat there with his chin on his hand, watching the
first glimmer of birth from within the larvae in the tank, he
did have a sensation, nevertheless, that there was something wrong in this line of thinking. Something perhaps
very wrong. Something that might backfire with a woman
who apparently wanted to be feely *and* trunky, and who
came across as bloody rooty when she wanted to be.

Perhaps he should insist that Chris listen to the tape.

The door opened suddenly. Malcolm jumped, and
almost fell off his stool. In the doorway stood Miranda,
the Trepantex woman who wore the leather shirt. She was
smiling broadly. Behind her were two men.

'Hi Malc,' she said breezily, walking into the lab.
'What's cooking today?'

He glanced at the men who had followed her in. 'We're
hatching,' he said.

She didn't seem to really grasp the importance of this statement. She flung her mobile on the lab bench right by the tank, glanced only briefly at the larvae, and turned her gaze on him.

He felt very uncomfortable. He looked down at her shoes, two thin strips of purple plastic.

'Just finished the quarterly profile, Malc,' she said.

'Oh,' he responded. 'Very good.'

'Just been considering the income genesis.'

'Income,' he repeated. 'Genesis.'

She smiled. 'Yeah.'

One of her colleagues was peering into the tank.

'Oh,' she said. 'This is Turk Brandenbruger. New York.'

Turk stuck out a hand. Malcolm shook it obediently.

'Brilliant work,' Turk said.

'Thank you . . .'

'And this,' Miranda said, 'is Charlie Muckensplit, from San Francisco.'

Another hand. 'Hi, Malc,' said Charlie.

'Charlie has a research programme into convalvular pre-gestation,' Miranda said.

'Oh,' said Malcolm. What the hell is that? he thought.

'We're putting a lot of capital into it,' Miranda said.

As if on cue, all three of them – Miranda in her purple shoes, Turk in his Armani suit, and Charlie in his West Coast tennis shirt, looked around at Malcolm's laboratory.

There was an uncomfortable silence.

Malcolm found himself blushing. With the toe of his shoe, he edged his carrier bag with his lunch box and paste sandwiches back under the bench. The tape, also stuffed inside it, clattered briefly against the tile floor.

Then, in the same steamroller fashion in which they had come in, the trio went out, pausing at the door for Turk to look back and say, 'Amazing.'

'If you wait a minute . . .' Malcolm said, but they had

slammed the door after themselves. Disappointed, he looked down into the tank, at the face of his emerging firstborn.

'Hello,' he said to the maggot. 'Don't get comfortable, now. I don't think it's going to be worth it.'

24

When Chris got to Prystock at half past six, she was surprised to see lights burning in the drawing room of the house, at the front. A comforting blaze of colour spread over the Cathedral Close pavement. As she parked the car in the bay opposite, Emily Villiers came to the window to draw the curtains and, catching sight of Chris, gave her a peremptory little wave.

It wasn't only the lights and the occupation of the front rooms that had changed, Chris found, as she opened the door. Almost everything about Henry's house was different.

The smell, for a start.

Chris had always thought that Henry's house smelled of carpet shampoo that hadn't worked. It wasn't just the soap, but a mixture of odours: damp, wool, strong tea, and Scotchguard. The kitchen would always be worse, reeking of old soup and shoe polish. Henry never opened a window, and he never had the curtains or furnishings cleaned. Every now and again he would get out an old Bex Bissell from under the stairs and attack the carpets with it. Hence the smell. And, mixed with the soap and Scotchguard and damp would be an overall air of Henry's outrage of being forced to do women's work.

There wasn't a whiff of mildewed carpet in the hall tonight.

Instead, there was an almost visibly vibrating tang of lemon Jif.

And, piled to one side in the hallway, Chris noticed a neatly folded stack of curtains from upstairs. Also, rolled tight, was the kitchen blind, a horrible flowery vinyl affair from 1972. Alongside it were the two basket-weave lampshades from the stairs, encrusted with the yellow muck of neglect. The flagstones in the hall shone, as if they had been treated with something, some kind of varnish or wax. The banister gleamed.

Emily Villiers exploded into the hall, her cape thrown around her shoulders.

'What a difference, Mrs Villiers,' Chris said admiringly.

'I've cleaned,' Emily responded, with some emphasis on the *cleaned,* and with one eyebrow faintly raised at the sight of Chris's shoes, encrusted with mud from Virginia's field.

Emily pointed to the pile in the corner. 'I'll take the curtains and drop them in at the dry cleaners,' she said. 'Everything else I shall put in the dustbin, if you're agreeable.'

'Well, I . . .' Chris wanted to be agreeable – after the day she'd had, which had been surprising to say the least, she was rather in the mood to be agreeable – but she doubted that Henry would be.

As if reading her mind, Emily Villiers started to pick up the stack. 'I've spoken to Mr Craven, and he's quite happy,' she said.

Happy, Chris thought. She had never seen Henry happy. 'Is he OK?' she asked.

'He's watching *Wheel of Fortune*,' Emily said.

Chris stared at her. 'But he hates it.'

'Oh, he's really enjoying it,' Emily insisted. 'He's pretending he's got a buzzer and everything.'

'But he only ever watches *Newsnight*,' Chris said. 'So he can shout at Jeremy Paxman and call him a jumped-up know-all.'

'We did *Countdown* together,' Emily continued brightly, 'and Mr Craven got the conundrum. Isn't that lovely?'

'*Countdown*,' Chris repeated. 'Has he got a temperature at all?'

Emily waved this remark aside. 'There's a casserole in the oven for you,' she said.

'Oh, that's kind. Thank you.'

'A very busy woman like you hasn't time to cook, I'm sure,' Emily said. 'Henry has had an egg and soldiers. I shall be here again at eight o'clock. Good night.'

'Good night,' Chris murmured. She opened the door for her and watched her go, a short little figure who looked like Moriarty, Master of Crime, from the rear, disappearing into the mists of Victorian London with his cape billowing about him.

She frowned, feeling the claws of lemon Jif settle on the short hairs on the back of her neck. She hadn't got time to cook and had, in fact, been dreading having to set to and make dinner, but at the same time, she bloody well resented Emily Villiers knowing this.

She closed the front door, and went into the drawing room.

Henry was propped in the straight-backed wing chair, looking very pink, as if he had been steam-cleaned. Perhaps he has, Chris thought, and an image of Henry in something like a car wash, being hosed down by Emily Villiers, sprang into her mind.

'Hello, Henry,' she said. She sat down on the couch in front of him. 'You're looking very spruce.'

'One thousand and DOUBLE POINTS!' screamed the TV set.

'Ha,' Henry said.

'Are you thirsty? Would you like a drink?'

'And a lovely designer dining suite that doubles as a games table . . .'

Chris put her hand on Henry's. 'Did you like Mrs Villiers?' she asked.

Henry at last turned his face towards her. 'Yes,' he said, quite clearly.

She smiled at him. 'I'm glad,' she said. 'Well, I'll just get out of these clothes, and have a shower. Is that OK?'

'Yes,' he said.

He turned back to the set with a very strange expression indeed, for Henry. It was one of contentment.

Standing under the dribble of warm water that passed for a shower in Henry's bathroom, Chris had time to consider her day.

All the way to Prystock, she had been thinking about the curious scenes played out at Virginia Pye's that afternoon, and the even curiouser reactions of John Donoghue and Owen Majolica.

When Virginia had finally let her in at lunchtime, Chris had been surprised to see that nothing was on the stove. She had grown used to Virginia's railway carriage being full of steam and the waft of sausages and coffee. Instead, Virginia had sat down heavily on one of the upturned packing cases, and folded her arms.

'I don't like it,' she had said.

Chris, removing a hen from the only other seat, sat down. 'Don't like what, Virginia?'

'It. All of it.'

'The filming?'

'Don't like it.'

An egg rolled under Chris's feet. She retrieved it, and put it carefully on the table. 'Was it something John said? John Donoghue?'

'No.'

'Owen, then? The man in the four-wheel drive?'

'No.'

'The crew?'

'No,' said Virginia. 'I haven't spoken to them.'

'Well, what is it?'

Virginia picked at the curling paint on the wall next to her. 'People looking,' she mumbled.

'At you?'

'Yes.'

'But everyone thinks you're marvellous,' Chris said. 'Your gift with birds. Living here . . .'

'I can't help living here,' Virginia retorted.

'No, I mean it's a wonderful place,' Chris explained. 'There are loads of people who give up houses in the city and buy places like this, little cottages and crofts, old chapels . . .'

'But that's it,' Virginia said.

'I'm sorry – *what's* it?'

'They give up houses,' Virginia said. 'They have *got* something to give up. They choose.' Then she promptly burst into tears.

Chris wasn't entirely surprised. She had seen all kinds of people dissolve into shuddering wrecks when television invaded their lives. She had seen teenagers on *My Life is Hell with a Teenage Daughter* weeping piteously in a floor manager's arms. She had seen grown men – if there was such a thing – develop a muted version of St Vitus Dance as the cameras rolled towards them. She had seen seasoned performers crack under the strain, throwing flower arrangements on morning television, forcing Lorraine Murphy to babble at length to a close-up camera about facial boils, while the sofa cushions hurtled from left to right in the shot behind her, and pages of script fluttered down like confetti. She had seen shy passers-by dry up when interviewed in the street; she had seen politicians helplessly blunder the words 'facts up at Westminster', while their agents mimed the *Psycho* shower scene behind them in a vain effort to get them off air.

And so she knew what Virginia was feeling. The excitement of being noticed, and raising a bit of money to keep Archie the duck in the style to which he would like to become accustomed, had worn off. Now reality had kicked in, and Virginia was faced with a lens through her window, and the sensation of having her flesh peeled from her bones for the sake of public amusement.

Chris handed Virginia a tissue from her handbag.

'I never had anything,' Virginia snuffled.

'But you've a lovely little retreat,' Chris said.

'I haven't,' Virginia said. 'It's a pile of shit.'

'You've got that marvellous painting.'

'Never asked for it. Don't want it.'

'Well, sell it, and buy a lovely house.'

'Don't want to sell it,' Virginia muttered.

There was a pause while Chris wondered what on earth to say to her.

'You see,' Virginia said, wiping her nose, 'it's all a laugh to you lot. Funny old tart banged up in a train . . .'

'It's not a laugh,' Chris said. 'It's interesting.'

'It's not bloody interesting!' Virginia shouted. 'You think I want to live here? I'd like one of those flats in Melcombe Whitechurch, that's what I'd like.'

'I see,' Chris said.

'You don't,' Virginia retorted. She gave a great sigh, balled the tissue, and threw it over her shoulder. She leaned on the table.

'I came here in 1954,' she said. Her voice was low, as if she had forgotten that Chris was there, and was thinking aloud. 'This was a chicken run in those days. Old man Brittal gave it me. My husband had thrown me out . . .'

'So you *were* married,' Chris said gently.

Virginia's lip trembled again. 'I married a man of fifty-two when I was seventeen,' she said.

'Fifty-two?' Chris said. 'Thirty-five years older?'

'He worked at the house where my father was born. He was gardener there.'

'This was some years after George Ransome went to America?'

'Yes,' Virginia said. 'It was sort of understood . . . my mother always had a job there. When I got old enough, they gave me a job in the kitchen.'

'And this would be when?'

'Fifty years ago. Just after the war.'

'And this was a house near here?'

'Hunscrete,' Virginia said.

The name rang a distant bell in Chris's mind. 'Is that anything to do with Sir Charles Hunscrete who's in the Cabinet?'

'My cousin,' Virginia said.

Chris stared a moment, then began to laugh. 'Cousins?'

'Half cousins,' Virginia corrected herself. 'Once removed or whatever it is.'

'So your father . . .'

'Was Charles Huscrete's uncle.'

'Holy cow,' Chris murmured. 'So, let's see: your father, the famous George who left in disgrace after getting your mother pregnant and went to Hollywood . . . he had a brother?'

'Older brother,' Virginia nodded. 'William. Born 1912. Died in Malaya in 1947 trying to shoot an elephant that got to him first.'

'Right,' Chris said. 'OK. Your Uncle William, who inherited the Hunscrete fortune, but then got trampled by an elephant . . .'

'Drowned by an elephant. It threw him in a river.'

'Drowned. OK. Drowned by an elephant . . .'

'Served him bloody right, an' all,' Virginia said. 'Bastard, he was.'

'I'm sure he was,' Chris said. 'But he had a son by then . . . the present Charles Hunscrete?'

'That's him.'

'The Cabinet Minister – and that's the same one whose wife tried to kill him last year?'

'Pity she missed,' Virginia snorted. 'They're all bastards, every one of them. Smug smiling bastards, you take my word for it.'

'Right,' Chris mused, accepting this quite happily. 'So this particular smug smiling bastard who's in the Cabinet now, he's your cousin?'

'He doesn't think so,' Virginia said.

'Why not?'

'Because I was born illegitimate.'

'Well,' said Chris smoothly, 'that just makes *you* a bastard too – which qualifies you as a regular Hunscrete, doesn't it?'

At last, like a ray of sun coming out from behind the clouds, a small smile lit Virginia's face.

'I was born ten years before him,' she told Chris. 'He was at public school by the time his mother gave me a job at the house.'

'This was the sister of the woman who had given George money to go to America and never darken her door again?'

'That's right. Well, sisters-in-law.'

'Happy family,' Chris commented.

'Still are,' Virginia said. 'This current one, he marries a nice girl, he uses her left, right and centre, he has a string of mistresses, drives his wife up the wall, loses her her job, lets her be thrown into prison.'

Chris leaned forward. 'String of mistresses?' she echoed.

'Yes. Five or six on the go at once.'

Chris stared at her with a similar sense of revelation that Sally Matthews was experiencing at almost the same moment five miles away in Hunscrete House. 'Well, I'll be damned,' Chris said. 'And he's the one always going on about families and protecting children and old-fashioned virtue, and all that.'

'That's him,' said Virginia.

'And yet he's got mistresses, and . . .'

'Illegitimate children. Two.'

'Has he,' Chris said. 'Has he indeed. But why doesn't everyone know about this?'

'Because he pays people off to keep quiet. Pays the mothers of his kids a fortune. I only know because I used to hear *his* mother ranting on about it to him in the house. She only died five years ago. Eighty-five, she was. Fearsome woman. Used to break horses. Didn't like horses, just liked breaking things. Horses. China. Lives.'

Chris raised an eyebrow. 'She sounds charming.'

'She once locked him – Hunscrete – she once locked him under the stairs.'

'Spare the rod and spoil the child.'

'He was twenty-two at the time,' Virginia said with relish. 'She kept him there three days.'

'Whatever for?'

'God knows,' Virginia said. 'She liked to thrash people, too. Seen her thrash the grocer once. Good for the circulation, she reckoned, a good thrashing. Thrashing and locking up. Whipping. Hitting folk with sticks. Oh, it was regular. Only things she never hit were her lurchers.'

'Her dogs?'

'Yes,' Virginia said. 'The first thing *he* did when his mother died was to take those dogs off and shoot them.'

Chris pulled a face. 'But Hunscrete went on TV last year and said how shocked he was by his wife stealing money, and how thankful he was that not a breath of scandal had ever touched the Hunscretes because they had always lived by such Christian standards . . .'

'That's him,' Virginia said. 'Smug bastard – I told you.'

Chris nodded slowly. 'I thought at the time he was tempting fate,' she said. 'I mean, every family has got at least one skeleton.'

'Runs in the blood,' the other woman said. 'He can't help it. It's like a family illness. Some families have got asthma and some have got arthritis, and the Hunscretes have got adultery.' She sighed. 'I'm not the only by-blow, you know,' she said. 'His father had six or seven that his wife didn't know about. Course . . .' she leaned forward, as if to share a secret, 'most of them are barking mad.'

'The Hunscretes?'

'No. Us kids.'

'But you're not mad, Virginia,' Chris said.

'Not mad,' she agreed. 'Just a bit half-baked.' She glanced over Chris's shoulder, out of the window. 'More people turning up,' she said.

But Chris didn't look around. She was still staring at the table top.

'Virginia,' she said, 'would you be prepared to say all this in the programme?'

'I won't say anything that isn't the truth,' Virginia said.

'But . . . everything you said just now, that's the truth?'

'Of course it is.'

'And you can prove it?'

'Got pictures and things, if you want,' Virginia said.

A long beat passed while Chris covered her eyes with her hands, then suddenly she looked up. 'Why don't you want older men on this film?' she asked. 'Is it because of your husband being so much older than you?'

Virginia tore her gaze away from the developing mayhem outside, and looked directly into Chris's eyes.

'It was like this,' she said bitterly. 'Gertrude Hunscrete – the whipping and thrashing one – had a gardener. She liked this gardener. Probably because he used to stand up to her, because he was as hard as she was.' A shadow passed over her face. 'Anyway, he was a widower, and she promised to give him three hundred a year and a cottage if he married me.'

'And you knew about that?' Chris asked, shocked.

'Didn't know a thing,' Virginia shrugged. 'He courted me, I said yes, because I was young and stupid . . .'

'And then what?'

Virginia looked away. 'Then all hell broke loose,' she murmured. 'He was a right bastard, too.'

Chris considered her for some time, full of sympathy.

'Virginia,' she said, at last, 'if I promised you that the man running this show *isn't* a bastard, would you feel better?'

'Can you?' she asked.

'Yes,' Chris said, meaning it. 'Owen is actually a decent person, I promise. Low boredom threshold, but decent.'

'And what about this John?'

Chris thought. 'He seems OK.'

'You're sure?'

Chris paused. How could she be sure? She hardly knew him – and yet she *was* sure. Perhaps her brain was decaying faster than Virginia's kitchen.

'I'm sure,' she said, crossing her fingers out of Virginia's sight.

Chris turned off the shower now, and dried herself on one of Henry's board-hard towels.

When she had come out of Virginia's railway carriage, she immediately saw Owen Majolica striding down the field towards her, towing the entire crew in his wake.

'Chris!' he yelled. 'How's the star?'

She had taken him by the elbow and led him a few yards away. 'She'll be all right,' she said, 'but you'll have to go slow. Don't make fun of her – be careful. This isn't *Whip My Butt*, Owen.'

'OK,' he said.

'I mean it,' she told him. 'You push her, frighten her . . . she'll just lock you out.'

'OK, Madeleine,' he said.

She stared at him, hands on hips. 'There you go again,' she said, annoyed. 'What's with this Madeleine?'

He affected innocence. 'Madeleine who?' he asked.

She gritted her teeth so hard that she felt her fillings bend. 'Please, Owen,' she said. 'Please listen to me.'

'Yes,' he said. 'I am listening, *Christine*.'

'Well, tell them.'

'Who?'

Chris had almost hit him with frustration. 'The crew, Owen. Tell the crew. Tell your scriptwriter.'

Owen's face suddenly lit up. 'Aha!' he said, and waved his index finger in front of her face. 'John's been telling me all about you,' he said. 'He's been telling me you've written a book.'

'Well, he's lying then,' Chris said.

Owen laughed. 'Am I in it?'

'No.'

'Aha!' he said, triumphant.

'Owen, please stop it,' she said. 'Before you turn into Alan Partridge.'

'Is it sexy?' he said.

'No.'

'Violent?'

'No.'

'Bit of scandal?'

'No. Look . . .'

'About anybody famous?'

'No.'

'About a man who whispers to horses?'

'No, Owen.'

'Woman who cuts up bodies?'

'No.'

'Spies and the Russian Mafia?'

'No.'

'Aliens and the FBI?'

'No.'

'Lady gardeners who don't wear bras?'

'NO,' she said.

Owen frowned. 'You'll never sell that, then,' he told her.

She tried to bite her tongue, and managed, instead, to bite the inside of her mouth. She winced with pain. 'I know that, Owen,' she mumbled.

He stared at her hard for a few seconds, then gripped her elbow suddenly. 'Chris,' he said, lowering his voice. 'I need help.'

She bit down the obvious reply. 'Help? What do you mean?'

'*Your* help.'

'But about what?'

Just then, John Donoghue walked up behind her and laid his arm across her shoulder. 'Will our Virginia talk to me now?' he asked.

Chris moved away from the arm. Something about it – something about both John and Owen's assumptions – had suddenly rankled. That, and being told that she would never be published, which was akin to a small stake in her heart. She took a deep breath.

'Mrs Pye doesn't want to talk to anyone just now,' she said. 'Only me.'

John and Owen looked at each other. 'That's a bit tricky,' John said.

'You'll just have to do location shots, atmosphere, the birds – all that . . . for now.'

'How long is for now?' Owen asked.

'A couple of days,' Chris said.

John's face fell. 'But she's talking to you?'

'Yes, she is.'

'How cosy.'

Owen slapped his hands together. 'Well,' he said, 'that's all right. You can get the info, and John can write it up.'

Fed up with the glare that John was giving her, Chris turned to go, but just as she was opening the door to her car to get her briefcase, she felt Owen's hand, once again, fasten about her arm. She jumped several inches in shock. 'For God's sake, don't do that,' she told him.

'I'm sorry,' he said. 'But I do need some advice.'

'What about?'

'Not here,' he said, glowering in the direction of the crew.

'Are you trying to be Austin Powers this time?' she said sarkily.

For the first time an expression of true irritation crossed his face. 'Will you meet me for lunch tomorrow?' he asked.

'Well . . .'

'I'll pick you up here at midday.' He gave her a watery smile. 'It's important, Chris.'

'OK,' she agreed.

He put his arms around her with real feeling. 'Thanks,' he told her. 'Thank you very much.'

She'd watched him walk away, feeling worried for him suddenly. Frowning, remembering this exchange now, Chris went downstairs.

The drawing room was silent: Henry had turned off the TV. The remote lay next to him on the arm of the chair.

Chris smiled at him. 'Tea?'

He nodded.

She went into the kitchen and, once having got over the shock of finding it pristine – even the inside of the cupboard under the sink had had its layers of grime removed – she noticed the stack of mail. Feeling guilty, she picked up the phone bill and took it into her father-in-law.

'Henry,' she said, 'I opened this yesterday, by mistake.' She held out the envelope. 'It's the phone bill.'

He took it with his left hand.

'I wasn't meaning to pry,' she said. 'I'm sorry.'

He pushed the bill into his pocket.

'Would you like me to pay it?' she asked.

'No,' he said.

'I couldn't help noticing the calls,' she said, sitting down. 'The long-distance ones.'

Henry said nothing.

'Is there anyone you would like to ring now?' she asked. 'Shall I plug the phone in here?'

'No,' he said.

Outside in the kitchen, as if on cue, the phone began to ring. Still looking back at Henry, Chris went out to answer it.

'Hello?'

'Hello. It's me.'

'Hello, Malcolm.'

'How are you?'

'Tired,' she said.

'*Are* you?' he replied, with emphasis. 'You need a *hug*.' Chris frowned. 'Sleep,' she said. 'That's what I need.'

'And how is Dad?'

She had never heard Malcolm call Henry *Dad* before. 'He's just finished watching television,' she said.

'Tell him I love him,' Malcolm said.

This was even more of a shock. So much so that Chris found a stool, hauled it over to the phone, and sat down heavily on it. 'Do I have to?' she asked.

Malcolm laughed. It was a hearty laugh, a manly, hairy, rugby team laugh. A laugh of unsettling jollity.

'Are you all right?' Chris said.

'You're so good at feelings,' he said.

'Good at what?'

'I love you,' he said. 'And I'm always here for you. Like a rock.'

'Are you?' she said.

He laughed again. 'You bring good things into my life,' he told her. 'Bright things.' There was a pause. Chris could, very faintly, hear a rustle of paper that sounded as if Malcolm were turning pages over. 'Bright things . . .' he repeated. 'And specialness.'

Chris hung, astounded, on the other end of the line. 'Malcolm,' she said at last, 'have you taken something?'

'Pardon?'

'Taken something. Drunk anything.'

'No,' he said.

'You haven't been prescribed those antibiotics again,' she asked. 'The ones that made you dehydrated?'

'Antibiotics?' he said, wounded. 'No. What antibiotics?'

'The ones that made you think my face was on upside-down.'

'No.'

'You're sure?'

'Look,' he said. There was a definite and rather desperate riffling of pages now. 'I haven't taken any antibiotics.'

'You've opened that bottle of retsina we bought four years ago, haven't you?'

'I have not drunk any retsina.'

'It won't have kept, Malcolm. It'll have gone off.'

'I have not!'

'Or soft cheese?'

'No.'

'That beer that makes your thumbs go numb?'

'I have not drunk any beer or eaten any cheese,' he said.

She heard him take a very deep breath. 'I have just rung to tell you that you are a very beautiful person.'

There was a long silence before Chris spoke again.

'Malcolm,' she said at last, 'if you won't tell me what you've taken, I can't help.'

And, furious, she hung up.

25

By ten o'clock the following morning, Sally was sitting in the offices of Boundhand Publishing in London. She would have been there at 6 a.m. if necessary, so hot was the letter of authorisation, signed by Alicia Hunscrete, in her briefcase. But then most people were only just getting up and going home at that time in the morning.

'Hot,' she murmured to herself. 'Hot, hot, hot.'

She tried to restrain herself from leaping to her feet and screaming 'Hot!' at the top of her voice. Instead, she gazed at the Boundhand logo – a clenched fist with a page caught in its grasp – that hung over Reception. Reception was manned by a very large girl in a very green jacket, who kept yawning, and whose tones were so upper crust – even when yawning – that they strangled every syllable. It was exactly the kind of voice you needed on a front desk – supercilious and laid-back, as if anyone visiting or phoning was being hopelessly gauche.

Sally would have bet money that half the frightened authors who dared to ring these offices put the phone straight back down as soon as they heard that voice – which was probably the idea. Boundhand was not in the business, after all, of being nice to authors. Boundhand loathed authors, and they loathed books. You didn't have to like something to sell it. Writers liked books, readers liked books, some of the rare and old-fashioned book-sellers liked books, libraries liked books. But publishers did not. They *marketed* them – a subtle difference which most of the writing and reading population failed to understand.

But Sally understood it. She knew that Alicia Hunscrete didn't even have to be a writer, didn't even have to be literate, to sell her autobiography. All she had to have was a pulse and to be married to Charles Hunscrete, liar, adulterer and Cabinet Minister. In fact, it wasn't even essential that Alicia *did* have a pulse. Plenty of books could be sold even if the former Lady Hunscrete were dead. Sally considered this point while she watched the receptionist routinely humiliating the delivery boys. If Alicia Hunscrete died of a documented broken heart or, better still, could be persuaded to commit suicide on the steps of Number Ten . . .

Sally shook herself. She mustn't think like that, tempting as the idea was from a marketing perspective. Instead, she tried to focus on the person who she was waiting to see. Alexandra Francis.

She dug her fingernails into her palm, thinking of what she would do if Alexandra wasn't interested in the book. She could take it to MacMordred Books. She could take it to UpperFollitt. Both of them had done stunning exposés last year. Both of them would kill to get this story.

She thought of the Senior Commissioning Editor at MacMordred, a very tall Oxbridge man whose terminally vague attitude hid a brain as sharp as ice. She thought of Irene Melk at UpperFollitt, an American of such bludgeoning avariciousness that she always made Sally's teeth ache. She had crossed both their paths at newspaper parties, back in the good old days when Sally had been a bright young name and weary old names had wanted to shake her hand, as if her starriness could brush off on them. No one had really wanted to shake her hand once she had got embroiled with Eddie.

Sally gazed upwards now, following the line of the

enormous palm tree that graced Boundhand's foyer. It stretched up through the building, fifty feet high. She remembered reading about it in the *Evening Standard*. On the day that it had been brought here and planted, its lorry had held up the traffic in most of North London. The Managing Director, pictured with it on the steps of Boundhand, had declared that it represented the living and growing heart of Boundhand's empire – an icon, conjuring images of tropical beaches, sex, sand, drink, money and strength.

And coconuts, of course. Great fat coconuts that periodically dropped on some poor agent's head.

Brilliant, Sally thought. *Brilliant*.

And, as she gazed at the little coconuts growing in the palm's fronds, getting ready to fall, she thought of Alexandra. It wasn't that Alexandra Francis was any the less avaricious or icy than Irene or the MacMordred man. If anything, Sally thought, Alexandra was tougher, having deposed several predecessors by back-door stealth. Tough and thick-skinned as . . . well, as coconuts. And that was going to come in very useful.

Alexandra was now on her fourth husband. It gave her an all-round glow of permanent incandescent fury. Standing near her was like standing next to a slow but irreversibly burning fuse. It wasn't that Alexandra didn't suffer fools gladly, it was that she didn't suffer them at all, especially the male variety. In fact, the woman had a nose for fools, was able to detect them from a great height and detonate them, like a smart bomb hitting its target from 20,000 feet.

And so it was really Alexandra that Sally wanted, as only she would be a match for Hunscrete. An outraged and exposed Hunscrete with his back to the wall. She knew how to flatten men.

And make money.

Thinking of money, Sally recalled the email she'd had from her former assistant Ellen that morning.

Don't bother to read Eddie's messages to you, it had said. *He's got creditors in here.*

That hadn't surprised Sally. She already knew that the Accounts exec had resigned soon after her.

Truth or Consequences . . . also in New Mexico, Ellen had typed. *Cheepie, Australia. Billings, Montana. Bye, love.*

In fact, Sally hadn't taken Ellen's advice. Intrigued rather than warned off, she opened Eddie's emails, of which there were three.

Sally, you selfish bitch! Yesterday lunchtime.

Sally, I'm suing you. I've got swellings, my toe is swollen, my feet are hurting. Yesterday, at 6 p.m.

I'll kill you dead. Last night, timed 11.32 p.m.

Sally actually felt sorry for Eddie. Let's hope Alexandra solves *my* money troubles before this morning is out, she thought. And crossed her fingers hard.

Suddenly, as if Alexandra had picked up this message telepathically, the chrome and smoked glass doors of Boundhand opened and Alexandra herself entered, with two assistants following behind. She was talking over her shoulder at one of them, a pasty girl who was taking rapid notes.

'And get him a decent wig,' she was saying. 'Not something his mother knitted, for Christ's sake.' Then she noticed Sally, and stopped. 'Hello darling,' she said. 'I thought you were dead.'

Sally got up, wearing what she hoped was a casual air. She returned Alexandra's air kiss. 'Who told you that?'

'Eddie Massingham.'

Sally shrugged. 'I resigned. That's dead as far as he's concerned.'

Alexandra frowned. 'But no, darling, really,' she

insisted. 'He told me you had been crushed by a freight lift in Liberty's.'

'I am not dead,' Sally said.

'But that explains it,' Alexandra said.

'Explains what?'

'Last week's edition.'

'*The Corker*?' Sally wondered. 'Why? What's he done now?'

'Four pages were blank,' Alexandra said. 'He told everyone they were in mourning for you.'

Sally sighed. 'Alex,' she said, 'I have an exclusive for you. We can stand here talking about Eddie, or I can take it somewhere else.'

Alexandra eyed her shrewdly for a second. 'Come up to my office,' she said, taking Sally's arm.

By three that afternoon, Sally was driving to Fulham.

In the glove compartment, she had a contract with Boundhand. On her face, she had a smile. The car windows were down and the radio on full blast, with Five entreating her to Slam Dunk Da Funk. She had a case of champagne in the boot and a cashmere top from Elspeth Gibson and a pair of sandals from Louis Vuitton and some Issey Miyake perfume that smelled like success. All around her, London was waking up to spring, and the horse chestnut trees unfolding great fists of leaves.

Sunlight dappled her face, and she felt . . . God, she actually felt happy. For the first time since Dermott had left, and she had dumped Eddie, she felt alive. She had value. Alexandra Francis had told her so. Alexandra Francis had written Sally's value in nice round figures on the contract. She was worth a whole chorus of 000s. Lovely big numbers with lots of lovely big 000s on the end.

At the set of traffic lights close to the house she had shared with Dermott, she leaned back in her seat and realised, closing her eyes temporarily to soak up the sun, that there was a chance of having a life. A real life, with good things in it. A life that had nothing to do with either Dermott or Eddie.

She sighed, changing gear as the lights turned green, and steered into the road where she had been living not so long ago, pulling up outside the house behind a tattered VW Golf. Before she could live another life, though, she had to put an end to this one.

She got out, the door keys in her hand.

An *Under Offer* poster was plastered over the For Sale sign. Yesterday evening, the agents had rung her to say that they had buyers.

Now all that remained was to clear the house.

A man was already standing on the doorstep. 'All right?' he asked.

She smiled broadly at him and toyed with the idea of giving the reply that she had always dreamed of giving when people said, 'All right?' It went as follows: 'No, actually, I'm not all right at all. I've got raging cystitis and I'm a part-time psychopath.'

But she didn't. She smiled sweetly and said, 'Yes, I'm all right, thank you,' to the man from the removals firm who had come to give an estimate of moving her stuff to Deadham Markham.

He grinned back at her, a nice fatherly-looking man in his late fifties, holding a plastic folder and pen with an air of importance and purpose.

She unlocked the door and stepped inside the house.

She bent down to pick up the post – a collection of circulars – and put it on the hall table. As she did so, she paused. Something suddenly struck her. Where Dermott's umbrella had used to be – and it was a great awkward thing, a Guinness umbrella that he had once pinched from a hospitality tent – was only a bare space. Her gaze

travelled up the wall. His framed front page of an early
Beano had gone. Ditto his picture of himself with John
Birt. His cartoon of Margaret Thatcher on a sinking ship.

She slowly turned her head.

'Where do you want to start?' the removal man said.

She gestured vaguely to the sitting room.

Walking down the hall in the man's wake, a creeping
feeling of shock began to wash over her. Funny, how she
knew.

She knew even before it spelled itself out to her in black
and white. A piece of the house had vanished, a piece of its
life, a part of its signature. It must be like the feeling, Sally
realised, of having been burgled – that uneasy, creeping
sensation of loss and violation.

But she hadn't been burgled. Not in the usual way.

She glanced into the sitting room. The CD stack was
empty. The CD player had gone. Gaps yawned in the
bookcase and she knew, without looking, that what was
missing was a whole sheaf of Dermott, a little library of
Dermott. And there was a gap in front of the fire, where
Dermott's prize possession ought to be – a prayer rug that
he had bought as a student when he went to Tibet and lost
most of his money and part of his mind on doing the self-
finding thing.

Of course, Dermott had never found himself. But he
had found lots of other people whose weirdnesses and
passions he had absorbed and used, as every good actor
should.

Sally tore her gaze from the empty stretch of floor.
'Excuse me,' she said to the removals man.

She rushed upstairs and into the double bedroom. In the
bright pool of sunlight that poured into the room, the
wardrobe doors all hung open. On Dermott's side was a
rack of empty coat-hangers, even the Mickey Mouse
hanger that she had bought him. Sally touched it briefly,

biting her lip. Turning round, she went to the chest of drawers, and opened it. The first three drawers were completely empty. She went into the bathroom, and saw that every single item of his toiletries had gone, even things that he rarely used, even the old soap tin with a sliver of Aramis in it, even his horrible half-rusted pair of nail clippers.

She stood feeling winded, breathless.

'Mrs Matthews?' called the man downstairs.

Even the disgusting flannel that sat on the side of the bath. Even his talc for his athlete's foot. Even his eyebrow tweezers that didn't work properly. Even the oatmeal and marmalade scrub she had given him for Christmas which he said he hated and had never opened, except to sniff it and pull a face.

She opened the laundry basket. Nothing in it but a sock. She reached down and took it out, slowly. One dirty red sock.

'Mrs Matthews?' the voice said again.

She turned round. The removals man was standing at the door of the bedroom.

'He left a sock,' she whispered.

The man walked hesitantly in.

'A red sock,' she said.

The man nodded.

'He said he wasn't leaving for a month,' she told him. 'And yet he's been here, and . . .'

'Been and gone,' the man said gently. 'Yes.'

Sally gazed at him. 'You see,' she said, 'he's gone to America.' She took a huge, gasping breath, trying to control the thudding in her throat. 'I knew that. I knew he was going to America.' She gave a tight little smile that somehow bent itself out of shape, into a grimace. 'I wish her luck with him,' she continued, 'because she'll need it. She'll never know what he's going to do next, or what time he's coming in, or who he's with, and he makes everybody bloody furious with him, and he—' At last she stopped.

Somewhere outside – outside this house with only one sock left in it, the one thing he had left after scooping everything up wholesale, ransacking the place of himself, ripping himself out of the country, in such a hurry to get away – another bloody bird was cheerfully singing.

She would kill it, that's what she would do.

Sally crumpled the sock in her hand, and held it to her chest. She sank down to the floor.

'Sock,' she said.

And the girl who had never cried throughout fourteen long years in the English boarding-school system, now began to cry again for the second time in two days.

26

Spring had truly sprung in Deadham Markham, a relief after the last three weeks of cloud and rain. And, as if to show that looking grey and godforsaken had only been a joke, the countryside around the village became green and lush, and the dandelions carpeted Virginia's field, and the bull in the farm two miles away could be heard championing the right of bulls to express themselves freely and indulge in a bit of genetic engineering with the cows outside.

Chris was sitting in the woods below Virginia's railway carriage. It was barely nine o'clock, and she sat with her back propped against a tree trunk, watching Virginia take to filming like Archie taking to water.

Virginia stood in the fragmented sun-and-shadow under the trees. Before her was the large pond where Archie lived with his other wives and two enemies. The enemies were squaring up to Archie at this moment, paddling around him and each other, looking masterful. Ducks, Virginia had told her, were the Gestapo of the bird world. Each duck considered himself to be the master of the universe, with qualities that far outweighed those of any other duck, and he would always be prepared to prove this with a bit of bruising, squawking and duffing up.

This morning, Virginia had decided to give the viewers a lesson in duck love.

Chris grinned. Virginia was quite recovered from her nerves. To prove it, she was wearing an orange jacket with

the word *Bovis Construction* on the back, a hideous pair
of leggings, a very large pink sweatshirt, and a butterfly
clip in her hair. Picking Archie up, she held him in a half-
Nelson while she explained his various lusts.

'A drake mallard attracts with ritual preening,' she told
the cameraman – 'You'll see him stop, and then he'll turn
his head and put his beak on his wing, as if to say, "Here,
look at this wing. This is a lovely wing, this is," because he
wants her to look at his speculum. Like, "It's a dead nice
speculum is this, it's a dead good one . . ."' She winked at
the camera.

'There's no such thing as straight sex,' she confided,
'not in the animal world. Look at dungflies. Go mad for a
cowpat. They sit on them to do it, they do. Right on a
cowpat, and then lay their eggs. Male wolf spiders? They
bang their teeth on the ground. Salamanders cover their
females' necks with spit . . .'

There was a movement behind Chris. She turned to see
John Donoghue creeping towards her, trying not to break
any twigs that would be picked up by the sound crew.

'Good morning,' he whispered.

'Morning.'

He squatted down next to her. She noticed an odd,
wary expression on his face. 'Is it true?' he breathed.

'Is what true?'

'That she's related to some MP or other?'

Chris frowned. 'Who told you that?'

'Well, is she?'

'Of course she isn't.'

John looked at her for some time, then shook his head.
'You're lying.'

'I am not.'

'Yes you are,' he hissed. 'I can tell. Your eyes go
together.'

'What do you mean, *together*?'

'Like this,' he said, and he squinted at her defiantly.

'I don't look anything like that,' she said.

'Come on,' he retorted. 'Someone in the catering bus heard you ringing the Houses of Parliament.'

'That wasn't about Virginia,' she lied.

'You're doing it again.'

'I am *not* doing it.'

'Oh,' John said knowingly. 'Maybe it's a secret between you and Owen?'

She turned towards him with a laboured sigh. 'I haven't got any kind of secret deal with Owen,' she said.

To her surprise, he suddenly looked furious. He got to his feet. 'Right, that's it,' he said.

She watched him stamp off through the trees, this time so purposefully breaking twigs that Chris heard a weary, 'Cut!' behind her.

She got up and went after him. 'John!' she called.

He had reached the gate from the woodland into the field, and momentarily leaned on it.

'What's the matter?' she asked, catching up with him.

'I can get bugger-all information out of her,' John said. 'Two days ago you spend half the afternoon with her, come out, and agree with Owen that all communication with her will be through you. Virginia treats me like some sort of sad git who's the only one who doesn't *know* he's got GIT written across his forehead . . .'

'That's not it at all,' Chris said.

With one arm on the gate, he turned to look at her. 'I'm sorry, Chris, but that *is* it,' he said. 'And I can't be expected to work without the full story. I can't get any sort of angle, you're filtering everything I *do* hear, and what's more . . .' He looked at the ground.

'What's more?' she prompted.

'What's more,' he said, looking up, 'I don't feel you appreciate my position.' He ran a hand through his hair, and then slammed his fist down on the top of the gate. 'No, that's not right,' he said. 'It's a damn sight more bloody personal than that. You simply don't like me. Now, I've worked with people who shit on me, and that was all right, because at least we agreed on the same eventual aims . . .'

Chris held up her hand to stop him. 'You've got completely the wrong end of the stick,' she objected. 'I don't dislike you.'

He considered her levelly. 'Well, show me the right end, then,' he said. 'The story of Virginia Pye, which you know, and won't tell me.'

She turned away from him. Up at the top of the field, Owen was talking to an RSPB man. There was much waving of arms, but their voices couldn't be heard. It looked exactly like the male duck-mating ritual in the pond below. Trouble in the making.

'John,' she said, 'have you ever felt that your life was falling apart?' She didn't look at him.

'Regularly,' he said.

'That whatever you do, you just can't stop it?'

She could see the RSPB man shaking his head. Owen was pacing up and down.

'Is it as bad as that?' John asked.

She picked at the splinters of wood on the top of the gate. 'I'm pasting over cracks. Things don't ever get sorted. Things never stay in my hand.'

'What is it that you want to hold on to?' he asked.

She paused. 'Something of my own, something I really want, something I can say I've done where no one else could.'

'You've stayed with Owen for five years,' John joked. 'No one else could do that.'

She smiled. 'Once you accept that you aren't dealing with an adult, it's pretty easy,' she said. 'And . . . you know, he has a certain charm.'

'Oh, Mrs Craven,' John said.

'Recklessness,' Chris said quietly. 'It has something to do with that.'

John leaned his head on one side, assessing her. 'I'm missing some vital bit here,' he said, at last. 'All this has some bearing on why you want Virginia's story to yourself.'

Chris shook her head. 'I want a change,' she said. 'Maybe that's what I want.'

'Recognition?' John guessed.

'Yes – recognition.'

'For smoothing the way?'

'Yes.'

'For being a good wife.'

'*Wife*?' she repeated. 'Who said anything about that?'

'You did.'

'I did not.'

He raised his eyebrows. 'There go the eyes again.'

'But I'm not talking about my marriage.'

'OK.'

'Which is absolutely fine, let me tell you.'

'Great.'

She gazed at him, frowning.

'And is *he* reckless?' he asked.

She didn't reply.

There was a sudden shout from up the field. The display behaviour between Owen and the RSPB man seemed to be over. They had dispensed entirely with ritualised postures, formal tail-wagging and bill-flicking, and had launched themselves straight into pecking each other's heads. Owen seemed to have the RSPB man by the throat. Papers flew up in the air.

'Oh God,' Chris breathed.

John looked closely at her. 'How many publishers has your novel been to?' he asked.

'Nine,' she said, watching Owen out of the corner of her eye.

'And have you ever had anything but a stock reply?'

'No,' she said.

'Can I read it?'

'No,' she said.

'Why not?'

'Because I suspect it's bollocks,' she admitted.

There was a squawk from the RSPB man, who was hopping on one foot.

'*The Day of the Jackal* went to eleven publishers before it was accepted,' John told her.

'I know,' she said. 'I buoy myself up with all those stories. But then so do a lot of other people who write books, who are all writing bollocks like me.'

John laughed. 'You've got all the qualifications for being a writer,' he said. 'Ego the size of West Lothian and confidence only visible under a microscope.'

The RSPB man began chasing Owen towards the trailers.

'I can write,' Chris said, slowly. 'I can tell a good story, John. But I'm somehow not doing it properly.'

'And not getting any help or credit.'

She shrugged.

The door of Owen's trailer slammed shut. Inside, he could be heard calling for help.

'And *that's* what's behind this,' John said, 'isn't it? Like any other normal person, you want credit. Credit for getting Virginia in the first place and credit for getting her story.'

'Well, I . . .'

John turned her towards him, his hands on both her shoulders. 'For God's sake, woman,' he said. 'For Christ's sake, stand up for yourself.'

'I *can* stand up for myself,' she retorted, stung.

'Well, bloody do it, then,' he said. 'This isn't Owen's project and it isn't mine. It's yours.' He saw the answer in her face. '*Now* we're getting somewhere,' he said. 'Is it a good story, this MP connection?'

Chris paused for only a second or two before deciding to spill the beans. 'It's a fantastic story,' she said. 'It's an unbelievable story. Not only is Virginia our own Hannah Hauxwell and Rolf Harris in one package, she's also George Bernard Ransome's daughter and Charles Hunscrete's cousin, and she knows the whole dirt on him. *And* she's got a Salvador Dali in that railway carriage of hers.'

John's eyes widened in disbelief for a second, then he clenched his fists in a gesture of victory. 'Great,' he muttered. 'Great . . . oh bloody marvellous bloody *GREAT*.' He opened the gate, and pushed her through.

'Where are we going?' she asked.

'To see Owen,' he told her. 'We're going to assign one of his daft Sloanes to look after him instead of you, and we're going to tell him that you will be writing the story, and I will be script consultant. We will say that you want screen credit and that you want to be paid accordingly.'

'But that's doing you out of a job,' she protested.

'Is it buggery,' he retorted. 'Change of title, that's all.'

'But . . .'

'Do you want to be given credit, or not?'

She smiled. He grinned back.

He started jogging up the field towards Owen's trailer. 'You'd better start behaving like a proper writer,' he said, over his shoulder. 'In the next thirty seconds, think of what else we can screw out of him.'

27

Two events improved Sally's life the next morning. Not by much, but some.

Her phone was connected. Her sludge was sucked up.

At 9 a.m, she was sitting on the bench in the garden, watching from a decent distance. The sludge man was enthusiasm personified. A relentlessly cheerful bloke, he had obviously found his vocation in life. He had snaked the hose from the sludge gulper tank right down the garden to the cesspit, whistling a strange garbled version of what Sally suspected used to be Vivaldi's *Four Seasons*. When he turned the machine on, a terrible grinding and slurping roar filled the air.

Sludge Man had stood over the cesspit and shouted progress up the garden to her.

'Got a bit of solid stuck,' he cried happily. 'Just shift it with a stick. Righto! Gone up the pipe . . . Blimey! Got a toad stuck. Bloody big toad down here . . . come and look at this bugger . . .!'

Sally had given him a wan smile. To her horror, a couple of minutes later, he had reached in his pocket and taken out a sandwich, and began eating it. Feeling queasy, she got up, and walked back to the house.

As she opened the back door, she heard voices at the front, and Steve appeared with his team in tow.

'Lovely morning,' he said, crossing his arms and leaning against the wall. Justin, the boy who loved horror films, looked over his shoulder.

'Got the slurry out front,' he told her.

'Yes,' she said. 'I know, Justin. I can smell it.'

Justin grinned, and made off down the garden at speed, swinging his spade in anticipation of seeing more solids hit Sally's filter pump, and more toads being shredded in the slime.

'Is there any tea going?' Steve asked.

'I expect so,' Sally said. Yet she stood stock still, smiling at him inanely, while he smiled back.

'I'll see to your patch today,' he told her.

She blinked. 'My what?'

'Your vegetable patch.'

'Oh,' she said, blushing. 'Yes, fine.'

In the kitchen, she had set up flat pieces of hardboard on upturned pallets, to serve as a kind of worktop. In these conditions, tea-making became a prolonged job, an art form worthy of any Japanese ceremony. She had learned to balance cups precariously on the hardboard, watching them sway.

'I hear they've got TV lorries up at Virginia's field,' Steve said. She glanced up to see him leaning on another post, this time the doorframe. She found the words, *You look nice* forming in her mouth and, horrified, stopped herself just in time. She replaced them with, 'Oh yes?'

'Filming Mrs Pye.'

'Oh.' She gazed out of the window.

Steve eyed her with lazy curiosity. 'Ever watch TV?' he asked.

'Not much,' she said.

'Only I see you've not got one,' he observed.

She turned to look at him. 'I used to have one,' she said. 'Believe it or not, I used to have a sink too. I had a table and chairs and I had an espresso machine and carpets and curtains and a husband.' She took the teabags from a box on the floor.

'Well, where are they?' Steve asked.

She set her face into what she knew, without even looking in the mirror, was in danger of becoming an habitual bitter line. 'The TV is on a lorry at the end of the week. The husband is in a Hollywood bed.'

Steve raised his eyebrows. 'Yeah?' he said, interested.

'Yeah.' She handed him a mug of tea.

'Not real Hollywood?'

She nodded wordlessly.

'Have you been married long?' Steve asked.

'No,' she said.

He drank thoughtfully. 'Neither was I,' he said. 'I was seventeen and she went off with my mate.'

'Oh?' Sally said. 'Sounds like some mate.'

'And some wife,' he responded.

'Do you see her?'

'Every week,' he told her. 'She lives down the road.'

Sally looked at him over her cup. 'I don't know what must be worse, seeing them every week, or never seeing them again.'

'Seeing them,' Steve told her quietly. 'With somebody else and somebody else's baby.'

They looked at each other sympathetically. It was in that moment that Sally knew, irrevocably, for ever, that Steve not only looked nice, but *was* nice. He was one of those pitifully rare people without rancour in his soul. And one of the even fewer men who could admit he had feelings. Her heart gave a little somersault of pleasure. She had found goodness in another human spirit. Hooray, she thought. Then, almost immediately, Do not even think of doing anything about it. He's too young.

'Oh – nearly forgot.' Steve said suddenly. 'I've got something for you.'

He put down his cup and went out. She heard him walk up the path, and the creak of the doors of the van. He reappeared a few moments later with a small yew box. Wearing an awkward, sheepish expression, he turned it round, and Sally saw that it was a cabinet.

'It's to go next to your bed,' he said. 'To put the alarm clock on.'

She stared at it. It was very plain and rather beautiful. She reached forward to touch its satin-like surface.

'It's lovely,' she said.

'I didn't pinch it,' he told her. 'I made it.'

'You made this?'

'Graham gave it me,' he said. 'The woodyard. We stacked a whole load of stuff there three weeks ago.'

'You made this for me?' Sally said.

'No,' he said. 'I made it for my mum, but she says it's too small, so I thought it'd go in your room.'

She smiled at his honesty. 'It's worth a bit of money, you know,' she said.

He shrugged. 'Maybe it won't go with your furniture.'

She put her hand on his arm. 'Oh no,' she said. 'It's lovely. Really lovely. I just—'

'I can take it away again.'

'No,' she said. 'Thank you very much. I would like to have it. It's wonderful.'

He put it on the floor between them and, to her surprise, she saw him blushing.

Justin appeared in the doorway. 'Here, Mrs Matthews,' he grinned. 'They're filming up at Mrs Pye's field.'

'Yes,' she said. 'Steve was just telling me.'

'Television,' he said. 'Big vans. Lighting van. Bus. Trailers.'

'You'd better go up there and see if they want any extras,' she said.

Justin's face was at once lit with a 1000-watt spot all by itself. 'You reckon?' he said.

'It's worth a try.'

'But not now,' Steve told him, grabbing his arm.

Sally picked up her car keys and laptop from the wide window sill. 'I have to go out,' she said. 'See you all later.'

'Can we go up Mrs Pye's?' Justin asked.

'It's not up to me,' Sally said. 'I'm not your boss.'

Justin pulled away from Steve. 'I'm going up.'

'You are not,' Steve told him.

'I bloody am.'

'The Reverend's paying your wages.'

'Get better wages up there,' Justin said, and made for the door, kicking over his spade as he went. Steve caught hold of his T-shirt. Sally edged past them, smiling apologetically at Steve. As she got in her car, she could hear Justin protesting that he could be Terminator 7, he could be Rocky 23, he could be on a boat with Kate Winslet, he was taller than Leonardo DiCaprio, he was thinner, he could kiss Julia Roberts better than Hugh Grant, he could show Gwyneth Paltrow a proper man's bits and buy her a frock with sleeves in.

Sally got into her car. As she put it into gear, she wondered who Mrs Pye was.

She pulled out into the lane, reaching for her sunglasses from the glove compartment. Just as she did so, a black shape loomed up out of nowhere, and she was forced to pull the wheel to one side to miss it.

'Bloody hell,' she whispered. The car stalled. She watched a BMW flash past. It circled the village green, its tinted windows giving no clue to the driver within.

Sighing deeply, Sally turned down the Hunscrete road.

Coming the other way from Sally, Chris was driving at speed. Beside her, in the front passenger seat, John Donoghue was reading the history of the Hunscrete family out loud from a sheaf of papers on his lap.

'Maniacs from the dawn of time,' he commented, turning a page.

Chris rounded a bend. The car passed at once from a blaze of mid-morning sunlight to a dark, deep-sided little valley of a road, with high hedges on each side. Suddenly, in front of her, Chris saw a little red car careering on what looked like two wheels straight towards her, and a cow, looking carelessly philosophical, standing right in the centre of the road.

'Jesus,' she muttered, standing on the brakes.

John's notes flew up in the air like a cloud of confetti. Through the pages, Chris saw the little red Renault jolt as it hit the bank of soil. She pulled the wheel to the right. The back of her car swerved gracefully to the left, presenting its rear to the Renault. There was an almighty thump, a shattering of glass, and a deafening blowing of a car horn.

'Are you all right?' she asked John.

'Elbow,' he said. He was nursing his left arm.

'Let me see.'

'I'm all right,' he said.

She released the seat belt, and got out. 'What the hell do you think you're doing!' she shouted at the Renault driver.

A small woman with white-blonde hair got out.

Great, Chris thought. *Just what I don't need – a dumb blonde.* She noticed Sally's designer suit, and immediately tugged self-consciously at the hem of her own skirt, which had escaped from British Home Stores several years ago, and ought to have long ago been put out of its misery by a fashion warden with a large gun.

'What the hell do you think *you're* doing!' shouted the woman.

'You're on my side of the road!' Chris yelled.

The woman gestured back at the cow. 'I've got a beef mountain on my side,' she shouted back. 'What am I meant to do – hit it?' She put her hands to her ears, reached back inside her car, and thumped the wheel a couple of times. When the horn continued, she took off her shoe and attacked the car furiously with the shoe heel. As abruptly as it had started, the blaring stopped.

Chris looked at the headlight of the Renault, now on the road in front of her. She looked back at her own car, sporting a huge dent in the rear wing. 'You could have killed us,' she said, in the new and unsettling silence. 'You must have been doing fifty.'

'I was not doing fifty,' Sally said, bearing down on Chris like a small limping tornado. 'I've only driven a hundred yards from the village, for Christ's sake. *You* were doing fifty. And you've broken the heel of my sodding shoe.'

'How could I be doing fifty?' Chris demanded, blushing slightly at this lie, because she probably had been doing fifty. 'I've just come through two hairpin bends. And you did that to your own shoe.'

'You were looking at your passenger,' Sally accused.

'I was looking at the road!'

'Is the road in his crotch?' Sally yelled.

'I was *not* looking at anyone's crotch.' Chris was puce with embarrassment.

'If you'd look at the road instead of your husband's genitals . . .'

'He isn't my husband.'

'Aha,' Sally said.

Chris clapped her hand to her forehead. 'Why is everyone saying "Aha!" all the time?' she demanded.

'If you'd had your hands on the steering wheel . . .' Sally said. 'Look at my car. Look at it!'

'My hands,' said Chris, 'were at ten to two.' She couldn't believe she had said this. It was what Malcolm always said. He maintained that the correct driving position was with hands at ten to two on the steering wheel, holding the rim firmly but lightly.

'Ten to two?' Sally echoed. 'Who are you, the speaking clock?'

Chris walked stiffly back to her car. John was in the slow process of getting out. Following a manly instinct which had been bred in him without his knowing it, he was coming to Provide Solutions to the Problem. Being a man, he would know exactly how to sort this out.

'Get back in the car,' Chris said.

He got out anyway.

Chris snatched up a piece of paper and John's pen. 'Give me your insurance details,' she told Sally.

'Give me yours,' Sally retorted.

'Ladies, ladies,' John murmured.

'You've damaged my car,' Chris said.

'What's *that*?' Sally demanded.

'It's a piece of paper,' Chris said. 'And this is a pen. The pen writes words on the paper. It's an old-fashioned activity called writing. We use it here on Earth. I don't think they have it in the Laptop nebulae.'

Sally's face froze. 'That,' she said, jabbing the Hunscrete crest, which was photocopied at the top of John's notes. 'That, *there*!'

'Ladies . . .' John said.

'Look,' Chris told her. 'this car's owned by Up-Line Cable. If you want to speak to—'

She saw the little blonde woman stiffen. 'Have you been at Hunscrete House?' Sally demanded.

'Is that anything to do with you?' Chris asked.

'Have you spoken to anyone at Hunscrete House?' Sally cried.

'Ladies . . .' John said.

Both of them turned on him. 'Will you shut the hell up!' they said together.

Chris turned back to Sally. 'There was nobody in,' she said. 'It was a spur-of-the-moment idea, not a bloody conspiracy.'

'Up-Line,' Sally went on. 'That's the grotesque one.'

Chris bridled. 'Give me your insurance details.'

'That's the *Billy Goes Bumming* one,' Sally sneered.

'Look . . .' Chris objected.

'What are you all doing down here?' Sally said. 'You're over this county like a rash.'

'I can't see that it's any of your business,' Chris said.

'It *is* my business,' Sally retorted. 'Lady Hunscrete is my client, and I want to know what you're doing with copies of Hunscrete letterhead.'

'Client?' Chris said. 'What are you, her hairdresser?'

Sally stared at her for ten long seconds. Behind them both, the cow began walking away, as if it had tired of the morning's entertainment and could have a much better time watching some grass grow.

John, groaning softly to himself, sat down on the verge to nurse his elbow.

'I,' Sally said imperiously, 'am Lady Hunscrete's business manager and biographer. Now, for the last time who are *you*?'

Suddenly, there was another screech of brakes behind them. The green van slid to a halt, and Steve and Justin piled out.

Justin came running towards Sally like a demented hen, flapping his arms. 'Mrs Matthews!' he was calling. 'Mrs Matthews!'

Steve jogged over. 'We heard the noise,' he said, as he reached Sally. 'The crash. The horn.'

'Mrs Matthews,' Justin gasped, 'she's on your step. She's sitting on it with her own bottom, on your step and everything.'

Steve turned Sally towards him. He lifted his hand to her face and, delicately, removed a small sliver of glass from her hair.

'My driving mirror,' she said.

He lifted her chin, and looked at her intently. 'Let me see your eyes,' he told her quietly.

'She's smoking a fag!' Justin cried.

'I'm OK,' Sally murmured.

'Got no tights on!' Justin foamed.

'Want to watch your eyes,' Steve said.

'I'm OK, really,' she whispered.

'Probably got no knickers either!' Justin screeched.

Sally, distracted at last, turned towards him. 'What are you talking about?' she said.

Justin clasped his hands to his chest, like a baby who has seen Father Christmas in the flesh. 'No bra,' he whimpered. 'No bra or nothing. Hairy armpits.'

Sally looked at Steve. 'What's he drivelling on about?' she repeated.

Steve smiled. 'Divina Delaney,' he said. 'She just drove up in a BMW, and she's sitting on your back doorstep.'

28

At one o'clock that afternoon, Malcolm was at a funeral. He thought that he had been invited out to lunch, but now that he was sitting in *Les Trois Tiques*, he realised that he had been mistaken.

To Malcolm, lunch meant a comfy chair, a tablecloth, and a couple of courses, of which one had to be a pudding. And by pudding he didn't mean kiwi fruit. He meant suet with a sauce on it. Something that steamed. Sauce or a nice thick yellow custard.

His previous boss, Mike Naylor, who seemed to have vanished into the jaws of Trepantex like Jonah into a whale, and had never been heard of again, had occasionally treated him to lunch. They had used to go round the corner from the office to a pub called the Darnley Arms. The Darnley Arms was regarded with quiet contempt even by those people who never went out to lunch, because it was so seedy, with its mildewed prints of sailing ships on the walls, and cutlery whose silver plating had long ago worn away.

But Malcolm had liked it very much. It served proper steak-and-kidney pie with gravy you could cut, and very wet cabbage that you couldn't, and swede. You never saw swede any more. The word swede wasn't even on the Spellcheck on his computer, for God's sake, as he had found out only last week. And yet he liked swede. He liked turnip and swede and potatoes before his two helpings of steamed pudding, and that was exactly what the Darnley

Arms served, and had served for the last thirty years.

He looked around himself now, at the restaurant where his new boss, the frightening Miranda, and the even more frightening Turk, had brought him.

Turk Brandenbruger sat opposite him now, his expensively-cut hair looking fashionably rumpled above his expensively rumpled linen jacket. Turk had gone for the informal look today, a jacket with an open-necked white shirt, and black jeans. Turk was so slim and toned that you could see his hip bones holding out the expensive seams of his expensive groin.

Turk smiled at him, but Malcolm still hadn't forgiven the bloke for showing him up when they arrived.

When Malcolm had come out, he had brought a coat, his trusty navy mac. Under the mac, Malcolm was wearing his navy wool suit. He had wanted to look his best for what he knew was an important meeting. Besides, it was vital to wear a suit and a mac because you needed somewhere to stow your wallet. Malcolm's wallet was huge, stuffed with receipts and torn bits from magazine articles, and lists, and a photo of Chris, and his cheque cards and credit cards. When they had got to the restaurant, Malcolm had let his mac be taken from him, and then had to make a fuss retrieving it to get his wallet. However the wallet was too big to fit in any of his jacket pockets, so he'd had to stuff it in his trouser pocket.

Turk, who had stood with his hands casually in his own elegant trouser pockets while the pantomime with the coat was going on, had given Malcolm a thoughtful, interested smile, like the smile one might give to a person fighting a terrific disability and being very brave. And then, Turk had ushered Malcolm ahead of him into the mirrored restaurant, and Malcolm had caught a flash of himself in the mirrors. He appeared to be moving like a giant land snail between the tables, trying not to touch anybody,

apologising needlessly, and shambling self-consciously
with a large bulging lump on the left hand side of his
trousers. His jacket caught on the wallet lump and stuck
out at right angles. Whereas, behind him, Turk was gliding
effortlessly along with his slender hips and chic rumpled
outfit.

Miranda brought up the rear, looking like an upside-
down exclamation mark in a black dress, with some sort
of weird black leather skull cap on her head. Words had
failed Malcolm when he had first seen her in the restaurant
reception. She looked like a glamorous executioner. All she
lacked was a bloody great axe.

As Malcolm had been shown to his seat, he looked
about him. Everything was black. The tables, the floor, the
ceiling.

All the women around him wore black. The men wore
either black or neutral, like Turk. Nobody wore a tie.
Except Malcolm, who had on his very orange-and-lime
one. Six months ago, during a rare sortie into Next, the
orange-and-lime tie had been trendy. Now, obviously, it
was not. That particular frisson in the world of fashion
had sputtered out like a dud firework, leaving him holding
the smouldering stub.

A waiter came up. Wearing black. He handed them
small black menus.

Miranda didn't bother to unfold hers. 'I'll have the
oysters,' she said off-handedly.

'Are they good?' Turk asked.

'Yeah,' Miranda said. 'Grilled with goat shank
shavings. Quite fun.'

'Hmmm,' Turk said, running his finger down the page.

Malcolm looked at the items listed, his heart sinking.
He couldn't possibly eat any of it, he realised. Onion tart.
Pumpkin risotto. Chicken liver parfait. Ostrich heart
brioche. Raw mollusc. His stomach rose and fell gently

under his suit. Brained mullet. Haddock bladderwrack in Stilton. Spinached udders. Sautéed aorta. Cabbage-wrapped oesophagus.

'See anything you like?' Turk murmured.

I like where it says FIRE EXIT over that door, Malcolm thought.

'I might have the soup,' he said.

'Yeah,' Miranda said. 'Cool. Squid in its own ink.'

'Or the lamb,' Malcolm said quickly.

The waiter came back. Turk ordered.

'So, Malcolm,' he said, leaning back, and draping one hand over the back of Miranda's chair. 'How are we doing, as employers?'

Malcolm began to sweat ever so slightly under the navy wool. What could he say? He could tell them the truth. He could say that he had never known his staff – what was left of them – to be so miserable. He could say that Trepantex was never going to be an academic organisation, or even a medical one, as it claimed. He could say that he longed to be in the Darnley Arms.

He opted for safety. 'It's been interesting,' he said.

'Really?' Turk echoed. 'You find it interesting?'

There was a little current in the conversational water, Malcolm realised. A kind of undertow.

'Challenging,' he added.

Turk looked at Miranda with some significance. 'Well,' he said. 'We find *you* challenging, Malcolm.'

The drinks arrived.

There was a terrible moment while the waiter stood the Perrier bottle between Miranda and Turk, and handed Malcolm a half of bitter.

'Do you follow the company's fortunes, Malcolm?' Turk asked.

Malcolm swallowed his drink as rapidly as he could. 'You mean the Stock Exchange?' he asked.

'That, and the media coverage.'

'Yes,' Malcolm said.

'And what do you think?'

'Think?'

'Of our public image.'

Malcolm's toes curled. Buoyed up, this time, by a few molecules of alcohol, he ventured the truth. 'You're having a bad press,' he said.

There was a short silence, during which the food arrived.

As the waiter withdrew, Turk nodded. 'We *are* having a very bad press,' he said.

They started to eat.

Malcolm had never seen anything remotely like the concoction on his plate. Whenever he had eaten lamb before, it was in slices with a bit of mint sauce on the side. But this lamb wasn't lying flat at all. It was a ball. A grey ball with veins of fat running through it, lying in a pool of water.

He tried to cut it. It seemed that some inspired chef had gathered up the offcuts from the floor of a tyre factory and compressed them into something the size of a billiard ball. He cut off a small piece and put it in his mouth. After a couple of chews, he swallowed it. The *agneau au Dunlop* slid only grudgingly down his throat.

Turk sat back after a couple of mouthfuls of his salmon fin salad.

He fixed Malcolm with an unwavering stare.

'Malcolm,' he said. 'You're married, aren't you?'

'Yes,' Malcolm said.

'To . . .' Turk looked at Miranda.

'Christine,' Miranda said.

'Christine,' Turk repeated. He nodded slowly. 'Malcolm,' he said, 'tell me about your wife.'

'Well,' Malcolm began, 'she works . . .' He was going to

say that Christine worked for a television company. Then he remembered the TV news a couple of nights ago, which had featured a field in Norfolk where Trepantex were trying to grow genetically modified broad beans. The field had been surrounded by banner-waving women wearing masks and tunics with a skull and crossbones painted on them. A good three minutes had been given over to several spokespeople from several environmentally-superGreen organisations who had condemned Trepantex as a bunch of abhorrent mutants.

Better not say that Chris worked in television.

'She's an assistant to a . . . managing director,' he said.

'Responsible job,' Turk commented.

'Yes. She's always very busy.'

'And how long have you been married?'

'Six years.'

'Six years,' Turk echoed. 'What a support to you she must be.'

Malcolm didn't answer. He sat looking down at his Dunlop billiard ball.

He had sent Chris flowers yesterday. To be perfectly honest, he hadn't wanted to do so. Flowers were expensive things, especially when you had them delivered. But whenever he had talked to Chris over the last few days, she had sounded weary and distant, and he had thought that she would like him to make some sort of appreciative gesture, so he had sent a bouquet to the house at Prystock. It had been ten-thirty at night before Chris had rung him.

'I'm sorry it's so late,' she said. 'I've been putting your father to bed.'

'Did you get the flowers?' he asked.

'Yes,' she said. 'What on earth did you send those for?'

At once, he felt aggrieved. He wanted her to gush out her thanks. Maybe cry a bit with gratitude. Women were

supposed to be overwhelmed by bouquets. That was the
only reason to send them in the first place.

'As a treat,' he told her.

'Oh,' she said.

He had frowned, deeply irritated. 'Didn't you like
them?'

There was a pause. On the other end, Chris was
struggling with the truth, which was that as soon as she
had got home, Emily Villiers had met her at the door, her
face darkened with disapproval, and told Chris that *the
flowers* had been removed to the back step, because the
pollen had irritated her father-in-law's mucus membrane.
It was very nice indeed to see flowers, she said frostily, but
really it was a little thoughtless to send lilies, for their
pollen fell everywhere and stained the carpets as well as
endangering Henry's recovery.

There was another reason for Chris's hesitation, too. It
was that she didn't like lilies. She had often said this to
Malcolm but, as usual, everything she said seemed to go
straight over his head. Or perhaps through it. She
suspected that, whenever she spoke, a small switch auto-
matically clicked in Malcolm's brain and turned off his
hearing. Like many husbands who have listened to their
wives – or, rather, been in the same room as their wives
when they were speaking – Malcolm did not actually
register most of what Chris was saying. There was no
need. In one form or another, he had heard it all before,
and besides, if it was very important, Chris would eventually scream and start to beat her head against the nearest
wall, and the little switch would flick back on in
Malcolm's head, like emergency lighting in a power cut.

Chris had swallowed down her own irritation at being
sent lilies she didn't want. She would have swapped every
flower that Malcolm had sent her for one hour of his real
attention.

'They're lovely,' she had lied into the phone. 'Thank you very much.'

Malcolm looked up at Turk now. He wondered if Turk was married, and what his wife was like. He glanced at Turk's hand, which was now gently stroking the small of Miranda's back.

'Yes, she's very supportive,' he murmured.

Turk seemed to suddenly move up a gear. He straightened a little in his seat, and leaned over the table towards Malcolm.

'That's great to hear,' he said, 'because a situation is coming up where strong partnerships pay dividends.'

Malcolm was well aware, now, of feeling very hot indeed in his suit. The rubber ball sat like a stone just below his diaphragm.

'Oh?' he asked. 'Why?'

Turk grinned. Miranda smiled.

'How'd you like to live in America?' Turk said.

'America?' Malcolm echoed.

'Los Angeles, in fact,' Turk went on. 'With the movie stars.'

Malcolm's rubber ball seemed to be interrupting his breathing. 'Los Angeles?' he said, bemused.

Turk nodded. 'There's an opening in that research facility,' he said. 'For your innovative programme.'

'My maggots?' Malcolm said.

'Starting next month.'

Malcolm stared at Turk. Then he stared at Miranda. 'But I can't possibly live in America,' he said.

Turk looked as if he'd been slapped. 'This is a great opportunity,' he told him.

'It's not that I don't want to take it,' Malcolm said. 'I can't.'

'Can't?' Turk was amazed. This was not a word in the Trepantex vocabulary.

'My father has just had a stroke,' Malcolm explained. 'Then there's Chris's job to consider.'

'But you just said how supportive your wife is,' Turk reminded him.

'She is, but—'

'Bring her to America.'

'But my father is ill.'

Turk gave Miranda her cue.

'Malcolm,' she said, 'we're closing research in the UK.'

He looked slowly from one to the other. 'But you said you'd be funding an expansion.'

'We are,' Turk said airily. 'In the States.'

'You said you were funding it *here*.'

Turk shrugged. 'We've had a reassessment since then,' he told him.

Malcolm now felt very hot indeed. He had a pain where the Dunlop ball had settled. His heart began to race.

'But you can't do that,' he protested. 'My work funds itself. Look at the figures. We recoup from hospitals and clinics . . .'

Turk shook his head. 'It's very small-scale.'

'But it's the future,' Malcolm insisted. 'Don't you know how resistant strains are becoming to antibiotics? Don't you know how virulent these viruses are? Have you ever seen a wound that won't heal?'

Turk looked pained at the raised voice. He signalled the waiter.

'Just a minute,' Malcolm said. 'This is pioneering stuff. Don't you get it? Don't you understand what you've got here? This is what Trepantex ought to be getting involved in!'

Turk signed the bill with a flourish. 'We will be getting involved in it, in Los Angeles,' he murmured softly.

A red mist seemed to gather behind Malcolm's eyes. He couldn't recall ever feeling this angry before. It had taken him years to produce what was ground-breaking medicine. As the world became more hooked on drugs, older methods would be reverted to. His project could not fail. Already his humble little maggots had saved lives. They had feasted on necrotising fascicitis, for instance, and stopped it stone dead in several patients. A disease that could not be halted even by penicillin.

'We need this work in this country,' Malcolm said. 'And don't tell me that you'll nurture it in the USA because you won't. You'll uproot me and uproot my family, and six months after I get there, you'll stop the funding. Don't think I can't see which way the wind is blowing.'

Several people in the restaurant had now turned to look at them.

'Malcolm,' said Miranda, 'keep your voice down.'

He stared at her. 'You knew about this,' he said. 'You knew about it weeks ago.'

He saw it written plainly in their faces. Trepantex had never intended to continue with his programme. Cutting his staff and computer time and academic contacts had been designed to squeeze him out. But he hadn't realised. He hadn't noticed. He hadn't believed anyone could lie to him so efficiently. Not when they brought in balloons and caterers.

'You pair of bastards,' he said.

Turk rose to his feet. He looked at Malcolm for two or three steady seconds, then turned on his heel, and left.

Miranda hesitated only a moment. 'That is what one would call burning one's boats, Malcolm,' she said.

Malcolm stood there in the black cavern, shaking. 'You had a welcome party,' he whispered, feeling pathetic. 'Banners. Champagne.'

Miranda smiled. 'We always have a welcome thrash,' she said. 'When we take over.'

Malcolm, finally, saw the truth. Chris had been right.

The party had not been a celebration at all. It had not been a wedding, nor a coming-of-age with a new parent. It had not been a gathering of friends, a christening of a new corporate baby. No, it hadn't been anything nice like that.

It had been a wake.

'Eat, drink and be merry,' he said. 'For tomorrow, you die. Is that right?'

Miranda had the grace, at least, to colour a little. Then she picked up her black bag and went after Turk.

Malcolm sat down again with a thump.

No one approached him.

No one looked at him.

For some time – he didn't know, afterwards, quite how long – he sat thinking about the tanks in the laboratory, feeling grief-stricken for their occupants, as if they were friends who had suddenly been made homeless.

Then he understood one more salient and devastating fact.

He understood that all those larvae in their mute and sterile containers *were* his friends. He thought about them far more than he thought about any living human being, even Chris.

Even Chris.

He put his head in his hands, thinking that he had, after all, been right.

Miranda *had* been an executioner.

It *had* been a funeral.

His.

29

At about the same time that Malcolm was staring down the twin barrels of corporate brutality, Chris had been hoping for a slightly more pleasant lunch with Owen Majolica. A five-star hotel would have done. Or a small manor house with a Michelin restaurant attached. Or anything, basically, that didn't serve food in a basket with a sachet of salad cream.

She had fancied herself sitting under a tree in a garden at a table spread with white linen, while the waiter discreetly uncorked a chilled bottle. She had counted on not being back from lunch for a long time. Preferably never. Perhaps the manor house would have rooms. A country restaurant with rooms. Big rooms with a big soft bed, rose petals scattered on the sheets that were soon crushed under their writhing bodies. And the dark-haired man would . . . she stopped her dream short. She had suddenly realised that the man in the dream was John.

'Shove up,' Owen said.

He plonked the half of lager on the pub table and she squeezed further into a corner, where the tacky wall promptly stuck to the arm of her sweater. She didn't like to touch the table itself. Something had died there, by the look of the stains.

'Do you come here often?' she asked Owen.

'Never been here before,' Owen said. 'Had to be out of the way.'

It was out of the way all right. It was so out of the way

that probably even the locals didn't know it was there. A back-street bar near a railway siding.

She looked at the food that Owen had brought. Scampi and chips in a basket with a sachet of salad cream with the lovely motto *Best Before October 1999*.

They stared at their respective meals for a moment, mesmerised by its awfulness.

'I'll take it back,' Owen said.

'Forget it.'

'Look,' he said, lowering his voice, 'I'll take you some-where good when this is all over. But this had to be secret. Top secret.'

'When what's all over?' she said.

He looked at her. He sighed once or twice, then bit his lip.

'Well, *what*?'

'Chris,' he said, 'how long have you worked for me?'

'Four years,' she said. 'Four interminable years.'

He smiled. Then looked down, and fiddled with the edge of the damp and tattered beer mat.

'Owen,' she said. 'Just say it, whatever it is.'

'I don't know where to begin.'

She picked up a chip, then put it down. 'If you don't hurry up, I shall be forced to eat this meal – and then you'll have a hell of a bill to pay at the Hospital for Tropical Diseases.'

He looked uncomfortable. Very uncomfortable. She was struck with an unpleasant idea. 'If you're going to fire me, make it quick,' she said.

His head shot up. He stared at her. 'I'm not going to fire you,' he said.

'Good,' she said. 'Are you going to propose to me?'

The colour drained from his face.

'OK,' she said. 'Just a wild card, that one.'

'Chris,' he said. 'I'm leaving Dad.'

'What?'

'Leaving the organisation. Up-Line. Majolica Industries. He's coming here tonight on his way to Brussels. I'm going to tell him then.'

'My God,' she said. 'Are you allowed to do that – just leave?'

'He can't stop me,' he said.

'Leaving the directorship of the company, resigning?'

'Yes.'

'But I thought you were Crown Prince, Owen,' she said. 'Destined for the throne. He who would be King.'

'I am,' he said.

She knew that Owen was an only child. His father had no one else to inherit from him. Owen had been groomed for greatness since the womb. 'He'll come after you with a Sherman tank,' she murmured. 'He'll gun you down before you get to the perimeter fence.'

'He can try,' Owen said, a note of steel in his voice.

She regarded him for some moments. 'You're really serious about this, aren't you?'

'Yes.'

'You must be pissed off with him,' she said. 'Is it that?'

'Not any more so than usual.'

'Then what?' she asked. 'I mean – why now? I thought you enjoyed it all – Up-Line . . . everything.'

He looked her straight in the eye. 'Do *you*?' he asked.

'Yes,' she said.

'Be honest.'

'I do enjoy it,' she pointed out, 'compared to the Inland Revenue.'

He nodded. 'At least you've had that,' he said. 'Something to compare it with. I've been force-fed the family firm since I could stomach solids.'

'And now you can't stomach it at all,' she said.

He frowned, leaning his elbows on the table, and

putting his head in his hands. 'I've got to get out from under his thumb,' he said. 'Ringing me up all hours of the bloody day and night. I've got to go where he can't get to me.'

'Is there such a place?' Chris asked, thinking of Majolica's media arms, which were knotted across the globe in a death grip. She doubted that you could even crawl under a stone in Outer Mongolia without some beetle or other catching sight of you, and promptly telling Jefferson Majolica through the Beetle Informer Internet.

'Yes,' Owen said. 'I know a place.'

A small but very bright light suddenly flashed on in Chris's mind. 'A boat,' she said. 'Madeleine.'

It was interesting to see just how much horror could be contained in one man's expression. 'You know,' Owen breathed.

'Just a guess.'

He grabbed her wrist. '*How* do you know?' he demanded.

'Repeating her name every five minutes is a bit of a give-away,' she replied.

'Don't tell him,' he said, looking terrified.

'Let go of my arm, Owen.'

'Promise me you won't tell him.'

'Tell him what?' she muttered. 'I don't know which boat, where boat or how boat. It was just a wild guess. A *guess*, Owen. Now let go of my arm.'

'Promise.'

'I promise!'

He dropped her arm, which she rapidly massaged.

'I'm sorry,' he said. 'But I'll go crazy if I don't get out.'

She shook her head. 'You always seemed to be enjoying it.'

'Bored,' he said. 'I'm bored rigid, Chris.'

She thought of the toys on his desk, the Oxford blue

above it. 'Yes,' she murmured. 'I could probably see that, but Jesus, Owen. Good luck.'

He leaned forward. 'Chris,' he said. 'I'm setting up another company. A little one. Not here – abroad.'

'Doing what?' she asked, aware of disappointment lurking in the pit of her stomach, and growing. She would miss him, she realised. She liked him very much.

'Marine archaeology.'

She stared at him. A reply of deep lunacy came to her lips. 'In water?' she said.

He grinned. 'In the Caribbean.'

'In a boat?' She pinched herself under the table, hard, on her thigh. *Stop being a fool.* 'This is the boat you were talking about?'

'My own boat, my own business,' he said. 'Spanish Rex, I'm going to call the new company.'

'Ah,' she said. 'Catchy.'

A smile of enormous satisfaction lit up his face. 'We've got this rig, there's a fucking great sonar on it, there's a fishing seat like on *Jaws* and there's a mini-sub—'

'Owen,' she said. This time it was she who laid her hand, rather more softly, on his. 'What about Up-Line? What about Virginia Pye? You told John and me yesterday to go ahead. The Hunscrete connection. Everything.'

'Yeah, go ahead,' he said airily. 'Fine.'

'But it's not as easy as that,' she objected. 'With you gone, your father will send in some team or other. A new face, head of company. He'll be steaming mad with everyone. What's to say he won't carve it up?'

'He won't do that,' he said.

'He will.'

'Not with you running it already,' he said.

The room tipped dramatically on its side for a second, then rotated gently, like a giant carousel coming to rest.

'Say again,' she murmured.

'You running it.'

'Me running Up-Line.'

'You do already.'

'I do not.'

'You set most things up already. You've got experience. You get on with everybody. You've got an economics degree.'

'Oh Jesus, Owen,' she said. 'A 2:1 from Sussex University doesn't qualify me to run a national company, for Chrissake.'

'It's more qualifications than I've got.'

'But . . .'

'It's only a little company.'

'But . . .'

'It's a breeze.'

'I can't do it, Owen,' she said. 'I don't know how. And your father will hate me. He'll blame me.'

'You don't have to do anything,' Owen said. 'Other people do it for you. You just sit in the top office and look at the view.'

She fixed him with a withering look. 'Owen,' she said, 'I hate to disillusion you, but running a company takes a bit more than that.'

He returned her gaze with a level, almost stony, expression, that she had never seen before. 'And I hate to disillusion *you*,' he said, 'but that's exactly what a piss-little company like Up-Line does, that exists in some bastard conglomerate's pocket.'

There was an uneasy silence.

'If it's such a piss-little company,' Chris said, 'your father could close it overnight, and I'd be out of a job.'

Owen shrugged. 'He won't close anything that makes a profit, and we make a big profit.' Again he took up her hand, and squeezed it. 'If he ever does that, Chris, I promise you I'll give you a job with Spanish Rex. You can come and make the margaritas every day.'

'Thanks,' she said.

'I mean it,' he told her. 'Every business needs a business head, and I haven't got one, so it might as well be you.'

'Thanks,' she repeated.

He smiled again.

'Owen,' she said. 'I don't want to run a company.'

'There'll be big money in it.'

'It's not what I want,' she said.

Afterwards, thinking about it, she couldn't quite believe that she had said it. No one in their right mind turned down what was probably a six-figure salary, but it was as if some little voice, the voice of sub-conscious desire, suddenly leapt out of her mouth. 'I want to write,' she said.

Owen looked perplexed. 'Like you described yesterday?' he said.

'Yes,' she said.

'With this John Donoghue?'

'With whoever. Or, preferably, on my own.' She knotted her fingers in her lap, amazed by her own suddenly expressed ambition. 'I don't want to sit in an office,' she said. 'I don't want to be secure.'

Owen grinned. 'Sounds very foolish,' he observed.

'Yes,' she said.

'Stepping off the high ledge without a parachute.'

'Yes,' she said.

'Or casting off in a little boat,' he said.

She smiled. 'Yes. Tell me about your little boat.'

Animation came to his features. 'She's a twenty-two-foot sloop called *Madeleine*,' he said.

'Nice name,' she said. 'How did I know that, I wonder?'

To her surprise, he began to blush. 'Well, that's the other thing,' he muttered.

'There's something else? Something besides leaving your father and dropping me straight in it?' she asked.

'There's this girl.'

Suddenly, the far-flung pieces of a rather large jigsaw dropped into place. 'Ah,' Chris said. 'Another Madeleine, maybe?'

'Yes.'

'Does she work for Up-Line?'

'No,' he said, looking horrified. 'No, she's an historian. I met her at the Schuylkill Navy Regatta over in Philadelphia last June. She rows.'

'Like you?'

'Better,' he said, with more than a trace of pride.

'And you and Madeleine . . .'

'We're going to the Caribbean together. The end of this week.'

Seeing the delight in his face melted her heart. She leaned over and kissed him on the cheek. 'I'm happy for you,' she told him, with sincerity. 'Really happy.'

'Thanks,' he said. His face was a deep shade of puce, with a schoolboy's embarrassment and pleasure.

Chris looked at him with renewed interest. She had always thought of Own as such a chip off his father's block. Someone who couldn't go to the bathroom without Dad's permission. But perhaps she had been more right than she knew when she described him to John as having a streak of recklessness. Although, when she had said that, she had been thinking much more of a plastic dog being sick on a conference table than Owen standing on the prow of a seagoing vessel shouting, 'Ship ahoy!'

'Owen,' she said, 'have you really thought this out? Have you got enough money, and all that? You can't run Spanish Rex on thin air. Your Dad will probably cut off your air supply when he hears about this, you know, never mind your money supply.'

He winked at her. 'My mother left me eight million,' he said.

'OK,' she replied. 'Just checking.'

He stood up, and dusted himself down. Together, they went out into the pale sunshine of the afternoon.

They stood on the bleak little street, looking down the nearby rail track, to a siding filled with ancient rolling stock.

'Will you come and meet Dad tonight?' he asked.

She looked at him. 'Must I?'

'Would you? Please?'

'Is there going to be much blood?' she asked.

'Yeah.'

'Mine, or just yours?'

He smiled. 'Don't say anything about Madeleine, Chris. He doesn't like her.'

'Doesn't he?' she said. 'Why not?'

He shrugged, scuffing an invisible piece of dirt on the pavement with the tip of his shoe. 'He's got this project,' he muttered. 'Wants me to marry some corporate heiress.'

'Anyone in particular?'

'Don't think so,' he said. 'Just a small merger of dynasties. That sort of thing.'

'And has Madeleine got any money?'

'Not a tin cent.'

'And this is what your father wouldn't like?' she asked.

He turned to her, frowning. 'She isn't after *my* money.'

'I didn't say she was.'

'She's a marine historian,' he said hotly. 'She's got a doctorate.'

'OK,' Chris said, holding up her hand. 'OK.'

He began to walk. She followed him.

At the end of the street, waiting to cross, she said, 'There's a problem with the Hunscretes, you know. Someone else is working on a biography. They want to be first to spill the beans on Sir Charles.'

'Someone?' Owen echoed. 'Who?'

She considered, for a moment, telling him about her short but vivid conversation with Sally Matthews. Telling him that she had never met a woman whose spikiness so closely resembled a giant cactus, and with whom it would probably prove impossible to negotiate.

Then she saw that familiar distant look in Owen's eyes. A look that she now knew had the name *Madeleine* stamped through it like a stick of seaside rock.

She took his arm as they crossed over towards the car park.

'Never mind,' she said. 'Leave it to me.'

30

Sally stood across the room from Divina, watching the other woman as she finished, and ground out, the most recent of her cigarettes.

When she was sure that the butt was firmly extinguished on Sally's kitchen floor, she looked up with a smile. 'Nice place,' she commented.

'It was, until you arrived,' Sally said.

'Minimalist, yeah?'

Sally ground her teeth. She hadn't done that since her maths GCSE.

Christ, to think that something as plastic as Divina Delaney could put all those porcelain crowns at risk. To think that Divina Delaney could revert her to Year 11, when the girl who sat in front of her in class – Chloe Blandford – had actually understood quadratic equations, as well as being a natural blonde. Sally had used to fixate so hard on Chloe's roots that she had started to unconsciously bear down on her back molars, and, after the exam, her jaw had seized up entirely. She could feel it happening again now. God damn her, this woman wasn't going to give her face cramps like bloody Chloe Blandford.

'Why don't you fuck off,' she heard herself saying.

Divina didn't move. 'Is this your famous British courtesy?' she asked.

'No,' Sally retorted. 'This is our famous British fucking rudeness and hostility, so fucking well fuck off. If you don't mind.'

Divina did nothing. Not even her eyelids flickered.

Sally turned away, leaning against the wall, her fist clenched. 'Look,' she said, without turning round, 'I just can't do this. I can't be witty. I can't even be civil to you. So if you've come here to gloat, or to try and mend fences, or be very cool and charming, please just go. Because I can't be any of those things, I can't even make much sense. So just go.'

In the silence of the room, she could hear the slow music of the garden, the whispering hush of the trees in the breeze, the water of the stream in the meadow, the bloody blackbirds being heartbreakingly beautiful.

A lump came to her throat. Oh Lord God, if You're really there, if there is any justice at all, she prayed, do not let me cry in front of this woman. I'll do whatever You want, OK? I'll put money in the Christian Aid packets. I'll go to church. I'll go on the days when no one goes, on weekday mornings in Lent or something. Please, *please* . . .

'Is he here?' Divina asked in a small voice.

It was such a small voice that Sally opened her eyes and looked around at her rival.

Divina was standing in a pool of sunlight, looking horribly photogenic, and very vulnerable.

'What?' Sally said.

'Where is he?'

'Who?'

'Dermott.'

Sally stared at her. 'He's in bloody California, where you are. Were. Should be.'

'He isn't,' Divina said.

Sally frowned at her, totally confused. 'Well, wherever they're filming this film.'

'He isn't there, either,' Divina said. 'I was just there.'

'What, Canada?'

'Yes. Last night.'

Sally shook her head. 'Well, what do you expect me to do?' she said. 'Find him for you?'

For a long time, Divina stared at Sally. Her eyes ranged sadly over Dermott's wife, as if the answer to his disappearance were written somewhere on Sally's body. Then, to Sally's utter amazement, Divina crumpled. She slid down the wall and folded in a heap on the floor, weeping.

Sally's mouth dropped open. Her immediate reaction was to run over and try to help her. But this thought was rapidly overtaken by a less noble one, which was that Divina was now in an ideal position to be kicked mercilessly to a pulp. Horrified at herself, Sally held back.

'I have to find him,' Divina sobbed.

'But I haven't seen him in over a week,' Sally said. 'When he went to America to see *you*.'

'I haven't seen him for three weeks,' Divina said. 'He didn't come. He said he would, he promised he would. But he never turned up.'

'But . . .' Sally's voice trailed away. Maybe Dermott had had some kind of accident. Maybe he had been hospitalised, and was too disfigured to be identified. Maybe he was dead. No – that would be too much to hope for. 'What makes you think he'd come here?' Sally said sternly.

'He told me he loved you,' Divina said.

The two women gazed at each other.

'When was this?' Sally demanded.

'On the phone. Last Tuesday.'

'But he *left* me last Tuesday!'

'I went to the London house,' Divina said, 'as soon as my flight got in this morning. There were men there, packing things. They gave me this address.'

'But . . .' Sally tried to get her head round what the other woman was saying, 'he cleared his stuff out, sometime between last Tuesday and now. Where's it all gone?'

'He told me he wanted another chance to make it up

with you.' Divina took a packet of tissues from her handbag.

'He told *me* to jump off the edge of the world without a parachute,' Sally retorted. 'All he left was a sock.'

The actress started to cry again. 'He left me mmmugmmnt,' she sobbed, into a balled wad of tissues.

'He left you what?' Sally said.

'Pregnant,' Divina said. 'I'm going to have a baby.'

Sally did the only thing any sane woman should do in a similar crisis. She opened one of the bottles of champagne.

Handing it to Divina, sitting cross-legged in the ruin of the kitchen, on the floor, she apologised.

'Not much of a celebration,' she said, 'but it's all I've got.'

'That's OK,' Divina said. 'It's all I ever drink.'

'Of course it is,' Sally replied. 'How stupid of me.'

They both looked down at the pockmarked lino.

'He didn't tell me he was married, you know,' Divina said. 'Not for a long time.'

Sally took a swallow of her drink.

'He was so funny,' Divina said. 'He treated me like a human being.'

'That's not exactly a big deal,' Sally pointed out. 'You *are* a human being. Just.' She still felt angry with Divina – and with Dermott.

'It's a big deal where I come from.'

'And where's that – Planet Silicone?'

Divina shook her head. 'You don't know what it's like. I've been treated like a piece of meat all my life – a performing seal. A meal ticket. A piece of arm kitsch.'

'You made millions of dollars being arm kitsch,' Sally said.

Divina eyed her, a dangerous spark in her glance. 'I earned millions of dollars *acting*,' she said. 'Millions of dollars I deserved for fighting my way up there.'

'Oh yeah,' Sally said. 'I read about that. How you fought for your art on your back.'

Divina put down her glass. 'You've never been on your back, for a job?' she asked.

'Certainly not.'

'For a roof over your head?'

'No.'

'To eat?'

Sally looked at her sceptically.

'Congratulations,' Divina said.

Sally shook her head. 'Don't give me that starving artists crap,' she retorted. 'Your family were WASP. You lived in Boston.'

'Yeah, I read that press release, too,' Divina said. She picked at a hole in the lino pattern. 'But my parents split up.'

'Or the child wounded by divorce crap, either,' Sally said harshly.

Divina raised her head and looked at Sally levelly. 'I wasn't wounded by divorce,' she said. 'I was glad to get out of that house, and so was my mother.'

'Glad to live off a considerable income from your father, I suppose.'

'Actually, no. My father paid a very poor allowance, a cheap fucking settlement, if you must know.'

'Oh? And why was that?' Sally said. 'I thought every wife in California had rights to keep her claws in her husband's cash until the day he died. And for several centuries afterwards.'

'My parents didn't live in California,' Divina said. 'My mother moved there to be near the man she really loved, George Bernard Ransome.'

'How sweet,' Sally said unconvincingly.

Divina looked as if she were having trouble keeping her

temper. 'It wasn't sweet,' she said finally. 'George Ransome – my *real* father, incidentally – was a very big name with a very small heart. He had a string of other women, and he didn't care much for either Mom or me. And I suppose you already know what a megalomaniac he was.'

Sally sighed. 'I'm sorry,' she said, relenting.

Divina got up from the floor. She leaned on the window sill and stared out into the garden. Sally poured herself another drink from the bottle.

'I'll lose six million if I don't start this film next month,' Divina said, at last. 'Not to mention the legal bills.'

'So do it,' Sally told her.

'I can't do it four months' pregnant.'

Sally shrugged. 'You must have solved that problem before.'

There was a long silence. Sally finally looked away from Divina's penetrating stare. 'I'm sorry,' she said. 'Really sorry this time. That wasn't very nice.'

'But you're right,' Divina said. 'I have been in this position before, and I have done something about it – and that's why I'm not going to do anything about it now. I'm going to have this child.'

Sally bit her lip.

'Go on,' Divina said wearily. 'Condemn me. Here's your chance. You have a right.'

'I can't condemn you,' Sally said. 'I've never had to face that.' She paused, looking at the wall through the distorted lens of the glass. 'I've never taken precautions, either,' she murmured. 'So the odds are, I'll never be in your position.'

Divina frowned at her. 'Meaning what? I don't get you.'

'I haven't seen a doctor about it,' Sally said softly, 'but I'm fairly sure I can't conceive.' She looked up, the expression on her face momentarily unreadable. 'Funny, isn't it?' she said. 'Here's you pregnant. And here's me, probably never will be.'

Divina came to kneel beside her. '*Is* it funny?' she asked.

'No,' Sally whispered.

'Did you tell Dermott?'

'No. I thought I'd wait, hope it wasn't so – see someone if I eventually had to.'

'But you never told him, even with all this talk of his having six sons.'

'He said that to you, too?' Sally said. 'Oh, the shit. The shit.'

And, despite her pleas to God, or perhaps because of them, God decided that Sally ought to cry in front of her own worst enemy. She tried hard not to, even then. She put her hand to her throat as if she could choke off the pain gathering there. Then she thought of Dermott in the *Tess of the D'Urbervilles* field with the squashed Panama hat on his head. And she thought of him falling into a pit of sand. And she thought of him quoting poetry, which she could not stand, even when she was fifteen.

And she found herself wrapped in Divina's embrace, sobbing.

'You know,' the actress said, 'I think maybe he really meant it, every time he said it. Having a family, being a stay-home Dad. All that scene.'

'I'm sure he did,' Sally wept. 'Pity that resolve didn't last a bit longer than the post-coital cigarette.'

Divina nodded slowly. In the silence of the room, the memories hung between them so heavily that you could almost touch them.

Sally wiped her eyes; Divina leaned back against the wall. 'I want this baby,' she murmured. 'This baby is damn well going to be loved. I'm going to forget his father.'

Sally stared at her. 'You can do that?' she asked. 'Just like that?'

'No,' Divina admitted, 'but I'm not running after him waving a diaper, either, pleading for help.' She gazed at Sally, trying to read her face. 'You think he's forgettable?'

'No,' Sally said truthfully. 'Dermott's like a permanent scar from a road accident. He'll never go.'

'Fade maybe,' Divina said. 'Maybe some day he'll fade.'

Sally emptied the last of the bottle into both their glasses. 'Here's to the next thirty years,' she said. 'Or however much longer it takes to forget Dermott Matthews. Fuck him.'

'Or not,' Divina said. 'Not again in this life.'

'Or not,' Sally murmured.

31

The last of the film crew left the field as the afternoon light began to fail. Virginia Pye stood at the window of her curious little house, watching the four-wheel drives churn out of the gateway, and the catering crew as they closed down the awning, put up the shutters, and switched off the lights. She saw the headlights threading their uncertain way down the hill and waited until the very final stray touches of light were soaked up by the encroaching night.

She sighed with relief. The field was hers again. Turning away, she lit the gas stove and put the kettle on to boil. Then, thinking better of it, she turned off the gas again, got down on her knees, and took a bottle of whisky and a large, crumbling shoebox from under the precariously balanced sink.

It was almost pitch black now.

She felt around the edges of the box, and lifted the lid carefully, as carefully as a mother folding back the blankets on a cot to check on a sleeping child.

The photographs were met by her fumbling fingertips; thick celluloid, the edges curled with damp. Slowly, she spread them, one by one, on the table. She knew exactly how many there were: fourteen. A life in fourteen pictures.

The first was large, its surface wrinkled and brittle, the film decaying. It was a group picture taken just before the war, on the steps of Hunscrete House: a shooting party, with the staff of the house lined up respectfully to one side. Somewhere in that group of faces was her mother, her forehead almost obscured by the white kitchen hat, her body a blur of white apron. She had moved while the picture was taken, and it was the only portrait that Virginia had of her mother, a misted square of white.

Her grandmother was there, too – although she had never once acknowledged the relationship. Gertrude Hunscrete sat centre stage on a large carved chair taken out of the hallway. Dogs surrounded her, closer than the humans.

In the dark, Virginia felt for the smeared glass with her fingertips, and, unscrewing the bottle purely by feel, poured herself a huge helping of Scotch. Her hands flattened on the spread images. Here was Hunscrete during the war, boarded up, with Virginia herself, as a child, playing with the very dogs that Gertrude adored on the same – now empty – front steps. Here was Virginia's wedding day, with Virginia's husband glowering at the camera. One other picture of her life at Hunscrete remained: Virginia and her husband at the back of Hunscrete House, a gun slung across his shoulder, a knee-deep pile of dead birds at his feet.

Her fingers strayed to the remaining photographs. These had a silkier sheen. They passed, she knew, from black-and-white to colour. They were all from America.

Every now and then – perhaps every seven or eight years or so – an envelope would arrive at Virginia's house. There would never be any letter in them, but there would be pictures. Promotional pictures from movies. George Bernard Ransome's movies.

Each time, the star would have signed the publicity still. Hedda Ramone, looking sultry in Ransome's *Girl from a Border Town*. Angela Hubbert in *Lizzie Takes Flight*. Clark Rutland from *Our Man in Chicago*. And every one inscribed the same. *To Virginia, with love*.

The largest was a picture of George Bernard himself,

taken with his child star, Beth Schreiber. Virginia turned the picture over. It crackled faintly in the darkness. In the gloom, she could just make out the outline of Beth Schreiber's impossibly perfect face.

On the back, George had written a message, the only one he had sent her. It said: *From one pretty little girl to another . . . to* my *little girl, from her Daddy*.

Virginia took another large gulp of whisky. It burned her throat, but the pain was a relief. It scalded away the memory associated with that picture, that message. The image under her pillow. The tears she had wept over it.

How would he know if he had a pretty little girl? He had never seen her at all.

Stumbling a little, Virginia got up and pushed the heavy table away from her. She heard one or two photos fall to the floor. She felt her way across the room, until she came in contact with the straw on the floor. Kneeling down, she reached out her hand, and stroked the back of the ducks in their open box. With her other hand, she scrubbed at her eyes, annoyed with herself, at her ability to still be hurt by pictures that couldn't talk.

The birds in the box stirred, submitting to her touch.

They weren't much of a family, these dumb creatures.

But they were all the family she had.

32

John pulled into the car park of Owen Majolica's hotel, found a space and switched off the engine. He sat for some time in silence, gazing at the ivy-clad facade of the sixteenth century manor house that must have been costing Majolica Industries an arm and leg.

On either side, for as far as the eye could see, the manicured lawns of the Manor spread away. There was the distant tinkling of a garden designer's waterfall and sculpted laddered ponds, not to mention the even more distant tinkling of money falling into the garden designer's bank account.

Owen's four-wheel drive was parked in front of the main doors, splattered with mud.

'Well, here we are,' John said. 'Are you sure you want me to come in with you?'

Chris turned to him, smiling. 'You don't mind?'

'No.'

'I need a hand to hold.'

'Hand on stand-by.'

They got out of the car and began to walk to the entrance. 'I still can't believe that woman,' John said, at last.

'Who, Sally Matthews?'

'Aggressive, or what?'

'Yes,' Chris said.

John shook his head. 'Five foot two of undiluted venom.'

Chris sighed. 'Well, she's only just signed a contract,' she said. 'I suppose she feels we're threatening it, trying to get Hunscrete House into the picture. Literally.'

'It's not as if we even want to interview Alicia Hunscrete,' John said. 'Just film the house.'

Chris started to laugh to herself. 'Rights to all Hunscrete intellectual property,' she said. 'Imagine! Hunscretes with intellects. What a terrifying prospect for the country.'

In the drawing dusk, the lights were slowly coming on in the hotel.

'And another thing,' John said. 'What was Divina Delaney doing there?'

'Well, I don't know, do I?'

'Is she a mate of hers?'

'Are you joking?' Chris said. 'Did you see the expression on Sally Matthews's face?'

John shook his head. 'In Deadham Markham, of all places. It's like the Pope turning up in B & Q. I thought film stars never went anywhere without bodyguards.'

They had reached the entrance steps.

'Come on,' Chris said. 'Let's get this over with.'

Owen was waiting for them in Reception.

He looked suddenly older, a tall figure standing alone. He stepped forward as Chris approached him, and enclosed her in a silent bear hug. She extracted herself only after several long seconds, blushing.

Owen smelled very good, and his body was wiry and hard. His embrace had been that of a steel trap – not comfortable, but skinny and fleeting. She wondered what hugging *her* must have felt like. Squashing a ripe banana in your fist, she decided.

I'm going to diet tomorrow, she thought.

I will lose five stone and look like Ally McBeal.

I will eat only fruit and drink eight pints of water a day.

Take cod liver oil.

Never touch another Twix as long as I live.

Go running.

Join the gym.

Do back flips.

This message was delivered marked *Urgent* to the command centre in her brain. Almost immediately the reply came back, flashed in neon letters on the inside of her skull. It said simply, *Bugger off.*

As he stepped backwards, and took her hand, she knew immediately and with absolute certainty what he was going to say.

'I've told him,' he said. 'He knows.'

'How did he take it?' Chris asked.

'Bad.'

They gazed at each other. Then, Chris turned to indicate John. Owen nodded at him. 'I brought reinforcements,' Chris said. 'But maybe you don't need us?'

'He wants to see you,' Owen said.

'Can I have any last requests?' Chris asked. 'Cream cake? Blindfold?'

'No, really. He's all right.' They started to go up the stairs. Then, after not more than three or four treads, Owen stopped. 'Actually, he's not all right,' he said. 'Just not throwing anything. He's gone very quiet.'

Chris suddenly felt sure that this was even worse than Jefferson Bluehorn's famous storm-force temper. 'Just a blindfold, then,' she murmured. 'Oh, and Keanu Reeves on a bed of asparagus, lightly oiled. That'll be fine.'

Owen smiled grimly. 'He started praying.'

'Uh oh. Is that bad?'

'My grandfather was a Baptist minister in Kansas,' Owen told them. 'Dad never really shook it off until he married my mother. But if something bothers him . . .'

'He regresses?' John asked.

'Yeah,' Owen confirmed. 'Fire. Brimstone. He regresses real hard.'

They had reached the door of the suite. 'He's not going to hit me with a Bible?' Chris asked, nervous.

Owen said nothing. He opened the door.

There in the room in front of them was a figure that Chris had seen a hundred times on TV. It was a face that had shone at her from balloons stranded on mountain ranges, from high-tech sleds on Arctic ice floes, from the labels of sauce bottles, from pension fund advertisements, from every window of the *Booted* chain of adventure clothing shops, from newspapers and magazines and biscuit wrappers and condom foil and computer software and ski salopettes and rugby balls and political pamphlets. Possibly, it was the world's most famous face. A face that wanted very much to look like Alexander the Great after a good pillage and which always looked to Chris, with its halo of wayward curls, more like Alexandra the Great after a bad perm.

Jefferson Bluehorn Majolica was kneeling on the carpet with his eyes closed and his hands clasped together.

Owen shut the door behind them.

'Dad,' he said, 'this is Chris Craven, and John Donoghue.'

Majolica's eyes snapped open. He got to his feet and walked over very slowly. He wore the expression of a man who has just been told he has a week to live. Chris, who had never actually met him, was surprised to see that he only came up to her shoulder.

Jefferson grasped Chris's hand. 'Chris,' he said, 'what's happened to my boy?'

Chris shuffled. 'Well, I . . .'

'For Christ's sake,' Owen muttered, walking over to the window and staring out at the shadows of the grounds.

'Do not take the Lord's name in vain,' Jefferson rumbled.

'*Christ*,' Owen repeated.

Jefferson took Chris's hand in his. 'You've done fine work for my son,' he said. 'Don't think I don't know that.'

'Well, I don't know,' said Chris, her crippling Britishness overcoming the proper response, which ought to have been, 'Fine work? I've done everything but wipe him down.'

'You know what this is?' Jefferson said. 'Rebellion. Pure and simple.'

'Well . . .' Chris began.

'I am not bloody rebelling,' Owen countered, from the window. 'I'm just choosing my own life.'

Jefferson had not taken his eyes from Chris. 'I've given my boy everything, Chris,' he said.

'Yes, I'm sure . . .'

'Every damned thing.'

'I just want my own life,' Owen said.

'I have torn my heart out,' Jefferson said. He thumped his fist against his chest. 'Torn out my own poor bleedin' beating heart. I put my own heart on a platter for that child . . .'

'Dad,' Owen interrupted, 'I am twenty-eight years old.'

Chris's hand was being slowly but relentlessly crushed.

'I have given him the keys to the kingdom,' Jefferson went on.

'Jesus H. *Christ*!' Owen yelled.

Jefferson raised his hand. ' "I put the Devil's words at my back," he intoned. "The ingratitude of my own child – I cannot cast my eyes on it, oh Lord *God* Almighty in Heaven, I cast not my eyes upon the devil . . ." '

Owen suddenly stormed across the room.

Chris stared at him. Never once, in four years, had she seen him storm. She hadn't even seen him squall. Not even a light rainfall. But now, there were definite thunderclouds racing over Owen's brow. He caught hold of his father's arm, and swung the older man round.

'You listen to me,' he said. 'I don't care what you believe, but don't you dare spout that sanctimonious shit at me.'

There was a second of absolute silence.

Then Jefferson opened his mouth.

'And don't tell me any old cod about me living with swine and then crawling back a prodigal son, because I won't,' Owen continued. 'As for me breaking your heart – that's impossible, because you haven't got one.'

He rammed his face close up against his father's.

Chris felt John tug lightly on her jacket, trying to pull her away from them. She took a step backwards, as anxious as he was to avoid any flying objects.

The two men said nothing at all, just stared at each other like two rutting moose, horns locked. The steam from their nostrils was almost visible.

'I, er . . . I wonder if I could just mention something,' Chris said. It was a valiant, if – as it turned out – misguided, attempt to defuse the situation. Or at least distract the Majolicas from tearing off each other's heads. 'This . . . um . . . thing with Up-Line, this programme with Virginia Pye . . .'

'I love Madeleine Hattersley,' Owen said, 'and that's why I'm going. And you can bloody well stuff it, Dad.'

'Yes, er . . . Virginia,' Chris gabbled. Jefferson Bluehorn had gone a wicked shade of white. 'Yes, it's quite amazing, Jefferson, because I don't know if you know Sir Charles Hunscrete at all, but Virginia is related to him, and it's all rather racy and very good . . . er . . . publicity for the programme.'

Jefferson slowly – very slowly – turned his head towards her. 'Hunscrete?' he whispered.

'Yes,' Chris said. 'She's related to Charles Hunscrete, and there's a woman already here doing Alicia Hunscrete's biography.' With relief, she saw Jefferson's clenched hands drop to his side. 'Virginia turns out to have some seriously famous relations,' she continued gamely. 'Not least George Bernard Ransome, who was her father and Charles Hunscrete's uncle.' She stopped.

Jefferson's face, known for being blond and smiling and dangerously bland, seemed to have suddenly frozen solid.

Owen, meanwhile, stepped back. He picked up his jacket from the chair. 'I love her, and there's not a thing you can do about it, so don't bother,' he said.

'Hunscrete?' Jefferson repeated.

John waded in to Chris's support. 'We wanted to pursue the links,' he said. 'The contrast between poverty and money, loss and fame, Virginia's standards and . . .' Then he, too, halted.

Jefferson was turning the shade of carbon monoxide poisoning.

'She's a kind of last innocent, a victim,' Chris ventured.

'Goodbye,' Owen said.

Jefferson tottered where he stood. 'Hunscrete,' he gurgled.

Owen opened the door. Jefferson's gaze faltered towards him, then back at Chris. 'Hunscrete?'

A shadow of a smile passed across Owen's face. He glanced at Chris, then blew her a kiss.

'*Hunscrete!*' Jefferson bellowed. Veins stood out on his forehead and neck.

The door to the suite softly closed.

'Oh Lord!' Jefferson cried. 'They that defile the flesh, despise dominion and speak evil of dignities!'

'Pardon?' Chris said.

' "Woe unto them, for they have gone in the way of Cain!" ' Jefferson whooped. ' "Spots in your feasts of charity when they feast with you, feeding themselves without fear, clouds without water, trees whose fruit withereth . . ." '

John looked at Chris. 'I think he knows him,' he said.

' "Waves foaming in their own shame!" ' Jefferson cried. ' "Murmurers and complainers walking after their lusts!" '

John whispered in Chris's ear. 'A light dawneth,' he said.

' "Woe unto them, brute beasts!" ' Jefferson bellowed, stamping up and down the room, waving his arms.

'What light?' Chris said.

John grinned. 'A light that sayeth that when Charles Hunscrete woth Foreign Secretary, he hath denied Jefferson Majolica British Citizenship, amen.'

'Woth?' Chris repeated.

Abruptly, gasping, Jefferson grabbed a small black case from the table. Opening it, he shook out two small white pills. He swallowed them dry, and Chris and John were treated to the interesting spectacle of seeing his face change from purple to pale pink in less than thirty seconds. The fury drained out of Jefferson's face like water swilling down a drain. Soon, the little ringlet-fringed choirboy returned to them.

He walked to Chris and John, and laid a hand on their respective shoulders. 'Children,' he intoned. 'Visit the wrath of the Lord upon the head of that abomination. Please.'

'Well,' said Chris, 'of course we certainly would like to, but there's a tiny fly in the ointment.'

'Fly?' Jefferson said.

'A woman,' Chris told him. 'She's digging the dirt on Hunscrete herself on behalf of his wife's biography. She's got a contract from Boundhand.'

'Is she,' Jefferson said. 'Has she.' He nodded a couple of times. 'OK, OK. So what's this about Ransome?'

'He's Hunscrete's uncle.'

A little smile began on Jefferson's face. 'I never heard that.'

'No one has,' Chris said. 'Virginia is the only person alive who seems to know it. Except Hunscrete himself.'

Jefferson's eyes had narrowed. 'Ransome's house was a pit of vipers and lepers,' he observed evenly.

'Oh. I see. Was it?' Chris asked.

'Lepers and whores,' Jefferson said. 'Offending in the ways of the flesh.'

'Did it?' John said. 'What ways?'

'A pit of revulsion and fornication until the day he died.'

'Fornication,' John said, writing it down.

'Beasts of the field,' Jefferson said.

'Right,' John said, scribbling. 'Would that be sheep?'

Chris, pulling a face at John, guided Jefferson gently away from him. 'Mr Majolica,' she said, 'we may be in conflict with this woman. She's a bit thorny. Possessive. I don't know if I can pursue the Hunscrete part.'

A glint came into Jefferson's eye. 'What's her name?' he said. 'Where's she live?'

Chris told him.

He laid a hand on her shoulder. 'You leave that to me, pretty face,' he said. 'Deals is where *I* live.'

The phone rang.

Jefferson picked it up, listened for a moment, then slammed it down. 'I got a ride to catch,' he said. Outside, they could already hear the chugging rotation of helicopter rotors. 'Need to get to Brussels.' He kissed Chris's cheek. 'Be talking to you in a coupla days,' he told her. 'You and me got a business to keep running.'

Before she could reply, he had shrugged on his coat and picked up a case. He glanced around the room, and his eyes registered a pen lying on the nearest chair. With great deliberation, he reached down, picked it up, and cradled it in his palm for a second before, colouring a little, stowing it away in his pocket. 'Forgot his pen,' he said gruffly.

For the first time, Chris felt for him.

'You know,' Jefferson murmured, 'I took off on a boat – Florida Keys, 1957. Scared the shit out of my daddy. Went to catch fish for a coupla years. Caught a woman or two. Caught dysentery. Went to Washington. Made a pile of money.'

He nodded slowly.

They followed him downstairs, where two men were waiting for him. One of them took the case. The other opened the door to the terrace.

Yet, just before running across to the helicopter, Jefferson Bluehorn paused one last time. 'She ain't got a tin cent,' he muttered. 'Not a tin cent.'

They watched as he got on board. They followed his progress as the helicopter rose into the sky, and turned east. They continued to watch until all they could make out was the whirring of the blades, just visible, wings above the trees in the twilight.

Then they turned to each other.

'He called me pretty face,' Chris said, beaming.

'Poor bloke,' John said, folding his notebook. 'Obviously as barking as Battersea Dogs' Home.'

33

It was half past nine in the evening when Chris got home. As she put her key in the door and opened it, she had a premonition that something wasn't right. The silence came ballooning out at her, so thick you could cut it.

'Hello?' she called. She put down her case and walked into the drawing room.

Emily Villiers was standing behind Henry, who sat in his wing armchair. Malcolm sat next to Henry. It looked to Chris exactly like one of those family portraits hung on the walls in stately homes: everyone looked slightly pained, as though someone had just farted.

'Hello,' she said again.

Malcolm got to his feet.

'What on earth are you doing here?' she asked.

Emily Villiers turned away. 'I shall make some tea,' she said. As she left, Chris noticed her hand stray for a moment to Henry's shoulder.

Malcolm came over and gave Chris a kiss on the cheek. 'We've been waiting,' he said.

'I rang four or five hours ago,' Chris said. 'Emily said she'd be glad to wait.'

Malcolm lowered his voice. 'Well, she hasn't been glad to wait,' he said.

Chris glanced at Henry apologetically. 'She was perfectly OK on the phone.'

'She's missed a bridge tournament.'

'Oh,' said Chris, 'I'm sorry about that.'

Malcolm looked her up and down. 'Where have you been until so late?' he said.

'Talking to Owen.'

'Oh,' Malcolm said. 'Owen, Owen.' He flung himself down on the nearest seat.

Chris looked at him. Then she looked back at Henry. Her father-in-law gave her a little smile. She was so astonished at this expression that she took a step backwards.

Emily came in with a tray. She put it down by Henry's side and fussed over handing him the cup. 'Well,' she said, straightening up, 'I shall get your father to bed and then retire myself, if that's suitable.'

'Retire?' Chris said.

'Mrs Villiers is staying over,' Malcolm told her.

'Oh,' said Chris. 'Why is that?'

There it came again. The silence so thick that it could be not only cut, but buttered, spread with jam, and used to feed the five thousand when the fish ran out.

Malcolm suddenly leapt to his feet again and grabbed Chris's arm. 'If you'll excuse us, Mrs Villiers – Father,' he said. He started pulling Chris towards the door.

'What are you doing?' Chris demanded, looking longingly at her tea.

'We're going upstairs,' Malcolm said.

She was pulled out of the door. Malcolm stamped on, rattling the pictures of the Fourth Rifle Regiment on the landing. Chris followed him, bemused and tired. As she got into the bedroom, Malcolm closed the door behind her.

'Where have you been?' he said.

She frowned. 'Working. You asked me that already.'

'Working until all hours of the night.'

'Malcolm, it's half past nine.'

'Working until half past nine.'

'Yes.'

He walked an almost complete circle on the rug in the centre of the room.

'Our dog used to do that,' Chris observed.

'What?' he said.

She gestured to the rug. 'Walk round in a circle when he had anal glands.'

He stared at her.

'Never mind,' she said.

'You're talking about your dog's piles?'

'It doesn't matter.'

'Ah,' he said. 'It's a joke. I get it.'

'It wasn't a joke,' Chris said. 'It was . . . never mind.'

'I've lost my job,' he said.

She had sunk to the bed, but at once stood up again. 'Now *you're* joking.'

'I don't joke,' he said.

'That's right,' she murmured. 'I forgot.' She took a step towards him. 'Oh, I'm so sorry.'

'Tell me you told me so.'

She tried to catch hold of his hand. 'I didn't think they'd do this,' she said.

He let her touch him, stroke his hand. She put her arms around his neck. He put his hands on her hips and then squeezed her tightly. Chris stood in his embrace, wondering how this expression of comfort could feel so desperately uncomfortable, as if he were strapping her into an iron maiden. She tried to gently push away from him.

'Someone else will take you on,' she said. 'One of the Universities.'

'There's no money,' he said.

'But there must be. Somewhere.'

'I doubt it.'

'There will be. Don't give up. Who needs Trepantex, for heaven's sake? You can make calls in the morning.'

He flashed her a dark look. 'There's no point.'

'But—'

He finally dropped his hands and turned away. He started emptying his pockets, lining the coins up with slow precision on the top of the chest of drawers.

'I'm sorry,' she repeated.

'I was here at five,' he said.

'I'm sorry.' She stopped, realising that she had done nothing but apologise since she had come in. Surely four apologies were enough. 'It's proving quite a tangle to work out, and . . .' She stopped. She wanted to tell him that she had been given a kind of promotion, at least a boost to her ego that had been overdue for some time. But in the face of his sacking, she stopped herself.

'It's more important,' he said.

'What is?'

'Your job,' he said.

'More important than what?'

'Than me.'

'That's not true,' she said.

'Keep your voice down.'

'I am keeping my voice down,' Chris said, her voice rising an octave or so. 'It's you who's shouting.'

'I am not shouting,' he said.

'You're doing it now.'

They glared at each other.

'You always do that,' Chris said. 'You say ridiculous things, and then you accuse me of shouting.'

'Will you keep your voice down. Mrs Villiers will hear you.'

'Oh *Christ*,' Chris muttered, furious.

'If I raise my voice, I've got good cause,' Malcolm hissed.

'Ah,' Chris said. 'If *you* raise your voice, you've got good cause. If *I* raise my voice, I'm being hysterical.'

'Mrs Villiers,' Malcolm said.

'Oh, *Jesus*!'

'And stop that.'

Chris stared at him. At last, she could stand it no longer, and looked away, taking deep breaths.

'Why didn't you tell me?' Malcolm said.

'Tell you what?'

'About her.'

She looked back at him. 'Who, Mrs Villiers?'

'Yes.'

'What about her?'

He raised his hands to heaven. 'I can't believe it.'

'Believe *what*?'

'Will you stop shouting!' he shouted. He got up and walked over to her. 'Come in the bathroom.'

'Eh?'

He pulled her up. 'She won't hear us in there.'

'Will you *stop* hauling me about like a sack of coal!'

'Do you want her to hear this?'

'Hear *whaaaat*!' she screamed.

'Sssssh!'

'I am going to kill you if you say that once more.'

'She's trying to win my father over,' he said.

'What do you mean?'

'You see?' he said. 'You haven't noticed the way she is with him.'

'No,' Chris said. 'I haven't noticed. So this is my fault, is it? What am I meant to have noticed?'

'When I came in,' Malcolm said darkly, 'she was washing his face.'

Chris started to laugh. 'My God!' she said. 'Call out the Riot Police.'

'I'm serious.'

'He can't hold the flannel properly, Malcolm. He can't close his fist.'

'You don't understand,' he said. 'She washing him like . . . like a child. And he *enjoyed* it.'

'Why shouldn't he?' Chris said. 'It must be lovely.'

'What on earth are you talking about?' Malcolm demanded.

'What I say,' Chris retorted. 'It must be lovely to be cared for and spoiled and watched and listened to.'

'Like a child!'

'Yes, like a child. Sometimes,' Chris said. 'Praised and admired, even if it's out of proportion, just occasionally. Seen. Heard.'

Malcolm's eyes ranged over her face, trying to figure her out. 'You're talking about me,' he said.

'It doesn't matter.'

'It certainly doesn't,' Malcolm said. 'I happen to be worried about my father.'

The slight stung more than Chris could have imagined. 'A woman is washing your father's face, and he likes it,' she said. 'What can be wrong in that?'

Malcolm's face began to flood with colour, an odd phenomenon that Chris had rarely seen, a sign of high emotion. 'He likes her,' he said. 'He likes *her*.'

'And?'

'Not like a nurse.'

Chris shook her head. 'Well, so what? If they like each other . . .'

'She's taking advantage of him.'

Chris began to laugh. 'She's doing nothing of the sort.'

'A sick and lonely old man.'

'But if it's what he wants . . .'

'It's not what he wants!' Malcolm protested.

Chris stared at him. 'How the hell do you know what he wants,' she said. 'You don't exist for each other except as cardboard cut-outs of people. You never talk to each other. You never talk to anyone.'

'I don't want to talk to anyone,' Malcolm said.

Chris did a double-take. 'What?'

Malcolm waved his hand. 'I don't want . . . all this talking. I mean, for God's sake, where does it get people?'

'It gets them closer,' Chris said.

'It does not,' Malcolm retorted. 'All this counselling business, all this endless yattering on . . .'

'It's called communication,' Chris said. 'You should try it.' She walked back to the bed, where she sat slowly down. 'You should try talking about something that matters.'

'Why?' Malcolm countered. 'What happened to just getting on with things? Look at the war. People didn't come back and talk about it. They got on with their lives.'

'And raised children who couldn't talk to anyone, just like them,' Chris snapped back.

Malcolm looked at her. 'Well, my father believed in that,' he said, very quietly. 'And I think he was right.'

'Yes,' Chris said. 'Don't talk about it. *Just look on the bright side.*'

A terrible silence descended between them.

They each looked at the few square inches of threadbare carpet in front of them – carpet which had once been high quality, bought when Henry had first been married, and which now had patches of wear. Something about the faded pattern of alpine flowers struck Chris as tragic.

'She's got him ringing marriage bureaux,' Malcolm said, not picking up the signals of Chris's distress, and talking to his feet.

Chris swallowed the knot of tears in her throat with difficulty. 'Sorry . . . what?'

'Marriage bureaux.'

'I don't understand.'

'Abroad,' Malcolm said. 'Thailand . . .'

Realisation dawned. 'The phone bill,' Chris murmured. She looked up at Malcolm. 'She didn't get him to do that,' she said. 'He's been doing it for ages.'

'Oh, so you know about it?'

'They were itemised on the phone bills, the foreign calls, but I didn't realise what they were, who they were to . . . my God,' she said. 'How lonely he must have been.'

They regarded each other for some time. Downstairs they could hear Emily Villiers saying good night to Henry, in a voice of affectionate sweetness.

'Let him do what he wants, Malcolm,' Chris murmured. 'Let him be happy.'

'Happy?' Malcolm said. 'Like that?'

'Yes,' Chris told him.

'No.'

'All right. So he likes Emily. What are you going to do about it?'

'Fire her,' he said. '*I'm* here now.'

Chris looked at him knowingly. 'I give you one day,' she said. 'One day of getting him on to the commode. Maybe not even a day.'

'I won't have him being treated like this,' Malcolm said.

'You won't have him being cared for?'

'Mollycoddled.'

'Jesus!' Chris exploded. 'He's just had a stroke, Malcolm. Bring on the dancing girls and feed him peeled grapes. Don't you think he deserves it?'

'You're quite mad,' Malcolm said.

She stared at him. 'Yes,' she said, finally. 'I'm married to a man who resents his father being loved, and thinks it's his wife's fault. I'm obviously quite deranged.'

'Now you're being facetious.'

'Mad and facetious. Anything else?'

'No,' he said.

She realised, quite suddenly, that she was talking to a brick wall. Perhaps more importantly, she was talking to a brick wall not in his own Brick Language, but in something entirely different. Fluent Reason, for instance.

'I'm not staying here,' she said. She started to put her shoes back on, which she had eased off while sitting on the bed.

'You can't go,' he said.

'I am going. Watch me. This is a shoe. I'm putting it on.'

'Take it off.'

'Oh, grow up,' she said.

'Fine.'

She dragged her portfolio and bag from the side of the bed where she had dropped them and went to the door.

'It's you who's being childish,' he said.

'I'm not to blame,' she told him. 'Not for you losing your job, or for having a job that I enjoy, or for your father being ill.'

'If you would just behave properly,' he said.

She stared at him. 'Malcolm,' she said slowly, 'I'm standing at the door. Say something nice. *I'm not to blame.* Say that.'

He didn't move.

'OK,' she said. 'So I am to blame. Fine. Fine! I'm obviously to blame for everything. I'm to blame for the weakness of your father's circulation. OK. Fair point. I engineered that deliberately. I'm to blame for Emily Villiers washing his face . . .'

'Childish,' Malcolm said.

'I'm responsible for Trepantex having the moral conscience of a virus. That's for sure.'

'Childish.'

'World poverty. Cliff erosion . . . oh, and I didn't forget the little things either,' she stormed. 'I arranged those traffic-lights that have a right-hand filter but not enough space for the traffic behind to get past, and there's traffic coming the other way . . .'

Malcolm rose from the bed with wounded dignity. 'I am

going to the toilet,' he said.

'The piece of foil on the top of the milk carton that you're supposed to peel off,' she yelled. 'But it won't peel off, and you have to cut it with a vegetable knife, and then the milk pours down the side of the carton.'

He went to the bathroom, and closed the door.

'The extinction of the white rhino,' she shouted. 'Tapeworms! Astrologers! Lice!'

Nothing but silence beyond the door.

'Anthea Turner,' she said, her voice cracking. 'William Hague.' She put her hands to her eyes. 'Oh shit, oh shit,' she grieved.

She looked at the closed door for some time. Then, snivelling, she tried to find a handkerchief in Malcolm's drawer. 'Bloody buggering hell,' she whispered to the floor. Then, in a raised voice, 'Malcolm, come out. I'm leaving.'

There was no reply. She went out of the room, then turned and came back momentarily, listening.

'Say something!' she called.

'I don't know what I'm supposed to say,' came the indistinct reply.

'Tell me not to go. I'm leaving. Tell me not to. Please.'

There was a pause. Then the door opened a crack. He stood there in his Y-fronts, clutching the *Financial Times*. 'Don't go,' he said.

'Oh, Malcolm,' she told him. 'You have to mean it.'

'You're never happy,' he said.

She looked at him. He looked at her for a second, then closed the door again, and shut her out.

She walked. Down the stairs slowly, and out into the darkness of the street.

34

Philippa Blood had an early meeting the next morning. These happened at least twice a week, and the most she usually saw of her husband before 7 a.m. was a muffled shape deep in the duvet – unless he had had early service, in which case the most she saw of him was a muffled shape deep in the newspaper, smelling keenly of damp hymn-books and bat droppings.

And so it was with some surprise that, as she reached the window seat at the curve of the landing halfway up the stairs, she almost tripped over Michael's feet. He was curled in the recess, his hands clasped over his knees.

She narrowed her eyes at him. 'Waiting for someone?' she asked.

'Nooo, nooo,' Michael said, affecting a casual air.

'Michael,' she said, 'if you don't get out of there, it'll be the worse for you.'

He got up.

'Even Angus can't look at you,' she said, nodding to the dog, who was lying with his head on the bottom tread of the stairs.

'It's in case she needs anything,' Michael coughed.

Philippa gripped his arm. 'If Divina Delaney needs anything in our bathroom,' she told him, 'it will not be a blessing and a chapter from the Epistle to the Ephesians, so get down these bloody stairs.'

'The shower tap sticks,' Michael protested.

'Don't be pathetic,' she hissed. 'You're a grown man.'

She stopped, eyeing him distrustfully. 'On the other hand, that's the trouble.'

She bundled him into the kitchen, where she deposited him in his chair and stuck the newspaper in his hands. 'Any more of that and I shall tell the Bishop.'

'He'd be over here like a shot,' Michael grinned. 'He likes actresses. The man's a walking "as the Bishop said . . ."'

Philippa held up her hand. 'I don't want to know.'

'He used to be a stagehand at The Windmill.'

'Don't tell me. I have enough trouble looking him in the eye as it is.'

'He used to comb the fans.'

Philippa covered her face with one hand. 'I won't be able to get that image out my head all day now,' she muttered.

There was a thunderous knock at the back door.

She glanced at the clock. 'Ten to seven. God help us.'

Justin's moonlike face appeared at the window.

'She's dead,' Philippa mouthed at him. 'Go home.'

The door opened. Justin was accompanied by two other lads from the scheme, in various stages of anticipation ranging from agog to extreme salivation.

'What's she doing?' Justin asked. 'Is she in your bed?'

'Don't torment the Vicar,' Philippa chided him. 'She has been sleeping in *a* bed. Now she's showering.'

'In the nude, like?' Justin cried.

Philippa ate two bites of her toast, picked up her bag and turned on her heel. 'Goodbye,' she said. She glanced pitying at the assorted male faces, all of which seemed to be turned towards the ceiling. A distant trickle of water could be heard, and a woman's voice singing 'I'm Jest a Girl Who Cain't Say No'.

Philippa sighed. 'Goodbye,' she repeated. 'For ever, probably.' Then she walked out, slamming the door.

Justin sank to a chair. 'I seen her in the nude in *Flotsam*,' he said. 'She's got a 38D. Both sides.'

'*Jetsam*,' Michael corrected. 'Double D.'

'She killed that bloke with a nail-file.'

'She got an Oscar for it,' Michael said.

Justin turned to him, eyes like saucers. 'You reckon she brung it with her?' he asked. 'You reckon she'd let me touch it?'

'I'd like to touch her Oscar,' one of the other lads said dreamily.

Michael nodded. 'Who wouldn't,' he muttered.

The room fell silent. Michael looked around at his tatty kitchen, at the sight of Angus lying full length in front of the Aga, steaming; at the half-tiled wall he was always promising Philippa that he would finish, and he wondered to himself what it must all look like to a woman who had everything.

Just then, they heard a footstep on the stairs.

The whole room froze. They all stopped breathing. Even Angus paused mid-stretch, one foot dangling mid-air and his ears on askew.

Divina put her head round the door. 'Hi guys,' she said. 'Have you seen what's in your front yard?'

No one said anything. No one moved.

'Front yard,' Divina repeated. 'This place outside, in front? Hello?'

Angus suddenly stirred into life. He wriggled upright, joyful that someone appeared to be talking about *outside*. *Outside* always meant a walk. He shot across the kitchen and launched himself at Divina's chest. Every eye in the place gazed at him admiringly.

Divina started laughing. Michael got up, feeling that his arms and legs weren't quite his. Someone had surely taken his own legs during the night, and stapled on another pair, but back to front. He forced himself across the kitchen in

Divina's direction.

'Sorry,' he said, trying to dislodge Angus without touching the heavenly body behind.

Divina didn't seem to care. She ruffled Angus's ears. 'Come and look,' she said. 'It's just a tiny little thing, but it doesn't look like a bird. Tell me what it is.'

They walked to the front door. Divina opened it, smiling at Michael. She was quite used to strangers freezing and staring whenever she came into a room, so her reception hardly fazed her. She walked down the steps on to the Rectory path, and kneeled down next to a small furry object.

Angus composedly sat down next to her and gazed at the ground, his ears dangling in his line of sight.

'Good heavens,' Michael said. 'It's a bat.'

'Is it?' Divina said. 'I never saw one before. It's awful small.'

At that moment, the front gate opened and Steve walked in, his bag slung across one shoulder. He looked twice at Divina, then grinned, and held out his hand. 'I know you,' he said.

Divina appraised him from head to foot, then returned the handshake. 'You're the guy from yesterday,' she said. 'Sally's guy.'

'Steve.'

Divina noticed, with some interest, and not a little disappointment, Steve's colour rise as she mentioned Sally's name. Oh well, she thought. Can't have 'em all. 'Hi, Steve,' she replied. She nodded down at the ground. 'Know what this is?'

He squatted on his haunches next to them. 'Pipistrelle,' he said.

'They're in the church,' Michael said.

'It's a baby,' Steve said.

They looked up. Justin and the other lads had drifted to

the front doorstep. They looked like extras from a *Thriller* video, drawn like zombies to where the action was. Justin looked as if he had been hit by a sandbag, his arms hanging loosely by his sides.

'Know anything about bats?' Divina asked him.

'Jinyer,' he muttered.

'A jinyer?' Divina asked. She looked, baffled, at Steve. 'Is that a kind of pipistrelle?'

'*Jinyer*,' Justin said, more loudly. He waved his arm in the direction of the hills behind the village, and clipped the lad behind him round the ear as he did so.

'It's come from Jinyer?' Divina said. 'Is that a place?'

Steve started to laugh.

Justin hobbled down the steps. 'Up top,' he said.

Steve helped Divina to her feet. 'There's someone who *would* know,' he said. 'Vir*ginia* – that's what he's trying to say. Virginia Pye, in the top field.'

35

Sally arrived at Hunscrete House at eight o'clock. Although she had rung Alicia the night before to warn her of the early start, she was still surprised to see, as she motored down the imposing sweep of the drive, that Alicia herself was standing at the front of the house, looking very dwarfed and vulnerable in front of the eighteenth-century façade.

She was dressed in the county uniform, as rigid a dress code as the Royal Enclosure at Ascot. To county women of right-wing political affiliation, there was only one possible outfit to wear, and it wasn't by Ralph Lauren. It was what Alicia had worn when elected to Parliament; it was what she had worn when she appeared in court; it was what she had been wearing on the day she left prison. A navy-blue pleated skirt, navy-blue jacket, navy-blue-and-white striped blouse and navy-blue court shoes, topped off with a large Hermès scarf.

Alicia had lost, however, the other trademark of Tory MPs. She didn't have a face of mildly astonished superiority any more. Instead, she looked very worried indeed.

Sally pulled up close to her, and got out. 'Ready for your day in Town?' she asked.

'I can't go,' Alicia said.

Sally walked around the side of the car. 'What's the matter?' she asked. 'Has something happened?'

'I just can't go,' Alicia repeated.

Sally frowned. 'Something *has* happened.'

Alicia looked away from her. 'I've simply had a chance to think about what I'm doing,' she said.

'Which is?'

'Letting myself down,' Alicia said. 'Letting everyone down.'

Sally shook her head. 'Just a minute,' she said. 'How can telling the truth be letting yourself down?'

Alicia paused a moment before she replied. 'I've had a visitor.'

'Who?' Sally asked, guessing already.

'Peter Wallington.'

'Who is . . .?'

'Charles's solicitor.' Alicia wound the Hermès scarf around and around her fingers. 'Charles got back from the West Indies the day before yesterday. I can't gamble on this, Sally.'

'Gamble on what?'

'My future,' Alicia said.

'But you're assuring your future,' Sally objected. Gritting her teeth, she crossed her arms, and leaned against the car. 'But tell me Charles's perception, for what it's worth.'

'He says that if I say anything about him – anything at *all* – he'll put an injunction on me. He'll stop the book. He'll stop the divorce settlement. He'll have me thrown out.'

Sally sighed. It was no more than she had expected, but it had come slightly earlier, that was all. 'Alicia,' she said, 'he's having you thrown out of here already, remember?'

'Without a penny. With no settlement.'

'You'll have the money from the book.'

'Not if he stops the book.'

'He can't stop it. On what grounds could he possibly do so?'

'National security,' Alicia said.

Sally started to laugh.

'I'm glad you find it so funny,' Alicia said, annoyed.

Sally shook her head. 'I don't. It's preposterous.'

'He's due to make a speech tomorrow,' Alicia said. 'It's a policy statement in the House.'

'Alicia, I know,' Sally said.

'I really don't want to bring down the Government.'

Sally stared at her, astonished. 'Pardon me?'

'The Bill is terribly important.'

'And Charles thinks that if you say anything about your marriage, that will destroy the Bill?'

'Yes.'

'But that's ridiculous,' Sally said. 'You've been an MP yourself – you know better than that. What he means is, it might destroy *him*.'

Alicia would still not meet Sally's eye. 'I don't want to destroy him,' she murmured.

Sally's heart dropped. She waited a moment, while Alicia looked everywhere but at her face. 'He doesn't deserve his position,' she said quietly. 'He bullied and bluffed his way into power. He's an incompetent Minister who doesn't give a damn for anything but his own hide. He's a cynical, selfish, two-faced adulterer. A five-star, gold-plated bully. Now he's threatening you again.'

At last, Alicia raised her face. 'I realise only too well what he's doing,' she said, 'and I realise that the book may well net me more than enough to live on. I also realise that it may serve to redress the balance a little.'

'Well, then . . .'

'But I'm being pushed.'

'By him.'

'No,' Alicia said. 'By both of you. By him *and* you.'

Sally stopped. Her mouth dropped open a little way. Alicia gave her a look that was almost sympathetic.

'Sally,' she said, 'I know how terribly important this is for you.'

'This isn't about *me*,' Sally objected.

'Isn't it?' Alicia asked.

Sally stared at her. 'Of course not. What do you mean?'

'I mean being rejected by one's husband,' Alicia said. 'Which, as we both know, is a most painful place to be, and one's reaction, naturally, is to hit back.'

'And you think I'm hitting back through you?' Sally asked.

'Aren't you?'

'No.'

'Not striking a blow for abandoned wives?'

'No.'

'Wronged wives?'

Sally put her hand to her forehead. 'How can supporting you hurt Dermott?' she said. 'Do you think he gives a tuppenny damn what I do?'

'No,' Alicia said. 'But that isn't the point. This isn't about making Dermott care. It's about making a man – any man, any husband – think twice. It's about showing the world what a terrible lousy deal a man can be. That's what *you* want.'

Sally looked hard at her. 'And you don't want that,' she said. 'Not an atom of you wants that.'

Alicia gave her a very small smile. 'Oh yes,' she admitted, 'I want that. I'd like to see him suffer very much. I'd even like to see him suffer at my own personal cost, at the cost of losing maintenance from him, at the gamble of supposing this book will sell. At the cost of humiliating myself once more. I would do all that if I thought that Charles would see the error of his ways, would be really hurt because he knew he had been wrong.' She laid her hand gently on Sally's arm. 'But you see, Sally,' she said, 'they will never actually see that they've been wrong. They will only see that they've been caught.'

'Then catch them,' Sally said. 'At least bloody well catch them.'

'And make myself as bad as him?' Alicia whispered.

Sally looked at her for some time, feeling all the noughts on the Boundhand contract draining swiftly away through her fingers. More awful still, she had a terrible feeling that Alicia was right. This was mud-slinging of a not very refined order. It wasn't that they, the mud-slingers, weren't perfectly justified to pick up their little bit of slime and chuck it as hard as they could. No one on earth would blame Alicia for landing a large lump of clay on Charles Hunscrete's lofty brow.

But, at the end of the day, Alicia would still have dirt on her hands.

Sally returned Alicia's hesitant smile. 'Oh why do you have to have principles, Alicia?' she mourned. 'MPs are supposed to grow out of them.'

'I'm sorry,' Alicia replied.

Sally looked around her at the sight of Hunscrete Park, a lovely piece of England that she had no doubt would soon be taken from Alicia for ever, principles or no principles. She was absolutely convinced that Charles Hunscrete wouldn't consider Alicia's capitulation as a strength, but a weakness. Once they withdrew from the book deal, he would only bear down harder, knowing that his wife had no defence.

Alicia would become that quintessentially English thing, the gentlewoman in distressed circumstances. With Charles Hunscrete's heel on her neck for the rest of her life.

'You're right,' Sally said. She patted the hand that was still solicitously lying on her own arm. 'But look . . . I'll have to go to London anyway to see Alexandra. Come with me. Boundhand are paying for a super hotel tonight. Let's live a little before Charles gets it all his own way. I give you my word we'll close this deal, forget the book. Anything you feel happy with.'

Alicia hesitated. Sally raised her hand in mock salute.

'Guide's honour,' she said. 'And I *was* a Queen's Guide, believe it or not.'

'I believe you,' Alicia smiled. 'Every Guide Leader I ever met was made from reinforced concrete.'

They beamed at each other.

'I *do* have an ulterior motive for wanting you with me, though,' Sally confessed. 'Concrete or not, I daren't face Alexandra Francis on my own.'

36

As Sally and Alicia drove away, they were not to know of the drama being enacted not half a mile from where they stood.

Chris and John had already decided that the Hunscrete connection couldn't be ignored. They needed to film on the estate, but they couldn't haul the vans up the main drive of Hunscrete Park without attracting just a smidgen of attention. And yet they wanted Virginia to talk about her father with at least some of the family landscape in shot.

And so early that morning, with the shooting schedule hastily rearranged, they found themselves standing on a boggy bank on the west side of the estate, where woodland swept down to the edges of the park. A rusty barbed-wire fence, embedded in wood stakes so ancient that they looked more like brown sponges than fence poles, separated the crew and Virginia from the sweeping vistas of Hunscrete land, across a small stream.

The great house could just be seen below, a pale cream brick square, one wing obscured by the long avenue of beeches that bordered the drive. As Chris looked down on the house from this vantage point, she saw a small red car driving away towards the gates.

John nudged her shoulder. She turned to him, and gratefully took the cup of coffee he was holding out for her.

'You know, this could work to our advantage,' he said. 'It'll look better, if anything, from here. We can voiceover how Virginia was excluded from birth from all the privileges, and even now she's excluded . . . blah blah.'

'Yes,' Chris said. 'I'd thought of that, too.' She took a sip of the coffee.

'Good light,' John said. 'Bright.'

'Yes,' she said.

He replaced the lid on his own cup and put it down on the tangled grass at their feet. 'What is it?' he asked.

She glanced at him. If she were honest, she had been afraid of this. That he would notice, and that she would have to explain. To him, to anyone. Put it into words. You think you're so good at description, she thought. Précis this in a paragraph.

'What's what?' she asked, in a low voice.

'Turning up here at six.'

'I couldn't sleep,' she told him.

'The excitement of television,' he said.

She looked away from him, at the far house, at the perfection of the day, and the loveliness of it – the tranquil half-mile of rolling parkland, the acid-leaf colour of the trees as they shed their winter nakedness, the more distant panorama of orchards and fields. It struck her heart. She put her hand to her eyes.

'Hey . . . hey,' John said.

The cup fell from her grip. She squeezed her eyes shut, but it wouldn't blot out the picture in her head.

She had spent the night in a Happy Little Traveller motor lodge just off the M20. It was quite possible that she would never get their hideous blue-and-orange-and-lime-green logo out of her head ever again. There had been no rest from it, except by shutting her eyes. Even then, the horrible grinning cheeseburger had danced in her private dark. Opening her eyes again, it screamed at her from the carpet, the tiles, the bedding, the curtains. For the rest of her life, she would associate a Cheesy Whopper with divorce. There was no major route in England now that she could possibly drive without the Happy Little Traveller hamburger leering out at her, wearing Malcolm's disapproval like a hat.

Standing here now next to John, she felt like the victim of some giant six-year-old con, in which she and Malcolm had colluded. She had been like the women who sometimes wrote to the TV station, convinced that the newscasters were in love with them. Convinced that the messages on air had been just for them. Sitting alone looking at a rectangle of transmitted sound and image, thinking that they had some sort of special relationship with the screen, never realising that they were terminally lonely.

Malcolm had transmitted into her life for six years – a dogged, dutiful presence. A decent chap, perfectly content with his lot – which was to keep her at arm's length, just outside his heart. And she had accepted the arrangement. For six years, she had let him think that it was all right.

She felt John's arms around her.

'No,' she said. 'Please . . . don't touch me.' The embrace at once slackened. She opened her eyes. 'I'm sorry,' she said. 'But don't. Just don't.'

'What happened?' he asked. He had stepped away a little, but not far.

'I don't know,' she said.

'Is it Malcolm?'

'Yes.'

'Want to tell me?' he asked.

'I don't know.'

'You don't know much,' he said.

She looked at her feet. 'Do you?'

'I think so,' he said.

'Congratulations,' she said.

'Is there anyone else?' he asked.

'No.'

'For you, or him?'

'No.'

'Has he hurt you . . . beaten you up?'

She waved her hand. 'No. Not Malcolm. Never.'

'Asked you to wear a rubber suit? Peed in your bathwater?'

She managed to laugh. 'God, John. No.'

He stared at her sympathetically. 'It's really bad, then,' he said.

She nodded. He took her arm. 'Come and sit down over here,' he said.

They sat together on a piece of damp turf and watched the water falling through its stony bed, reflecting the sunlight, singing obliviously to itself.

'Have you got any children?' he asked.

She dug her nails into her palm. 'No.'

'I have,' he said. 'Two girls.'

She turned to look at him. 'Have you?'

'I don't see them often,' he said. 'They live in Brittany, with their mother.'

'You were married?'

'No,' he said, 'but she's married now. She wanted commitment. Steadiness. To be sure.'

Chris gave a small, half-laugh. 'That's just what I don't want,' she said.

'There's no pleasing women,' he commented.

She looked at him. 'You're really sure of yourself, aren't you?' she said.

'I'm a realist,' he replied.

'With all the answers.'

'Yes.'

She shook her head. 'Malcolm thinks I'm a bit of a liability,' she murmured.

'That's very convenient,' John observed. 'He's got someone to blame, then.'

'He doesn't blame me,' she lied. 'He saved me once.'

'Saved you?' John echoed. 'What from?'

'Debt.'

'Saved you from debt,' John said. 'And what else?'

She thought. 'Being used.'

'I see,' John said. 'He's a pretty nice person, then. Never to use you.'

'Yes, he is.'

'So you got married to this safe person, this nice person, and now you're fed up of being safe and nice.'

'It's not like that,' she said.

'It is, from where I'm standing,' he said.

'You don't know anything about it,' she retorted.

'I do,' he said.

She punched the grass next to her. 'You don't.'

'Look,' he said. 'My partner was a very nice woman, she still is a nice woman, she's a wonderful mother, but I couldn't live with her, because I woke up every day feeling like I had asthma. I mean, I just couldn't draw breath. I would want to bang my head against a wall. And I'd treat her like shit, which she didn't deserve, because I was torn up inside, and I'd see all this reflected in the faces of my children, and I was teaching them that this was what marriage was.'

'I'm not you,' Chris said. 'I'm not like that.'

'Yes, you are,' he said.

Chris got to her feet. He caught hold of her arm.

'Let go of me,' she said.

'It's a matter of being honest,' John said. 'With yourself, with him.'

'Let *go*.'

'Have you tried?' he asked.

'Tried what?'

'Tried to improve things. Love him.'

She stared at him with her face streaked with tears. 'Yes.'

'Genuinely?'

'For a long time, yes.'

'And nothing worked?'

'Yes . . . a little. Sometimes.'

'Overall?' he persisted.

'No,' she said.

'And when you get home, are you dying to see him?' he asked.

'No,' she said.

'Wanting to touch him?'

'No,' she said. 'He wants me to be near him, but when I am, he's . . . not there. Not there, inside. I can't really explain it. He wants me, but only so far. Only half of me. Only half of him. It sounds nothing . . .'

'But it's everything,' John said.

'Yes,' she said. 'Yes, it is.'

'Then go.'

'How can I?' she said. 'It's not right.'

He shook her. 'Whoever said it's right?' he demanded. 'It'll never be right. But tolerating each other . . . that's life? *That*'s right?'

She put her hands to her eyes. 'I don't know,' she said. 'I just don't know.'

Standing looking at her downturned face, he suddenly put his arms around her and kissed her. He felt her astonishment and resistance for a moment, then something like hesitation. Then, without any warning at all, a hundred-thousand pound Catherine Wheel of delight starting whirring in his head. He pulled apart from her abruptly.

'What is it?' she asked him.

'What was that?' he said.

'What was what?'

He stared at her face, at the traces of tears, at the lips still parted in surprise.

'I don't know,' he told her weakly. 'I just don't know.'

37

Malcolm thought that the slope back to the field was very steep. It hadn't seemed that bad when he'd come down it half an hour before. He had followed the tracks left by the television team, followed the directions given to him by the girl in the trailer at the gate of the field. Followed the slight hum of voices far down below, in the trees.

He'd emerged by a small stream, slightly higher than the spot where they were filming. He saw an elderly woman standing near the water, dressed in a lurid pair of pink trainers, a pair of army fatigues and a yellow coat. Then he saw Chris, standing under the trees with a dark-haired man. They were talking, sipping coffee from polystyrene cups.

The sound man had stopped him, catching his arm and asking him to wait while they did something called 'atmos'. He stayed where he was obediently, looking at Chris through the overhanging branches.

He saw her gazing at the view beyond, at a large house in the parkland. He saw her put a hand to her face, and then suddenly drop the cup that she had been holding. Over the heads of the crew, he strained to catch her movement. He saw the dark-haired man put his arms around her, and her push him away a little. But not far. They talked a little more. The man took her arm and led her to a piece of turf bank, where they sat down.

The elderly woman began talking to one side of him. She, too, was staring out towards the house in the parkland. She, too, seemed to be having difficulty saying something. Her hand, too, went to her eyes. The cameras kept turning. The mike boom hovered over her head. Malcolm tried to catch her words, and heard only a soft, apologetic cadence.

He looked back at Chris. No sound there at all. Only the mime of the man deep in some kind of explanation. Chris was listening to him, her face intense.

'Cut and print,' a voice said.

Malcolm glanced back at the crew, a small knot gathered around the older woman. Someone was handing her a handkerchief. He looked back at Chris. She had got to her feet, shaking her head.

He registered the expression in her face without understanding it at all. Anguish mixed with anger. Resistance. Hesitation. He took a step forward, wondering if she needed his help.

And then he saw that she didn't need his help at all.

He turned away.

He began to walk up the slope, suddenly such a gradient. Suddenly so slippery. Brambles caught at his arms. All the way, he saw the exact correlation between Chris's bent head and the curve of the dark-haired man's shoulder. He saw those two lines. Two lines, etched against sunlight. Two shapes with a bright green backdrop. An arm across a shoulder. The way Chris's neck had arched as she dropped back into the embrace. He saw two lines, two lines. Leaves. Green. Slope.

Gate.

Field.

But he didn't see the boy until it was too late. A ball careered into him, a five-foot five-inch rugby ball with arms and legs attached. A red face loomed into his.

'Where is it?' the face demanded. 'The filming, like?'

Malcolm gestured behind him, into the trees. 'Down there.'

The boy punched his shoulder. 'Thanks, mate.' He rolled into the trees, then suddenly stopped and turned round again. 'She down there?' he yelled. 'Jinyer?'

'They're all down there,' Malcolm said sadly.

He had parked his car by the gate. He got his keys out of his pocket, a remote control working sluggishly in his head. *Car keys. Drive home. Car keys. Drive home.*

Then he saw the van parked across him, blocking the way. A green van with rusted wheel rims, no tax disc, and a toy stuck to the windscreen that showed an arse appearing from a pair of trousers.

A woman was sitting in the back of the van, her legs swinging. She was holding something in her lap. As he walked up, she lifted her head and smiled at him.

'Found her?' she asked.

'Yes,' he said, without thinking.

'Is she coming up?'

'No,' he said.

'Ah, goddamn,' she muttered. 'This thing's gonna bite me. See his little teeth? Real small teeth. Look.' She held out the bundle to him. In a cardboard shoebox, stuffed with a ragged towel that had once been yellow, a tiny furry face glared back at him.

Malcolm hesitated. He felt he ought to know the woman. Her face was vaguely familiar. 'Do you work with Chris?' he asked.

'Uh . . . no,' Divina said.

'With Up-Line?'

'No,' Divina said. She looked at him closely. 'You're not one of the church team, are you?'

'No,' Malcolm said, confused.

There was a slight pause while each wondered who the other was. Then Malcolm leaned over the box. 'Pipistrellus pipistrellus,' he said. 'Of the genus pipistrellus.'

Divina raised her eyebrows. 'Oh, right,' she murmured. 'So I guess that makes it a pipistrelle, right?'

'It does,' Malcolm said.

'A baby bat.'

'It's not a baby,' Malcolm said. 'That's an adult.'

'But it's teeny!'

'The adult pipistrelle is the size of an average human thumb,' he said. 'So that's really quite a large one. Where did you find it?'

'Down in the village. At the Rectory.'

Malcolm looked at the extremely angry little face swathed in its yellow shroud. 'Probably lives in the church, then,' he said. 'Or some warm place under slates or lead.'

'It's sleepy,' Divina said.

'Stunned, more like,' Malcolm observed. 'Is it injured?'

'I don't think so.'

'A cat might have swiped it,' Malcolm said. He sat down next to Divina in the back of the van. 'It needs to go home. It'll start getting restless and disorientated.'

Divina smiled. 'You a biologist?'

'Not exactly,' Malcolm said. 'I did my doctorate in insects. These things eat their bodyweight in insect life each night.'

'You work round here?'

'No . . . London,' he said. 'Well, not really London actually. Not really anywhere. I'm research. Medical.'

'Into what?'

He gave a grim smile. 'You don't want to know,' he said. He frowned at her. 'You're American,' he said.

She laughed. 'Yeah, right.'

'Which part?'

'Los Angeles.'

He nodded. The penny still hadn't dropped. In fact, there was very little hope of it ever dropping, because Malcolm had no interest at all in films. His idea of hell was being dragged to a cinema by Chris to see *Sleepless in Seattle*. Or, worse still, *Shakespeare in Love*, which was about the most bloody two hours he had ever experienced, seeing as he didn't know one end of a sonnet from another and, if pressed, would have guessed that *Titus Andronicus* was some sort of bacterial infection. He couldn't for the life of him see what the fuss was all about. He couldn't understand a word of Shakespeare. He didn't care if the latter *was* one of England's greatest playwrights and poets, because he couldn't understand *any* poet, not even modern ones, who all seemed to shout louder than the bloody fools in *Romeo and Juliet*.

He wished that Juliet had taken poison in the first five minutes. Think what trouble it would have avoided. No one would have wasted time observing lights from yonder window breaking. There would have been time for several more swordfights. And then they could have all gone home happy.

'I'm between jobs,' Divina said.

Malcolm looked down the field. 'Don't get involved with this lot,' he told her darkly. 'They're all mad.'

Divina bit her lip. 'Film people usually are.'

Malcolm tapped the edge of the shoebox. 'You see, with creatures like this,' he said, 'it's really very simple. They eat, they copulate, they give birth, they sleep, they die. They don't do anything else.'

'Like what?' Divina asked.

'Like argue about phone bills, or want to get married,' he muttered.

Divina smiled to herself. 'There sure is a lot of energy wasted doing *that*,' she said. 'I've been married twice.'

Malcolm stared at her. 'But you're much too young,' he said.

She laughed. 'Yeah, much,' she agreed. Then she sighed, and looked down the field. 'I wish I were a bat.'

'I always wanted to be an anigozanthos,' Malcolm said.

'A what?' Divina said.

'A kangaroo paw plant,' Malcolm told her. 'Or maybe an amaranth.'

'What is *that*?' Divina asked, turning to look at him.

'A type of plant that can be used as a diuretic,' he explained. 'Useful, you see? Constructive. Take this chap here . . . his saliva contains an anticoagulant which is being developed to treat heart conditions.'

Divina leaned forward, fascinated. 'You mean bat spit can cure heart attacks?'

'The botanical and zoological world has a lot to offer the human species,' he said. 'Not showy things – not your average elephant or gazelle, but the unglamorous infestations. Worms, spiders and so on.'

'But we don't give a hell of a lot back,' she replied. She considered him with some interest. 'You married yourself?'

'I don't know,' Malcolm said. 'I thought I was once.'

'I know that place,' Divina said. 'It sucks.'

'Does it?' Malcolm replied. 'Yes. I suppose it does.'

Divina laughed. 'You know what I'd like?' she said. 'I'd like it real simple. I mean a *real* simple arrangement.'

'Like bats?'

'Yeah, bats,' she agreed. 'No promises, no fantasies, no fucking up.'

'Up,' Malcolm said. 'Quite.'

She looked past him, into the distance. 'No weekends in Paris,' she murmured. 'No white roses, no poetry, no shit.'

'Shit. Yes.'

'Just a guy. No complications. Just a real, quiet, useful, wallpaper guy.' She sighed deeply.

'Wallpaper, right,' Malcolm said.

Divina looked closely at the box. 'So we ought to take this back, put it in the church?' she asked.

'Yes,' Malcolm said. 'Outside near the church, at dusk.'

'Will there be other bats around?'

'A couple of hundred.'

'Cool.'

Malcolm got up. 'Well, it was very nice to meet you,' he said.

She put the shoebox down. 'You're not going?'

'Well, I . . .'

'I thought you'd help me with this little guy.'

'Well, I . . .'

'Important things to do,' she said. 'Yeah, I understand.'

He looked down at her. He thought of the things he had to do. All so very important.

He had to go back into London and clear his desk. He had to ring up his pensions department. He had to sign a form handing his desk keys back to Trepantex. He had to give them his security pass. He had to go and see his father and wean him off Asian women. He had to face the iron resolve of Emily Villiers. He had to wait for Chris to come home. If she ever came home and, if she didn't, he had to look at an empty bed.

Important, yes.

So important.

'Breadfruit relies on bats for pollination,' he said.

Divina nodded, fingering the edge of the towel.

'Bats are prone to extinction because they are the slowest reproducing mammals on earth for their size,' he murmured.

She didn't reply.

'Disk-winged bats can walk up windows.' He shifted uneasily from foot to foot. 'I'm sorry,' he said. 'I'm told that I'm a bit of a bore. At least, I'm not told that, but I gather that I am.' He looked at his feet. 'Yes, I gather that I am,' he murmured.

Divina looked up. She considered him seriously for

some moments before she spoke. 'If you worked with some
of the people I've worked with, you'd know what boredom
really is,' she told him. She held out her hand to him.
'Divina Delaney.'

'Divina,' he said, taking the outstretched fingers in his.

'I know,' she said. 'It was meant to be, like a goddess?'
She saw the expression on his face. 'Look,' she said. 'call
me Anne, OK? Or Annie. That's what I was christened.'

'Annie,' he said, shaking her hand. 'Malcolm Craven.'

'Hi, Mal,' she said. She picked the box up, tucked it
under her arm, and linked her other hand under Malcolm's
elbow. 'You can walk me over to that shed,' she said.
'Some woman lives there I was supposed to see. We'll leave
a note.'

They picked their way across the cables and the
cowpats.

The mid-morning sun was now hot, and the smell was
becoming indescribable. Across the field, the awning was
pulled out over the catering van, and two women emerged,
spraying air fresheners.

'The next time I'm buying a packet of Bold,' Malcolm
heard one of them say, 'for God's sake remind me not to
get the meadow-fresh.'

Malcolm and Divina knocked hesitantly on the half-
open door of Virginia's railway carriage. There was no
reply.

'Got a piece of paper?' Divina asked.

Malcolm did. In his pocket he had paper, a pen, a card
to call out the breakdown services to his car, a timetable of
the buses between Barking and Ilford, fourteen pence of
which one was a 1935 penny, and a piece of string. He
gave her the pen, and hastily stuffed the rest back into his
jacket.

'Can't write on a door,' Divina said. Giving him the bat
box, she pushed the railway carriage door open and

walked inside a pace or two, looking for a flat surface.

Standing outside, all Malcolm could hear was silence. Then there was a little gasp. Then there was nothing at all above the buzzing of the horseflies and the fluttering of wings in Virginia's makeshift aviary behind him.

Then he heard Divina murmur, 'My God, my God . . . God.'

She came to the door, ashen-faced, her hand to her throat. 'Where is she?' she asked.

'Who?' he said.

'Where is the woman who lives in here – where is she?'

Malcolm shook his head. 'Down the hill?' he said. 'I don't know.'

Divina jumped down the two steps from the carriage. Without another word, she started out across the field, running hell for leather.

'Annie!' Malcolm called.

She waved her hand at him, without looking back.

'What is it?' he shouted. 'What's the matter?'

38

The afternoon was drawing in, with a lurid and brassy-coloured sky, by the time that Owen reached Weypool Harbour.

It had been one of the longest days of his life, yet, as he drove down through Dorset, he felt more alive than he had done for years. The first evening lights of the coast came into view as he breached the line of hills and cut down the narrow winding lanes to the sea. Five years since Up-Line had been set up; four years since Chris had come to his rescue by joining the firm; three years since he realised he was never going to be the next Rupert Murdoch.

And just one year since he had met Madeleine.

A smile came unconsciously to his face. Negotiating the last piece of road, he caught sight of his boat, a business-like and understated piece of seagoing artistry. He was proud of the fact that, unlike his father's enormous white floating palace, now currently moored in St Tropez, the *Madeleine* was built for sailors – and not for showing off and sunbathing.

He brought the four-wheel drive to a stop on the dock, got out and locked it. For a few moments, he stared at the Up-Line many-tongued logo on the driver's door. He hesitated only slightly before throwing the keys gracefully over his shoulder into the water.

Madeleine was waiting for him on deck.

A slight woman of twenty-five or so, she stood with one hand on her hip, and the other holding back her long hair from her face. He stopped at the top of the gangplank and looked appreciatively at her. She had never been to a gallery opening, book launch, or a party to celebrate fifty years of making outrageously expensive clothes. She had more productive things to do with her time. Things that, to his delight, involved diving in nil-visibility waters holding a silt pump, or – joy of joys – sitting on a rolling deck in a force nine gale piecing together medieval drainage pipes. She leaned now on the rail, returning his gaze with a lazy smile. She wore tattered jeans, a sweater of uncertain age, and her feet were bare.

He ran down, dropped the holdall he was carrying, and held her in a tight hug for a few seconds before they went below. All was silent on the dockside for a couple of minutes. Then Owen re-emerged, carrying something.

He staggered to the guard rail, balancing the object against his hip while he manoeuvred it on to the rail. For a second, he was outlined against the reflecting water against the setting sun, a tall man holding a large square box.

Then, he jettisoned the whole thing over the side.

It made quite a splash before it sank.

It would be several years – years that Owen and Madeleine spent happily in the West Indies, where they raised two children – before a puzzled boat owner in Weypool, trying to unsnag an underwater line, found a set of car keys next to a television set on the bottom of the dock.

39

On the very same evening, five other people were changing their lives for ever.

In the Trepantex office block in London, Malcolm was packing the contents of his laboratory desk into a cardboard box. He made sure that his experimental notes were uppermost – twelve years of meticulous records on the development of his larval strain. He switched off the electricity supply to the empty hatching tanks, and even unplugged the already-dead phone. But, just before he turned out the light, he looked again at the piece of paper on which a woman called Annie, who lived in Los Angeles, had scrawled an instruction. Beside the words was a telephone number in England. He considered the looping, exuberant handwriting with his head on one side and a more than disbelieving expression on his face. *Call me tomorrow. I mean it*, it said. *Call me.*

He closed the door to the office and started down the corridor, holding the cardboard box that contained his previous life. And he allowed himself a smile – just a small smile of the most hesitant optimism – as he waited for the lift.

Meanwhile, in a small pub in Kent, in front of a log fire, Christine Craven sat opposite John Donoghue, watching him as he read a manuscript.

And not so very far away, two women who had been strangers until that day – two women who could not have been more unlike each other, and yet were linked for eternity by their past – pulled up in a taxi outside an hotel.

It was ten o'clock, and the frontage blazed with light. Virginia Pye peered out of the taxi, then caught Divina's arm.

'I can't go in there,' she whispered, stricken.

Divina, half out of the cab, stared at her in amazement. 'Why not? You're with me, remember.'

'I can't,' Virginia repeated. 'Look, it's got big doors.'

Divina grinned, hauling on Virginia's arm. 'Things are gonna be different from now,' she said.

'I've got my wellies on,' Virginia whimpered.

Divina herded her into the foyer like a sheepdog snapping at the heels of a particularly stubborn ewe. Once inside, Divina's face opened a host of other doors as if by magic. Doors to a private lift to the penthouse. Doors to a suite of such breathtaking luxury that Virginia clung to the doorpost, taking off her Wellingtons.

'What're you doing?' Divina demanded.

'I don't want to muck up these carpets,' her half-sister told her.

'For Chrissake,' Divina said, heaving her inside. 'Forget the friggin' carpets. You deserve some spoiling, Ginny. And from hereon in, I'm going to make sure you get it.'

They sat on a roof terrace an hour later, shielded by trees and palms. Virginia had inspected all these minutely at first, transfixed that a full-grown tree could spring from a pot. Swathed in a hotel dressing gown, and pink from the hot tub, Virginia was reeling a little from her two glasses of champagne. When Divina came out to join her, she looked up, her eyes fixed on the younger woman's face.

Divina smiled. 'Penny for them, sis.'

'We don't look alike,' Virginia said. 'That's what they'll all say: "She's never her sister, that lump of lard".'

Divina sat down. She looked critically for some moments at Virginia. 'We've got his nose.' She leaned forward and touched Virginia, gently, between the eyes. 'This part, this narrow bit.'

'It's not much to go on,' Virginia said.

Divina pursed her lips. 'Moles,' she said. 'Got any moles?'

'One on my knee.'

'Show.'

Together, they looked at Virginia's knee.

'Got nothing there,' Divina said. 'Got two on my shoulder.'

Virginia shook her head.

'We're the same height,' Divina said. 'Same colour eyes, same hair.'

'I'm not blonde,' Virginia said.

'Neither am I,' Divina admitted.

'Got this on my palm,' Virginia said, extending her hand. 'Like a bump, in the middle, both hands.'

Divina sighed. 'Nope.'

'Got high insteps,' Virginia said. 'Can't keep shoes on without they got straps.'

'No.' Divina stretched her legs in front of her and showed her perfectly proportioned feet.

'Have you got papers?' Virginia asked. 'Proving things, like?'

Divina gave a twisted little smile. 'Oh yeah,' she said. 'He admitted he was my father. Went to court, got a paternity ruling. My mom was determined.'

'And you got that written down?' Virginia said.

'Yep,' Divina replied. 'But we never received a cent for all that. We chased him across four states, he sent cheques that bounced. He once even did thirty days for non-payment. I got letters he sent to Mom saying he'd pay . . . you know, the whole thing.'

'Letters,' Virginia echoed enviously. 'He wrote to you?'

Divina's face clouded. She picked up the glass in front

of her, stared at it for a moment, and then put it down. She pulled her dressing gown around her, suddenly chilled. 'No,' she said. 'He never wrote. Not a line. Not a card.'

Suddenly, she got up and went back into the room behind them. As she waited, Virginia's heart began to sink. Maybe in the morning, this lovely girl would regret her enthusiasm, she thought. Maybe she would wake up and come in to see her in her vast satin-covered bed, and take one look at this dumpy, weather-beaten face, and think, I made a mistake. No half-sister of mine could look like that.

She took after her mother, really. That was the trouble. Oh, maybe she had some of that lofty Hunscrete brow, and that narrow frowning space between the eyes, that Divina had already pointed out. Maybe she had it, and maybe she didn't. But the rest of her face was plain and broad and permanently flushed. It was Divina who seemed to have picked up that aristocratic expression, that pale skin, that sensuous mouth. In fact, Virginia thought, Divina, when you looked hard at her, looked quite like her cousin Charles Hunscrete. She had inherited that same imperiousness, that air of calm superiority. But Virginia had never had that, and never would.

Bloody Nora, she thought sadly. I'm the ugly sister. Like Cinderella and the Ugly Sisters.

She's going to wake up in the morning and hate me.

This is a joke.

She was getting hurriedly to her feet as Divina emerged on to the terrace again.

'What's happening?' Divina said.

Virginia blushed. 'I don't want to show you up,' she said. 'I'd better go home.'

'Show me up?' Divina demanded. 'What do you mean?'

Virginia's embarrassment grew. She fiddled with the thick towelling tie of the dressing gown. 'Show you up, looking a mess,' she muttered. 'Maybe I'd best go home. Maybe it's a mistake. Maybe my mum got it wrong.'

Divina put the package she was carrying down on the table. 'Are you saying your mother is a liar?' she asked.

Virginia was almost at the suite door when she turned. 'No, I bloody well am not,' she retorted. 'My mother never told a lie in her life.'

Divina slowly opened the package. Inside it, Virginia saw, were a strange assortment of things. A man's handkerchief, laundered and neatly folded. A pressed pink rose. A sheaf of papers with some sort of official legal stamp. And several photographs.

Virginia glimpsed Clark Rutland, and a signature.

And George Bernard Ransome with child star Betty Schreiber.

'He used to send me these,' Divina murmured.

Slowly, Virginia edged closer. She saw Divina turn over the picture, and she read the message on the back.

From one pretty little girl to another . . . to my *little girl, from her Daddy.*

When Divina finally lifted her eyes from the photograph, she saw that, beside her, Virginia was weeping, the tears running unchecked, dripping from her cheeks on to the dressing gown.

'What is it?' Divina said, getting swiftly to her feet and holding Virginia by the shoulders. 'What's the matter?'

Up to that very moment, Virginia had doubted that she belonged anywhere near Divina. She doubted even more that she belonged in a hotel like this. She doubted that she deserved anything more than a token piece of attention, culled from the absurdity of marrying a duck. She had doubted, deep in her heart, that she should dare to mention her connection to the almighty Hunscretes. Or to the icon that was George Bernard Ransome, a very cruel man who, in reality, did not actually deserve to have a redoubtable daughter like Virginia.

But then, everything changed.

She thought of the damp shoebox under her sink.

She thought of the endless hours holding her own photograph of Betty Schreiber.

She thought of the years of envy and shame and loss.

And she flung her arms round Divina, and hugged her for all she was worth.

'Oh, it's really true,' she whispered ecstatically. 'Oh, at last I've got family, dear. I've got *family*!'

40

The next morning, a small and unremarkable woman stood in the queue for the Strangers' Gallery. She had been there for some time, her brown handbag clasped in front of her, waiting in a sea of tourists for her place in the public seats of the House of Commons. As others brushed past her, she gave them apologetic glances, a shrinking figure in the vast and heaving ocean of the seat of Government.

Allocated her place, she sat down at the front of the gallery and looked down into the debating chamber. It was almost midday, and the House was half-full, racing through its business as the weekend loomed. The MPs were all anxious to be away to their constituencies, where their mistresses awaited them in the sand bunker off the ninth hole of the golf course.

The woman looked hard at the Government front row.

The Prime Minister wasn't there, of course. He was in Australia, making patronising noises to the colonies. But his deputy was lounging on the green leather, looking like a formidable bear that had been crammed into a suit. Alongside him was a petite and outrageously gorgeous blonde, the Transport Minister.

On the other side of the deputy Prime Minister sat a man whose languid nonchalance drew the eye. Unlike his colleagues, Charles Hunscrete looked as if he'd been made for the task of sitting, with one arm draped over the seat, his legs crossed, and his head raised as if he were listening.

This posture, however, was actually designed to show off his profile to the TV cameras.

Charles always wore a little smile when sitting on the Front Bench. He loved the attention. He loved looking blasé. He loved his bright white cuffs beneath his tailored suit. He liked his polished shoes. He liked his manicured hands with the rather nice fingers. He loved his expensive Caribbean tan. In short, he admired himself tremendously. Especially for his defection last year from the Tories to Labour, to receive a Cabinet Post.

And the Minister for Family Affairs was feeling even more in awe of himself than usual today. He was due to make a speech on teenage pregnancies, and, while not really having any grasp at all of the policy, he had made what he thought were some rather amusing little asides. Nothing too controversial, of course. Nothing that would register with any of the hacks sitting in Annie's Bar. But just a few nuances culled from the classics, to show how urbanely witty he was. What an asset for a once-Socialist Government. What a delightful yet intelligent representative of the upper classes.

Only this morning he had been at Privy Council and made a little joke within Her Majesty's hearing. Her Majesty had turned to look at him with slightly less severity than usual, a fact that would keep his ego warm for many a month to come.

The woman in the public gallery looked hard at Charles Hunscrete. She looked at the speech which he held loosely in that fabulously-manicured fist. She looked down at her own little book, a book that she had bought about the Palace of Westminster, which told her that one of the statues in St Stephen's Hall had a repaired sword, because a suffragette had once chained herself to it.

She closed her eyes momentarily against the sea of green and the recurrent images of the portcullis. You couldn't get

away from either in here, it seemed. A portcullis gate with
its vicious spikes, and chain winding through it. For the
past ten years, she thought desperately, she had been
chained and spiked. Held behind a drawbridge.

She was the original Princess in the Tower.

Except the Princess wasn't twenty-two any more. She
no longer had hair halfway down her back. The Princess
was thirty-three, and had grown plain and dumpy, the
result of being kept in a windowless room. She grew hot
inside her grey jacket. Its polyester mix was bringing her
out in a rash – she could feel it creeping up her neck. Or
perhaps that was only her fury, which had been kept
simmering for so long and was ready, now, to explode.

She had accepted her imprisonment because the Prince
had always come to see her and given her money and
assurances that one day she would be let out into the
fresh air. One day when the time was right. One day when
the Prince had finished all the other business that
consumed him, slaying dragons and putting Liberal
Democrats to flight. Releasing virgins from the clutches
of other men.

The small Princess's face crumpled at the memory.
At her own guileless stupidity. At ten years of keeping
very quiet while her Prince galloped around the
countryside.

It would still have been all right, of course. She would
still have put up with it, had she not received a visit two
days ago from a man called Peter Wallington. Wallington
was the modern equivalent of the troll gaoler – the one
who would occasionally leer into her airless room and
rattle the keys meaningfully at her before he would hand
over her dinner.

A visit from the troll with a letter from the Prince.

The woman's hands closed tightly over her handbag.
She gave Charles Hunscrete one last look, a look of

unmitigated venom, before she gently eased the catch of the bag open.

Twenty minutes later, Sally and Alicia were negotiating the morning chaos of Parliament Square.

Sally glanced across at Alicia. 'Look,' she said, 'I know what you're thinking, but it's not true.'

'You couldn't have chosen a worse place,' Alicia said.

'I didn't choose it,' Sally told her, slamming on her brakes while a motor-bike courier expertly cut them up, followed by four taxis. 'Alexandra chose it.'

Alicia said nothing. She sat with her arms crossed, gazing at the edifice of the Houses of Parliament with a curled lip.

Sally tried to sneak their car between a Mother's Pride van and a Mothercare juggernaut, the drivers of which were shouting at each other in a very *un*maternal fashion.

'No one's going to interrupt her while she's in a meeting with Boundhand's owner,' Sally said, giving two well-manicured fingers to the Mothercare man, and standing on the accelerator. 'Then she came straight here. It was her idea to have photos of you outside Parliament, not mine.'

'But you knew about it,' Alicia said.

'Yes, I knew about it,' Sally admitted. 'Where else would you take publicity shots of an ex-MP who is going to spill the beans on a Cabinet Minister?'

Alicia gave her a withering look.

'OK,' Sally said. 'Listen. I'll park by the kerb and I'll get out and tell Alexandra and the photographer that it's off. You don't even have to get out of the car.'

'You said Guide's Honour,' Alicia muttered.

Sally grimaced. 'I know,' she said. 'But actually, I was drummed out of the Brownies for dancing the wrong way round the toadstool. Sorry. Maybe they'll still buy you lunch.'

'You're all the same,' Alicia murmured, staring at the crowds on the pavement.

Sally bit her lip. Then she leaned forward. She had got past a lumbering four-wheel drive, but there was a still an unholy mess of people crowding the pavement and spilling out on to the road. She scanned Old Palace Yard for a glimpse of Alexandra's fearsome shoulders. The traffic came to a resounding halt. Horns blew. Two policemen ran across the road towards the House.

'What's going on?' Sally wondered.

Suddenly, a photographer sprinted in front of the car. Then he stopped. He wheeled around and stared at Sally, then at her passenger. A kind of ecstatic light dawned in his face, and he leapt to the side of the car and banged on the window.

Sally pressed the electric control, and the glass rolled down. 'What is it?' she said.

'Any comment?' he asked, and started flashing the camera at Alicia. 'Any comment, eh? Comment, love, eh? Eh?'

Sally rapidly rolled the window back up, almost severing the man's hand. 'Jesus,' she muttered. 'What the hell's going on?'

'You did this,' Alicia said.

Sally turned to her. 'I swear to you, I did not do this, whatever it is. Alexandra's photographer is called Chris Brown, and he's very nice, sixty if he's a day, and he was coming to do a few low-key portrait shots of you with the House as a background, on the lawn over there.' She waved her hand vaguely in the direction of the grass and trees opposite the House, where MPs were routinely inter-viewed for TV. 'It was going to be ten minutes, max. And we *were* going to lunch, Alicia. Hopefully with Alexandra, if she didn't get too incandescent and threaten to remove my bile duct and throw it in the Thames.'

She stared all around her. The car was being swamped by a tidal wave of faces. Someone banged on Sally's window. The little Renault shook. Alicia put her head in her hands. 'Get me out of here,' she whispered.

Sally started the car and put it back into gear. 'I can't move forward,' she said.

'Then go back.'

Sally looked behind her. To her astonishment, she saw Alexandra Francis running, actually *running* up the road, waving. With a deftness she didn't know she possessed, Sally managed to wheel the car round towards her. The photographer yelped. 'My bloody foot!' he screamed.

'Oh Jesus,' Sally muttered.

She pulled up alongside Alexandra, released the door locks, and watched in amazement as the unutterably cool, steam-pressed and iron-willed Senior Editor flung herself into the back seat, sweating like an Olympic hammer-thrower. 'How did you do it!' Alexandra cried. 'It's marvellous, marvellous!'

'What is?' Sally said.

'Absolutely fucking marvellous!'

'*What* is?'

'How the hell did you manage *that*!'

'Manage what?' Sally yelled. 'We've only just got here. We've been stuck in traffic right back to the Brompton Road. What in God's name is going on?'

Alexandra Francis gazed at them both in amazement. 'You mean you don't *know*?' she demanded. 'You weren't in on it? I thought you'd arranged it to coincide with Alicia's pikkies!' She started to laugh. 'Oh, it's marvellous. Absolutely *brilliantly* marvellous!'

'What don't we know?' Alicia asked suspiciously.

They were hurtling around and around Parliament Square, dodging trucks like a demented fairground dodgem.

'Hunscrete!' Alexandra said. 'Having a fight with some bloody woman and her handbag! On the *floor of the House*!' She was thrown back in her seat as Sally tore between two buses. 'Oh, it's priceless,' she said. 'Peter Hall couldn't have staged it better, he really couldn't.'

Sally made a violent and sudden lunge along Victoria Embankment. With one wheel on the pavement, she turned left again, and slewed to a halt by Horse Guards. Both she and Alicia turned round in their seats and stared at Alexandra.

'What bloody woman?' they said, together.

The bloody woman in question had hung by one arm from the Strangers' Gallery for at least fifteen seconds before Charles Hunscrete had even noticed her.

He had been too busy thinking of his lunch, and wondering if anyone would introduce him to any of the horribly lascivious and promiscuous single mothers that he was planning to talk about. The murmurs of surprise, the riffle of laughter, had passed in one ear and out the other. Until someone had nudged his elbow.

The woman in the grey jacket was lowering herself out of the gallery. She was already over the rail, and hanging mid-air above the Commons. She was, with quite a practised air of calm, jolting downwards on what appeared to be a nylon rope and which, she would reveal afterwards to the press, was actually a line of Marks & Spencer tights which she had spent the last few minutes knotting together under a newspaper in her lap.

'Excuse me,' she had said, from her swinging vantage point. It had been a very soft voice, and the tone was almost apologetic. 'Excuse me,' she continued. 'But that man is a liar.'

The MPs looked at each other, each one feeling a momentary rush of panic. After all, they were *all* liars.

The woman seemed to gather strength. Her soft tone went up several decibels. 'Charles Hunscrete is a professional liar,' it rang out.

Most of the MPs – relieved that it wasn't *them* in the spotlight – got to their feet. People in the Gallery were hanging over the side, delighted with this unexpected exhibition of freestyle abseiling.

'Him, there,' the woman added, as if anyone could still be in any doubt. And she pointed at Hunscrete.

The world suffered a minor explosion in the following moments. Security rushed into the Gallery and tried hauling the woman back. Opposition MPs started yelling for her name. The Speaker called for order. Only Charles Hunscrete stayed absolutely immobile, staring up at her, his face frozen in an expression of sick disbelief. He could feel his heart thudding in his chest. The air in the Chamber suddenly felt very thick and sweet and overpowering. It was like trying to breathe through custard. His vision swam. He vaguely registered the police trying to pull the woman back up while she produced a small penknife, cut the line of tights and fell in a heap to the floor.

For a few glorious seconds, he thought she had killed herself, but she got up, dusted herself down, and walked over to him.

He gazed up at her, fear curdling his soul. And then he did a very stupid thing indeed.

She said, 'Hello, darling.'

And he said, 'Hello, Helen.'

And then she hit him with her handbag.

Alexandra Francis was in full flow in the back of Sally's Renault.

'Apparently she caught him an absolute corker,' she said. 'Cuffed him to the ground. Black eye. Tried to stamp on him.'

'Didn't anyone stop her?' Alicia asked, in a very small voice.

Alexandra began laughing all over again. 'Well, this is the funny thing,' she said. 'Nobody on the Front Bench lifted a finger. It's almost as if they were perfectly happy to see him slaughtered. It was the police who finally got her off him and took her out. By this time she was kicking and screaming all the way. Calling him a miser and a cheat, an adulterer and God knows what else. Gave the press plenty of time to wake up in Annie's Bar, I can tell you. They swarmed all over her. When I got here, she was hanging on to the railings while the police tried to get her into a van.'

'And she's . . .' Sally's voice tailed away. She glanced at Alicia's totally expressionless face.

'She's Hunscrete's mistress,' Alexandra said, apparently oblivious to any effect this might have on Charles Hunscrete's wife. 'Been kept up in Lincolnshire for the last ten years. They've got a nine-year-old daughter. Of course,' she added, wiping the corners of her eyes, 'when she started yelling that he had another child by some other woman in Haverfordwest, and that he'd threatened *both* of them, and cut off *both* their allowances this week . . .'

Alicia suddenly turned back in her seat, and faced the windscreen.

For a moment, Sally thought that Charles's wife was going to faint.

Alicia's face went a deathly chalk-white. Her eyes narrowed. Her hands curled into fists, and a small vein began throbbing at her temple. She appeared to have stopped breathing, until she took one almighty gasp of air.

'Sally,' she said quietly, 'take me back, if you please, to Parliament Square. I would like to talk to that charming journalist about a book I have planned.'

Postscript

It was two years later that Sally Matthews got married. It was a very quiet affair – so quiet, in fact, that only six people knew about it.

Michael Blood, who performed the ceremony in the beautiful little church in Deadham Markham.

Philippa Blood, his wife.

Justin, steaming in the summer heat in a suit two sizes too small for him that he had borrowed from his brother.

Alicia Hunscrete, newly divorced and never happier, having retained Hunscrete House in her settlement. She had, to her immense satisfaction, not heard from her ex-husband Charles for some time. Ever since seeing his picture in the *News Of The World*. It had been taken in Marbella, in a nasty little villa, over the garden wall. Sir Charles had been snapped lounging by the poolside, a paunch overhanging his shorts, and a copy of *Poor Man's Investments* spread over his face. By all accounts he was being besieged by the lawyers of his mistresses, but Alicia didn't give a damn. She was too busy counting the money that was rolling in since she had let half the parkland to a holiday company. She was investing most of it in an exceptional wine cellar.

To make up the wedding party, of course, were the happy couple themselves, Sally and Steve.

Sally Matthews, author of the best-selling biography *The Decline and Fall and Rise of Alicia*.

Stephen Bentley Bristol Rovers Cross, fixer of broken hearts.

In fact, they might have been married much earlier if it had been left up to Steve. To say that the man was besotted was an understatement, though he did a creditable job of hiding it while Sally sorted out her record-time divorce from the adulterous Dermott. Even after the divorce, Steve had tried to keep a low profile to give her space, space that Sally soon found she didn't need. In fact, she had begun to get quite irate at Steve's absences until one day she had met him outside the village shop.

'What do you mean by avoiding me?' she had demanded as she staggered under the weight of a bag of rose fertiliser for the back garden.

'I don't want to avoid you,' Steve had told her, trying to take the bag from her. 'I just don't want to . . .' he searched for the right-sounding phrase '. . . get in your face, sort of thing.'

Sally had given him a piercing look. Then she had looked at her shoes. A small, catlike smile crept over her face. Eventually, trying to rearrange her expression into one of relative innocence, she told him, 'Actually, I can't think of anything nicer to happen to my face.' She'd opened her car door, leaving him blushing furiously. She'd glanced over her shoulder. 'Tomorrow evening?' she'd asked him. 'Seven-thirty for eight?'

On the night of the wedding, in good honeymoon tradition, the happy couple stayed awake until four in the morning. Because they couldn't see Dermott until then. 'Will you stop dropping crumbs in this bed,' Sally complained, trying to pull her pillow into a shape comfortable enough to prop her up and see the television. 'And give me the remote, I can't hear a thing.'

There followed a short and pleasant wrestle over the remote, until Sally finally managed to turn up the volume, and the American commentator's voice came booming into the bedroom.

'And the nominees for Best Actor are . . .'

'Oh God,' said Chris, six thousand miles away. 'I'm going to be sick.'

John glanced at her in the seat next to him. Then he looked around for a second at the row upon row of famous faces, and at the Oscars stage, where Jude Law was lounging casually against the podium, causing most of the female audience to suffer from sudden and severe oxygen deprivation. 'You've already been sick,' John told Chris. 'Once at the hotel and once in the Hollywood Oscars Lifetime Achievement Lavatory.'

Chris gave him a helpless look. Down the rows of seats, she could just see the top of Jack Nicholson's head. 'If they call us,' she whispered, 'you'll have to go. I can't go. I can't be sick on Jack Nicholson.'

John pinched her arm, hard. 'Will you shut up,' he hissed.

'Bruce Willis for *Frantic Calm* . . .'

A torrent of applause.

'Everyone will look at my arse,' Chris whispered desperately. 'They'll say, "For Christ's sake, look at that mountainous bloody pack of cellulite." It'll be broadcast across America. No one will remember that I wrote anything. They'll just remember my arse.'

'Why shouldn't they look at your arse?' John remarked. 'You've put a lot of hard work into it. You always said you wanted a big one. I *like* your arse.'

'Look,' she smirked, 'I like it, and you like it, but America will show it in *Freaks USA*. They'll sell the rights to it. They'll build shopping malls on it. They'll make it a National Park.'

'Will you shut the hell up,' John sniggered.

'Sean Connery for *Under White November* . . .'

'We won't win,' Chris moaned. 'Why did we ever come here? Why did I ever have to meet Virginia Pye? Why did she have to be Divina Delaney's long-lost half-sister? Why couldn't I have stayed in the Inland Revenue?'

Off to the right-hand side, she could just glimpse Virginia's head.

Virginia Pye was loving every minute. Arriving on Divina's arm earlier in the evening, she had been dressed in a disastrous pink meringue, and was sporting pink feathers in her hair. Her violent waving had revealed an acre of under-arm hair. The long camera shots as she walked down the red carpet had shown that she had blue carpet slippers on under her frock, but Virginia didn't give a damn. She was famous, as famous as she could ever have hoped for, with her TV series topping the ratings and her face on every magazine cover. Almost as famous as her sister, who had set the gossips on fire by bringing a new man to the Awards Ceremony.

'A radical biologist, currently carrying out astonishing breakthroughs as a new partner at The Hills Bacterial Clinic,' the introduction had run, down every news wire in the world.

Followed by a picture of the trio.

Divina in a suicidally low-cut dress, her figure fully recovered from the birth of her adored daughter, Pippa.

Virginia, in full windmill mode.

And Malcolm, looking anything but cool, wondering if his father would be watching, and knowing that he wouldn't because his wife, Emily, insisted he was in bed by half-past eight.

'Oh God,' Sally had said, sitting upright in bed at the sight of Virginia on screen. 'Did you feed the ducks?'

'Fed the ducks, yep,' Steve replied.

'Archie?'

'Pining.'

In Hollywood, the roll call of nominees was over. Among the four faces pasted on to the screen was Dermott Matthews's.

'And the winner of Best Actor is . . .'

Three seconds of excruciating silence, followed by a name.

Famous name, great choice.

Not Dermott Matthews.

Three seconds of Dermott's face, falling to pieces.

'Oh dear,' said Sally.

'Ah, shame,' said Steve.

An ocean away, Chris was holding John's hand.

'Will you get off me,' he told her. 'You're crushing my fingers.'

'And the nominees for Best Screenplay are . . .'

'Oh Christ,' Chris whimpered.

'Smile,' John said. 'They're all looking at us.'

'Oh *Christ* . . .'

In the Deadham Markham bed, Sally squealed. 'John and Chris! Look!' She thought of the recent frantic emails from Eddie Massingham, who, after his spell in The Priory, was now back in business making everyone's life a misery. *Can you get me Chris Craven?* had been his latest try. *Somebody said you're mates.*

She hadn't even bothered to reply.

She leaned forward to look at Chris's image, now, on the screen.

'Christine Craven and John Donoghue and Jefferson Bluehorn Majolica for *A Bridge Between Two Worlds*, the heartwarming true life story of the reunion of two sisters . . .'

'Hurray!' yelled Virginia, from the depths of the theatre. 'Yes!'

There was a muted drumroll. Followed by what felt, to Chris, like four hundred years of complete silence.

Then, three rows down, she saw Malcolm turn round in his seat. They gazed at each other for a long moment. Then, very slowly, Malcolm raised his hand in a small, victorious fist, while Divina, next to him, looked over her shoulder and grinned.

'They know something,' Chris muttered. 'They know something, John.'

She saw the camera in the aisle below swing round. 'Please God,' she said. 'Not my arse.'

The envelope was opened.

The winner announced.

And all she remembered, all she remembered for years afterwards, was the brightness of the lights that flooded over her, and the feeling of John's hand tightly holding hers.